COLT DISPATCHED EVERY GOBLIN within sword's reach, oblivious to where his momentum was taking him. He might have followed the deadly rhythm that had taken ahold of him forever, except he caught sight of something that made him pause.

During his time as prisoner, Colt had scarcely been able to tell one goblin from another. They all looked the same—like evil incarnate. Every crescent-shaped pupil, dark as the Pit, had glared at him with a palpable hatred. Each mouth, lined top and bottom with pointed teeth, had grinned with the promise of horrors to come.

But there was one goblin Colt had gotten to know better than the rest, one who had wanted to keep him alive. Paralyzed by the magic of the vuudu staff, Colt had lain lifeless in a tent on the outskirts of the camp with nothing to do but stare upward. The only reprieve from the tedium had been visits from his merciless captor.

Drekk't.

Everything seemed to slow around him as his eyes met those of the general. Drekk't must have seen him too because he suddenly advanced in Colt's direction.

Colt forgot about the surging throng of enemies around him, and the other goblin warriors seemed content to ignore him and his enchanted sword. They gave him a wide berth as they hurried past.

The crystal sword held out before him, its blade slick with dark blood, he regarded Drekk't with a calm that belied the raw emotion gnashing at his soul. This is for Cholk, he thought, as the general drew nearer.

THE RENEGADE CHRONICLES

Rebels and Fools

Heroes and Liars

Martyrs and Monsters

Martyrs
and
Monsters

David Michael Williams

To Kate,
I hope you've
enjoyed the
adventure!
-DMWilliams

ONEMILLIONWORDS

Martyrs and Monsters is a work of fiction. Names, characters, places, and incidents either are products of the author's imagination or are used fictitiously. Any resemblance to actual persons, living or dead, business establishments, events, or locales is entirely coincidental.

ONEMILLIONWORDS

Inquiries can be directed to onemillionwords@hotmail.com.

First published by One Million Words, LLC, Wisconsin, USA

First printing, March 2016

ISBN 978-0-9910562-3-1

Written by David Michael Williams (david-michael-williams.com)

Cover art copyright © 2016 by One Million Words, LLC

Cover design by Jake Weiss (jacobweissdesign.com)

Author photograph by Jaime Lynn Hunt (jaimelynnhunt.com)

Interior art copyright © 2016 by One Million Words, LLC

Map by David Michael Williams and Jake Weiss

Martyrs and Monsters is dedicated to the One True Author for so many, many blessings.

Rydah
and the Celestial Palace

WINDY
BAY

Port
Gust

Cresta Wood

Fort
Valor

Fort
Faith

Hylan

Port
Stone

The Rusty Crags

Steppt

Travelers'
Stop

Ispian
Lake

The Ruins of
Baklah

ADEN OCEAN

Prologue

The stiffness creeping into his long limbs made each stride more difficult than the last. Rivulets of sweat tickled his cheeks, but the cold night air was no match for the heat that consumed his skin and burned his lungs—a fire that rivaled the inferno he had left far behind.

He knew they were back there. Every now and then, a cry rent the stillness of the forest, a sound that resembled nothing so much as the baying of hounds. Even when they were silent, he sensed their nearness.

Othello was no stranger to the hunt, though usually the roles were reversed.

His empty quiver pounded against his back with every exhausting stride. He refused to cast aside his longbow, which he clutched awkwardly against his breast. The bow was one of his few possessions, and tossing it aside would only give his pursuers proof of his passing.

The predators—foreigners to the island until recently—stuck to his trail with a persistence he begrudgingly admired. He had done his best to conceal his path in the beginning, but they had found him anyway.

Now his flight was chaotic, desperate.

The shouts were growing louder by the moment. He wondered if they could smell him. The creatures certainly resembled animals in their ferocity, and some said they could see in the dark. But they weren't mere beasts. They spoke a language he didn't understand, and they knew magic. Perhaps they were using spells to track him now.

He ran so far he might have outpaced dawn itself. When he glanced over his shoulder, he saw not the welcoming rays of morning light, but rather his first unobstructed view of the hunters. Some called them monsters. He couldn't disagree.

Looking ahead once more, he focused a dense copse of aspens a few yards away. The forest had thinned out without his noticing. If he could only make it to the trees, he might be able to alter his course and lose them.

Othello cried out in pain as the arrow tore through tendon and muscle. His wounded leg buckled. His momentum sending him tumbling to the ground. He came down hard, skinning his elbows and biting his tongue. His longbow clattered against the trunk of a tree.

He rolled unto his back to assess the damage. The shaft was crude in design but effective. Blood glued his buckskin pants to his leg.

There wasn't even time to remove the arrow. The creatures were already closing in on him. The six of them were breathing hard as they loped toward him. Spearheads and sword tips preceded their advance. A seventh goblin hung back, fitting a second arrow into its bow. If there had been more than one archer, he would already be dead.

Then again, he would likely die anyway.

Swallowing the metallic tang in his mouth, Othello tucked his legs beneath him and sprang forward. The pain that coursed through his injured leg nearly sent him back down to the ground, but he pushed through it. He grabbed the shaft of the nearest spear with his left hand and drew his one remaining weapon with the right.

The goblin would have been wise to let go of the spear. As it was, the creature ended up the victim of its own slow reaction and Othello's momentum. The goblin could do little more than pull a surprised face as Othello's hunting knife slid into the hollow beneath its sternum.

He shoved the dying monster into one of its compatriots while avoiding the descending blades of the others. He then launched himself knife-first at the closest goblin. A dark, horizontal line appeared across the creature's neck. An instant later, black blood oozed down the goblin's chest.

Othello didn't even see the second corpse hit the ground. He was already turning to face the remaining foes.

The four held their grounds, alternating their glances between him and their fallen comrades. They had underestimated him, and he wondered if their taste for self-preservation would slake the thirst for vengeance.

Although outmatched, Othello knew he could take at least one more of the monsters with him to the grave. So...who will it be? he silently prodded.

The goblins seemed to be considering that very thing. They eyed his blade, slick with dark blood. Adrenaline or exhaustion caused the creatures to undulate before him. The shadows dancing in the distance were making him dizzy.

It was only when a second shaft planted itself just below his clavicle that he remembered goblins were wont to poison their arrows.

The impact sent him staggering backward, but he somehow managed to stay on his feet. The goblins kept their distance. With their toxins in his blood, he was as good as dead. They wouldn't risk getting gutted by his knife.

He thought he heard a goblin laugh as he pushed himself, unsteadily, toward where the archer stood, reaching for another arrow. He dove at the creature's chest with all of his might, planting his knife hilt-deep into the goblin's body.

But his aim had been off, and the wound wasn't fatal.

The goblin rained down a series of blows about Othello's head and shoulders, splintering its bow for its trouble. The creature's gangly arms possessed great strength. The howling, flailing monster raked its claw-like nails across his face before he could pull away.

Othello kicked out with his uninjured leg, connecting with the handle of the knife still lodged in the archer's chest. The creature let out a pathetic yowl and pitched forward. Slumped but still standing, he turned to the remaining goblins.

None of them had made a move to help their companion. They were, at that moment, exchanging words in their strange tongue while glaring mercilessly at him. Then, as one, the four stepped apart and waited for him to come forward so that they could surround and slay him—or for the poison to finish the job for them.

Othello wiped the sweat and blood from his eyes with a filthy sleeve. The toxin burned in his veins, and he shivered in spite of himself. The ground beneath him pitched back and forth like the deck of a ship in a squall.

The goblins smiled in cruel delight. Confident he was no longer a threat, the four of them came forward, giving him a wide berth as they spaced themselves evenly on all sides.

Weaponless, nauseated, Othello fingered the wooden object he had unconsciously removed from a small pouch at his belt. With one finger, he traced the symbols that were carved into the reddish surface of the coin-like token. He didn't know what the glyphs meant, but his father had insisted it was elfish writing.

He hadn't asked his father why he had given him the token when he had left home. And he didn't question his sudden need to caress the heirloom's smooth surface. If it was a good luck charm, as he had long suspected, he needed its magic now more than ever.

Something sharp tore into the back of his shoulder. With a wild cry, he lunged at his adversary, groping for the goblin's sword arm. It was all he could do to hold the blade down and away from him. As they struggled, he used his opponent for support.

Somewhere in the back of his mind, he wondered if he would have been able to defeat the hunters if they hadn't drugged him. That thought evaporated when the other three goblins made their presence known, their jagged blades biting into his flesh.

Othello roared, but the sound came from someone—or something—else. He forgot all about his missing friends and the burning war camp as he grappled with the predators. There was only pain and the need to survive.

The primal game of kill-or-be-killed lasted mere seconds.

Part 1

Passage I

Alone in his private pavilion, Drekk't wanted nothing more than to lie down on the worn-out cot, close his eyes, and pretend that day's events hadn't happened.

The stench of fire hung heavy in the air, though the last of the flames had been snuffed out more than an hour ago. Subduing the hungry flames had been no easy task. They hadn't had a great quantity of water at their disposal. The general had refused to sacrifice the army's drinking water, and thus, the fire had been left to burn itself out, consuming a good many tents—and soldiers—before finally dying.

Drekk't's army had reduced the island's capital city and one of its fortresses to rubble. Neither battle had been easy. Those victories had come at the cost of many goblin lives, even though the humans had been caught by surprise both times. Yet tonight's fire had caused more damage than an organized counterattack would have.

Of course, the blaze hadn't started itself...

Though his scouts had yet to return, Drekk't had little hope of capturing those responsible for the unexpected offensive. He was too exhausted to be angry. The humans' audacity would not go unpunished—of that he was certain—yet for now, there was nothing to do but sleep and dream of revenge.

He was limping over to his cot when a freezing wind filled the tent, causing the rawhide walls flap madly. Drekk't reached for the broadsword at his hip, thinking the humans had returned. Then he realized what the unearthly breeze portended. His hand stopped halfway to his weapon.

His enemies had not returned, but he trembled nonetheless.

It was impossible to tell whether the tent flaps opened or not because an impossibly dark shadow suddenly occupied the space between him and the only way out. Drekk't gawked, dumbfounded, as the coalescing blackness took shape.

The shrouded figure standing before him was roughly the same size as the general, though Drekk't felt much, much smaller. Wrapped in a robe as dark as crow feathers, the newcomer exuded a tangible aura of power. So strong was the sensation it might have knocked him off his feet had he not already fallen to his knees.

"Arise, General."

"Yes, *n'Kirnost*. Of course, *n'Kirnost*," Drekk't groveled, keeping his eyes downcast.

It wasn't the first time he had cowered before the great personage before him. Before his providential promotion to campaign general, Drekk't had taken his orders from another, one of T'Ruel's many arrogant princes. Drekk't had advanced in rank thanks to that prince's costly mistakes.

These days, he took his orders directly from the top.

Drekk't had many reasons to feel apprehensive before the Emperor of T'Ruel. Not the least of which was the Emperor's intolerance for failure of any degree. Even if the general had great news to impart this night—which he certainly did not!—Drekk't would have found it difficult to keep a tremor out of his voice.

The Emperor's absolute authority in T'Ruellian society was matched only by his godlike magic. Drekk't had no idea whether the Emperor had used *vuudu* to cross the ocean and visit him in person or whether he had created an illusion of himself to manifest on the island. Not that it mattered.

Drekk't knew very little about how *vuudu* worked, and that was just fine with him. He bore no love for spells or the shamans who wielded them. He was a warrior. He won his victories through cunning tactics, relying on the sword and the strength of the arm wielding it.

As a rule, shamans did not impress Drekk't. The Emperor, however, was the one exception.

"Tell me what has transpired here."

Still looking down at the ground, the general took a deep breath and took a couple of seconds to search for words to describe the tragic events that had transformed his war camp into a scene of disorder and destruction.

His mouth refused to cooperate. He would have rather stabbed himself in his good leg than confess his failure to the

Emperor, but outright lying wasn't an option. Drekk't had to practically spit out each sour-tasting sentence as he related how a handful of humans had sneaked past the perimeter guards, rescued a valuable prisoner, and covered their retreat by igniting the army's stockpile of explosives.

He decided against mentioning the part where two of the humans had bested him in close combat, wounding him badly before making their escape...

The Emperor said nothing as the general imparted his ill tidings. When Drekk't reached the end of his report, he was forced to wait several uncomfortable minutes before the Emperor spoke.

"And they all escaped."

Unsure of whether his sovereign lord was asking him a question or stating a fact, Drekk't muttered, "They did, *n'Kirnost*."

The Emperor then made a noise that sounded like a growl. Drekk't glanced up in spite of himself. His gaze was drawn to the only color within so much black. Deep within the Emperor's cowl, two small orbs of fiery scarlet flickered like candles in a gale. Even though he knew the Emperor was a goblin underneath it all, Drekk't felt as though he were standing face to face with Death.

Under the scrutiny of the Emperor's unnatural eyes, Drekk't was assailed by the sudden need to fill the terrible silence. "I sent my best trackers to hunt the humans down," he added, "But all except one of the ghost-skins fled on horseback, *n'Kirnost*. They couldn't hope to catch them."

There was another long pause, during which the general could do nothing but squirm inwardly and remember how his predecessor, Prince T'slect, had been punished. If the Emperor could treat his own son so mercilessly, what chance did the general have of walking away unscathed?

Finally, the Emperor spoke. His voice was deep—deeper than any voice Drekk't had ever heard. There was an echo-like quality to the tone as well, as though the Emperor were standing inside a cave rather than a tent.

"I am most displeased, General Drekk't. T'slect's incompetence forced our hand against the humans. You and your army have enjoyed two major victories, but your counterpart in the west has not fared so well. I have sent reinforcements to aid that army, but that is the last ship I send to this island until it has been conquered and annexed to T'Ruel."

"Yes, *n'Kirnost*."

"Is there anything else you wish to report before I leave you to clean up your mess?"

Drekk't hesitated. He had glossed over another aspect of the humans' raid on the camp. Now he wondered if the Emperor had read between the lines—had read his mind, for that matter—or if that question had been mere routine.

General Drekk't summoned every ounce of courage he possessed and uttered the words that could well prove to be his last.

"*Peerma'rek*...it was taken by the humans."

The temperature inside the tent dropped so drastically Drekk't saw his breath pouring from his nostrils in frantic puffs. A veteran soldier of countless campaigns, Drekk't counted himself among goblinkind's bravest deadliest specimens. Yet given a choice between facing a regiment of berserker dwarves or the wrath of his sovereign lord, he would pick the bearded bastards every time.

Rumor had it that the Emperor was the son of Upsinous, the goblins' patron god. Others said that he was Upsinous in disguise. At that moment, Drekk't would have believed either was true.

"I promoted you to campaign general despite the fact that you were not granted Upsinous's greatest gift," the Emperor said at last. "Though you are not Chosen of the Chosen, I put my faith in your abilities as a leader and as a warrior. I lent you *Peerma'rek*, the greatest of the Goblinfather's talismans, to make up for your shortcomings.

"It was a mistake to give you the staff. I should not have bestowed upon you the gift of *vuudu* when Upsinous himself deigned not to do so at birth.

"I do not enjoy being proven wrong, General."

To Drekk't's astonishment, the Emperor did not follow his statement with a fatal blow.

"You lost *Peerma'rek*, and you will recover it," the Emperor said. "If you do not, you won't live long enough to regret it. I don't care what it takes. Being the fine tactician that you are, I am confident you will find a way to accomplish both of your objectives...regaining the staff *and* conquering the island."

Drekk't could barely move his lips to reply. "Yes,

n'Kirnost."

The Emperor's silhouette started to fade. The effect resembled nothing so much as a desert mirage vanishing upon closer inspection. The deep voice was as strong as ever, however, as it spoke some final words:

"You made the same mistake as T'slect. You underestimated the humans. Do not do so again."

The red, unblinking spheres were the last to disappear, leaving Drekk't alone in darkness.

A path cleared before Ay'sek as he strode through the rows of tents. The soldiers' conversations ceased one by one, resuming only when they assumed he was out of earshot. He paid them no heed. They were unlearned louts, the lot of them. He was above them all, and they knew it.

On another night, Ay'sek might have strained to hear the resurging dialogues on the off chance a soldier dared speak ill of him. He couldn't begrudge those born without Upsinous's gift their jealousy, but insubordination would not be tolerated.

He knew he had a reputation for being short-tempered and rigid—even for a shaman. The goblins now bowing and averting their eyes as he passed by did so out of fear as well as respect.

But tonight he had better things to ponder than useless underlings. The quenching of the fire had been in no small part his doing, and the measures had taken their toll, leaving him weary and eager for rest. He had only just fallen asleep when the messenger—an obsequious imp, to be sure—roused him back from the realm of dreams.

Here and there, tendrils of smoke spiraled up to the heavens, which was an indecisive gray. Whatever late night or early morning, it was hardly an appropriate time for a Chosen of the Chosen to be disturbed. True, he was living in an army camp, but was nothing sacred?

The closer he got to his destination, the more irritated he grew. Gritting his teeth, he craned his neck in search of a tent unlike its neighbors. He had never had any use for Drekk't, but after tonight, his estimation of the general had sunk to new lows.

When he finally reached Drekk't's pavilion, he did not hesitate. Sweeping past the sentries, he stormed inside the tent and leveled a look at the general that, he hoped, expressed the full measure of his displeasure.

Drekk't leaned over a small, wooden desk, scratching at some parchment with a quill. The furniture—all of the pavilion's accoutrements, in fact—were spoils of war, but whether they had been acquired from the wreckage of Rydah or taken from some other land, Ay'sek couldn't guess. Drekk't's residence wasn't lavish per se, but it was spacious.

Space, however, was a luxury in itself. Even Drekk't's highest-ranking officers shared their tents with others, and after tonight's fire, quarters were bound grow even more cramped. The general lived better than anyone else in the camp—aside from a certain shaman.

"Ay'sek," Drekk't grunted, not deigning to look up from his writing. "Thank you for coming so promptly."

Ay'sek narrowed his eyes. No, he had never liked Drekk't. Smug, insolent Drekk't, who held no regard for proper etiquette. Disrespectful Drekk't, with his blatant disregard for Upsinous's gift and the gifted. It was a wonder that some shaman hadn't killed the arrogant brute long ago. Though murder was an unforgivable crime in T'Ruellian society, it was also dangerous for anyone to accuse another of murder—especially if the murderer were a shaman.

"Your lack of respect wears on my patience, General," Ay'sek snapped. "You will address me as *n'feranost* or Master Ay'sek."

Drekk't looked up from his work, blinking stupidly, then dropped the quill and rose to his feet. He wore the expression of a sleepwalker woken in the midst of a late-night stroll, leaving Ay'sek to deduce that the general hadn't meant any offense. Drekk't was simply distracted.

But that only annoyed Ay'sek more. Most goblins possessed a healthy dose of fear for their betters. Drekk't, however, was so accustomed to ignoring his place within the hierarchy that he lacked the instinct to kowtow.

"My apologies, Master Ay'sek." Drekk't gave a slight nod of his head, a sad excuse for a bow.

Ay'sek didn't reply. He was curious about the document that had so captivated the general's attention, but he wouldn't give Drekk't the satisfaction of asking about it. Instead, he studied the warrior.

Dark circles surrounded Drekk't's dull orange eyes, though

the rest of his complexion looked waxen. His grayish yellow skin had lightened to a color resembling the ash blowing around the camp, and while most all goblins hunched a bit, Drekk't's above-average build appeared to be too much for the general to support just then.

Forget spells, Ay'sek thought, I need only blow on him, and he'll topple over!

Drekk't's wretched condition was almost enough to bring a smile to the shaman's face. The general's present state could well have been the result of the humiliation that the humans had dealt him, but something told Ay'sek that there was more to it than that. Come on and spit it out, he silently demanded. I don't have all night.

Drekk't tore his tired gaze away from Ay'sek's and spoke. "As you know, the Emperor saw fit to bestow upon me the talisman *Peerma'rek*. You also know that the humans stole it from me this night."

Ay'sek nodded, and now he did smile, albeit slightly. He had never liked the idea of Drekk't—or any mere solider for that matter—possessing *vuudu*. Upsinous's gift was reserved for the Chosen of the Chosen alone. He had often wondered why Upsinous suffered such a blasphemous tool to even exist.

Seeing Drekk't with *Peerma'rek* had been like watching a rabbit test out a pair of wings. And it irked him even more to think of humans handling one of Upsinous's greatest relics.

"I want you to recover *Peerma'rek*."

Ay'sek scoffed. "And whom do you mistake me for...one of your witless lackeys? You were the one who lost it, Drekk't. *You* retrieve it."

Had anyone else in the camp spoke to Drekk't that way, he would have been justified in skewering him on the spot. Drekk't was the campaign general, after all. He commanded the thousands of soldiers that made up this battalion, and he would govern the combined forces of the eastern and western armies once the two regiments rendezvoused at the center of the island.

Militarily, Drekk't was the highest-ranking officer on the island. But an ungifted goblin never outranked one of the Chosen of the Chosen.

The general didn't seem overly bothered by Ay'sek's harsh words. If anything, he looked amused.

"I am the campaign general," Drekk't stated. "I have a war to win. I cannot be in two places at once, and you are the only other person I trust with this task."

"And what makes you think I will do it?" Ay'sek challenged.

"The Emperor has commanded it."

Ay'sek couldn't quite suppress a startled snort. Only Upsinous himself held more authority than the Emperor of T'Ruel. Drekk't could have ordered Ay'sek to clean his boots with his tongue, and as long as he had the Emperor's blessing, Ay'sek couldn't refuse.

He did not doubt Drekk't had spoken with the Emperor. While the shaman had never conversed with T'Ruel's sovereign lord himself, he had seen people who had, and all of them—shamans and the ungifted alike—had been shaken by the experience. They had all been physically and mentally sapped—just as Drekk't clearly was.

Ay'sek understood now that he was trapped. Oh, he might take up the matter with the Emperor, but Ay'sek valued his life far too much to risk second-guessing an order. If the Emperor wanted *Peerma'rek* back, Ay'sek wasn't going to be the one to deny him it.

"Why not send one of your lieutenants?" Ay'sek demanded.

"We underestimated the humans," Drekk't replied. "To attempt to take the staff by force would be folly. I'm certain of that. Even if they didn't use *Peerma'rek* against us, we would lose valuable lives in the struggle.

"But I have devised a way to get it back without sacrificing a single soldier. Prior to the invasion, you disguised yourself as a human. You posed as the Renegade Leader of Rydah and tricked the rebels into opening the gates of the capital city. You lived among humans for almost a year. You know how to act like one."

Not to mention I'm the only shaman in your gods-forsaken army, Ay'sek groused.

Drekk't added, "You will track down the humans who stole *Peerma'rek*, and you will take it back."

Ay'sek might have argued. He could have pointed out that the army needed him. Without its cache of explosives, the battalion would have a difficult time with the remaining fortifications and walled cities. They needed him. They needed *vuudu*.

He might have pointed out that, with him and his spells in the vanguard, a small unit could regain the staff by force, but

Ay'sek also was wary of the fearless humans who had strode boldly into the war camp and walked out again in one piece.

In other circumstances, Ay'sek would have jumped at the chance to extricate himself from the army. At least while pretending to be the Renegade Leader of Rydah, he had lived comfortably. A war camp was not his idea of fine living—not like the upper echelon who resided at T'Ruel's finest temples—but neither was Ay'sek eager to return to the humans. Despite their many flaws, goblin soldiers were far better company than the ugly ghost-skins.

Ay'sek glared at Drekk't. "For your sake, General, I hope you bring this conquest to an end soon. The Emperor is not the only one hoping for a quick triumph over the humans."

Without another word, Ay'sek swiveled on his heels and stomped out of the tent. He was due for a long holiday back in T'Ruel once this war was over. If disguising himself as a human—again—would bring the end that much closer, so be it.

Ay'sek directed his steps back toward where his private tent—and its precious solitude—awaited. What he needed now was time to think and, of course, sleep. Unlike some goblins he could name, he preferred careful planning to spontaneous displays of force. An enemy killed by a knife in the dark was just as dead as one ripped apart by a barrage of spells.

Drekk't probably expected him to leave a trail of gutted humans on his trail to *Peerma'rek*, but if Ay'sek was going to take on this mission, he would do things *his* way.

As he lay down on his pallet, an ancient goblin axiom came to mind:

"Never cause more killing than you must, lest the last death be your own."

Passage II

Outside the window, the tree-strewn landscape grew darker by the minute. A few flurries danced on the wind, tiny harbingers of the winter to come. The meager candlelight inside the cottage lent the pane of glass a mirror-like quality, framing the countenance of the man who stood before it.

Colt's face had regained some of the shape and color it had lost during his time with Drekk't. Generous nourishment and plenty of rest would do much to improve his appearance, the young commander knew, but he had no appetite, and his sleep had not been restful these past two nights.

While scrapes and bruises would fade, some scars might never heal.

Although he stared out the window, Colt saw neither his reflection nor the woods beyond. In his mind's eye, he saw Cholk straddling his chest and pounding his fists meaty fists into Colt's face.

The goblins were all around them, their shrill cheers building with every blow. Colt hadn't the strength to defend himself. And he couldn't bring himself to fight for his life, *wouldn't* give the goblins the pleasure of watching him battle his friend. If the dwarf wanted to destroy the life he had saved so many months back, it was his right...

Cholk procured an arrow, a bolt that had been shot at Colt to motivate him to fight back. But instead of plunging the arrow-head into Colt's breast, Cholk used it to slit his own throat. Colt would never forget the dwarf's final words before he sacrificed himself:

"Suicide is a great crime among my people, but to give your life so that another might live...well...I'd say that's honorable enough. Sorry I had to make it look so real..."

Colt's eyes caught movement. So caught up in the memory was he that he couldn't immediately discern whether it had come from the inside or the outside of the cottage. When he felt a hand on his shoulder, he turned suddenly to regard the person who had stolen up on him.

At the sight of Opal, he exhaled a breath laden with too many emotions to count. He had been infatuated with the beautiful archer since he met her back in Continae. Even then, he couldn't say no to her. She had enjoyed free passage with him and his Knights to Capricon. He wasn't sure when he had started to truly love her, but he could admit it now, if only to himself.

He had thought his heart would burst when their eyes had met in the goblin tent that had served as his prison.

Opal smiled at him now, though Colt recognized it for the front it was. She was worried about him, and he loved her all the more for her concern. While he had been lying in that tent, paralyzed by the *vuudu* of Drekk't's staff, he had had plenty of time to think. He vaguely recalled swearing he would confess his feelings to Opal if he survived the ordeal.

But caught in her dazzling green eyes, beholding and beholden to her full lips and the braid of golden-red tresses, Colt didn't know where to begin. And so he did what he had done every day since their miraculous escape from the goblin camp. He swore that he would tell her the next time they were alone.

Since there were currently twelve other people residing at the cottage, the private conversation would not come soon.

"Are you all right?" Opal asked, careful to keep her voice low. No less than nine people were sharing the single, communal room with them at the moment.

"I'm just eager to be on our way," Colt replied, which was more or less true.

Ever since his promotion to Commander of Fort Faith, Colt had suffered from chronic indecision. He had second-guessed every decision during the conflict with a local band of Renegades and, later, with the goblins who had instigated the rebellion in secret.

Colt had been all too eager to leave Fort Faith and the responsibility that went along with being a commander. He had led a small party—a group that had included Opal, Cholk, and two rebels who had been enemies just days before—to Rydah.

But their warning of a goblin invasion came too late. The

capital city was now little more than several square miles of ruins. Colt knew it was his duty return to the fort and prepare his men for the attack that would inevitably come, but he had come to this cottage instead, to regain his strength and get his thoughts in order.

Now was time to vanquish doubt once and for all.

He knew what he had to do, and he was resolved to do it.

Opal broke eye contact and glanced out the window. Colt wondered if she was looking for the only other person who hadn't made it back to the cottage.

Othello had run off when Opal and the others had rescued him from the goblin camp. They had been forced to leave the forester behind in order to save themselves. Colt knew almost nothing about the man, which made him feel even guiltier that his liberation had likely come at the cost of Othello's life.

Opal, apparently, had come to know the forester during their trek to the goblin camp. She had cursed Lilac—the third member of the rescue party—for losing track of Othello in the chaos that ensued. He suspected the forester's absence was partly responsible for Opal's subdued spirits. Colt couldn't deny he was a little jealous of the absent forester, though the man was almost certainly dead.

That Othello was a Renegade made the situation still more puzzling to Colt; Opal had never masked her disdain for the rebels.

He felt as though he should say something to comfort Opal, but just then a third person joined them at the window.

"Are you all ready, Commander?" Sir Dylan asked.

They all had been restless today, but Dylan Torc was the edgiest of them all. Dylan, one of only a few Knights to escape Rydah's destruction, had a reputation for being impatient. That was probably why he had been allowed to lead a motley team to the cottage in the first place.

Dylan, a handful of other Knights, and some characters of lesser repute had all volunteered to leave the safety of Hylan—a sprawling farming community that had yet to face the full brunt of Drekk't's army—and return to Rydah. The troupe had combed the ruins for survivors before pressing their luck with some reconnaissance work.

It had been Dylan and his companions who had stumbled upon the goblin camp moments before Colt, Opal, and Lilac had needed to make their getaway. Dylan himself had convinced Colt to go back to Hylan with him and his men, after a few days' rest at the cottage.

"I am ready and eager," Colt told Dylan.

Dylan nodded vaguely and said, "Allow me, Commander..." The fair-haired Knight stepped forward, wedging himself between Colt and Opal, and drew the curtain shut.

"Even a single candle can act as a beacon when it's black as pitch outside," he explained. "No need to bring the goblins down on us now...not when we've remained hidden this long. We'll be heading out as soon as the sentries return..."

Alternating his gaze from Colt to Opal, Dylan apparently came to the conclusion that he was intruding for he turned and walked away again. Almost immediately, the Knight resumed the erratic pacing that had occupied him for the past hour or more.

Colt couldn't hide a smile. None of them had more than an armful of possessions, and yet Dylan had insisted on reminding them all—repeatedly—to prepare themselves for the journey ahead. As a matter of fact, Colt didn't even own the coat on his back, as the saying went. His clothing had been donated by the man who had once lived at this cottage before goblins stained the floorboards with his blood.

Colt had lost his armor when he had been taken into the goblins' custody. By sheer chance, Opal, Othello, and Lilac had found his sword, which the goblins had discarded on one of the many game trails that crisscrossed the forest.

He was relieved beyond words to have the sword back in his possession. *Chrysaal-rûn* had been in his family for centuries, and the weapon's strange, crystalline blade had proven to be quite a valuable tool against the goblins.

Aside from the crystal sword, Colt would bring only one other object to Hylan, an item so nefarious that few others in the group would dare to touch it.

Colt glanced at Opal, who continued to look at the window even though the curtains blocked any vantage of the scene outside. Both she and Lilac had wanted to stay at the cottage one night more to give Othello more time to find them. But everyone else had voted to move on, lest the goblins show up in lieu of the missing forester.

Not knowing what to say to Opal, Colt turned his attention to the others in the cottage. Dylan was exchanging words with Lilac. Colt supposed the woman warrior was assuring him she was ready to go.

Like Othello, Lilac had been a Renegade up until the true menace—the goblins—had made themselves known. Colt didn't know her very well either, but he had faced her in battle on one occasion and knew her to be a capable swordswoman. If Lilac was bitter about having to leave Othello behind, she did well to hide it from the others.

Near Lilac and Dylan sat the cottage's unexpected couple. Mitto O'erlander and Else Fontane had been reunited before Colt arrived at the hideout. From what Colt had gathered over the past couple of days, Else had owned an inn in Rydah, where Mitto, a traveling merchant, was wont to stay. Apparently, the two had acknowledged their love for each other only after believing the other had died at the hands of the goblins.

Else and Mitto sat very near each other, sharing softly spoken words. Colt frowned, though he knew he should be happy they had found love in these troubled times. And yet their affection served as a reminder of how things could be—*should* be—between him and Opal. He so desperately wanted Opal to look at him the way Mitto and Else looked at each other.

Suddenly, the door to the cottage flew open. Colt reached for *Chrysaal-rûn*, but it was only Gomez.

The old man, called Loony Gomez by some, was clad in a long black cloak. He pulled back his hood, self-consciously patting down his wayward strands of gray hair, and then brushed off the light layer of snowflakes from his shoulders. Gomez looked more like a befuddled beggar than a master burglar, but as the former leader of Rydah's Thief Guild was wont to say, incompetence was a fantastic disguise.

A Knight entered the cottage next, followed by a second thief, a surly fellow who went by the name of Tryst.

Dylan was on the trio in a flash.

"Get your things. We leave at once," he announced. Colt thought that the Knight looked more excited than a boy on Yuletide morning.

"Yes, Sir!" Tryst barked sarcastically, pushing his way past Dylan over to where a pot of hot water sat atop a rundown stove.

Gomez also went for the stove. "In a moment, Dylan. I'm half frozen…an' the other half's stiff from standin' for three hours straight."

Dylan let out a loud sigh. "You have five minutes. We dare not linger any longer without a perimeter guard."

Of the three newcomers, only the Knight voiced his agreement. Gomez and Tryst were already bringing steaming-hot mugs to their mouths.

Thanks to the small stove, the cottage was temperate, if not overly warm. Colt wondered how cold it was going to get that night. It probably would have been a good idea for everyone to imbibe some of the hot liquid before venturing out into the chilly night.

As the three sentries enjoyed their drinks and a bit of leftover supper, everyone else watched and waited in silence. While the hike to Hylan would not be terribly long, Colt found himself considering the various problems that could arise along the way. Not the least of them was the goblin army.

"You're not taking *that*, are you?"

It took Colt a second to realize Tryst was talking to him, and it took even longer for him to understand what the thief was referring to. Glancing down at his right hand, Colt was astonished to find he had been holding the *vuudu* staff the whole time.

The *vuudu* staff—Colt had no idea what else to call the wretched thing—was comprised of a grayish rod resembling petrified wood, a yellowed skull that rested atop one end, and some black feathers sprouting out beneath the jawbone to make a macabre beard.

The goblin general had used the staff to render his prisoners helpless. The staff had also allowed Drekk't and Colt to communicate, despite the fact that they spoke two very different languages. The staff could do other tricks too...

In stealing the *vuudu* staff, Colt had robbed the goblins of a great weapon, and at the same time, he had stripped Drekk't of the ability to wield magic.

"Let's just bury the damn thing and be done with it," Tryst said. "Thing gives me the willies."

Colt, who had been absentmindedly studying the staff, now held it protectively against his chest. Although he loathed the *vuudu* staff—despised it for what it had done to him—he would never relinquish it willingly. They had gained the staff at the cost of Cholk's life. He'd not dishonor the dead dwarf by throwing it away.

To Tryst, Colt simply said, "No."

"For all we know, the goblins might be able to track us because we have it," the thief argued.

"All the more reason why we shouldn't leave it lying around where they can easily get it back," Colt replied.

"It's not worth dying for!" Tryst spat.

"If the goblins could track us with it, wouldn't they have come by now?" Opal pointed out.

"She has got a point," Dylan said to the thief, whose face settled into a deeper scowl.

"Fine then," Tryst said. "But don't expect me to save your asses when it starts raining black arrows."

"Gods above and below, where's Lucky?" Gomez asked.

So loud was the older thief's shout that Tryst spilled some of his drink on the front of his shirt. Tryst started swearing, but everyone else looked around for the missing man.

"He's probably just fertilizing the forest." Tryst punctuated the comment with a curse as he dabbed at the scalding mess on his chest with one of his sleeves

Gomez's face was a portrait of unadulterated distress. "Darclon smite me, I must be slippin'. I can't even keep track of me boys anymore!"

Although Gomez was a master criminal—or had been, until the Renegade movement in Rydah had edged out the Thief Guild—it was clear the old man genuinely cared for his cohorts. Gomez was already donning his wet cloak and walking back to the cottage's entrance when the door opened again.

Gomez's face provided Colt with all the confirmation he needed. The old man's eyebrows, which had been furrowed beneath a relief map of wrinkles, shot skyward. His mouth curled at each end to form an enormous grin.

The next moment, Gomez gave the newcomer a not-so-gentle shove.

"Gods damn you, Lucky. You nearly gave me a heart attack!"

Beside Colt, Opal let out a quiet laugh, and Colt found himself smiling too. Everyone watched as Gomez dragged Lucky over to the warmth of the stove, all the while berating the thief for being "pokey."

Rolling his eyes at Gomez and Lucky, Tryst took another sip

of his tea. Though he had never said a word to him, Colt liked Lucky better than Tryst. Where Tryst was pushy, cynical, and just plain rude, Lucky was quiet and easygoing. The man wasn't a mute, but Lucky was clearly comfortable with letting others do the talking.

Five minutes later, the cottage was empty, and fourteen riders with little in common except a grudge against the goblins followed a narrow trail through the expansive forest that covered northeastern Capricon. They were companions by circumstance, allies out of necessity.

Although Colt outranked Dylan, the commander had no qualms with letting him lead the way. For one thing, Dylan knew the quickest route to Hylan.

Colt took up position behind Dylan and Lilac, who rode together since there weren't enough horses to go around. Colt had been more than happy to partner with Opal. Even though this wasn't a pleasure trip, he basked in every moment he was near the woman.

Each and every one of them kept a wary eye on the shadow-strewn forest, an eerie environment that could conceal all manner of predators. A wan sliver of a moon lit their way, its light bleeding through the sheet of clouds stretched across the sky.

In silence, the troupe trudged forward…

To Hylan.

To hope.

Passage III

Dylan had predicted they would reach Hylan by late morning, but the sun had passed its pinnacle hours ago and was now making a slow but steady fall to the western horizon.

Lilac couldn't blame Dylan for his miscalculation. For one thing, the impatient Knight had probably never made the trip without running his horse at a full gallop. She knew racing through the woods at night would have been suicidal, yet even after dawn, the company maintained a conservative pace.

They stopped every few hours, giving the horses the chance to graze and providing the riders an opportunity to stretch and empty their bladders. No stranger to long stretches in the saddle, Lilac grew impatient with the frequent breaks, but she never voiced her complaints.

Not everyone was in as good shape as she was.

While Colt, a Knight of Superius, might have pushed through his weakness on pride alone, Mitto suffered through every minute he spent on horseback. The middle-aged merchant had earned a vicious wound en route to Rydah, and he was not fully recovered—though he did his best to hide it, especially from Else. If it hadn't been for Othello, Mitto would have died in the woods, never knowing Else had survived the fall of Rydah.

Othello...

He was back there somewhere. Logic told her that he was dead, but her heart wanted to believe otherwise. There had always been something uncanny about the man. If anyone could outmaneuver the goblins in the thick forest, it was Othello.

When they finally reached the end of the trees, Lilac couldn't help but cast a final glance back, half expecting to find that the silent forester had been following them all along. Of course, he was not there.

As they left the forest behind, the land sloped up and then down, which slowed them even further. At some point—she had lost all track of time—Dylan announced that they were very near their destination. Lilac scanned the hilly landscape for signs of civilization. She thought she saw a squat, stone building off in the distance, but she couldn't be certain.

As reluctant as she had been to leave the cottage—and Othello—behind, Lilac was now eager to reach Hylan. Her eyelids grew heavier with each passing minute. What she needed was sleep, preferably in a bed. She had had her fill of hard planks.

Her time at the cottage seemed more like a dream than reality. She had done her part to help with sentry duty, but mostly she had just been waiting for Othello to make a miraculous reappearance. She also thought a lot about the other Renegades back at the fort. And she had considered trying to talk Colt into going back immediately.

But she never did work up the courage to confront Colt, who looked like he had been to the Crypt and back. As a matter of fact, the only person she had really talked with was Dylan. The older sister of a Superian Knight, she had found common ground with Sir Dylan Torc, though their conversations hadn't delved too deep.

None of the other Knights seemed interested to chat with her, possibly because she was a Renegade. She might have gotten to know Else and Mitto better, but the recently reunited couple treasured what little privacy they could get. And Gomez, Lucky, and Tryst formed their own clique.

Which left Opal...the last person Lilac would have approached for companionship.

Lilac suspected Opal was still holding a grudge against her for an incident that had happened back when the Renegades and the Knights were still at war—before anyone knew the goblins were working the two political factions against each other.

Moreover, Opal blamed her for Othello's absence. The forester had taken off during their raid on the goblin war camp. While Opal rescued Colt, Othello had slipped away and started an enormous fire for a much-needed diversion. If they had waited for the forester, they all would have perished.

What Lilac couldn't figure out was why Opal cared so much about Othello at all.

Whatever her reasons, Opal seemed to accuse Lilac with every glare. But what Opal didn't know was that Lilac also blamed herself for deserting the forester. She wondered how she would tell Klye and the others when they finally returned to the fort.

Her peripheral vision picked up movement in the elms lining the path. Lilac's hand went for her weapon a moment before her brain could register that they were being ambushed.

Her fingers wrapped around the hilt of the vorpal sword. Whatever enemy had caught her unawares would soon learn the peril of crossing her. Between her skill at swordplay and the enchanted blade that could rip through the strongest of materials with little effort from its wielder, Lilac Zephyr was no easy mark.

She was on the verge of vaulting off the horse to confront the goblins, when she felt Dylan's hand press on her leg to keep her in place.

The ambushers were not goblins, but men—Knights, judging by their costume and demeanor. Swords drawn, they regarded Dylan's company with suspicion. Lilac spotted three archers among their ranks, which meant there were probably a few more hidden somewhere back in the trees.

She silently commended the Knights for their stealth. They wore dun-colored overcoats to better blend in with their surroundings, and some had even dulled the shine of their mail with mud.

"State the pass-phrase!" one of the Knights hollered.

To Lilac's relief, Dylan answered without hesitation. "Larks dally away this fine autumn day."

When none of the surrounding Knights eased off, Lilac began to worry Dylan was mistaken. The Knight who had first spoken, a hale specimen with arms the size of fence posts, look a step toward Dylan, keeping the arrow in his crossbow trained on the man's chest.

"A goblin spell-caster might have been able to pluck the pass-phrase from the true Dylan Torc," the crossbowman stated.

"Then why even bother having a pass-phrase?" Dylan snapped. "You know who we are. Did you think we weren't coming back...hoping maybe?"

His brash reply caused Lilac to flinch. The Knights of Superius were not known for having a sense of humor.

The unfamiliar Knight merely returned Dylan's stare, however, as though his shrewd eyes might penetrate the imagined *vuudu* enchantment.

"Let us pass, Sandros," Dylan said, crossing his arms. "Or would you rather I prove my legitimacy by disclosing intimate details about your time as a squire?"

Still, the crossbowman—Sandros—did not budge.

Dylan cleared his throat dramatically. "Your first night away from home, you cried like a—"

"Lower your weapons!" Sir Sandros called. He lowered the crossbow to his side and gave Dylan a half-hearted salute, which Dylan returned without enthusiasm.

"May I introduce you to Sir Saerylton Crystalus, Commander of Fort Faith," Dylan said, indicating Colt with a wave of his hand.

Colt mimicked Sandros's stiff salute. "*Former* Commander of Fort Faith," he corrected. "Fort Faith has been renamed Fort Valor in honor of the original Fort Valor, which has been destroyed."

Sandros's face paled. "Fort Valor is no more?"

Dylan cleared his throat. "We come bearing important news…"

Sandros nodded and stepped off the path. "May the Warriorlord watch over you," he said as the group of fourteen started forward once more.

Tryst muttered something sarcastic in response to Sandros's reference to the Knight's patron god. She glanced over her shoulder and watched the Knights return to their hiding places between the stalwart elms.

Removing her hand from atop the vorpal sword's pommel, she turned her attention ahead and watched as the distant structures grew in size. As they crested a final hill, she got her first unobstructed view of Hylan.

Taking in the single avenue lined with several small buildings, Colt might have called Hylan a one-horse town, except he could see two steeds tied to a post outside what appeared to be a store.

When they reached the first building, Dylan dismounted, and everyone else followed suit. Dylan told his Knights to take the horses to the stable, which they did without comment. Colt's eyes followed the men as they walked the animals over to a building farther down the dusty road.

"This place was never intended to house an army," Dylan said, though Colt wasn't sure whom he was addressing. "The local farmers would come here to buy supplies, trade, and socialize. I would wager the stable has never been so full."

They bypassed the store Colt had noticed earlier and came to a stop outside one of the few two-story buildings in the village.

"The Knights of Superius have never had much of a presence here," Dylan stated, turning to regard Colt. "There are no walls or towers, no barracks. There isn't even a proper office since the mayor works out of his home.

"And since Hylan has its own militia, there was never a need to station Knights here. The villagers would call upon the Knights in Rydah only if things got out of hand, which didn't happen often in a place so small."

The whitewashed building's sign had faded beyond legibility, but Colt was certain it was an inn. He had done some traveling in Superius before joining the Knighthood. With their father's coin, he and his brothers had always opted for the finest lodgings.

In spite of its rundown appearance, Colt thought the inn looked like a palace. The prospect of a straw mattress alone was a blessing from above.

"There wasn't enough room for everyone to stay here," Dylan continued after a thoughtful pause. "We had to ask the local farmers and huntsmen to put up most of Rydah's refugees."

As Dylan spoke, Opal gravitated toward the inn's door. Colt had invited her to lean against his back and sleep during their ride, but the jostling horse—or the threat of a goblin ambush—had kept her awake throughout the night and the start of the day.

Dylan quickly positioned himself between Opal and the door. "My apologies, miss, but it wouldn't be proper for a lady to enter what has become the barracks."

"Then where in the hells are we supposed to sleep?" Opal demanded. "If you think I'm going to hike to some homestead and share a room with a brood of brats, you're sadly mistaken."

Dylan's tanned complexion took on a rosy hue. "Actually, we converted the back of the storehouse into quarters for the women."

"Female Knights?" The question had come from Lilac.

Dylan looked even more embarrassed. "Ah, no, not exactly. Some of Gomez's thieves had been staying there, but they were assigned to border patrol not long before we left for Rydah."

"Good lasses, ev'ry one of 'em," Gomez boasted. "Quiet as cats, with eyes…and claws…just as sharp."

"I can attest to that," Tryst laughed while making a show of rubbing his back.

"Good…we'll have the place to ourselves," Opal said to Lilac. "Not that I'm picky. I'm so tired I'd share a room with an ogre."

An ogre but not a handful of farm children? Colt thought. He tried to imagine Opal raising children of her own but couldn't. The notion left him feeling sad. He had always liked kids…

"Where is this storeroom?" he heard Else ask. Colt glanced back at the middle-aged woman and found her looking as bleary-eyed as the rest of them.

"In the back part of the shop," said Dylan, pointing back the way they had come.

"Why didn't you say *before* we walked past it?" Opal demanded. "If I don't get some sleep soon, I'm bound to get cranky."

With that, Opal started walking toward the shop. Lilac flashed Dylan a sheepish smile, and then she and Else left the group.

Dylan, his face clouded with bewilderment, said nothing as the woman departed. Colt figured Dylan—whose reservoir of nervous energy never seemed to run dry—that the other members of the company were weary after their long ride. If the young Knight was at all tired, he didn't show it.

Dylan looked at Colt and the others as though really seeing them for the first time that day. "Um, why don't we see if there is any vacancy in the barracks?"

No one argued.

The seven men entered the inn and trudged up the creaky, wooden steps. They came upon a hall of doors. Dylan tentatively peeked inside the first one, only to find it occupied. The next room was also full, but the third was empty.

Well, not exactly empty, Colt realized. There were clothing and other belongings strewn about, but the owners were nowhere to be found.

"Finders keepers," Tryst intoned as he plopped himself down on one of the beds.

Dylan cleared his throat. "I suppose we can rest here until the sentries return for the night. I'll find out where we should stay when I give the report."

If the others heard what Dylan was saying, they didn't respond. Tryst was already wrapping a blanket around himself. Colt thought he saw the glint of steel before the thief's hand slid beneath his pillow. Lucky and Gomez chose beds nearest Tryst's.

Mitto sat upon a bed next to Gomez's. The merchant gingerly reclined, grimacing in discomfort as the wound in his side stretched. When he found a suitable position, Mitto let out a contended sigh and closed his eyes.

"Commander," said Dale, "perhaps it would be best if you came with me. They will want to hear what you have to say about Prince Eliot...the *false* Prince Eliot...and about Fort Valor."

Although he had known the request would come, Colt couldn't hold back a sigh.

"Lead on," Colt replied.

Dylan hesitated a moment, glancing down at something. Colt followed the Knight's gaze to the *vuudu* staff, which Colt still carried. Dylan looked like he was going to say something but then thought better of it.

Colt briefly considered leaving the staff behind. He entertained the idea for no more than a second, though. With one hand steadying *Chrysaal-rûn*'s scabbard against his leg and the *vuudu* staff in the other, Colt cast a longing look back at the empty beds and followed Dylan outside.

Once inside the shop, Lilac paused to take a look at her surroundings. The space behind the counter was unoccupied, and the shelves were all but bare. The place smelled like a blend of cinnamon, sage, and old wood. Ahead of her, Opal lifted a portion of the countertop and was about to cross through the threshold of what, presumably, led to the storeroom, when someone appeared in the doorway, blocking her way.

"Well, well, well. If I knew you were comin', I woulda tidied up a bit."

The woman didn't seem surprised to see the three of them, but her hazel eyes narrowed as she scrutinized her new roommates. Lilac took the opportunity to study the woman in return.

She had a pretty face with a deep cleft in her chin. Despite the season, she wore summer slacks and a short-sleeved shirt that stretched tight across her small breasts. Her muskrat brown hair was cropped tight against her neck. Lilac saw scars of varying size and color dotting her muscular arms.

"The name's Hunter. Don't believe I ever seen any of ya before, which means you ain't from around here."

"I'm Opal, and she's Lilac," Opal replied, indicating Lilac with a halfhearted wave of her hand. "We came from Fort Faith, but Else here is from Rydah."

"Fort Faith? I didn't think anybody lived there, let alone a couple of handsome fillies like yerselves," Hunter said.

Lilac didn't have the energy for an explanation; and neither, apparently, did Opal.

"It's a long story. We've been on the road all night, and I fear I might fall over at any moment."

Hunter stepped out of the doorway, and made a sweeping motion with her hand. "Well, be my guest, ladies. There'll be time to chat later on. With those monsters lurkin' out there, ain't none of us leavin' anytime soon."

One by one, Opal, Else, and Lilac entered the storeroom, which, Lilac saw, would prove to be a snug dormitory. But she was too exhausted to care. She wasted no time in unfolding one of the bedrolls piled in a corner. Opal and Else did the same.

Hunter watched them from the doorway. "Welcome to Hylan," she said, an enigmatic smile curling her lips. "The odds are great if you're lookin' for a man. 'Specially if you like Knights."

Hunter's grin vanished as she added, "Just don't get any funny ideas about Pillip. He's spoken for."

Lilac exchanged a puzzled look with Else Fontane. When she glanced back at the doorway, Hunter was gone. From the adjacent room, she heard a candy-sweet voice exclaim, "Sweet dreams, girlies."

The sentiment was punctuated by the slamming of the front door.

"She wasn't around the last time I was here," Else said, crawling under her blanket. "She seems like a...colorful

31

person."

Opal scoffed. "That's one way of putting it."

Lilac was too tired to put her thoughts into words. Her eyes closed the instant her head hit the makeshift pillow that was more boot than bedroll. Seconds later, all memory of the woman named Hunter was buried beneath the imaginary adventures of her sleeping self.

Lilac's sleep was deep and long.

Passage IV

Colt had gone to great lengths to escape Fort Faith.

Stifled by the confines of his command, he had exploited a loophole in the Knighthood's laws. By changing Fort Faith's name to Fort Valor and transferring all of his men to the authority to Stannel Bismarc, the commander of the *original* Fort Valor, Colt had freed himself of his responsibilities, enabling him to take an active role in the fight with the goblins.

The only reason the maneuver was legal was because no one had ever thought to do it before.

But in hindsight, Colt hadn't escaped his responsibilities. He had led the party charged with delivering news of the goblin invasion to Rydah. As the company's leader, he was responsible for those who had lost their lives on the mission.

Everyone from the goblin Drekk't to Sir Dylan still called him "Commander," even though his fort—Fort Faith— technically no longer existed. And while Gomez, Mitto, and the others were allowed to sleep in Hylan's provisional barracks, Colt was expected to report to the village's authority with Dylan.

Once the two of them exited the inn, Dylan stopped. Not understanding the reason for delay, Colt shot his companion a look that said, "Now what?"

Dylan cleared his throat. "There are some things I should tell you before we go."

Colt waited, all but tapping his foot.

"There are three factions struggling for control of Hylan."

Taking in the meager assembly of buildings that made up Hylan's center of commerce, Colt might have found Dylan's words humorous. As it was, Colt was too tired to be good-humored about anything, let alone a lengthy explanation that was bound to complicate his life further.

"Quillan Dag is the Mayor of Hylan," Dylan told him. "By law, he is the village's highest authority and commands Hylan's militia. But Quillan is no warrior, and so far he has been content to let those more experienced in the ways of battle manage the village's defenders."

As he spoke, Dylan's eyes fixed on a structure farther down the road. Colt followed his gaze to what looked like a large house. He assumed it was the home of Quillan Dag--and their destination.

"Sergeant Dale Mullahstyn is the highest-ranking Knight to survive the fall of Rydah," Dylan continued. "He speaks for the Knights here in Hylan. Ever since our arrival, Dale has been trying to convince the mayor to evacuate everyone from the region."

"Evacuate to where?" Colt asked, intrigued in spite of his weariness.

"Kraken," Dylan answered. "Or Steppt...anywhere, really. As you've surely noticed, Commander, there would be no stopping the goblins if they set their sights on Hylan. The farm-steads are spread out across miles, and even if we managed to gather everyone into the village proper, we have neither walls nor men enough to defend them."

Colt nodded. While he hadn't seen the ruins of Rydah, he had seen the army that made them. Hylan wouldn't last an hour.

From the way Dylan had spoken, Colt presumed Dylan agreed with his commanding officer. What the man said next, however, changed Colt's mind.

"Dale is a far-removed member of Superian nobility. He was one of a dozen sergeants stationed in Rydah. He has always lorded over his subordinates, and now that he has no one to take orders from, he's acting like he's the gods-damned King of Capricon."

Dylan's eyes were narrowed, as though he were glaring at the sergeant through the wall of the mayor's house. Colt wanted to ask Dylan what *he* would do in Dale Mullahstyn's place, but asked a different question instead.

"You said there were three factions in Hylan. Who is the third?"

"Ruford Berwyn. He was Rydah's Captain of the Guard."

Colt had all but forgotten Rydah was a port city, but upon hearing "Captain of the Guard," he was reminded that in a city as large as Rydah, the Knights weren't the only enforcers of peace and justice.

Since Superius's inception four centuries ago, the Knights had protected the realm from wrongdoers in the capacity of governors and soldiers. But as Superius grew in size—territory-wise and population-wise—there were simply too few Knights to oversee so vast an area.

Hence, local constabularies had been developed. Lord Knights gave up their civic authority to mayors and magistrates. Constables maintained law and order in populous cities as well as in towns too small to warrant a barracks for Knights.

Today, the Knights of Superius served primarily as the nation's army, defending coastlines and political borders against foreign invasions.

The man Dylan had mentioned, Ruford Berwyn, was a Captain of the Guard. Port cities like Rydah presented unique challenges. With so many people coming and going, smugglers and pirates could easily lose themselves in the hustle and bustle. It was the guardsmen's responsibility to keep the city's harbor free of crime.

Then, all at once, Colt understood the crux of Hylan's dilemma.

In most instances, the Knighthood and the coastal guards—or pier guards, as they were sometimes called—complemented each other, working together but functioning as separate entities. Neither organization had authority over the other. Thus, neither Dale Mullahstyn nor Ruford Berwyn could be said to outrank the other.

"If the mayor is content to let the warriors plan Hylan's defense, then the problem must stem from the fact that Dale and Ruford don't see eye to eye," Colt concluded out loud.

Dylan flashed him a wry smile. "Captain Berwyn argues against making any rash decisions. He didn't want to abandon the village until we learned more about the goblins' strategy. He wants to coordinate Hylan's efforts with those of Fort Valor…"

Colt knew that Dylan was referring to the original Fort Valor, which had been demolished almost two weeks ago.

"Even though he is not a Knight of Superius, I personally think Ruford Berwyn is better equipped to lead Hylan's resistance. But after he learns the fate of Fort Valor, he might concede to Dale."

Colt caught and held Dylan's eyes for a second, but then the other Knight looked back at that same house down the street.

Dylan must have known that by bringing Colt to Hylan he was upsetting the already precarious structure of power. Colt outranked Sergeant Mullahstyn, and even Ruford Berwyn, a Captain of the Guard, might willingly concede to a commander's leadership.

But had Dylan brought Colt to Hylan to cure the government's paralysis or to further his own agenda?

"Dale won't be happy to learn a commander has arrived in Hylan," Dylan said, his wry smile returning.

"Then we had better not keep him waiting," Colt replied softly.

As he followed Dylan to the home of Quillan Dag, Colt stared at the back of the Knight's head. He might have asked Dylan why he had worked so hard to get him to come to Hylan. He might have asked what Dylan hoped to accomplish by pitting him against Dale and Ruford.

If Colt was going to be used like a tool, he wanted to know to what ends.

But Colt kept silent. He didn't want to offend the Knight with clumsy accusations; he needed all the allies he could get. Somehow, he thought he could trust Dylan, who wore his heart on his sleeve.

Colt had never asked to be a leader of men, but he had seen the goblin army with his own eyes, and he knew what had to be done.

Unconsciously leaning on the *vuudu* staff for support, the exhausted commander mentally prepared himself for his encounter with the erstwhile triumvirate.

Hylan's three leaders were already gathered in a spacious room in the mayor's home when Colt and Dylan arrived. No one seemed surprised to see them, which left Colt to assume one of the Knights from the cottage or some lookout had brought word of their coming.

The first thing Colt noticed upon entering was the large head of a buck mounted above an idle fireplace. The decapitated beast's antlers were so long they nearly touched the ceiling. Other curiosities decorated the walls—including an ancient-looking spear and dead animals of various kinds—but Colt dismissed them all after one glance.

Instead, he fixed his eyes on the three men who quickly rose to their feet. Although Dylan introduced them one by one, Colt could have guessed who was who.

A middle-aged man who had been sitting on a padded wooden chair off to one side, approached Colt with surprising alacrity. The man's belly protruded so far it half hid the brass belt buckle beneath. A bushy brown beard covered the man's chin and cheeks. His polite smile and the laugh lines framing his jovial eyes remained even after shaking Colt's hand.

Colt instantly liked Quillan Dag. He pitied him too. Beneath his friendly manner, the Mayor of Hylan looked anxious and eager for the whole affair to be over with.

Colt muttered a greeting to the mayor and was immediately confronted by a second man.

Ruford Berwyn also had a paunch, but the difference between Ruford's and Quillan's builds was about twenty-five pounds of solid muscle. Ruford's thick, brownish-red mustache billowed out from under his nose and curled at each tip. The skin on his face and hands was dark and leathery, undoubtedly the result of spending so much time in the sun by the sea.

Ruford was bedecked in the red-and-white striped uniform of a guardsman. He wore golden epaulettes and a tall, rounded hat. A curved sword hung from his belt; it was the only visible weapon on Ruford's person.

"Good to meet you, Commander." Ruford's voice was deep and husky—just as Colt had imagined it would be.

"The pleasure is mine," Colt replied.

Ruford's handshake was tempered steel, compared to Quillan's doughy grasp.

Then Ruford stepped aside, making way for the final officer.

Dale Mullahstyn was immediately recognizable as a Knight of Superius. He carried himself with a stiffness a scarecrow might envy. No trace of emotion disturbed the sergeant's statuesque countenance. He looked like every portrait Colt had ever seen of the Knights of yore—serious to the point of stern and seemingly above those he was charged with protecting.

Dale's blond hair looked as though it had been trimmed recently. So fair was the Knight's hair that Colt almost missed the mustache perched above his small mouth. Dale's dark brown eyes were given prominence by his light hair and skin, and Colt felt those dark orbs bore into him as the two of them exchanged bows.

Sergeant Mullahstyn hardly deigned to glance at Dylan as he returned to the straight-backed chair he had been sitting in before Colt and Dylan's arrival. Thanks to Dylan's earlier comment, Colt couldn't help but see Dale's tall-backed chair as throne. He imagined a gilded crown resting atop the "King of Capricon's" head.

No one offered Dylan or Colt a seat. Three pairs of eyes looked to them, waiting for some sort of an explanation. It was Dale Mullahstyn who eventually put their questions into words.

"Sir Dylan, you were sent to Rydah to search for survivors and learn what you could about the enemy. Please…enlighten us."

Dylan shot a brief glance at Colt, as though he would have been happy to let Colt have the floor. Colt returned the look calmly. Then Dylan launched into the report of his eleven-day mission.

The animosity between Dylan and Dale filled the room with nervous energy. Dale interrupted Dylan throughout his story, challenging his subordinate's decisions, which Dylan, in turn, defended with unrestrained vehemence. Colt noticed Quillan Dag spent most of the meeting staring down at his fidgety hands.

As Dylan told of how he and his men had found Opal, Lilac, Mitto, and Othello in Rydah, Dale stole probing glances at Colt.

Colt didn't flinch beneath the sergeant's gaze. In fact, he returned the stare, resisting the urge to look away. The son of a nobleman himself, Colt had met more than his fair share of arrogant aristocrats.

I may be younger than you, Colt thought, but I'm not weaker. I've seen things that would make you mess those fancy trousers of yours…

When Dylan got to the part where he, Gomez, Tryst, and Lucky went off in search of the goblin army, Sergeant Mullahstyn interrupted him with an upraised hand.

"Let me see if I understand you, Sir Dylan. You left Rydah to go look for the enemy?"

"Yes, sir. I—"

"Your orders were to go to Rydah, not to the enemy encampment."

"My orders were to learn more about the goblins," Dylan argued.

"In the vicinity of Rydah, where you were to be looking for those injured or in hiding," Dale said.

"We *did* look for survivors, but didn't find any."

The sergeant appeared not to hear Dylan's rebuttal; he started talking before Dylan even finished his sentence. "And you say you went to the enemy encampment in the company of three thieves?"

"Yes, sir."

"What if they had turned on you?" Dale demanded.

The question must have taken Dylan aback. He opened his mouth, but no words came forth. Colt didn't know the details of how Gomez and his "boys" came to be allies with the Knights and guardsmen in Hylan, but he understood the gist of it. Much like how the Renegades and the Knights at Fort Faith had joined forced, the thieves had banded with their former enemies to fight a greater threat.

"I had no reason to doubt the thieves' loyalty," Dylan said at last. "The goblins destroyed the Guild's home when they destroyed ours."

Dale snorted. "When I let that crazy old man tag along with you, I half expected…and half-*hoped* the rogues would run off. What could have motivated them to seek the invaders' camp, I wonder? Perhaps they didn't find enough loot in the capital's ruins."

Dylan did not reply, but Colt could read the Knight's unspoken words in the violent glare he shot at Sergeant Mullahstyn.

"You may continue with your report," Dale told Dylan, settling back in his throne.

Colt listened as Dylan related how he and the three thieves had helped "Commander Crystalus" and two of his companions escape the goblin war camp.

"That was days ago. Why didn't you make for Hylan at once?" Dale asked.

"One of the commander's men was unaccounted for. We hoped he would find his way to the cottage, but after two nights, we decided we couldn't risk our lives any further."

"You were foolish to stay as long as you did," Dale said. "You had a responsibility to bring the information back to us immediately. What if the monsters had found you and killed you before you could report?"

Dylan said nothing. Colt recalled how Dylan had wanted to leave for Hylan the very next day, but Lilac and Opal had talked him into giving Othello another night. Now the Knight was being remonstrated for his compassion, for compromising.

Colt's respect for Dylan swelled.

"You may continue, Sir Dylan," Dale Mullahstyn bade.

"As you can see, Sergeant...gentlemen...I convinced Commander Crystalus to return with us to Hylan, where he could recuperate from his ordeal...though I must admit I had an ulterior motive in bringing him here.

Colt held his breath.

"Commander Crystalus knows the enemy better than anyone. With his unique intelligence, we might concoct a plan to—"

"What is there to know about our enemy?" Dale interrupted. "They are savage creatures whose only thoughts are for killing."

Colt could have argued that point, but he remained silent.

"I have to admit I am amazed to learn the beasts bother with taking prisoners...unless they were saving you for dessert, Commander."

Again, Colt forced himself to hold his tongue. He wasn't about to tell Dale how Drekk't had used the *vuudu* staff to peel information from his mind. Possibly Dale suspected he had spilled his guts under the duress of torture. In truth, the goblins couldn't have hurt him any more than they had when they stole his will.

After several seconds of silence, Ruford Berwyn spoke.

"Five thousand of the creatures...five thousand *goblins*," the guardsmen said, using the terminology Colt and Dylan had brought with them to Hylan.

Quillan Dag echoed the sentiment with a huge sigh and wiped the perspiration from his forehead.

"It is as I have said all along," Dale said. "We are impossibly outnumbered without any viable options for defending ourselves here."

"How many warriors are there in Hylan?" Colt asked.

"Now that Sir Dylan and his men have returned, there are forty-eight Knights of Superius," Dale replied evenly.

Ruford shot a sidelong glance at Dale Mullahstyn and crossed his arms. "In addition to the *Knights*, there are twenty-seven guardsmen...myself included...roughly fifty militiamen, and a dozen or so thieves from the Guild."

"Less than two hundred against five thousand," Dale summarized, his lips curling into a humorless smile. "And our allies at Fort Valor are all dead."

The sergeant paused for effect. Looking directly at Ruford, he added, "Can there be any argument against evacuating the village now?"

The Captain of the Guard only frowned.

"There are other options," Dylan insisted.

"We have already heard your ideas, Sir Dylan," Dale snapped. "Your opinion has been noted and dismissed. We will not waste time with talk of suicide."

"But—"

"Sir Dylan Torc, I am your commanding officer, and I will not permit insubordination. Is that understood?"

Though he spoke to Dylan, Dale looked directly at Colt. The sergeant was testing him, *baiting* him. Colt nearly surrendered to the indignation burning beneath his skin.

"I suggest we take some time to reflect on this new information before we make any decisions," Ruford said.

Dale rolled his eyes. "Waiting is all we have been doing, Captain. The Warriorlord alone knows why the enemy has not made a move against Hylan, but every second we dally pushes our luck even further. We now know we can expect no help from Fort Valor, and there are not enough men at Fort Faith to make a difference. We must make a decision *now*!"

The quiet that followed Dale's declaration seemed more pronounced than his shouting. Dylan Torc looked as though he plenty to say, but he kept his mouth clamped shut. Be patient, Colt silently bade the Knight. Dale hasn't won yet...

To Colt's surprise, it was Quillan Dag who finally spoke. "This isn't the Knighthood, Sergeant. The people of Hylan won't leave their homes just because you tell them to. They need to know what's going on."

"So let's go tell them," Dale countered, suddenly rising from his chair.

"It...it will take some time to gather everyone," Quillan said, visibly flustered. "And look at poor, Commander Crystalus. He and Sir Dylan have ridden all night without rest. They must be exhausted."

"How soon can you arrange an assembly?" Dale pressed the

mayor, speaking through clenched teeth.

"Tomorrow night."

"Very well," said Dale with a sigh. "We shall tell the masses of our decision tomorrow night."

Colt might have pointed out that a consensus had not been reached, but he was too tired to argue. Let Sergeant Mullahstyn think he bullied everyone into his plan. Though Colt had remained quiet for most of the meeting, he would have his say before long.

Passage V

When Lilac awoke, she would have sworn she had never seen the four bare walls around her before. But when she spotted Else's sleeping form, she recalled the exhausting trek from the cottage to Hylan.

Of Opal there was no sign, and since there were no windows, Lilac couldn't decide if Opal had gotten up early or if she and Else had overslept.

But what was oversleeping to Lilac? What did she have to get up for? She supposed that even though she was a Renegade, whoever was in charge in Hylan might put her to work somewhere. After all, the thieves from the Guild were pitching in.

Folding up her bedroll, she decided that if anyone was going to boss her around, it should be Colt. He had allowed her to join the mission to Rydah in the first place. She would find the young commander and ask him what the plan was. As she ran a hand through her greasy hair, she only hoped she'd have time to clean up before they left for the fort.

If they were going back to the fort.

Lilac walked outside. The chilly air cleared the cobwebs from her mind. A washed-out sun hung near the center of the dull gray sky. Night and morning had come and gone while she rested.

The street that bisected the village of Hylan was empty. Lilac was seized by the irrational fear that the goblins had come and killed everyone while she and Else slept through it all. She shook the notion from her head and reminded herself that Hylan wasn't a populous place to begin with.

Not knowing where else to go, she started toward the converted inn. She had almost reached the door when she spotted Colt, Opal, and Dylan farther up the road, walking away from her. She had not seen where they had come from, but it appeared as though the trio were angling across the street, possibly heading for the stable.

Lilac ran after them, holding her scabbard tight against her thigh so she wouldn't trip over it. As she neared the stable, she realized that there was more to Hylan than the buildings that lined the village's solitary street. Beyond the stable, sprouting up on the other side of a hillock, was an assembly of tents that stretched for a quarter of a mile.

Colt, Opal, and Dylan came to a stop at a largish tent that stood at the fore of the gathering. One by one, they entered the tent. Lilac arrived a few seconds later. Drawing back the flap at the opening, she found Dylan's back blocking her path. She tried to squirm past him, mumbling an unheard apology.

Dylan didn't budge, but she managed to make a space for herself in what proved to be a bit of a crowd. The smell of iodine and the row of cots suggested she was in Hylan's infirmary. She had joined a ring of strangers in standing around a cot occupied by someone of great importance, apparently. The only problem was that a squat man, presumably a healer of some sort, was kneeling over the body, completely blocking Lilac's view.

"Othello!"

Opal left Colt's side, shoving her way to Othello's bedside. Lilac was right behind her. She crouched down by the patient's head and realized with amazement that it was, in fact, the missing forester.

When Lilac had first met Othello, he had been clean-shaven. Now, a full blond beard, soiled with mud and, possibly, blood obscured his chiseled features. His face had lost much of its color and was slick with sweat. His eyes were clenched shut as he threw his head from side to side.

"What's wrong with him?" Lilac asked the healer.

The man did not answer, and in the space that followed, Lilac heard someone ask, "Who is this guy?"

The healer was examining a wound on Othello's leg. Lilac didn't know whether to be grateful that the forester was alive or worried that he looked to be lingering on death's doorstep. How could the gods reunite them only to take him away?

"One of the border patrols found him earlier this morning," someone behind her said. "They called out to him, but he didn't seem to hear them. When they approached, he collapsed."

"He looks done for," opined another, earning him a baleful glare from both Lilac and Opal.

Dylan told the group that Othello was a member of Commander Crystalus's team and how the forester had been lost after he started a devastating conflagration in the goblin camp.

"He's a true hero," Dylan concluded solemnly.

Lilac would have voiced her agreement, but the statement sounded too final, like the memorial carved upon a gravestone.

"Is he going to die?" Opal demanded, grabbing the healer by his sleeve.

"I don't know," the man snapped. "He's lost a lot of blood. These're arrow holes, by the looks of 'em. He's got a high fever, which may melt his brain if I can't bring it down."

"Poison," Lilac whispered.

On their way to Fort Faith, Dominic Horcalus had been stuck with a goblin arrow and had been similarly debilitated. Othello had concocted a brew to battle the Renegade's fever, but only the clerics at Mystel's Temple had been able to cure him.

Sizing up Hylan's healer, who wore the duds of a rancher, Lilac feared that the man was no match for the clerics of the Healing Goddess. For all she knew, he was an animal doctor.

Before she knew what she was doing, Lilac was following the healer's every command, dipping a rag in a bucket of well water, squeezing the excess liquid from it, and wiping Othello's brow. She helped the doctor remove the forester's buckskin shirt and winced at the sight of his injuries.

She couldn't bring herself to question how Othello had crossed the miles between the goblin camp and Hylan in fear that scrutinizing the miracle would somehow nullify it. All the while, she was conscious of Opal's presence. The woman was holding Othello's hand and staring down at him with tear-filled eyes.

Lilac let out a startled cry when Colt drew his sword suddenly and lunged forward. Down came transparent blade of *Chrysaal-rûn*, stopping just inches from Othello's face.

The crowd around her was abuzz with questions, but Lilac realized, then, what Colt was doing. Goblin shamans possessed the ability to take on human form. T'slect had fooled everyone into believing he was the Crown Prince of Superius. But Colt's crystal sword could dispel the goblins' *vuudu*, showing the shaman's true form beneath the enchantment.

Judging by the fact that Colt sheathed his weapon seconds later, he had not seen a goblin face through glassy blade.

Slowly, the tent began to empty out. Dylan lingered a while longer, staring grimly down at Othello. Colt left soon after. Meanwhile, the village's healer worked tirelessly, cleaning and bandaging Othello's wounds, examining his bones for breaks.

At one point, Lilac glanced over at Opal and saw that the woman's eyes were closed. Whether Opal was praying or weeping, Lilac did not know. But she didn't begrudge Opal for her presence there; Othello needed all of the help he could get.

Lilac did what she could to bring him comfort, wiping the sweat from his forehead with the cool rag and trickling water into his mouth with another. Although Othello's eyes flickered open every now and then, he never truly awoke from his fever dreams. The healer, who was in and out of the tent throughout the day, would only shrug his shoulders when either of the women asked him whether Othello would survive.

Her mind wandered as the hours passed. Back at the cottage, she had been annoyed with Opal for how much she worried about Othello, as though she, Lilac, had some claim over him. True, Lilac had fought beside Othello on several occasions. They were allies certainly and companions too, but were they friends?

Did the reticent forester have any true friends?

Othello had joined Klye's band of Renegades months before Lilac. According to Klye, Othello had killed some Superian woodcutters in self-defense. Klye, Ragellan, and Horcalus came to his rescue, saving him from a mob. Othello had remained with the rebels thereafter.

She could add up all she knew about Othello on one hand. He had been a hermit, making his home in a forest. He was an excellent shot with a longbow. He knew something about concocting natural remedies. He seemed to possess a sixth sense for detecting danger.

And he had chosen to follow Opal's plans instead of hers when Opal had wanted to search for Colt and Cholk.

Lilac was still sore about that last point, but she couldn't hold a grudge against a man fighting for his life. She had thought, at the time, that Othello had gone along with Opal because he had romantic feelings for the redhead.

Beside her, Opal gazed down at Othello's face. Lilac might

have given her vorpal sword to know what the woman was thinking.

Sometime later, a man barged into tent. His wide eyes took in her and Opal before coming to rest on Othello. Lilac didn't recognize him—and yet there was something familiar about him. The man let out a sigh that befit his great size.

"Are you looking for someone?" Lilac asked. "The healer should be back shortly."

"Looking for someone," the man repeated. "That I am, missy. I was hoping my boy had finally turned up. This *is* the new arrival, right?"

The man pointed down at Othello, and Lilac nodded.

He let out another sigh. "My boy run off this past summer, and he hasn't come back."

Though not a parent herself, Lilac could imagine the poor man's distress. Anyone would worry over a missing child, but the fact that there was an army of goblins on the island must have made it ten times worse. The man was wringing his hands—which were practically the size of pumpkins—and shifted his gaze from Lilac to Opal.

"My son killed another boy," the man said. "Wasn't his fault, though. He was only trying to save a girl from some unwanted attention, or so she tells it. And no one doubts it. That Llede Hendorm was a bully from the day he was born!"

The man punctuated the exclamation with yet another sigh. "I just wish he'd come home. My boy, I mean. We were able to follow his tracks for a while, but…gods, he could be anywhere by now. And if he was staying in Rydah at the time of the… the…"

He trailed off, and Lilac politely looked away. If this man's son had gone to hide in Rydah, he was surely dead. But there were plenty of other places the kid could have gone. Lilac was about to tell him that very thing, but when she opened her mouth to speak, no words came out, and she all but choked on thin air.

She *had* seen the man before!

Or, rather, she had seen a version of his face that was decades younger. Yes, those were the same clear, blue eyes that revealed more than they could ever hope to hide. The hair was the same too, though the man had patches of white mixed in with the red.

"You're Arthur's father!"

The man pulled a baffled face that probably resembled Lilac's own, confirming her suspicion without ever saying a word.

Arthur's father was perhaps a full foot taller than his son, and he was nearly twice as wide. But there was no denying the resemblance. Now that she saw it, she wondered why she hadn't seen it right away. And it all made sense when she thought about it. Arthur had never explained why he was working as a dockhand in Port Town—which was about as far away as one could get from Hylan without leaving the island.

"You...you know my boy?" the man whispered, his eyes glistening with unshed tears.

"I know a young man named Arthur Bismarc—"

"That's him! Tell me, where'd you see him?"

Lilac was already regretting opening her mouth. She wanted so much to put the man's worries to rest, but she couldn't. For all she knew, the goblins had moved on to new Fort Valor after destroying the original one.

She wanted to help the man, but was it her place to tell him how Arthur had gotten mixed up with a band of rebels?

"It was more than two weeks ago...at Fort Faith," she told him.

"Fort Faith?" the man laughed. "What, he thinks he's a Knight?"

Lilac shrugged, unwilling to say more. The man—whose name, she learned, was Glen Bismarc—did not press her for too many details. Clearly, he was relieved to hear Arthur was about as safe as anyone in Capricon could hope to be. She told him Arthur was one of several misfits who had sought sanctuary from the goblins at new Fort Valor, which was true enough.

"Praise be to the gods," Glen said with another chuckle. "You don't know how happy you've made me, girl. Will you be returning to that fortress soon?"

"I wish I knew," Lilac replied.

"Pardon?"

"I have friends back at the fort, so I hope to return as soon as I'm able," she clarified.

Glen Bismarc fixed his eyes down at his feet, which were taking small steps to nowhere. "If you see Arthur again, would you do me a favor and give him a message from his family?"

"Of course."

"Could you tell him that we all miss him terribly and that we hope he comes home as soon as it's safe? And tell him...tell him it wasn't his fault..."

"I will," Lilac said.

Glen's mouth couldn't decide whether to smile or frown. A single tear freed itself from his lashes, only to lose itself in the thick hairs of his beard. "I'd go there myself, but I've got seven other youngins to look after...and my wife...she's been sick with worry. I'd better go give 'em all the good news."

The bear of a man made an awkward bow to Lilac and another to Opal before wrestling his way past the tent flaps. Lilac stared at the opening for several minutes after his departure and then glanced over at Opal, who was already looking at her.

"That was weird," Opal said.

And for once, Lilac couldn't disagree with her.

Rather than follow Dylan to wherever the Knight was going, Colt wandered over to an alley between Hylan's inn and what turned out to be a blacksmith's shop. He glanced furtively around him, but no one was paying him any notice.

Colt steps took him to a woodpile at the far end of the alley. The slightest trace of apprehension surged through him as he approached the stack of lumber. Tossing a quick glance back the way he had come, Colt stretched out his arm and reached into a tight niche between the hewn wood and an old fence.

With his shoulder pressed hard against the pile of wood, Colt gingerly explored the space, his fingers scraping along the jagged edges of the timber. The longer he stood there, searching, the faster his heart beat.

But then the tips of his fingers found a smooth surface. Like everything else, the object felt like wood, but unlike the felled trees around it, this pole was cool to the touch. Colt let out a sigh.

It was still there.

For a moment, he considered pulling the *vuudu* staff out of its hiding place—just to be sure that it wasn't broken—but then decided against it. Finding a place to stash the vile relic had been difficult enough, but finagling the thing into the tiny space between the woodpile and fence had been a frustrating endeavor.

Colt withdrew his hand and stared at the blackness of the

space, imagining the skull watching him in return. The thought gave him goosebumps.

He had almost walked into the meeting with Dale, Ruford, and Quillan Dag with the staff in hand, but Dylan had talked him out of it. Colt had left it out in the hall, where, fortunately, no one had found it.

If he hadn't been so tired, Colt probably would have come to the same conclusion as Dylan. After all, bringing a goblin talisman before the three leaders of Hylan would not have made a good first impression.

Thinking back to the meeting, Colt wondered if he had made the right decision. He felt terrible for not standing up for Dylan, though it couldn't be helped. The Knight had said almost nothing to him since then.

Colt had wanted to reassure Dylan that Dale Mullahstyn had not won yet, but neither of them had been in a mood to talk last night, and this morning had lent them no privacy. And even if he trusted Dylan with his plans, Colt was not ready to make them known to the public.

The time for that would come soon enough.

Colt leaned his back against the rickety fence. This was the first time he had been alone since his captivity at the goblin camp. He quickly banished those dark memories into a far corner of his mind and tried his best to enjoy the solitude, the refreshing afternoon breezes. But the truth was Colt didn't want to be alone.

He knew he ought to be overjoyed by the miraculous return of Othello Balsa. He had had enough of a burden to carry without the guilt of the forester's death compounding it. Of course, the Renegade might die anyway. He was in pretty bad shape…

Colt hated himself for the small part of him that hoped Othello *would* die.

He imagined Opal combing her fingers through the forester's hair, brushing the tangled bangs from his eyes. Colt had no claim on Opal as a lover, but even their friendship seemed somehow threatened by Othello's arrival. Not for the first time, Colt wondered what had transpired between the two archers during his absence.

He had hoped to speak with Opal prior to the village assembly planned for that night, but Othello had unwittingly spoiled that. There was nothing stopping him from going to her now, he supposed—nothing except hurt feelings and suspicions.

Maybe it's for the better, he thought. She'd be safer with Othello than with me.

Tears burned at the corner of his eyes, but he forced them back. He had more important things to worry about than romance. He had a mission.

Colt started back toward the road but stopped after a few steps to look back at the woodpile. What if someone found the *vuudu* staff and stole it while he was away? Perhaps he should bring it with him to the meeting. Though he was loath to admit it, he felt braver, *stronger* when holding the staff, as though it were a trophy symbolizing his small triumph over the goblins.

And he would certainly need courage in the hours to come.

Eventually, he turned his back on the skull-tipped staff and exited the alleyway. He had nowhere to be until the rally that evening, so he kept on walking. He had no destination, and yet he couldn't help but notice his steps were taking him in the opposite direction of the infirmary tent and Opal.

Passage VI

Across the road from the colony of tents, at the spot where Hylan's commercial center came to an abrupt end, a crowd had gathered, forming a semicircle around a wooden dais that looked like it had been there for quite some time. Though the sun had not yet set, the torches flanking the scaffold were ablaze.

Lilac stood alone in a sea of strangers. She had no idea whether the people around her were refugees from Rydah, citizens of Hylan, or members of some other category. With the drone of speculating, anticipating voices in the air, Lilac felt more than a little lost.

How did I end up here? she wondered.

She saw Colt and Opal standing near the front of the crowd. Opal had left the infirmary tent a few minutes before she had. Lilac had not wanted to leave Othello, who had yet to regain consciousness, but neither did she want to miss the assembly.

If nothing else, she might learn what was coming next.

A moment later, she spotted Sir Dylan Torc beside Colt. This didn't surprise her in the least. Ever since he had met Colt, Dylan had not let the young commander out of his sight for long. She was also beginning to suspect Dylan didn't have many other friends within the Knighthood.

Lilac thought she saw Mitto and Else somewhere up ahead, but the undulating sea of people made it difficult to be certain. It seemed like everyone had someone to talk to—everyone but her. She hoped the meeting would commence soon and conclude not long thereafter. She found herself wishing that Othello were there beside her, never mind he was always a silent companion.

Lilac jumped when someone clapped her on the back. She spun around to find Hunter regarding her with a friendly smile and wearing the same clothes as the day before.

"Howdy, neighbor," she said. "Where've you been hidin' all day?"

Lilac had all but forgotten about the woman. Not knowing what else to say, Lilac told her the truth: that she had spent most of the day with a friend who had wandered into Hylan that afternoon and who was fighting for his life in the medical tent.

"I wouldn't fret overmuch 'bout it. If he's lasted this long, he'll mend," Hunter assured her.

Lilac wasn't convinced, but she thanked Hunter just the same. She waited, expecting Hunter to say more, but apparently the woman had no other business with her—and was not at all uncomfortable with the lag in conversation.

Lilac pretended to search for someone in the throng.

"Say, there's Bly Copperton." Hunter pointed off to the right. "See him? Over there...the heavyset bloke in the cap...the one with the black beard...no? Well, you'll probably get a better look at him later. He's sure to have his say before the meeting's done."

In a milder voice, she added, "His wife and daughter were killed by the fiends."

Though Lilac couldn't see the man Hunter was referring to, she nodded solemnly and asked, "The goblins have come this far south?"

Hunter's face wrinkled in confusion. "Goblins? Is that what yer callin' 'em?" She paused. "I s'pose it's a fitting enough name. Naw, the fiends...the *goblins*...haven't showed their ugly faces 'round here yet. Bly and his family's home was further north, not far from Rydah."

Lilac's mind flashed back to the cottage Dylan had commandeered.

Hunter spoke on. "If I'm not mistaken...ah, yep...there he is. That's Pillip Bezzrik next to him. He's Bly's brother-in-law, and he's just as angry as Bly is about his sister being dead, but he's a lot quieter 'bout it."

A few seconds later, Hunter, still staring off into the crowd, added, "Pillip and I've been on-again-off-again for some time now...."

Lilac concluded from the fact that Hunter wasn't with her beau now that they were currently "off." Which is probably why she felt the need to strike up a conversation with a complete stranger, Lilac reasoned.

"Did you come from Rydah too?" Lilac asked.

Hunter snapped her eyes away from Pillip and looked back at Lilac. "Huh? Oh, no. Do I *look* like a city girl? No, ma'am, I've been livin' here 'most all my life.

"My old man wanted to be a farmer, you see, only he didn't make much of a go of it. After he passed on, I gave up on the ol' family business but stuck around here anyhow. It's a good place to earn a living if you're into…"

Hunter gave her a sly smile. "Hey, guess what it is I do."

"Um…" Lilac stalled, trying to think of a profession that wouldn't insult the woman.

"I'm a *hunter*," she proclaimed. "And a damn good one too. But that's not why I'm called Hunter. It's my actual name."

"I see."

Hunter glanced back over to where Bly and Pillip were. "My house is a few miles away from here, but I've been staying in the village lately. It ain't safe livin' by yourself these days. Plus I'm a member of the militia. It's my duty to protect Hylan in times like these."

Aside from a knife hanging from her belt, Hunter was unarmed. Lilac wondered how she—or any other hayseed warrior, for that matter—intended to hold back the goblin army.

"Both Bly and Pillip are in the militia too," Hunter continued. "Bly's a hunter and trapper like myself. But Pillip, he runs the general store."

Hunter met Lilac's eyes once more, and her face flushed a little. "But listen to me go on. Tell me about yerself. That ginger friend of yours said you were from a fort?"

Lilac hardly knew where to begin, but she was saved from a lengthy narrative when a sudden hush swept over the crowd. Both women turned to watch as a balding, middle-aged man with a sizable gut climbed the stairs of the dais.

"That's Quillan Dag, the mayor," Hunter whispered.

Lilac listened as the Mayor of Hylan told them all what Dylan and his team—which included Lilac herself—had learned about the invaders. He used the word "goblin" with visible awkwardness.

When the mayor related the estimated number of goblin in the army, the silence that had fallen over the multitude vanished immediately.

"Five thousand of the bastards?" someone cried. "We're

doomed!"

Hunter scoffed. "That can't be right. I mean, how could so many of them have snuck onto the island without anyone knowin' it?"

Else Fontane herself had seen the goblins' tower-like ships and how their cannons had reduced Rydah and the magnificent Celestial Palace to rubble. The former barkeeper had spoken of the massive flotilla in hushed tones, her eyes reflecting the horror of that night. Lilac didn't know how the ships had gotten so near without anyone seeing them, but she had her guesses, *vuudu* being one of them.

"It's true," Lilac assured Hunter. "I saw their camp with my own eyes."

And that's not even all of them, Lilac thought. Some had surely remained with the fleet. And then there were the goblins Klye and Scout had encountered in Port Town and the ones that had ambushed them outside Pillars...

Hunter shook her head, speechless. Meanwhile, up on the platform, the mayor made several unsuccessful attempts to restore order. Lilac feared that the proceedings would degenerate into pandemonium, perhaps even panicked violence.

Just then two men separated themselves from the crowd and joined Quillan Dag on the stage.

"Who are they?" Lilac had to shout for Hunter to hear her.

"The one who walks like he's got a sword up his arse is Dale Mullahstyn," Hunter said. "He speaks for the Knights of Superius. The other one's Ruford Berwyn. He commands the other warriors from Rydah...pier guards, I guess you'd call 'em."

Lilac watched as the Knight, Dale, came to stop beside the mayor. Ruford stayed back a few paces. At the sight of the new-comers, the crowd begrudgingly calmed.

Sir Dale Mullahstyn addressed to the crowd in a loud voice. "Thanks to this newest intelligence, we now know exactly what we are up against. The goblins have already destroyed our capital and Fort Valor."

The Knight paused, sweeping his gaze over the crowd.

"Hylan is a village without walls and without an army to defend it. From the very start, I recommended an evacuation of Hylan...an orderly retreat to either Steppt or Kraken, since both of those cities are more defendable than this village.

"But there were those who thought my plans hasty and ill-conceived. You wanted to wait until we knew more about the army that leveled Rydah in a day. Well, we now know the extent of the enemy's power, and it is considerable."

Dale waited again, but this time the break was immediately filled up by noise from the crowd. Some of those gathered grunted their agreement with the Knight, though Lilac could hear the disparaging mutterings of several others.

"Many would sooner die than abandon their homes," Hunter said to Lilac, glaring up at Dale Mullahstyn all the while.

Ruford strode forward then, eclipsing Dale and Quillan Dag. The Captain of the Guard waited until the people settled down before beginning a speech of his own. He needn't have bothered though, so booming was his voice.

"I urged Sir Mullahstyn to wait for the reconnaissance reports, hoping we might be able to unite our forces with those of Fort Valor. But that fortress and its defenders are gone.

"If five thousand goblins turn their sights on Hylan, we won't be able to stop them from razing the settlement. I realize not a one of you wants to leave, but your lives are more precious than anything you'd be leaving behind. Retreating to Steppt or Kraken is our only realistic option."

The dissenting voices of the crowd grew louder, but Ruford kept going.

"Having said that, I believe simply handing Hylan over to the enemy would be a tactical error."

The throng quieted some at this statement, and Dale jerked slightly.

"Leaving Hylan for the goblins would be equivalent to putting food in their mouths and roofs over their heads for the winter. Which is why I recommend that before we leave, we put everything to the torch."

The furor of the crowd reached new heights, and Lilac worried that the agitation and frustration would manifest itself in violence after all. Ruford Berwyn didn't try to speak over the din. He simply crossed his arms and took a step back beside the mayor.

Dale Mullahstyn raised a hand, which was ignored. The Knight's mouth began to move, but his words were swallowed up by the outrage and fear of the crowd. After sever minutes, the people finally quieted enough for Lilac to make out a few words.

"...sooner the better...only what you can carry...could be on their way even as we..."

If Dale was at all bothered by the fact nobody was listening to him, he gave no outward sign of it. He continued to talk, until the hissing and shushing from one portion of the crowd forced him into submission.

Lilac couldn't make out what had caused the silence. Like those around her, she craned her neck, trying to peer over the heads of the people in front of her. She could hear someone talking. The voice was familiar.

"There is another way!" the voice repeated again and again until he had everyone's attention.

A man stepped out of the crowd. He picked a spot in front of the dais, though he did not ascend it, and turned to face the assembly.

"I know him, but I can't recall his name," said Hunter beside her. "That Knight's no friend of Dale's, that's for sure. This should be interesting."

"What happens when we get to Steppt?" Sir Dylan Torc shouted. "What happens when so many new mouths empty the city's cupboards with all of winter still ahead? What happens when the goblins shatter the walls...or the very mountains that cradle Steppt...with whatever explosives they have left?

"And what happens when we flee to Kraken, and the goblins follow us there too? What happens when their ships cut off a retreat to sea? What happens when there's nowhere else to run?"

No one said a word as Dylan's intense gaze landed on one after another of them. Lilac glanced back up at the dais and saw Dale Mullahstyn staring frostily at his fellow Knight.

"I will tell you what happens," Dylan said. "After the goblins have chased us from one end of Capricon to the other, we die. With our backs pressed to the wall, we die. Unable to swing our swords for fear of hitting each other, we die. Cornered and overwhelmed, we die."

"And how is that any different from staying here and dying?" Dale Mullahstyn snapped.

"Indeed!" Dylan replied, turning to face Dale. "We might as well save ourselves the trip! Better to die defending your homes than burning them down *for* the enemy!"

More than a few shouts from the crowd supported the sentiment.

Dale Mullahstyn rolled his eyes. "The circumstances are dire, but not hopeless. There are reinforcements in Steppt—"

"Not nearly enough," Dylan argued, which earned him another glare from Dale. "And why wait for the goblins to come to Hylan? I say we've done enough waiting as it is!"

Dale let out a sharp laugh that stole everyone's attention. Standing behind the Knight, Ruford and Quillan Dag exchanged uncomfortable looks.

"Ever the hot-blooded lion, aren't you Sir Torc? Ready to charge into a pack of hyenas, even if it means your death…"

Even from her distance, Lilac could see Dylan's face redden.

"I, for one, do not fear death," Dylan fired back. "And what I am posing is not suicide. The goblins expect us to run. If we strike them without warning—"

"Are you calling me a *coward*?" His face drained of color, Dale rushed forward to the edge of the stage. His hand rested on the hilt of his sword.

Dylan ignored Dale and was now looking out at the crowd once more. "I have been to the goblins' camp. I saw a brave man start a fire that made the fiends howl in confusion and rage. We don't have to be many to be effective. We need only to—"

"You are not in command here, Sir Torc, and I have half a mind to have you arrested for insubordination!" Dale cried. "Even if you would throw your life away for no good reason, I would never allow you to take any other Knights with you…though maybe those thieves you have become so friendly with would join you in your folly."

The crowd was growing restless again, with individuals calling out cheers or jeers at random intervals. At Dale's mention of Gomez and his boys, Lilac heard a voice that sounded suspiciously like Tryst's say, "I've seen sewer rats with bigger balls than this guy's. How'd he get to be a Knight anyway?"

As the mob grew louder and louder, Dylan turned his back on the people and began arguing his point face-to-face with Dale. Although she couldn't hear him, Lilac saw Dale yell back, emphasizing his words with violent hand gestures.

So chaotic had the scene become that Lilac didn't even see Colt until he had climbed the final steps up onto the dais.

Colt walked past Ruford Berwyn and Quillan Dag—who regarded him with vague curiosity—and came to a stop a few steps behind Dale. He waited until the crowd noticed him and simmered down. Then, he spoke.

"It is true that you outrank Dylan, Sergeant Mullahstyn, but as Commander of Fort Faith, I outrank you. If anyone has the authority to command the Knights here, it is I."

Dale Mullahstyn reeled as though physically struck. He spun around and leveled a hateful glare at Colt, who affected a mask of indifference. Colt hoped his expression was a passable impersonation of his father, the heroic Laenghot Crystalus, who had disciplined errant soldiers and delinquent children with the same professional detachment.

At that moment, Colt knew Dale hated him more than anyone else in the world—including Dylan—but Colt buried the swell of emotions that threatened to burst forth. Even if he had never felt like a great leader, it was time to start acting like one.

"You have no jurisdiction here, *Sir* Crystalus," Dale hissed. "By your own admission, you abdicated your authority to Stannel Bismarc. *He* is the Commander of Fort Faith, not you."

Colt's face remained impassive. "And tell me, Sir Mullahstyn, when was the last time a mere sergeant was honored with the command of a fortress?"

Dale's eyes widened and then narrowed dangerously. He sputtered for a few seconds, his rage rendering him speechless.

"I was never demoted," Colt added. "I still hold the rank of commander."

Colt felt a hand on his shoulder. He tore his eyes away from Dale's and found Ruford Berwyn standing beside him. In a voice that was meant for only Colt and Dale to hear, Ruford said, "You need to settle this in private. These people have enough instability to contend with."

Dale looked like he was about to argue. Instead, he pulled himself together, smoothing the material on his impeccably clean doublet, and gave a sharp nod.

"We will discuss this at the mayor's house," Dale told Colt.

"No."

The single word sent Dale recoiling. Ruford's eyebrows rose.

"No," Colt repeated. "There is nothing to discuss, Sergeant. You are no longer in charge here. I am."

Dale trembled, and Colt thought the Knight would surely draw steel. Colt didn't want to fight the man, but he would if he had to. Dale would be put in his place one way or another, and thanks to *Chrysaal-rûn*, Colt knew he would come out on top in a trial by combat.

Ruford Berwyn placed a restraining hand on Dale's shoulder. Colt locked eyes with the Captain of the Guard, whose expression was that of concern and perhaps wariness. Before any more words could pass between them, they were interrupted by a question that rose above the clamor of the crowd.

"And what'll *you* do, Commander?"

Trusting that Dale was not, at present, a concern, Colt turned around. When his gaze landed on a rotund fellow whose arms, crossed though they were, were the thickness of fallen timber, Colt knew that he had found the owner of the voice.

A surge of uncertainty coursed through him. All of his injuries seemed to complain at once, and he wished he had the *vuudu* staff to lean on. But he had come too far to start doubting himself again.

When Colt spoke, he was talking to himself as much as to the man in the crowd.

"I too have been to the goblin war camp. I was one of two prisoners the goblin general kept alive. Through their foul magic, they learned everything about the island's defenses. They know our tactics."

"And where would you have us run, Sir Knight?" the same man asked.

A second man, who was leaner and taller than the first, nudged the speaker in the side and said, "Quiet, Bly. Let him talk."

"I would have us run *toward* the goblins," Colt stated.

Those eight words were enough to produce a new wave of shouts. From on the ground beneath the dais, Sir Dylan Torc looked up at him and smiled.

Passage VII

Lilac had intended to go back to the medical tent to sit with Othello some more before retiring for the night. When Hunter insisted she join her for a drink, Lilac could have refused. Yet she had acquiesced after the slightest bit of arm twisting.

Truth to tell, a stiff drink sounded too good to pass up just then.

After making a quick stop by the medical tent—only to find Othello unconscious—Lilac left the forester in the doctor's care. She supposed Opal would return before long...

Lilac followed Hunter into the flock of tents. They soon came upon an open-air pavilion that was so full of people, she couldn't immediately make out what was inside. Hunter forged a path through the crowd, paying no mind to whom she jostled. As they got farther into the tent, Lilac saw a makeshift bar that had been erected using a long plank and piled-up crates.

Hunter called the barkeep by name, demanding two mugs of lager "right quick." Lilac guessed lager was the only thing on tap, which was all right with her. She gulped down the cool, foamy liquid, relishing the chill that spread down her throat. Even in Superius, Hylan was renowned for its flavorful beer.

Lilac, who hadn't had any alcohol since leaving Continae, the drink tasted downright heavenly.

She took several big swallows from the stein. By the time the cup was half-empty, she was already feeling lightheaded. This surprised her until she remembered how many hours it had been since she ate. Not that she was complaining; already the lager was making her feel more relaxed—in spite of recent events.

Lilac had been as surprised as anyone when Colt announced his intention to lead an army against the goblins. She didn't know where she fit into the young commander's plans, but she supposed she would join him and all of the others—so many others!—who had volunteered for the crusade.

She was, after all, still his prisoner.

One thing Lilac *did* know was Colt would not likely allow her to return to Fort Valor on her own. And as much as she wanted to get back to the other Renegades, she knew it was far too dangerous a journey to undertake alone. And with so few capable fighters to be had in Hylan, there was no one to spare to accompany her.

Besides, Colt needed every warrior he could find. The fact that she possessed an enchanted sword only made her more valuable to the cause.

Lilac took a long pull of her beer.

She wasn't a coward, but neither was she eager to face the goblins again. She had seen the size of their army with her own eyes, had witnessed their battle-hungry ferocity firsthand, and had survived all encounters with the goblins only by the skin of her teeth.

Logic told her facing the goblin hoard head on would mean certain death for her and everyone else in Colt's army.

Lilac wiped the foam from her mouth with her shirtsleeve. She had left Fort Valor knowing it could well mean her death. She had joined Colt's cause willingly, and she would continue to follow him willingly. She didn't want to die, but she wouldn't back down.

Colt wasn't the only one who had lost a loved-one to the goblins. Were it not for the monsters, both her brother and Chester Ragellan would still be alive…

"Easy, girl," Hunter laughed, collecting Lilac's empty glass. "The night's still young."

Lilac chuckled in spite of herself. "I suppose you're right."

Hunter tried to signal the busy barkeep, but the man had his hands full in more ways than one. When he walked away to deliver a fistful of mugs to other patrons, Hunter leaned over the bar and helped herself, refilling Lilac's mug and topping off her own.

The rustic woman had been chatting with an older one she hadn't bothered to introduce. Lilac might have thought Hunter rude for the neglect, but she didn't say anything. Probably Hunter had brought her there so she wouldn't have to drink alone. Enjoying a pleasant buzzing in her brain, Lilac contented herself with watching the people around her.

A few minutes later, she spotted someone familiar.

She hadn't gotten a good look at Bly Copperton before the meeting had started, but when the man had asked Colt what he planned to do with his authority over the Knights, Hunter had identified him again.

She had described Bly as a hunter and trapper, and he certainly looked the part. What Bly lacked in height, he made up for in girth. Though he wore his hair cropped quite short, his bare arms and cheeks were covered in thick dark hair.

If Glen Bismarc was reminiscent of a big brown bear, then Bly was of the black variety.

Standing beside Bly at the other end of the bar was a man who looked somewhat less wild than the people around him. He was Bly's opposite in almost every way. Tall and slim, his hair combed neatly forward, Pillip Bezzrik sipped unenthusiastically from his drink. He appeared to be listening to Bly, whose boisterous words could be heard above the ruckus, but Lilac noted how Pillip stole occasional glances in their direction.

"So," Lilac said, turning to Hunter, "what happened between you and Pillip anyway?"

She knew she was being bold, but she didn't care. The alcohol had loosened her lips, and she figured the worse thing Hunter would do was tell her to shut up. Or maybe hit her.

Hunter took another swig of her drink. "Men can be such dolts sometimes. I don't think they know what they really want." She emptied her mug. "We got into a stupid fight almost a month ago, and all he had to do was apologize. It wasn't even anything important. He just hurt my feelings, is all. But Pillip can be damn stubborn in his own way."

Hunter made to take another gulp, only to find a mug full of suds. Leaning over the counter to refresh her drink, she added, "Then his sister and niece get killed, and all I want to do is *be* there for him. I eased up on the cold shoulder…and we *have* talked some since then, but it's not like before.

"I ain't even mad anymore, but…well…I guess I'm even stubborner than he is."

"Having a drink together sounds like a step in the right direction," Lilac suggested. "But you need a reason for going over there. That way it won't look like you're caving. Why don't you introduce me to Bly? He's your friend too, right?"

Hunter considered the plan. "Yeah. I've known Bly longer than Pillip. He introduced us, in fact." She giggled. "Come to think of it, it's usually Bly who gets us back together after we break up. Guess he's been preoccupied lately…"

"Judging by the way Pillip keeps looking over here, I'd say he's ready to make up."

The woman's face flushed. "Well, let's get this over with then."

Hunter led Lilac over to the two men and introduced her. Bly clamped his hand around Lilac's own, grunting a hello.

"Nice to meet you." Pillip cleared his throat before adding, "How've you been, Hunter?"

"Can't complain," she replied. "You?"

"All right…considering."

There was an awkward pause during which Bly drained a large percentage of his mug.

"So…what were you two talking about just now?" Lilac asked, hoping to spur a new dialogue into being.

"Actually," Bly said, "we were talkin' about that kid commander. Don't remember his real name. Everybody just calls him Colt, it seems. I was sayin' how he's got more guts than that Dale Mullahstyn'll ever have. Of course, bein' one of his friends, you probably know all about that, huh?"

Lilac didn't really want to talk about Colt, since it would bring her thoughts right back to the inevitable march on the goblin camp. Still, she supposed she should be grateful for the conversation—and the company.

"I've known Colt for a little more than a month," she said. "He's a good man…but not your typical Knight in some respects. As for his real name, it's Saerylton Crystalus."

"Well, all I can say is that I'll be the first the first in line tomorrow night," Bly said. "And I won't be alone. You were there. You heard the crowd. Hylan ain't gonna burn itself down, not as long as her militiamen are still alive."

"It's like Dylan Torc's been saying all along. Better to die fightin' than hidin'," Pillip added, his voice a soft baritone to Bly's booming bass.

"Best not to die at all," Hunter argued.

"You're not coming?" Pillip asked.

"'Course I am! Even if I wasn't in the militia, I'd go. If ever there was a time for folk to defend themselves and their land, this is it. That Dale Mullahstyn must think us Hylaners are as soft as our cheese.

"Besides, if I stayed behind, you guys'd lose all respect for me."

Pillip gave a wry smile. "Since when do you care what anyone thinks of you, Parth?"

Hunter's easy smile vanished instantly. "Don't call me that, Pillip, least of all in public!"

"Here we go!" Bly roared, throwing up his hands and sloshing his drink on himself and those around him.

"Sorry," Pillip was quick to add. "It slipped, Hunter."

Lilac brushed spilled beer off of her arm. "Wait, what did he call you?"

"Never mind," Hunter mumbled, burying her face in her stein.

"It's her real name," Bly explained. "She hates it."

"You said *Hunter* was your real name," Lilac said.

The bottom of Hunter's mug tipped higher.

"That's her last name," Bly whispered.

"Just drop it, Bly," Pillip said.

"Fine by me. Less talkin' and more drinkin'. Won't be long, and we'll all be as sober as sober can be."

Lilac couldn't refute the man's reasoning, so she took another drink…and another…and another after that.

Colt descended the stairs of the dais, cheers still ringing in his ears.

At best, he had hoped to win over the other Knights of Superius who had hitherto been taking orders from the sanctimonious Dale Mullahstyn. He knew there was a chance that some of Hylan's militiamen would join his company, but he had not expected the get the overwhelming approval of the crowd.

It seemed the Hylaners would do anything to prevent their village from being burned to the ground. Then again, he wouldn't know until tomorrow how many men and women would actually throw in with him.

Quillan Dag came forward to dismiss the assembly, but most of the crowd had already dissipated. Colt veritably floated among the stragglers. He felt lightheaded. His skin tingled with equal parts apprehension and exhilaration.

Colt started over to where he had last seen Dylan and almost ran headlong into Opal. He was glad to see her—he always was—but judging by her frown, the feeling was not mutual.

"We need to talk," she told him, planting her hands on her hips.

"Very well."

Without another word, Opal turned and headed for a secluded area behind the makeshift barracks. Colt followed, more than a little confused. He wondered if this had something to do with Othello.

When Opal came to a halt near a gnarled oak, Colt stopped too and waited for the woman to explain herself. He didn't have to wait long.

"And just when were you going to tell me about your plan to lead an army against the goblins?"

Colt couldn't help but flinch. The angry glare she leveled at him would have stopped a charging minotaur in its tracks. At one time, the look might have sent him into a stammered apology, but while Colt loved Opal more than anything in the world, his sense of purpose was too strong to back down.

"I wasn't aware I had to run everything past you," Colt replied thickly.

Opal's green eyes narrowed, but Colt held her gaze. "You don't, but I thought we were friends, and friends aren't usually so secretive about decisions that will have such drastic effects on both of their lives."

"I am a Knight of Superius," Colt said with a helpless shrug. "On top of that, I am a high-ranking officer. I'm sorry, Opal, but I couldn't tell you everything even if I wanted to."

"I'm not asking you to share secret information," Opal was quick to reply. "I'd just like to know what you're thinking every now and then. I followed you...Cholk and I *both* followed you to Rydah because we were worried about you. You decided to leave Fort Faith on the spur of the moment, and we wanted to make sure you weren't getting in over your head."

Colt chuckled humorlessly. "Too late for that."

The comment did nothing to assuage Opal's temper. Gods, he thought, she's even beautiful when she's angry.

"Your friendship means so much to me, Opal. As did Cholk's. Cholk gave his life for me, for the mission—"

"The mission that you have forsaken!"

"How so?"

Opal uncrossed her arms and let them drop down to her side. A good sign, Colt thought.

"We came here with the intension of spreading word of the goblin invasion to Rydah so that we could coordinate an offensive with the capital," she said. "We now know more about the invasion than Stannel and everyone else back at the fort, but instead of returning and updating your men, you're planning on going against the goblins alone."

Colt chewed at his lower lip. "I had thought about that, but there's simply no time to go back to the fort. The goblins could even now be on their way to Hylan. At least Stannel and Petton and the rest are safe behind stone walls."

"Safe?" Opal scoffed. "Like the Knights from the original Fort Valor?"

"What would you have me do?" Colt demanded. "I can't be in two places at once. I'm trying to do the honorable thing here."

"Oh," muttered Opal, "and here I thought you were going after revenge at the expense of more lives, including your own."

Colt tasted the bile rising in his throat. "You can stay behind if you like," he told her quietly. "That way you won't have to leave Othello's side."

Now it was Opal's turn to look struck. Her lips moved in a silent rebuttal but then pressed together firmly. Colt ached to know what it was the woman couldn't say—though he knew the answer might destroy him. Then again, could knowing be any worse than *not* knowing?

"What is it between you two, anyway? I thought you hated the Renegades."

Opal seemed to shrink before his very eyes. He couldn't remember a time when he had ever seen her speechless, and the unusual display seemed only to confirm his worst fears.

"Do you love him?" he asked, his voice almost failing him.

The question was like a splash of cold water against Opal's face. "What in the hells kind of a question is that to ask?"

"You said yourself that friends don't keep secrets…"

Opal sucked in her lips, then sighed. "I really don't know how to answer your questions, Colt. There *is* something about Othello…it's like he's…familiar."

Colt didn't follow at first. Then he remembered Opal's

amnesia. She had no memories of her childhood and had gone on a quest to find out who she was. After a year of fruitless searching, she had given up.

Opal had covered much of Continae in that time, but she was no closer to knowing her true identity now than she had been at the start. That Othello seemed familiar was no small thing.

"Do you think you knew him…from…from before?" Colt asked.

Opal's eyes explored the contours of an overarching branch. "I don't know, Colt. It's like when you're trying to think of a word or a name. It's at the tip of your tongue, but you just can't say it."

"Have you asked him about it?"

Opal shook her head. Her long, scarlet locks looked brown in the darkness.

Colt might have asked her why she hadn't confronted Othello, but he was already feeling as though he had pressed her too far. He hated seeing her so vulnerable.

"If you want to stay in Hylan for personal reasons, I'll understand," he told her.

She studied him for a moment. When she finally replied, a familiar half-smile tugged at the corner of her mouth. "You're not getting away from me that easily. I didn't rescue your sorry butt from the goblins just to let you run off and get captured all over again."

Colt doubted she would ever know how happy those words made him.

"I know that you're in charge," she added, "but for the record, I think going to the goblin camp is a big mistake."

To Colt's absolute astonishment, Opal took a step forward and wrapped her arms around him. So stunned was he by her actions that, for a moment, he just stood there, his arms stiff at his sides.

"You're my only friend on this island, Colt. I don't know what I'd do if I lost you."

Her whispered words tickled his earlobes. Belatedly, he patted her back. His tongue felt swollen in his mouth, and before he could say anything, Opal broke away.

"Good night, Saerylton."

Colt's heart swelled as he watched her go. He wanted to shout that he loved her, but he had once again missed his chance.

He stood there for a long time—his pending meeting with Dale, Ruford, and Quillan Dag all but forgotten—as he pondered her words and the portent of the hug.

Passage VIII

Lilac awoke with no memory of how she had gotten back to the empty stockroom and a headache that reached all the way down to her toes. She forced herself to rise and dress. When she stepped into the storefront, daylight assaulted her eyes like daggers.

Walking down Hylan's only road, she kept an eye out for Hunter, though she figured the woman was probably with Pillip. She reached the medical tent without seeing anyone familiar. The light inside was blessedly dim. There was no sign of the doctor, but at that moment Lilac didn't care.

Othello was awake and sitting up.

It was all she could do to keep from smothering him with a great hug.

"Thank the gods," Lilac said. "We feared we would lose you!"

"I'll be fine," Othello insisted, his voice cracking.

Oddly, Othello seemed pretty close to fine. Were it not for the scarlet-stained poultices covering his bare chest like patchwork, she might have doubted he had been hurt at all. In fact, he looked far better than Lilac was feeling just then.

The color had returned to his face. His tangled blond hair had been brushed back, away from his eyes, which had lost the glint of fever's madness.

"When did you wake?" she asked. "When I was here yesterday, it seemed likely you'd be out for days."

"Very early this morning."

"How are you feeling now?"

"Better," he answered, and Lilac couldn't help but smile at his customary curtness.

She asked if he was hungry or thirsty, to which he shook his head. She wondered whether Opal had visited him that morning but instead asked, "Did the doctor fill you in on what's been happening?"

Othello shook his head again. "He told me to take it easy...not to talk."

Lilac's smile grew. Telling Othello to be silent was like telling a Knight to stand up straight. She did her best to summarize the events of the past few days. Othello's face betrayed no emotions as she concluded with last night's assembly.

"Colt challenged Dale's authority and declared his intentions to lead a force against the goblin war camp. And he had a lot of supporters.

Still no reaction from the forester.

"I'm going, too," she added a few seconds later. "Thanks to my vorpal sword, I might even be of some help."

Before we all perish, she silently added.

The thought was sobering to be sure, and she was suddenly overwhelmed with fear. She needed to run, to get as far away from Hylan and the goblins as possible. You shouldn't be here, her mind screamed. Superius is your home, not this island.

But she knew the goblins wouldn't be content with conquering only Capricon. T'slect, the goblin prince, told them T'Ruel had designs on all of Continae. By staying and fighting alongside Colt and the others, she would be defending her homeland, albeit indirectly.

And she could never forget that the goblins had killed her brother, disposing of him after he grew suspicious of his commanding officer's odd behavior. The poor man never knew the goblins were, in fact, the ones responsible for the Knighthood's immoral activities.

Lilac herself wouldn't learn the truth until months after her brother's death. Gabriel had written her a letter shortly before he was caught snooping. The missive told of how the Knights had hired a wizardess assassin to hunt down Chester Ragellan and Dominic Horcalus, his former comrades who had been labeled Renegade sympathizers.

Lilac had "borrowed" the vorpal sword, a family heirloom that had done little more than collect dust over the years, and sailed to Capricon in hopes of saving the rogue Knights of Superius. She had found Ragellan and Horcalus in the company of a band of Renegades. In the end, she killed the assassin, but not before the spell-caster beheaded valiant Chester Ragellan.

She could have returned to Superius at once. After all, she wasn't a rebel, not really. Yet she had formed a bond with the unusual band. And she hadn't realized how much she wanted to make a difference in the world.

Her father, a baron, would have told her that power lay in politics, but Lilac had learned during her time with the Renegades that history was often decided by people who just happened to be in the wrong place at the right time.

If she returned to Superius, she would undoubtedly marry a nobleman, earning the title of baroness or countess or something equally useless. She had envied her little brother in following his dream to become a Knight of Superius. If the Knighthood allowed female squires, wouldn't she have enlisted right along with him.

Lilac Zephyr could never be a Knight, but she was a warrior —and the vorpal sword made her a formidable warrior indeed.

"When do we leave?"

Othello's question broke the spell of her daydreaming. At first she could only blink stupidly, having forgotten the forester was there.

"Colt wants everyone gathered in the square by—" She stopped suddenly. "What do you mean by 'we'? You're not fit to go anywhere, especially not to another battle!"

Othello didn't say anything. His bold green eyes bore into hers, somehow making a stronger argument than words ever could. She knew Othello's accuracy with a longbow would be a valuable addition to the troupe, but no one—not even Colt— could ask the forester to return to the fray. Not so soon.

But if Othello was determined to go…

She wondered if Othello's desire to join Colt's army was a matter of pride. The man *had* taken quite a beating. Studying the forester's chiseled, almost statuesque face, she found it difficult to believe any emotion could penetrate Othello's being, least of all pride.

Then again, Othello's motivation had always been a mystery to his companions. Why should now be any different?

"We're to set out at dusk," Lilac said at last. "I strongly recommend you stay here and recover…even though we need all of the help we can get."

As soon as she said that last part, she realized how much she hoped he *would* come. If she were to die in battle, she wanted at least one friend beside her.

"You should get some more rest," she said. "I'll come back later and see if you've changed your mind."

Othello nodded and lay back on his cot.

Lilac intended to take her own advice. Her head was throbbing. The mere thought of beer made her stomach roil. She left the tent, heading back to the store. Physical ailments aside, her mood was currently at the mercy of two warring factions: relief at Othello's remarkable recovery and apprehension of what was to come.

As she crossed the dirt road, she saw Opal exit the general store. She muttered a cool greeting as she walked past. Lilac didn't have to turn around to know where Opal was going. Idly, she wondered if the woman would try to talk Othello out of leaving Hylan. Or maybe she wanted the forester to come along.

For all Lilac knew, Opal might offer to stay behind and nurse him back to health.

Not for the first time, she wondered what Colt thought of Opal's behavior regarding Othello. Surely the young commander was not at all pleased with the ambiguous relationship. It was obvious to Lilac that Colt had feelings for the woman.

Opal had to know that.

They were the only ones in the room that had formerly been reserved for travelers but was now a part of Hylan's barracks.

Colt lay on a cot, his hands clasped behind his head. Dylan was making a show of packing his things into a knapsack. The restless Knight had already rearranged the items inside more than half a dozen times, but that didn't seem to bother Dylan at all.

Several times, Colt found himself on the verge of engaging Dylan in conversation, only to think better of it. While he considered Dylan to be a worthy soldier and ally in his cause, he worried that Dylan saw him as nothing more than a means to an end. Thanks to Colt's support, Dylan had accomplished what he could not have done alone.

It was a depressing thought, one of many that had been swimming around in his head that morning.

Watching the other man out of the corner of his eye, Colt

wondered why Dylan Torc was so eager to engage the goblins. Probably, Colt thought, his reasons aren't so different from my own. He has surely lost countless comrades during the fall of Rydah. Worse, the Knight had seen the invaders slaughter hundreds of innocents, unable to save those he was charged to defend.

And yet Colt suspected Dylan would have acted no differently had he been stationed in Hylan all along. The man simply seemed to enjoy being in the thick of things. It was just the type of man he was.

Colt had been half-dozing for nearly an hour when he heard a knock at the door. He sat up and looked toward the threshold, expecting to find someone standing there, partially revealed by the half-open door. But he saw only a vacant hallway.

"Hello?" Colt called.

"Is everybody decent in there?" Opal asked.

Colt glanced at Dylan, who was indeed fully dressed. Not caring a bit what the other Knight thought about admitting a woman into the barracks, he said, "You can come in."

Opal entered, taking in the mostly empty room with a quick glance.

"Where is everybody?"

Before Colt could reply, Dylan said, "Gomez, Tryst, and Lucky went out for some 'refreshment.' From what I overheard, the old man wanted to say goodbye to 'his boys.' I guess he won't be coming along."

"But Tryst and Lucky are?" Opal asked, her voice rich with disbelief.

Dylan nodded, but didn't look at her. As he spoke, he polished the blade of a small dagger with a stained rag. "They're coming, and so are some of their colleagues. But Gomez is worried he would slow us down. 'I ain't as young as I used t' be,' he said."

When Opal didn't respond, Dylan glanced up from his work. Sheathing the dagger, he added, "I had better go and make sure they don't get carried away. It will be time to leave before we know it."

All but bowing as he hurried past Opal, Dylan left the room. Colt was thankful for the privacy, but his cheeks burned at the thought of being alone with Opal. Sometimes, he feared she could see into his mind and read every one of his impure thoughts.

He swung his legs over the side of the bed and stood up, facing the oblivious love of his life.

Opal's long hair was held in place by the thick braid she always wore while traveling. A freshly stocked quiver clung to her back, and her crossbow hung from her belt. She didn't at all resemble the soft woman he had held last night, but Colt would have hugged her even if she were covered head to toe in plate mail were the opportunity to present itself.

"I just wanted to see if you're having any doubts," Opal told him. "And if you are, I plan to nurture them."

His mind still fixed on that woefully brief moment of intimacy, Colt was baffled by her statement. When he realized she was talking about the mission, he flashed her a rueful smile.

"That's what I was afraid of," Opal said with an exaggerated sigh.

He appreciated her support despite her personal misgivings. If anyone could have talked him out of advancing on the goblin camp, it was she. Of course, Opal didn't seem to know how much sway she held over him.

"You look like you're all ready to go," he said, gesturing at the crossbow resting against her shapely hip.

"It's all I have with me," she laughed. "For that matter, it's all I own...except for my horse. Gods, I wish I could have brought Nisson along. I am not looking forward to a three-day hike through the wilderness."

Colt didn't have the heart to tell her the trip would take closer to five days than three.

"I guess the good news is that if we fail, we won't have to worry about walking back."

Opal crossed her arms, which caused the furrow between her breasts to become more pronounced. Colt forced himself to look her in the eyes, which happened to be narrowed.

"That's not funny, Colt. I'm the pessimist here, not you."

"You must be rubbing off on me."

Opal rolled her eyes. "I don't know about that...though you *have* changed a lot since we met in Port Errnot."

Colt's mind jumped back to that fateful day. His uncle, Sir Rollace White, had introduced the two of them, after he had tried to rescue Opal from some street toughs. Not that she had needed his help.

It had been no more than two months ago, though Colt almost couldn't believe that. It was difficult to believe there had been a time in his life when Opal wasn't around.

"I've changed since you met me?" Colt repeated. "For the better, I hope…"

Opal regarded him thoughtfully. "I suppose 'matured' might be a better word. You're certainly not second-guessing yourself as much as you used to."

At least not aloud, Colt thought.

"When a man knows the right course, it's easy to be confident," he replied, thinking of men like his father and Dylan Torc.

"Are you going to take that with you?"

Colt glanced down at the staff he hadn't realized he was holding. A chill ran down his spine as he gazed into the hollow eye sockets. The disembodied head had made appearances in his dreams ever since Drekk't had used the *vuudu* staff to make him spill secrets about Capricon's defenses. A part of him wanted to smash the skull into a thousand pieces.

"I'd like nothing more than to be rid of it," he said. "I know it's an instrument of evil and that it ought to be destroyed, but I can't bring myself to do it."

When Colt did not elaborate, Opal asked softly, "Why not?"

He studied the wretched rod. "When the goblins made Cholk and I fight each other for sport, I was angry at Cholk for attacking me. But when I realized that he was just making it look realistic…and then killed himself so that they wouldn't kill us both…well, I was even angrier with *him*.

"Drekk't made me tell everything I knew about Fort Faith and the rest of the island. I wasn't strong enough to resist his spells, and I began to think Cholk had made a terrible mistake in giving his life for me.

"I wanted nothing more than to give up and die. I wasn't worthy of his gift. But you gave me a second chance too, Opal, and something good came out my incarceration after all. We have this staff. Neither Drekk't nor any other goblin is going to use its vile magic against a human again."

"So why not be rid of it once and for all?" Opal asked.

Colt met her eyes and saw they were full of worry.

"I know it should be destroyed," Colt said, "but it seems like a waste, especially if we could somehow use it against them."

"You're thinking about using *vuudu* against the goblins?" Opal asked, astonished.

Colt shook his head. "No…I don't know…if they see us with it, maybe they will think we can harness its power. Besides, we're not even sure we *can* destroy it, and if it's to remain whole, I'll be the one to hold onto it."

"Even if you'd be taking it back to the one place you don't want it to end up?"

"Even so," Colt sighed. "Truth to tell, I don't trust anyone else with it, and I must lead the attack on the goblins."

"For vengeance?" Opal ventured.

Colt searched her expression, wondering if she was trying to goad him, but her face was without guile. "It's true that I want to pay Drekk't and his soldiers back for all that they did. But this is more about making the best use of Cholk's gift than revenge."

"How do you know you're not wasting that gift by putting your life at risk?" Opal pressed.

"I suppose I don't, but I know I have to do *something*. I suppose I can't expect you to understand. When someone gives their life for you, it's as though you're living for yourself and for them. If you don't do something spectacular…something worthy…"

"I don't think Cholk meant to put more pressure on you, Colt."

Colt smiled with one side of his mouth. "Regardless of his intentions, I know this is something I must do."

Opal produced a half-smile of her own. "Well, you can't blame a girl for trying. I'll be there with you every step of the way, Colt. I too owe those gray-skinned sons of bitches for what they did to Cholk."

Colt took a step toward Opal, wanting nothing more than to initiate a sequel to last night's hug. She was all he had left in Capricon. His family back in Superius might as well be in another world. But he hung back.

"Else and Mitto are staying," Opal said, "though you probably already knew that. Mitto's injuries haven't mended entirely. Anyway, neither of them are warriors."

Colt watched her pink lips form the words. How he desired to silence them with a long kiss! He took a step closer.

"Lilac is coming," Opal stated, sounding none too pleased. "But I suppose it's better she stick that sword of hers in goblins rather than Knights."

Upon mentioning the Renegade woman, Opal pulled a sour face, but not even a frown could mar her beauty—the fullness of her lips, her shimmering green eyes, her womanly form...

"Othello is coming too," she added.

Colt stopped mid-stride and jerked as though slapped.

"What?" he demanded.

"I know that he's in bad shape, but he refuses to be left behind. And he's still your prisoner, technically."

Colt could think of a thing or two he'd have liked to do with the prisoner just then, but he forced the dark thoughts from his mind.

"Just as long as he doesn't slow us down," he mumbled.

"I wouldn't worry about that," Opal said. "He's looking much improved, and I'll keep an eye on him."

I bet you will, Colt thought.

"Well, like Dylan said, we'll be heading out soon," he said quickly. "I'd better finish getting ready."

"Oh, yeah, all right," Opal said. Colt thought she looked confused, but he couldn't quite enjoy her discomfort at being so abruptly dismissed, even though it was a small sliver of pain compared to what she had unwittingly caused him.

"I'll see you later," he said, turning around and walking back to his bed.

Colt continued to stare up at the ceiling long after her footsteps echoed through the inn. He tried to keep his mind off of the beautiful archer, but it was not an easy task. He did his best to focus on the mission, though that topic was only slightly less depressing than his relationship with Opal.

Man-to-goblin, his company couldn't hope to compete with Drekk't's forces.

All their hopes lay in surprise.

Passage IX

He stole through the lengthening shadows, his pace unhurried but steady. Aside from the occasional shout from the ale tent carried by the chilly breeze, all was quiet. He put more than a mile between himself and Hylan before coming to a stop.

Ay'sek made a cursory examination of his surroundings. He was flanked on all sides by middle-aged conifers. Except for an owl whose eyes glowed white in the darkness, he was quite alone.

The shaman picked up a stick from the ground and traced a circle in the dirt. His mantle covered most of his body, but as he looked down, he caught sight of the pale flesh of his hand. He shuddered.

Ay'sek doubted he would ever get used to the sight. The ghastly skin seemed to hang loose around the thick digits, which themselves were tipped with rounded, useless fingernails. By Upsinous's black heart, he *hoped* he would never grow accustomed to being human!

When finished, he discarded the stick and seated himself in the center of circle. He chanted the words of a familiar incantation, a spell that would insure no one could enter—or shoot anything into—the circle.

Supremely confident in his enchantment, Ay'sek wasted no time in uttering the words to a second, more complicated spell.

He felt the power of the Goblinfather flow into his body, an elating sensation that made him feel as though he might burst like an overripe melon. His brain flooded with images. He saw himself turned inside out while a pair of enormous red eyes scrutinized every inch of him. Talons raked his flesh like a lover in the throes of passion.

Ay'sek shuddered in agony and rapture.

When he opened his eyes, he was no longer surrounded by trees, but inside of a tent. Drekk't looked surprised to see him, which was to be expected. Ay'sek had, after all, materialized out of thin air.

Drekk't appeared to be in the midst of a meeting. A handful of other goblins, whom Ay'sek recognized as officers, stood before their general. Upon seeing Ay'sek, Drekk't ordered them to depart, which they did hastily, eyeballing the shaman warily as they scurried from the tent.

When the last of them was gone, Drekk't said, "I feared something ill had befallen you, Master Ay'sek. You left nearly a week ago, and this is the first I hear from you."

"You need not concern yourself with my welfare, General," Ay'sek replied dryly. "I know how to take care of myself."

"I am more concerned with your mission. Do you have *Peerma'rek*?"

Ay'sek's heartbeat quickened. How he longed to snuff out Drekk't's smug expression! He could think of at least a dozen ways of accomplishing it, everything from tearing off his lips to melting the flesh from his face. And he might have done it—except he was miles away from Drekk't and the army.

"I do not have the staff yet," Ay'sek said, quickly adding, "though I could take it at any time."

"Then why *don't* you?" Drekk't demanded.

Ay'sek was about to reprimand the general for his impudence—*no one* talked to a Chosen of the Chosen like that!—but he had seen something buried beneath Drekk't's irritation: fear.

The shaman smiled inwardly. If he failed in his mission, Drekk't would not survive a second visit from the Emperor of T'Ruel.

Which meant that even though his magic could not reach Drekk't currently, Ay'sek had absolute power over the wretched general. I control your fate as surely as if there were a noose around your neck, he silently boasted.

Drekk't was practically trembling with impatience when Ay'sek finally answered his question, "It was no great challenge locating *Peerma'rek*. A talisman of that magnitude exudes an aura of power. A first-year acolyte could have found it."

"Commander Saerylton Crystalus still has it?" Drekk't asked.

"He does," Ay'sek said. "He and his allies have brought it to a village called Hylan, where the refugees from Rydah have gathered."

"So why haven't you taken back the staff? Does it have anything to do with the commander's magical sword?"

Ay'sek had been mindful of the sword ever since he had infiltrated Colt's party, but not for the reason Drekk't was probably thinking. While the crystal sword possessed a miraculously keen edge, Ay'sek was more concerned with the blade's reflective surface. Prince T'slect's illusion had been exposed by the sword's magic, and T'slect had been a mighty shaman.

"I do not hesitate out of fear, General, but out of prudence," Ay'sek said at last. "The men of Hylan are planning a counterattack. As long as I was there, I decided to learn something of their plans."

"And?"

"And your former prisoner, Commander Crystalus, intends to lead a small army to the war camp. They leave tonight, in fact."

When Drekk't asked for the number of Colt's battalion, Ay'sek estimated one hundred men.

Drekk't laughed, displaying a mouth filled of yellow pointed teeth. "What could he hope to accomplish with so few? He must be a suicidal fool."

The general grew silent then, staring at something beyond Ay'sek.

"I trust that the army is equipped to deal with the humans," Ay'sek said to Drekk't when it was clear the general was not going to say more. "Of course, they might be delayed or not come at all when they discover the staff is missing."

Colt had stashed *Peerma'rek* somewhere in Hylan, but Ay'sek knew that when they left the village, the commander would bring the staff with him. No, he wouldn't part with it easily, but with Ay'sek's own *vuudu*, it would be little trouble for the shaman to sneak over to where Colt slept.

But he wouldn't kill Colt—not as long as he had a purpose for the man and that sharp sword of his.

"No, Master Ay'sek," Drekk't said suddenly. "You will not make a play for the staff. Not yet."

Ay'sek's confusion was almost instantly replaced by anger. He bit into his lip so hard he could taste blood. "What?"

"I want you to continue to spy on the commander and his

pitiful army. Do not reveal yourself until I give the order."

"But—"

"That is an order, *n'feranost*." Although Drekk't had used the title of reverence for a Chosen of the Chosen, Ay'sek heard the word for the mockery that it was. "Stay with the commander at all costs. There will be time enough to recover the staff. After all, he is bringing it right back to me."

Ay'sek's mind reeled. Why did Drekk't care so much about the small contingent of humans? He already knew they were on their way. What more information could Ay'sek glean? It was almost as if Drekk't wanted Ay'sek to make sure Colt and the others *did* come. At once, he realized the truth of it. The commander had scored a terrible hit on Drekk't's pride when he escaped with *Peerma'rek*.

Drekk't wanted a rematch.

"But how will I know when the time comes to strike?" Ay'sek asked, trying valiantly to keep his composure. "If I am to remain among the humans, I won't be able contact you and learn what it is *you* are planning."

Drekk't shrugged his shoulders. "You, a Chosen of the Chosen, ought to be clever enough to figure out what to do. But for now, I would suggest you get what rest you can. It sounds like you have some long, tiring days ahead."

Ay'sek hands shook at his side. Not wanting Drekk't to know how much he was upsetting him, the shaman said, "Very well, General."

He spat the words that would take his consciousness back to his body. When he opened his eyes, he noticed it was darker than when he had closed them. Not wanting his supposed friends to grow suspicious of his absence, he went back to Hylan at once.

A wave of nausea sent him falling into a sapling for support. Gorge rose in his throat. Spots danced before his eyes. Being a Chosen of the Chosen came with a price. Wielding the power of a god was a heady experience, but every spell took its toll.

He felt as though his body were being stretched out to impossible dimensions. The pain was exquisite. After several long minutes on his knees, bracing himself against the excruciating cramps rippling through his stomach, the shaman was finally able to stand.

The magic made him strong, a formidable warrior; suffering

for *vuudu* made him even stronger.

He wiped the sweat from his forehead and forced his wobbly legs to take him back to the human village. A burning that had nothing to do with magic roiled in his belly when he thought of Drekk't.

"Gods damn that sorry excuse for a goblin," he muttered.

By the time he neared Hylan, Ay'sek's pulse was already returning to its normal rate. He thanked Upsinous that he had not been there—physically—in the tent with Drekk't. He probably would have killed the general. And that would have been a mistake.

Ay'sek wasn't one of the mindless brutes comprising Drekk't's army. He was a shaman. His weapon was his mind, and the more he thought about the course ahead, the wider his smile stretched. If he were going to orchestrate the general's death, he had to make sure he wasn't implicated.

Drekk't wanted a second chance to face Colt in battle. Colt wanted the same.

"You will not return to T'Ruel a hero for this campaign, Drekk't," Ay'sek promised. "You will not return at all!"

He only hoped he would be present to witness Drekk't's final moments in this world.

Colt stood atop the dais, looking down at the throng gathered below. The first had arrived nearly an hour ago with newcomers arriving sporadically. Most carried hunting spears or long-bladed knives that had been hitherto used for skinning game. A few had bows and quivers.

Those who had no weapons were ushered over to a modest pile of castaway swords and hastily crafted pikes. Colt's heart swelled with pride as he watched members of that last group accept whatever tool was given to them and join their comrades in forming ranks.

These people were not warriors, but they were willing to give their lives in defense of their homes.

The Knights of Superius were immediately recognizable by their armor, which caught the flickering torchlight. Dylan and the others worked diligently to organize the assembly into companies of ten. Although Colt was eager to be off, he knew it was necessary to establish order from the start. He intended to lead an army, not a mob.

The Knights would serve as officers, and gods willing, their subordinates would do as they were told. Colt had told Dylan—his unofficial second-in-command—to keep things as simple as possible. As soon as the army was divided into manageable units and the basic orders were explained, they would begin their march.

Colt busied himself by studying the crowd, scrutinizing the faces of the men and women who had pledged allegiance to his cause. Most were strangers, thought he thought he recognized the burly man having a conversation with Lilac and Othello.

Predictably, Opal stood at the fringe of that group. She had promised Colt she would keep an eye on "the Renegade"—meaning Lilac. How convenient, Colt thought, since Lilac wouldn't likely stray far from Othello.

His gaze lingered on the forester for only a moment longer before looking away. He wouldn't waste his energy worrying about Opal and Othello. A good commander could not afford to be preoccupied by matters of the heart, not when so many lives were depending on him.

Colt spotted Loony Gomez a few minutes later. The old man appeared to bidding his former charges farewell. Colt didn't know how he felt about allowing the thieves to come along, but he supposed he should be thankful for every sword arm he could get. And yet contention was something he would not—*could not*—tolerate.

The belligerent Tryst came to mind…

Beyond the crowd, his arms crossed before his broad chest, stood Ruford Berwyn. Colt felt certain the Captain of the Guard was watching him, though he was too far away to be sure.

Ruford had made his decision the night before: he would stay in Hylan with Dale Mullahstyn and those Knights who remained loyal to the sergeant. None of Ruford's twenty-some guardsmen had forsaken their captain; Colt saw not a single uniformed man among his army.

At first, Colt had been frustrated by Ruford's lack of support, but the more he thought about it, the more he believed leaving Ruford to watch over the village wasn't a bad idea after all. Although Dale had vowed he wouldn't put Hylan to the torch, Colt put more stock in Ruford's promise.

The Captain of the Guard gave Colt a sudden, stiff salute.

Colt let out a sigh and returned the gesture. Ruford Berwyn then spun on his heels and tromped back toward the mayor's house. Colt watched him go, doubting he would ever see the man again.

"Commander."

He hadn't heard anyone ascend the platform, so he did his best to hide the fact he had been taken unawares. When he turned and saw who it was, however, he couldn't help but gape.

"Sergeant Mullahstyn," Colt said after a pause.

What was he doing here? Was this a desperate ploy to steal back the authority Colt had stripped from him? He eyed Dale warily, waiting for the Knight to make his move.

"You and I did not meet under the best of circumstances," Dale said after a nervous cough. "I have heard it said that war brings out the best in a man...courage, honor, love for his countrymen...but I have come to believe otherwise."

Colt did not know what to say.

"Please accept my apology for the way I behaved," Dale continued. "I realize, now, that you are acting in Hylan's best interest, as you see it. I hope you believe me when I say I am doing the same."

Colt smiled a mostly genuine smile. "You wish to defend the villagers."

Dale stared at him for a moment longer before breaking eye contact. "No one could ever doubt your bravery, Commander ...or that of your followers. Surely you know your course will lead to their deaths."

The sergeant looked at Colt once more. "You cannot win, Commander."

"You might be right," Colt conceded, "but if I must die doing my duty, then so be it."

"Spoken like a true martyr, but what of *them*, Commander?" Dale indicated the crowd with an outstretched hand. "They are not Knights of Superius. They are simple men and women. It is a Knight's privilege to protect them, to fight *for* them...not *beside* them."

"Even when they don't want our protection?"

"*Especially* when they don't want to be protected." Dale took a deep breath before continuing. "The gods alone know which of us is making the bigger mistake. If our fate is to lose to the invaders, I don't suppose it matters what we do in the mean-time."

Colt studied the man for signs of sarcasm, but Dale had apparently meant what he said. Colt wanted to tell the sergeant not to lose hope, but he could not bring himself to commit hypocrisy. At least he wasn't the only Knight sparring with doubt.

"Maybe it's what we do in the meantime that truly matters," Colt said. "What else can we control but our own actions?"

Dale's smile was almost imperceptible. "You are wise beyond your years, Commander Crystalus."

"Thank you," Colt replied, trusting the statement had been meant as a compliment. "What will you do once we are gone?"

Dale chuckled softly. "Well, thanks to that rousing speech of yours last night, I shan't be able to talk any of the hayseeds into fleeing for their lives. Ruford and I will stay in Hylan as long as we must. You can think the worst of me, Commander, but I would never leave the villagers undefended."

The two men stood in silence as Dylan and the other Knights of Superius made the final preparations for their late-night trek. A little while later, Sergeant Mullahstyn excused himself, making his way back to the home of Quillan Dag.

After what felt like hours, Dylan approached the dais and said, "We are ready, Commander."

"How many are we?" Colt asked, his voice nearly a whisper.

"Eighty-eight in all."

Colt nodded vaguely. It was more than he had expected and probably more than he deserved. But it was not nearly enough.

It's not too late to back out, Colt thought. I could stay in Hylan and make a stand with Dale and Ruford. Maybe I should follow Opal's advice and leave for Fort Valor at once. By now Stannel and Petton would have begun to worry about us...

"Are you well, Commander?"

Dylan wore a worried expression, which told Colt a lot about he himself looked.

I am their leader, Colt reminded himself. I no longer have the luxury of entertaining doubt. The gods alone know what we will find at the end of our march. All I have to worry about is getting them there in one piece.

Colt patted Dylan on the shoulder, drawing strength from the Knight's unwavering confidence. While he missed Stannel's coolheaded reason and limitless faith, he was grateful for having a companion like Dylan Torc, who seemingly would have taken on Upsinous and the rest of the gods of darkness without hesitation.

Colt looked out at his army and smiled in spite of himself. He had no energy left for a second oration. Whatever zeal his words had inspired last night would have to sustain the troops a while longer. Time was of the essence.

"All right," Colt said to Dylan. "Let's go."

If any wondered about the macabre staff their leader handled as casually as a walking stick, they must have dismissed it as just another idiosyncrasy of the man they had come to call Commander Colt.

Part 2

Passage I

The first thing Petton noticed was the Renegade Leader carried himself with a sturdiness and self-assuredness that had been lacking during their last meeting. Petton frowned. If Klye Tristan had regained his full strength, it meant that he would have to keep a closer eye on the rebel.

Klye, meanwhile, spared Petton only the briefest of glances. In that half-second, an effluvium of emotions passed between them. Along with contempt and unabashed arrogance, Petton saw in Klye's eyes the look of the victor.

Petton swallowed a sour taste in his mouth. You haven't won yet, Renegade, he thought. Make one false move, and Stannel will have no choice but to toss you and the rest of your band of criminals into the dungeon.

At the commander's request, Klye took the chair beside Petton's. Petton eyed the rebel for a moment longer before he too turned his attention to the one who had called for the awkward meeting in the first place.

Commander Stannel Bismarc shuffled a few sheets of parchment to one side of the desk and settled his gaze on the Renegade Leader. Stannel looked as comfortable in the presence of the Renegade Leader as he did with any of the Knights at the fort.

"Thank you for coming," Stannel said to Klye. "Your condition seems much improved since last you were here."

Klye shrugged. "You brought one hell of a healer with you. If not for Sister Aric, I'd probably still be spending my days in the infirmary."

Petton bristled at the Renegade's harsh language, and he searched Stannel for signs of displeasure. Sister Aric was, after all, one of Stannel's dearest friends. But if the commander was at all offended, he didn't show it.

Before either Knight could respond, Klye added, "The last time I was in this office, it was because one of my Renegades had disappeared. But since I was just with my men...those that are still here, at least...I'm guessing this is about something else."

Petton's heart beat faster beneath his breastplate. He wanted nothing more than to smash his fist into the insolent rebel's face. Klye's disrespect for Stannel might have been understandable if Stannel had somehow mistreated Klye and his men. But in reality, the Renegades had lived more like guests than prisoners since their capture nearly a month ago...except for the pirates.

"You and Dominic Horcalus were of great help in recovering those who had gone missing," Stannel said at last. "And before that, Commander Crystalus had asked you to make recommendations for his company."

Petton wanted to point out that there was no way of knowing whether the two Renegades had proved a help or a hindrance to Saerylton Crystalus's party. For all they knew, Lilac and Othello had fled the first chance they got. Or worse.

He saw Klye's lip curl into a lopsided smile. "Lilac and Othello were chosen by default. You and Colt didn't trust anyone else to go."

"Be that as it may," Stannel replied evenly, "your thoughts on the matter were valuable."

"But not so valuable when it comes to Pistol and Crooker," was Klye's flippant answer. "Unless you called me here to say you're letting the pirates out of the dungeon?"

Petton seethed and wondered what it would take for Stannel Bismarc to lose his temper.

"I do not wish to discuss any of your Renegades, in fact," Stannel continued, evoking a raised eyebrow from Klye. "Would you be good enough to tell the lieutenant and I a little about how you came to know Noel?"

For the briefest of moments, arrogant Klye Tristan lost his composure. He opened his mouth, only to close it again an instant later. Petton beamed inwardly, taking satisfaction in the fact he was responsible for Klye's discomfiture. Stannel had not known that Klye and Noel were acquaintances prior to their separate arrivals at the fort.

Ever a skeptic of coincidences, Petton had never forgotten that detail.

Klye cleared his throat. "Are you asking me whether or not you can trust Noel? Because if you are, I'll tell you what I'd tell anyone else. When you deal with a midge, you do so at your own risk."

"That is *not* what the commander asked, Renegade," Petton said, earning a swift glare from Klye.

Ignoring Knight and rebel alike, Stannel said, "But you have 'dealt' with this midge before. Noel thinks of you as a friend, does he not?"

Klye's crooked grin returned. "I suppose so."

"And do you consider him a friend as well?"

The Renegade Leader crossed his arms. "I suppose that would depend on your definition of 'friend.' Noel and I have been allies on two different occasions, but if he were to depart from my life as suddenly as he recently reentered it, well, I wouldn't be surprised…or saddened."

"You have trusted Noel with your life."

Petton didn't know whether Stannel had intended that as a question, and neither, apparently, did Klye, who was staring hard at Stannel, waiting for him to go on.

"Noel was responsible for helping you breech this fortress," Stannel said. "You put your life and the lives of your men in his hands. That implies faith in the midge and his magic."

"He knew the prince was evil, though none of the Knights would believe him," Klye explained blandly. "He thought he was doing the right thing by letting us in. Anyway, I think he likes Colt better than me. I'm surprised he didn't go east with him."

"*Commander Crystalus* had enough to worry about without having a midge underfoot," Petton stated.

"With all due respect, Stannel," Klye said, "maybe if you told me what this was all about, I could tell you what you want to know about Noel."

Stannel studied Klye for a moment—a scrutinizing look that unnerved Petton whenever it landed on him—before saying, "The Kings of Continae need to know the realm is in danger. Even if our forces in Capricon cannot repel the goblins, we might keep their armies occupied while the Continent United rallies for war.

"I have written a letter to King Edward, informing him of the goblins' intent and accomplishments. I would like Noel to deliver the missive."

Petton had heard a similar speech not long before Klye's arrival, and he had been no less surprised than Klye appeared to be now. The Renegade Leader's expression turned thoughtful as he scratched his arm absently. Petton had no way of knowing what Klye was thinking, but he was certain it wasn't anything good.

For all of his prejudice against the Renegades, Petton trusted Noel even less. Like most Knights, Gaelor Petton had no use for wizards. In addition to being a spell-caster, Noel was known for switching sides at the drop of a hat.

Noel had the same freedom at the fort that Klye and his Renegades enjoyed—against Petton's advice. This made the lieutenant's job far more difficult since it was nearly impossible to keep tabs on the midge. For all they knew, Noel could, at that moment, be hiding in a corner of the office, invisible.

As former Commander of Fort Faith, Saerylton Crystalus had been somewhat unconventional in his methods, but that was mainly because he had been a novice in the ways of leadership. Stannel, however, ought to know better than to let rebels walk the fortress unchecked.

"Noel is our sole means of communicating with Superius? Gods help us," Klye muttered.

"Perhaps they will," Stannel said with a faint smile. "Tell me, Klye, do you believe he is capable of carrying out the mission?"

Klye thought for a few seconds and came up with the same answer Petton had given earlier. "Well, if he fails, we're no worse off than before...except we won't have Noel's magic to aid us when the goblins come."

Petton had seen the midge wield his spells against the goblins firsthand and couldn't deny that Noel might prove a useful tool against the invading army. If the midge didn't throw in with the goblins, of course...

"It doesn't look like we have much of a choice, does it?" Klye said.

We? thought Petton.

"Do you think he can do it?" Stannel repeated.

Klye's half-smirk vanished as he said, "If there's one thing I've learned about Noel, it's that he's full of surprises. Given the chance, I'd say he's capable of anything."

The ambiguous statement did nothing to banish Petton's

doubts, but he knew the matter was out of his hands. He had the feeling Stannel had made up his mind before summoning the Renegade Leader.

Klye was dismissed a few minutes later, though not before he made yet another petition for the imprisoned pirates. Petton asked to be excused soon after.

Outside of Stannel's office, Petton cast a glance at the closed door. Although he spoke with the commander every morning—going over strategies and contingency plans—Petton knew very little about the man.

Stannel Bismarc had been the Commander of Fort Valor for almost fifteen years, but not *this* Fort Valor. The original Fort Valor had stood a day's hard ride to the east before the goblins destroyed it. Fort Faith had been renamed Fort Valor so that Colt could relinquish his responsibilities to Stannel without having to clear his transfer of power through the proper channels.

If Fort Faith had kept its true identity, Petton would have been the rightful replacement.

The lieutenant could admit he was jealous of Stannel and that that was natural reaction to the circumstances. But while Petton was possessed of a competitive nature, he wasn't a sore loser. Anyway, there were far more important things to think about during in a time of war.

And yet…

Rumors were circulating about Stannel, who had personally sought out the missing residents of the fort. Stannel had taken a few of the Renegades along with him, though Petton had argued against it. The rebels had returned from Wizard's Mountain with tales of a battle between Stannel and an unnatural creature made of stone.

According to the Renegade who always wore a black hood—Scout, was it?—Stannel had saved the day by shattering one of the monster's boulder-sized arm with his one-handed mace, forcing the thing to retreat.

Stannel had never denied the details of the fantastic story, but neither had Petton pressed him on it. Some of the Knights chalked up Stannel's feat to the magic of the highwayman Ruben, but Petton was almost certain Ruben was a fraud. Where the magic had come from, Petton could not say—if there had been magic in the first place.

Regardless of what had really happened, the Knights of *new*

Fort Valor were starting to speculate about their new commander. Petton reminded Ezekiel Silvercrown and the other higher-ranking officers that now was not the time for distractions, but as he turned and walked away from the commander's office, he realized he too had been spending an awful lot of time thinking about Stannel.

As though he didn't have enough people to keep an eye on!

Klye made almost no sound as he crossed one corridor after another. He had been searching for Noel for almost two hours, and the chore was beginning to take its toll on his body. He felt as though he were playing hide-and-seek with the midge, only his supposed playmate had no idea that the game was going on.

He wasn't trying to be stealthy; it was simply habit.

Klye was nearing the end of his sweep of the fort's second story, having started from the bottom and worked his way up, when he reached a certain intersection where the hallway branched into two perpendicular avenues. Klye chose the left path without hesitation.

As he approached the base of a staircase, he remembered the last time he had been there, when he and his men had followed Opal to the fort's western wing—and to the false Prince Eliot Borrom. Back then, the tower had served as castle's war room and Colt's personal office. Now, thanks to T'slect's spells, the place was no longer habitable.

It was probably the most dangerous place inside the fort, which was why Klye was suddenly certain he would find Noel there.

Upon reaching the top of the stairs, Klye chuckled. At the end of the hall, where a pile of fallen lumber and stony rubble had replaced the door to the war room, sat the midge. Noel had his back to the wreckage, seemingly oblivious to the fact that a minute shift behind him might result in a small-scale avalanche.

Then again, Klye thought, the little bugger probably *had* thought of that. Perhaps an unseen wall of magic was holding back the fallen masonry…

Klye had learned long ago not to underestimate Noel. The midge, as a people, could manipulate magic with intrinsic ease, accomplishing feats that human wizards might spend their entire lives trying to perfect. Thus, in a world where every spell-caster was subject to the scrutiny of the masses, the midge earned disdain even from their human counterparts. He supposed most wizards thought the midge squandered their extraordinary powers, dismissing them as simpletons—albeit dangerous simpletons.

Once upon a time Klye had thought Noel a simpleton. But while the short spell-caster was possessed of an almost child-like rationale, he had proven time and time again he was no fool. The fact that he was still alive was testament to his shrewdness.

As he drew nearer, Klye saw Noel was staring down at a book on his lap. The midge's legs and feet were completely covered by his light blue robe, and the brim of his pointy straw hat hid his face completely. Were those two small hands not in plain sight, gripping the edges of the book, a passerby might have mistaken Noel for a pile of clothes.

The midge didn't look up as he approached, which made Klye pause. There were worse things than startling a midge, but at the moment he couldn't think of any. Now that he was standing directly beside him, he could see Noel's mouth shaping the words to what Klye assumed was a spell.

Feeling more foolish by the moment for simply standing there, Klye cleared his throat noisily. Without glancing up, his lips still forming the unheard syllables, Noel held up a hand, indicating Klye should give him a moment.

He hadn't stolen up on Noel after all—though he had, once again, underestimated him.

After a few more seconds, Noel slammed the two halves of his book together in a loud clap. Strange glyphs had been etched across the front cover, which was a dull gray color. Judging by the yellowed pages within, the cover had probably been a bold black at one time.

There was something in the angular script that seemed malignant to Klye. Sometimes it was easy to forget that friendly, good-natured Noel was a caster of black magic. Not that Klye knew much about the differences between the three types of magic. For all he knew, white and red spell books used the same alphabet.

"Hiya, Klye," Noel smiled, not bothering to get up. "What are *you* doing up here?"

Klye had half a mind to ask Noel the same thing, but on second thought, he wasn't in the mood for a lengthy explanation.

"I was looking for you."

"Really?" The midge's smile broadened. "We haven't talked in a while. Did you miss me?"

"Ah…"

"I was going to visit you, Klye, but I thought I should do some studying first. I know…I know…most midge don't use spell books. Some don't even know how to read! But I'm in a hurry, and I don't think there's anything wrong with shortcuts. When it comes to transportation rites, one little mistake can land you in a Meridian cannibal's stewpot…well…that's just an expression. I don't think Meridians eat people anymore."

Klye opened his mouth, hoping to interject, but Noel was quicker.

"But I really *was* going to see you before I left. Oh, did you hear? Stannel has chosen me for a secret mission. Imagine, a midge working for the Knights of Superius! I guess the gods knew what they were doing when they sent me here…not that *I* ever doubted them. Don't tell anyone, Klye…" He lowered his voice into a loud whisper. "I'm going to see the King of Superius so I can warn him about the goblins."

Klye shook his head in exasperation.

Noel's eyes doubled in size. "Um, maybe I shouldn't have told you…you being a bad guy and all."

"I'm *not* a bad guy!"

"Yeah, yeah, the Renegades and Knights are on the same side now. I remember. But I can't take any chances. This is important business!"

Klye rolled his eyes. "I already knew about your mission. That's why I was looking for you. I wanted to speak with you before you left."

"All right."

With the midge staring expectantly up at him, Klye suddenly felt self-conscious. He almost wished Noel would take off on another tangent. "It's just that…I was hoping you could do me a favor, do the *Renegades* a favor."

Noel's big blue eyes narrowed, and his smile fell into a frown. "I'm not a rebel anymore, Klye. I'm working for the Knights now…again…"

Klye wanted to point out that Noel never really was a Renegade. Instead, he said, "Actually, you'd be helping the Knights too."

The midge lifted a fair-haired eyebrow and regarded Klye skeptically. No, Klye thought, he's no simpleton.

"As you may have heard," Klye began, "my band ran afoul of some goblins while we were in Port Town. I have reason to believe the goblins are using the city's sewers as a base. Meanwhile, the Renegades of Port Town and the city guards are fighting each other, much like we were fighting with the Knights of Fort Faith when you got here."

Noel's expression did not alter.

"What I'd like for you to do, Noel, is to make a quick stop in Port Town before you magic yourself to Superius. If you could get word of what the goblins are planning to Leslie, she might be able to talk some sense into her father, the mayor..."

Klye trailed off, gauging the midge's reaction to his words. Noel's face gradually relaxed, and then, to Klye's surprise, the wizard's mouth curved into a wide grin that rivaled its predecessors in size and emotion.

"Who's this Leslie person?" he asked.

"What? Oh, Leslie Beryl...she's the Renegade Leader of Port Town. She helped me and my band when we were in a tight spot, and I owe her one."

Noel veritably giggled. "Is she your *girlfriend*?"

"She's a *colleague*."

"Is she pretty?"

Klye knew Noel was only trying to egg him on. He wouldn't give the midge the satisfaction of watching him squirm. "Are you going to help me or not?"

Noel's expression turned serious. "I'd love to help you, but I can't. I've never been to Port Town."

"So?"

"So," Noel said, "I can't magically transport myself to a place I've never been. I have to be able to see...in my mind...where I want to go. I have no idea what Port Town looks like. I might be able to extract the image from your memory, but that could be dangerous for both of us."

Klye swore. Like most people, he knew very little about magic. In his younger days, he had thought magic gave wizards godlike abilities. More and more, however, he was realizing that magic, like everything else in life, had plenty of limitations.

"Wait a minute," Klye said. "I'm pretty damn sure you've never been to Castle Borrom. How do you intend to magic yourself to the King of Superius?"

"You're right. I can't go directly to Castle Borrom. The closest I can get is Therrat, Ristidae."

"That's not even in the same country!"

"I *know* that. But I have a friend in Therrat who owns a shop for wizards. I'm hoping he might have a spell that can take me closer to Castle Borrom. Usually, I don't bother with transportation spells. They take all of the fun out of traveling. You don't get to see any of the scenery. But since I'm going on an important mission…hey, are you listening to me?"

Klye said he was, but in truth, he had tuned the midge out.

"I'm sorry I can't help you, Klye. I hope your girl—I mean *friend* will be all right."

"Yeah, well, thanks anyway. Good luck with your mission. I'd better go and check on my men."

Klye turned and walked away. He could feel his face burning and told himself it was due to frustration with magic rather than embarrassment. He supposed Leslie and her Renegades would just have to watch out for themselves for the time being.

He might have said a prayer for the Renegades of Port Town if he thought it would do any good. At times like these, he envied people like Stannel and Sister Aric, who put so much faith in the gods. But since he couldn't bring himself to talk to imaginary spirits—and since there was nothing he could do to help—he pushed Leslie and her cohorts out of his mind…

…but not before wondering whether she ever thought about him.

Passage II

Arthur's whole body trembled, sending trickles of perspiration running down his bare arms. He lay there for a moment, trying to suppress his quick, heavy breathing. His heart thudded like a bass drum that would surely awaken everyone else in the room.

He rose to his feet and, still gasping for air, tiptoed to the exit. Once the door was closed behind him, he let himself fall against it. Sweat or tears tickled his cheek, and he wiped away the water with the back of his hand.

Arthur glanced gratefully at a nearby torch, which tossed its light far down both ends of the hallway. For a full minute, he stared straight ahead at the gray stone walls around him and told himself over and over again he was safe inside the fort. It had only been a dream.

But not even the wavering torchlight could banish the dark visions burned into his mind.

Arthur was no stranger to nightmares. He had been having the same dream for more than three months, a vivid terror that was made all the more terrible by its basis in reality. The nightmare was more than just a bad dream; it was a memory, one he couldn't escape even in sleep.

But the past few nights had seen a change in the nightmare. New components included a stony giant, a demonic little girl, and a horde of goblins always on the edge of sight.

Despite the sweat coating his skin, Arthur felt like he was burning up. He needed to find some fresh air, fast.

The young man stumbled barefoot through the dimly lit fortress, searching for an open window but finding only yard after yard of solid wall. It occurred to him the last time he had wandered the fort at night he had ended up in the very misadventure now complicating the old nightmare. He kept walking anyway.

Arthur found a small window in a random nook, but he wasn't the first person to have found it.

The Commander of Fort Valor turned at his approach, watching him impassively. Arthur would have fled back the way he had come, except he was certain the commander had already identified him. While Stannel had never mistreated him—though he was a Renegade—Arthur always felt uncomfortable around the Knight.

Then again, he felt nervous in the presence of any authority these days.

Not knowing what else to do, Arthur continued on toward his destination and came to stand sheepishly beside Stannel.

"It would seem that sleep eludes us both tonight." The commander's tone was gentle.

Arthur nodded. He wondered about Stannel's insomnia. Was it the stress of being in command of a new fort that kept him up?

"I don't believe I properly thanked you for what you did," Stannel said suddenly. "You must forgive my negligence, but ever since we returned from Wizard's Mountain, I have been…preoccupied."

Arthur had thought a lot about the incident. He and Ruben, a former highwayman, had followed the insane Toemis Blisnes and his granddaughter through a hidden tunnel from the fort and to the nearby foothills. They had tracked the old man all the way to Wizard's Mountain.

What had happened next still baffled Arthur.

"It's me who should be thanking you, Commander. If you hadn't shown up, Ruben and I would probably be dead."

The stone creature had knocked him unconscious before Stannel, Horcalus, Scout, and Sister Aric arrived. Ruben certainly would have been crushed to death. As it was, Toemis Blisnes hadn't survived the encounter, and Zusha, his granddaughter, was missing.

"We have never been properly introduced, you and I," the commander said after a moment. He held out his hand. "I am Stannel Caelan Bismarc, and it is an honor to meet you, Arthur …?"

Arthur tried to reply, but his tongue rebelled. Finally, he stammered out, "B-Bismarc?"

"That is correct."

"*My* family name is Bismarc!"

Stannel's eyes widened ever so slightly. "Is that so? How fortuitous."

"I've never met a Bismarc outside of my immediate family," Arthur told him. "And I thought only nobles used three names. Are you a lord?"

Stannel smiled warmly. "It is true the Superian monarchy uses middle names, but having three names is long-standing tradition in Glenning. It has been that way since before Superius existed."

"But you are Superian." Arthur didn't know much about the Knights of Superius, but he knew the Knighthood didn't admit foreigners into their ranks.

"I was born in Superius, but my father and my mother were Glenningers," Stannel explained. "My father was a Knight of Eaglehand, Glenning's equivalent to the Knights of Superius."

This was all news to Arthur, who had thought the Knights of Superius were the unparalleled defenders of Continae. All he knew about Glenning was that it was directly south of Superius.

Stannel continued, "My father's name was Caelan. Hence, that is my middle name. As a Knight of Eaglehand, Caelan Bismarc fought alongside the Knights of Superius during the Thanatan Conflict. After the ogres were pushed out of Continae, he joined his Superian comrades in what came to be called the Wilderness Crusade, even though Glenning's king did not support the effort.

"So impressed was my father by the honor and courage of the Superian Knights, that he sent his pregnant wife to Superius instead of Glenning. The Knights of Eaglehand were already a waning presence in Glenning by then, just as the monarchy was…and is."

After a brief pause, he said, "The name Bismarc is native to Glenning. Did you know that, Arthur?"

"Um, no…no, sir…I did not."

"Your parents never spoke of Glenning?"

Arthur flinched at the mention of his parents. He did his best to keep his voice steady when he answered, "Not that I can remember, sir."

Stannel seemed interested by this, or perhaps it had been Arthur's initial reaction that piqued his interest. The commander massaged his chin as he said, "It is possible your parents are unaware of their roots, I suppose. Capricon was once owned and governed by Glenning, but enough time has passed that many of the islanders identify more with Superius than Glenning. You are from Capricon, are you not?"

"Yes," Arthur said, "I'm from Hylan. My parents are farmers. They wanted me to be a farmer too."

Arthur could hardly believe he was chatting with a Superian commander. Moreover, he couldn't believe how much personal information he was telling the man. He hadn't even told Horcalus some of these things!

"Doesn't every father secretly hope his son will follow in his footsteps?" Stannel asked with a chuckle. "I suspect my father wanted me to enlist with the Knights of Superius. Unfortunately, he died before I was born. By the time I became a Knight, Ristidae had been liberated from the ogres, and the Wilderness Campaign was at an end."

Arthur wondered if every Knight of Superius knew the history of Continae as well as Stannel did. Maybe they learned it as a squire. He decided to ask Horcalus about it later.

"I'm sure he'd be proud of you," Arthur said quietly. He looked down at the floor as he spoke, as much to remain unobtrusive as to hide his watery eyes. How he wished he could say the same of his own father!

"To tell you the truth, Arthur, there are times when I think I was not cut out to be a Knight at all."

"I think you're a good Knight. Scout said you fought off that stone giant all on your own."

Arthur glanced over at Stannel to find that the Knight's expression had gone as hard as a statue's. Gods above, what did I say? he wondered. Maybe Stannel was upset over losing the girl, Zusha. In Arthur's dreams, the shadowy throng of goblins carried her away, though sometimes he saw her sitting upon the rock monster's shoulder.

"That is not entirely true," Stannel muttered.

At first, Arthur didn't know what Stannel was referring to, but then he recalled the comment he had made about Stannel defeating the giant single-handedly. Scout had retold the story again and again over the past few days, describing in great detail the golden light that had erupted from Stannel's mace.

Arthur very much wanted to ask Stannel about his mace, but he didn't want to put more distance between them. Both Horcalus and Scout were convinced Ruben had cast a spell on Stannel's weapon, but Ruben had admitted to Arthur earlier that he knew no magic whatsoever.

Perhaps like Colt and his crystal sword, Stannel owned an enchanted weapon.

"Do you think we'll ever get to the bottom of what happened out there?" Arthur asked Stannel, adding quickly, "I mean…where did that stone creature come from anyway? And where did Zusha go?"

Stannel stared out the small window into the night. "We may never know. I only pray that the girl is safe."

Arthur hoped for the same. In addition, he hoped he would never see the rock giant again.

"It was nice talking with you, Arthur," Stannel said. "But the night wanes, and you and I should make another attempt at sleeping."

Arthur nodded. He didn't want their conversation to end but had no excuse for prolonging it. Soon after Stannel was out of sight, Arthur started the walk to back to his room. He worried about having the nightmare again, but he felt stronger for his talk with the Commander of Fort Valor.

If he dreamed of Wizard's Mountain again, he decided he would keep an eye out for Stannel Bismarc and his mace.

Opal awoke with a gasp. Her heart pounded in her chest, and her breath came in quick, desperate gulps. At first, she could only lay there in the darkness, afraid and not knowing why. Eventually, her eyes began to adjust to the dim light that colored the sky a pale yellow.

It wasn't the first time she had woken in a fit of panic. But what was more frustrating than the chronic nightmares was the fact she could remember absolutely nothing about them upon waking. It was as though all traces of the dream evaporated the moment she opened her eyes, leaving not a single clue as to the nature of the night terrors.

Opal supposed her amnesia was to blame. A healer had once told her that memory loss often resulted when a person suffered something very traumatic. It stood to reason that the event she continually dreamed about was the same event that had triggered the amnesia in the first place.

Which made her inability to remember it all the more maddening.

The same healer had told her she might one day, out of the blue, remember her past, including the one terrible memory causing her nightmares. He had said she would regain her memory when she was emotionally ready to deal with whatever it was that had happened to her.

Thinking back on the conversation, Opal doubted the healer's reasoning. She couldn't imagine anything worse than not knowing her past, not knowing who she really was.

Besides, she *felt* ready for a revelation. She wasn't some fragile maiden afraid to step in the mud. As a matter of fact, she had lived through some rather distressing ordeals in recent memory. An image of Cholk's head hanging from a tree, his mangled body parts scattered beneath, came unbidden into her mind.

Even though she knew it would do no good, Opal closed her eyes and willed her mind to break through the barrier separating her from the realm of unconscious thought. She struggled to grasp onto an image from the nightmare, any lingering impression, but found nothing but a great black void.

Opal continued to lie there even after her heartbeat and breathing returned to normal. The nightmare always left her feeling weak and pathetic. She had sneaked into a goblin war camp without hesitation, had engaged Drekk't—who turned out to be the goblin's general—in combat, and was on her way back to face those savage warriors again.

So what in Abaddon, the Crypt, and the Pit had happened to her that had caused her mind to close in on itself like a frightened turtle?

Judging by the low level of light, sunrise was still an hour or more away. She briefly considered going back to sleep—there was to be another long day of walking ahead—but decided against it. She couldn't recall having ever had the dream twice in one night, but she didn't want to risk going through the frustration again so soon.

Opal climbed out of her bedroll and immediately began to shiver. The Superian calendar had heralded the advent of winter almost a week ago, and Capricon was beginning to show signs of the season. The grass around her glistened with frost, and her breath danced in the air. Wrapping her coat tightly around her,

Opal decided an early-morning walk would do wonders for her circulation and her mood.

She tiptoed around the slumbering bodies that stretched between her and the trees. As per Dylan's recommendation, the women had made their own separate camp not far from the men's. She had shared a fire with Lilac, Hunter, and a few other women from the village's militia. She had not said much to any of them last night—though Lilac and Hunter seemed to have hit it off—and she wondered if the strangers thought her rude for her reticence.

Not that Opal cared what they thought of her. It just didn't make sense to make new friends when they were all likely going to die in a day or two.

She banished the depressing thought to whatever abyss had swallowed her dreams. If today was destined to be the last day of her life, she was determined to enjoy it as best she could. And at that moment, a peaceful walk through the woods sounded like a small piece of Paradise.

A chorus of sparrow songs drifted through the evergreens. She wandered for a time as though in a trance, captivated by the beauty around her. Eventually, she happened upon a doe, nibbling at the remaining leaves on low-lying branches. Her hand instinctively reached for her crossbow.

But she stopped before her hand got anywhere near the weapon. Although fresh meat would be a blessing to Colt's army, she could not bring herself to shoot the deer. Perhaps it was because she knew her own death would almost certainly come soon. Perhaps it was because she just didn't want anything to ruin the morning's tranquility.

The doe must have caught her scent for the muscles in her thick neck tightened suddenly. One dark, liquid eye fixed on her. For a long moment, neither of them moved. Opal let her warm breath out slowly into the crisp air, not wanting anything to startle the magnificent animal.

The doe took one last bite of her breakfast before walking farther into the forest. Opal reflected a moment longer before renewing her own hike. She guided her path in another direction, not wanting to disturb the deer again.

It occurred to her that none of them—neither humans or goblins—belonged there. The wilderness had children of its own, beasts who cared nothing for foreign armies.

Opal had gone a little farther when she heard the sound of trickling water. Deciding a drink of fresh water—not to mention a good washing—was in order, she followed the burbling to a stream no more than four feet wide. The water splashed over and around rocks that looked like they might have been there since the beginning of time. The creek was shallow and clear.

She cupped the chilly liquid in her hands and poured it into her mouth. The water numbed her tongue. The coldness swam down her throat and into her stomach. Though the drink caused her to shiver, it was refreshing nonetheless.

She brought her wet hands to her face in hopes of removing some of the grime from yesterday's day-long trek. She felt so isolated she might have stripped off some of her clothes and performed a more thorough washing, but she feared the cold would seep into her bones. Better to die at the end of a goblin spear than in bed from an illness, she thought.

Someone was standing on the other side of the stream.

This time she grabbed her crossbow and brought it up to aim. Startled though she was, she noted from the start the intruder was a man, not a goblin. Her heart racing, she peered at him with one eye, ready to fire if he made any move to harm her.

"I surrender," the man said in a low, calm voice.

Lowering her weapon, Opal wondered how she hadn't recognized Othello immediately. Standing at least six and a half feet tall, the forester was the tallest member of Colt's company. He carried a longbow and wore the same buckskin attire he always wore, despite the holes and tears from goblin arrows and blades.

Even from across the stream, she could make out his bold green eyes.

The forester's habit of appearing when one least expected it was just one of the man's many mysteries. It was no small miracle he had made it all the way to Hylan, and watching him fight through his fever, Opal had been reminded of her first encounter with the archer.

The Renegades had taken her as a prisoner to their hideout at abandoned Port Stone. Klye and his gang had all but forgotten about her as they made their plans to strike out against the Knights of Fort Faith. Only Othello had cared enough to treat her wound, one that his arrow had caused it in the first place.

She remembered his gentle touch as he bandaged her leg…

Not only had Othello made the best first impression of all of Klye's Renegades—in spite of the arrow—but also, he seemed possessed of a kindred spirit. She had spent much of the past few years accompanying merchant caravans along Ristidae's untamed highways. Othello too had lived most of his life in the wilds. And they were both archers.

Opal knew Colt worried about her getting mixed up with a Renegade, but while she was undeniably fascinated with the forester, she did not attribute her feelings to love or even sex. She had told the truth when saying Othello reminded her of her forgotten past. Her attraction to Othello was strictly related to her obsession with recovering her past.

Though the forester was handsome in a rugged sort of way...

Opal's face grew warm in spite of the wintry air.

"I didn't mean to startle you," she said awkwardly.

"Likewise."

Othello crossed the stream in two strides, using a protruding rock to keep from getting his feet from getting wet.

"You shouldn't be out by yourself," Opal scolded. "You've barely regained your strength."

"I insisted on helping with the perimeter watch," he said. "You're lucky I didn't mistake you for a goblin."

"Are you calling me ugly?" she shot back, unable to hide her smile.

She realized too late that she was flirting. Being the only woman in the company of mercenaries and, later, the only female at a fortress full of Knights, Opal was no stranger to the art of flirtation. She considered it harmless fun.

That she was teasing Othello should have been nothing unusual, except for the fact she was oddly aware of it.

Othello just stared back at her, and she lost herself in his eyes. A sensation not so unlike that which she had experienced earlier this morning swept over her. There was a memory—or perhaps *all* of her memories—hiding in the back of her mind. The mere sight of Othello seemed to evoke this indescribable yet wholly exasperating feeling.

Only recently had she started associating the two—Othello and the dream...her attraction to him and the repulsive nightmare.

"I know this is going to sound crazy," Opal said, "but have we ever met before...outside of Capricon, I mean?"

A faint wrinkle appeared between Othello's eyebrows, as he considered the question. A moment later, he flashed a rare smile and said, "No. I think I would remember a woman as ugly as you."

Before Opal could recover from her shock—she had thought the forester incapable of humor—Othello walked away, following the shore of the stream. She stood there a while longer, trying to puzzle out his place in her past as well as his place in her present. No answers came.

Passage III

After three glasses of elf water, Noel was feeling a bit silly.

He hadn't had any liquor since before leaving for Capricon—everyone at Fort Valor was always too busy to share a drink with him—so he supposed he was making up for lost time. The sweet, tangy liquid warmed him from the inside out.

Feeling quite cozy in spite of the tall drifts of snow outside, Noel would have liked nothing more than talk the day away inside the mageware shop, exchanging tales with his good friend. But even with the pleasant buzzing in his head, he couldn't forget he was on a very important mission.

With an exaggerated sigh, Noel put cork in their gossiping—and the bottle of elf water—and got down to business. He forced himself to skip many details, which pained him greatly, as he told the midge seated across from him the reason for his visit.

"So you see, I really need to find a way to get to Castle Borrom so I can warn King Edward Borrom III and the other Kings of Continae about the goblin invasion of Capricon," Noel concluded, taking a deep breath afterward.

Avuru clapped his hands together and laughed. "Wonderful story! If anyone else walked in here spinning a yarn like that, I'd pay him a crown for the entertainment and send him on his way. But you're not joking, are you, Noel?"

He shook his head. "'fraid not. And it's im-per-a-tive that I succeed in my quest. There are many lives at stake," he said, doing his best impression of a Knight of Superius.

As Avuru stroked his beardless chin, it occurred to Noel that many midge would find his dilemma perplexing. After all, humans weren't known for their kindness toward midge. Even though Pickelo South, the midge homeland, had joined the Alliance of Nations, the men and women of Continae, Ristidae, and the rest didn't really want anything to do with them.

Avuru probably wondered why a midge would go to so much trouble to help humans.

"Tell me again what the goblins look like?"

Noel poured another glass of elf water—he was awfully thirsty—as he launched into a lengthy and gruesome description of the monsters that were invading Capricon. When Noel used four fingers on one hand to imitate the goblins pointy teeth, the two midge ended up nearly choking on their drinks. They laughed for five full minutes.

When Avuru caught his breath, he said, "Well, just as long as those beasties don't come tromping all the way to Therrat. It'd probably stop business altogether.

Noel smiled, taking back what he had thought earlier about Avuru not caring about humans. Avuru not only got along with humans, but he was the only midge Noel knew of to set up shop in a human city.

Of course, most of the locals didn't know the store was owned and operated by a midge. Neither did they know the true nature of shop. On the surface, Hidden Treasures was a dry goods store, but wizards from all over the continent were known to stop by to purchase special ingredients, potions, and new spells.

Therrat was located on a major trade route between Superius and Huiyah. There were so many merchants coming and going in this Ristiadaen city that various guilds governed prices to ensure that everybody could make a profit. It was a mystery to all but a few how Hidden Treasures stayed in business.

"Someday, I'm gonna walk right up to Oswaald Stelwar and the rest of the guild members and tell them the truth," Avuru was wont to say, especially while drinking elf water.

Noel doubted Avuru would ever do it. The Guildmaster would probably run him out of town.

"So...can you help me get to Superius?" Noel asked, wiping a tear from his eye and doing his best to contain the giggles that threatened to burst free whenever he thought of his own goblin impersonation.

Avuru swirled the transparent liquid in his glass. "I'm thinking, I'm thinking."

As the shopkeeper made a mental sweep through all the spells he owned, Noel glanced around the room. His eyes took in all manner of magical equipment—black, white, and red candles; glass jars of every shape and size; shelf after shelf of rolled-up scrolls.

Noel always cherished his visits to Hidden Treasures. Although Avuru didn't let him play with his inventory, the storekeeper was known to allow Noel an occasional glimpse at the spell books for free. He never left Hidden Treasures without a new incantation in his collection.

He squinted, trying to read what was written on the spines of the books on a nearby shelf. He jumped in surprise when his eyes met those of a man, who quickly looked away. The lad then made a show of measuring out a quantity of dark powder.

Noel had noticed the man on his way to Hidden Treasures' secret, lower level, but he had forgotten all about him during his chat with Avuru.

"Never mind Orin," Avuru said. "He's a good kid. And he's my apprentice. Just between you and me"—the midge lowered his voice to a whisper—"he's got a lot of potential."

Noel nodded absently. Orin didn't look like much of a kid to Noel. He suspected the sandy-haired apprentice was an adult, though perhaps not yet twenty. Then again, it was so hard to judge ages when it came to humans.

"Well," Avuru said, "I don't have a transportation spell that will take you directly to Castle Borrom, but I do have one that will get you as far as Tourney. It's an ancient spell, scripted in the Eight Century of this era by a red-robe who had a penchant for watching the Knight's jousts. Tourney's a two-day ride from the capital. South by southwest, if I'm not mistaken."

Noel, who couldn't even remember what he had had for breakfast that morning—or *if* he had had breakfast—was amazed by the other midge's memory. Avuru had to be the smartest midge in the world.

I'll have to come back and visit Avuru after the war with the goblins is over, Noel thought. Maybe I could even help teach Orin some spells. I always wondered what it would be like to be a teacher…and to teach a human! Why—

"Noel?"

The midge blinked his eyes and snapped out of his reverie. "Uh, yeah?"

"Do you want the spell or not?"

"Of course I do, but, um, I don't really have any money. I

spent it all on the way to Fort Faith. I didn't think I'd be leaving so soon. I was in such a hurry to get there...because the gods sent me, if you'll recall...and—"

Avuru waved his hands dismissively. "When was the last time I charged you for anything, you gnome-minded fool?"

"*Gnome*-minded?" Noel sputtered. "Bah, you wouldn't know a gnome if one came in here and took a hammer to your thick skull."

"He'd trip over his beard before he got past the threshold!" Avuru shouted back.

Both midge burst into uncontrollable laughter.

Tears filling his eyes once more, Noel declined when Avuru attempted to pour more elf water into his glass. By the Three Goddesses, he wished he could spend a night in merriment with his old friend, but he would never forgive himself if anything happened to his friends back in Capricon.

Noel followed Avuru past Orin and into Avuru's private study. The shopkeeper headed over to a wall made up of small cubbyholes. After a few wrong guesses, Avuru extricated the correct scroll and handed it to Noel.

"I'd better help Orin finish with the security wards and what-not so we can close up," he told Noel. "You're welcome to spend the night if you'd like."

Noel was sorely tempted to accept. Just thinking about a soft, warm bed evoked an enormous yawn. But it would take only a few minutes to learn the transportation spell, and if he used an acceleration spell once he got to Tourney, he could sprint the rest of the way to Castle Borrom.

Wouldn't Stannel and the others be surprised at how quickly he accomplished his mission!

"Thanks anyway," he said, patting Avuru on the shoulder. "Some other time."

Avuru smiled. "Next time, *you* can bring the wine."

"I'll bring you some gnomish mushroom beer," Noel laughed.

Avuru stuck out his tongue before leaving the room. Alone at last, the fair-haired midge let out a great sigh and settled onto a stool. His heavy-lidded eyes glanced over the mantra that would magically devour the miles between Therrat, Ristidae, and Tourney, Superius.

When Avuru poked his head into the study a few minutes later, he wasn't too surprised to find the scroll lying on the table. The only sign Noel had ever been there was the distinct shape of a pointy-hat-wearing gnome traced in the dust.

By the time Noel reached Castle Borrom, the half-moon was low in the sky, and the sun was mere hours from rising. A slew of spells had launched him across the Strait of Liliae to Ristidae, then from Therrat to Tourney, and finally from Tourney to his final destination. But the magic had taken its toll.

Noel was finding it increasingly difficult to keep his eyes open.

His heart still pounding from his supernatural sprint to the capital of Superius, Noel took a moment to get his bearings. From the look of things, Castle Borrom was as much a palace as a big city nestled between the castle and the towering walls surrounding it all.

The walls both surprised and dismayed him. He had hoped to simply walk up to the castle's front door and ask for King Edward Borrom. As it was, he still had a long walk through the city ahead of him, and the speedy enchantment he had cast in Tourney had already worn off.

A lesser midge would throw down his staff and give up, Noel decided. But he was on a mission, and he wasn't about to let barred gates and miles of cobblestone stop him.

Since the Knights of Superius always asked too many questions—and never liked his answers anyway—Noel spoke the words to another spell that allowed him to float, feather-like, over an unwatched section of wall. The incantation made him light-headed as well as weightless. His energy fading fast, Noel knew casting one more spell would probably cause him to faint.

Sticking to the shadows, Noel dutifully placed one foot in front of the other, following what he hoped was a direct route to the palace. The streets were all but deserted at that hour. Some early risers were getting a start on business, and an occasional Knight marched past, patrolling the city for bad guys.

Noel did his best to avoid the latter. He didn't have time to argue with know-it-all Knights, and somewhere in the back of his mind, he worried that maybe word had reached the capital of his involvement with Klye's Renegades.

He practically collapsed to the ground in relief when he

reached a stairway leading up to the palace. He gave a friendly smile to the two Knights standing on either side of the path and tried to walk past them. But the men's gasps made him stop in his tracks.

"What in Abaddon?" swore the Knight on the left.

Both men reached for their weapons.

Noel took a hasty step back, nearly tripping over the bottom of his robe. I must have startled them, he thought. As the Knights drew their swords, Noel tucked his staff into a loop on his belt. He then rolled up his sleeves and placed his hands palms out to show he was unarmed.

The gesture caused both men to draw back. The Knight on the left flinched and cursed again.

"Don't let him cast a spell!" the man on the right shouted, diving forward.

Noel made a noise that, under other circumstances, might have been funny. He tried to backpedal, but the butt of his staff jammed into the ground, stopping him with a jerk.

"Wait!" he yelled. "I didn't do anything wrong!"

While he tried to wrestle the staff out of his belt, Noel hopped backward, doing his best to stay out of the Knight's reach. The second man had not moved. He looked like he couldn't decide whether to help his friend or run in the other direction.

At last, Noel freed the staff. He held onto it for all of two seconds because the oncoming Knight then struck the wooden rod with his sword. Noel yelped at the sting and involuntarily dropped the staff.

"I was sent here by Stannel," Noel said over his shoulder as he tried to evade the Knight's grasp. "He's the Commander of Fort Valor...well actually it's Fort Faith, but they're calling it Fort Val—hey!"

The Knight now had a handful of Noel's sleeves. The midge yanked with all of his might, but the man gave a great tug, pulling Noel off the ground and into the Knight's armored chest.

"Quit your squirming," the man barked. To his comrade, he shouted, "Get over here and help me, you coward!"

His face pressed up against the cold metal of a breastplate, Noel couldn't see the other Knight, but he heard his approaching footsteps. Noel struggled all the harder.

"I have to see the king!" Noel cried. "I must warn him! The

goblins are coming! The goblins are—"

The second Knight grabbed hold of his other arm. "Shut him up! If he casts a spell, we're dead!"

A gloved hand clamped tight over Noel's mouth. The hand smelled—and tasted—like leather and made breathing a chore. Noel tried to voice his indignation, but the muffled sounds that escaped through the glove only made the Knights tighten their hold on him.

Tears dripped from the corners of Noel's eyes. Why wouldn't the two idiots just stop and *listen* to him? He didn't want to fight them, but he had to get some air. Growling in frustration, Noel opened his mouth as wide as he could and bit down hard.

If he had had goblin teeth, Noel might have pierced the glove and the flesh beneath. As it was, his desperate attack simply surprised the Knight, who pulled his hand back. Noel's lungs filled with blessed air.

"Little monster," the gloved Knight spat as he gave Noel a sharp slap across the face.

By this time, Noel was beginning to think talking his way out of the situation was an impossibility. His head was spinning from getting struck, and it was only a matter of time before the leathery hand covered his mouth again.

The words to a spell flashed in his mind, and before he knew what he was doing, he was pronouncing each and every syllable.

Noel was dropped to the ground. The Knight who had been holding him cried, "Bloody hell, we're done for!"

Meanwhile, the Knight with the smelly gloves lunged forward, wrapped his arms together under Noel's armpits and wrenched him off the ground.

"Lemme go! I didn't do—oof!"

The Knight was squeezing so hard Noel feared he'd soon hear his ribs cracking one by one. All he could do was gasp for air that wasn't there. His cheek was once more pressed against the cold metal of the first Knight's armor. In spite of the tall torches lining the stairway ahead, everything started getting very dark.

The next thing Noel knew, he was lying on the ground, his chest heaving up and down. It took him a second to understand what had happened, but a cursory glance at the Knights on either side of him provided the answer. Both men were lying flat on their backs, their eyes closed.

Noel's sleep spell had taken effect in the nick of time.

He tried to sit up, but the motion sent another wave of dizziness through his mind. He had pushed himself too hard. Sheer will alone was keeping him from passing out.

Don't do it, Noel. You can't sleep yet. You still have important work to do. He knew, now, he would not get to King Edward so easily, but after some rest, he'd have a lot of different incantations to choose from.

All he had to do is find a place to hide, a safe hiding spot where he could rest...

The midge crawled toward his discarded staff. Behind him, he heard the voices of men and a crescendo of footsteps. His scuffle with the two sentries had alerted more Knights. In a matter of seconds, they would be on him, and neither his magic nor his own two legs could save him.

He was too tired even to cry.

"I'm sorry," he muttered. "I tried...I didn't do anything wrong...Stannel..."

Passage IV

The closer they drew to the goblin camp, the more difficult it was for Colt to combat the second guessing that had become second nature for him ever since he had first learned of his promotion to Commander of Fort Faith last summer.

Throughout the nearly two and a half-day trek, a voice had whispered in his ear, growing louder with each passing hour, that it wasn't too late to turn back. A second voice, that of his father, the heroic Laenghot Crystalus, reminded him that fear was a natural response to an impending battle.

"Great men are defined by great deeds," Lord Crystalus was wont to proclaim, and Colt found himself summoning the maxim again and again to fight back against his mounting doubts.

He tried to keep his mind busy with thoughts of strategy, but though he pushed his men to the brink of exhaustion each day, he could not wear out his brain. With so much time to walk in silence, Colt couldn't help but evaluate his actions—and inactions—as the Commander of Fort Faith.

Saerylton Crystalus had taken on the mantle of leadership with the grace of a toddler tying his shoelaces for the first time. He had made many mistakes, but nothing hurt worse than remembering those who had lost their lives under his command.

Sir Gregory Wessner and Sir Phance Swordsail had been crushed when T'slect's *vuudu* dropped the ceiling on them. Colt hadn't known either man well—just well enough to remember their names when ordering them to remain and guard the false prince. He knew that he would never forget them for as long as he lived—however long that would prove to be.

He thought a lot about Cholk too. How he wished he had pried for more information from the dwarf. How had he come to join the Renegades? What had prompted him to leave his homeland, Thanatan, for Continae? He would never know any more than he already did about the friend who had sacrificed everything for him.

No matter which course his overactive mind chose, the path always wound back to the same sorry fact: he was leading nearly one hundred men and women into a hopeless battle.

When they were but a few miles from the goblin camp, Colt found that he could not look at his companions' faces. There were times during the past couple of days when he had prayed death would be the worse fate any of them found. The goblins were not wont to take prisoners, but rumor had it that the foreign army had a taste for human flesh.

Colt briefly considered sending out scouts to gather information about the enemy encampment but decided against it. His entire strategy depended on the element of surprise, and besides, he had seen the goblin army with his own two eyes. How much could have changed in nine days?

Taking those final steps toward the clearing that housed a thousand or more tents—with no sign yet of enemy sentries or patrols—Colt could scarcely breathe. His heart was beating so powerfully in his chest that it physically pained him.

It occurred to Colt, then, that the only difference between a great deed and an incredibly foolish one was the outcome, which no mere mortal could ever know. Maybe even brave and brilliant Aldrake Superior, the first warrior-king of Superius, had struggled against such a storm of uncertainty…

With Opal on one side and Dylan on the other, Colt tightened his grip on *Chrysaal-rûn* and used its crystalline blade to sweep aside the gnarled branches blocking his view of the camp. He steeled himself, but nothing could have prepared him for what met his eyes.

According to Dylan, the area had once been home to a company of woodsmen who sent their lumber to Rydah's ports. The goblins had supplanted the woodcutters, claiming the secluded area as their own and filling the man-made clearing with their own tents.

But now the only evidence that either encampment had ever existed was the acre of well-trodden earth, blackened fire pits, and the occasional bone. A surreal dizziness overcame Colt, and if the air hadn't been perfectly still, he surely would have fallen over.

Beside him, Dylan muttered, "Gods above, could we have passed them without realizing it?"

A picture of Hylan's villagers falling beneath the horde of savages flashed in Colt's mind. He swallowed the gorge in his throat with a grimace.

"There's no way," Opal said. "A group of that size couldn't have come anywhere near us without our hearing them. And we took a mostly direct path from Hylan to here, so we certainly would have run into them if they had been anywhere along the way."

"So where in the hells did they go?" Dylan demanded.

By that time, whispering and mumbling could be heard behind them, as the civilians and militiamen of Hylan tried to figure out what was going on. The Knights who had chosen Colt over Dale Mullahstyn exchanged puzzled looks while awaiting their orders. As the seconds passed by, the soldiers' voices grew louder.

Then the unmistakable thundering of hooves interrupted them.

The bastards are behind us! Colt thought. He couldn't explain it, but somehow the goblins had orchestrated an ambush, doubling back in a most unlikely—and arguably impossible— manner. It was only when the first of the riders came into view, with Dylan attempting to wrangle the troupe into formation, that Colt remembered the goblins didn't have a cavalry.

The sight of Captain Ruford Berwyn, sitting astride a dappled charger and leading a company of red and white-clad guardsmen, might have won an award for the day's most unlikely vision, were it not for the disappearing goblin army.

"We had hoped to catch you before you met the enemy," Ruford said, his horse wading through a sea of people.

"You need not have worried," Dylan replied. "The goblins are gone."

"Gone!" Ruford repeated. "Gone where?"

Colt glanced back at the empty field that had formerly contained the greatest threat to Capricon. The goblins had left few signs of their occupancy, but apparently not even *vuudu* could hide the path they had taken. There was a noticeable gap in the trees on one side of the clearing, and from his vantage, Colt could see the hole spread farther into the woods.

Following the army wasn't going to be a problem. Answering Ruford's question was as easy as identifying the direction that the goblins had chosen.

"South and west," Colt whispered. "To my fort."

It was all so puzzling.

Stannel had faced the goblins in combat on three occasions. His last confrontation had taken place two weeks ago while on his way to Fort Valor—the original Fort Valor. He had over-come the ambushers, only to find his fortress in ruins.

In his mind's eye, he could still see the smoldering remnants of that once-noble castle, the remains of its loyal defenders. All signs had indicated the struggle had been quick, devastating, and recent.

So why weren't the goblins employing the same winning tactic against new Fort Valor?

The lookouts had first spotted the enemy army earlier that afternoon. The goblins had not bothered to mask their move-ments; they had swarmed out of the eastern woods and brazenly encircled the fortress. Rough estimates numbered the goblins at five thousand. But rather than attempt to overwhelm the fort—or reduce it to rubble with their explosives—they had set up camp.

It was all so very puzzling.

After more than an hour of waiting for the invaders to make a move, Stannel had finally called for a conference, reluctantly pulling his officers from their posts. Since the war room was still in shambles and since Stannel's office would have made for cramped quarters, he called them to the dining hall.

Gaelor Petton was the first to arrive. The lieutenant was clad head to foot in armor and wore his customary frown. Petton's entrance was followed almost immediately by the arrival of Ezekiel Silvercrown and Chadwich Vesparis. The rest of the lower-ranking officers would remain on the ramparts, ready to issue orders if the goblins attacked.

When Klye Tristan and Dominic Horcalus walked in the room, Petton lifted an eyebrow in surprise, but to Stannel's relief, the lieutenant did not utter any of the criticisms that were surely on the tip of his tongue. The two Renegades—*former* Renegades, Stannel corrected—took their place, sitting opposite the three Knights, while Stannel remained standing at the head of the long table.

He didn't have to tell them, Knight or Renegade, the reason for the meeting. Anyone who happened to glance out a window knew Fort Valor's peril.

"To begin with," Stannel said, "can anyone proffer a guess as to why the goblins have not yet volleyed their explosives at our walls?"

None of the Knights said anything, though Zeke and Chadwich exchanged a look.

"Maybe they used up all of their ammunition on the first Fort Valor," Klye offered. "Or maybe they're just prolonging the fun."

"This is hardly a joking matter," Petton grumbled, not deigning to look in the Renegade Leader's direction. "As for the original Fort Valor, we still do not know what razed it. It might have been a new type of siege engine or magic—"

"*Vuudu,*" Klye corrected.

Petton waved a hand dismissively. "We should assume that the goblins have not yet bombarded the fort because they are unable to do so."

"But why delay?" Horcalus asked. "They have nothing to gain, whereas we now have time to prepare."

"It doesn't make sense to hold your winning card if you know you can take all the tricks," Klye added. "Either their machines broke down somewhere along the way, or the shamans are off on holiday."

"We cannot assume anything," Petton insisted. "They might be trying to lull us into a false sense of security."

"Security? Did you see how many of them are out there?" Zeke Silvercrown posed the rhetorical question at Petton, who stared hard back at him.

"Anyway you look at it, we're in trouble," Klye said. "With or without a secret weapon, we're vastly outnumbered. Why *would* they bother dropping the roof down on us when they can starve us out? Don't the besiegers always have the advantage over the besieged?"

Though every Knight in the room knew the answer, Dominic Horcalus was the first to speak. "Not necessarily, Klye. By cutting off our food supply, the goblins could force us out, but depending on our supplies, that could take months.

"Long sieges can be detrimental to both sides. The invaders have little protection from the elements, such as the heavy snowstorms that are bound to roll down from the Rocky Crags."

Petton looked like he wanted to argue, but instead he looked away from Horcalus and said, "Perhaps they are simply waiting for nightfall. Didn't that dwarf say they could see better in the dark?"

There were mutters from the other two Knights, confirming that they too had heard such a thing. That the goblins had eyes like cats was just one of many rumors circulating the fort. There were men who swore the goblins were demons incarnate, and others were convinced garlic would keep the fiends at bay.

"We shall remain at full alert," Stannel stated at last. "Our watchmen have spotted no evidence of siege engines, but we ought to be prepared for collapsing masonry and fires nevertheless.

"It stands to reason that they are waiting because they hope we will ride out against them...though surely they have overestimated our size if they believe we would do that."

Stannel took a deep breath. "One thing I do know for certain is that if we leave the fortress, we will surely die."

The word "die" echoed through the mostly empty hall.

"So we stay cooped up in here and wait for frostbite to win the war for us," Klye said, a half-smile curling his lip. "I can live with that."

"They will attack long before then," Petton predicted. "Mark my words."

Klye moved in before the lieutenant had even finished his sentence. "Then you can certainly see the need for us Renegades to be armed."

"I don't see that at all," Petton replied. "In fact, I would say it is high time you rebels were put somewhere out of the way. The dungeon, for example..."

"But that would be tantamount to murder," Klye argued. He alternated his gaze between Stannel and Petton as he spoke. "If the goblins *do* get inside the fort, we'll need to defend ourselves. If you don't give us our weapons back, then you might as well kill us now yourselves."

Petton's expression did not change, though Stannel thought he detected a bemused glimmer in the lieutenant's eyes.

Klye continued, nonplussed, "No Knights are going to want to babysit us, Commander, and there's no reason they should have to. We've proven ourselves as capable warriors, and it's damn obvious you need every man you can get."

"We have enough to worry about without having to watch for knives in the back," Petton said.

"Enough!" Stannel shouted, cutting off Klye's retort and evoking a start from everyone present. To Petton he said, "Klye is correct in his reasoning, and I, for one, would not give the goblins an easier time in their killing. Mark *my* words, Lieutenant, there will be enough killing before this is finished.

"Klye and his men have promised to do us no harm, and I respect that oath. Trust is a two-way street, after all."

"So Pistol and Crooker will be let out of the dungeon?" Klye pressed.

Horcalus winced at the Renegade Leader's audacity while Gaelor Petton openly glowered at Klye.

Stannel hesitated only a moment before saying, "The pirates also have the right to defend themselves. They will be released and allowed to carry their weapons, provided you will vouch for them, Klye Tristan."

"I've been vouching for them all along," Klye said, but there was no venom in his words.

Stannel glanced over at the Knights, measuring their reactions. Both Ezekiel Silvercrown and Chadwich Vesparis wore neutral expressions. Gaelor Petton, however, had gone pale and veritably trembled.

"This is ridiculous!" he exclaimed. "Protocol—"

"Protocol demands that a subordinate follows the orders of his commanding officer," Stannel interrupted. "Now, if we are finished fighting with one another, I suggest we move on to discussing our tactics."

Petton sat back and folded his arms, the scowl not quite fading from his face.

Throughout the rest of the conference, Stannel did most of the talking. He outlined the key elements of fortress's defenses, pausing only briefly to ask for verifications on his facts. He had not been the Commander of new Fort Valor for long, but he had lived as a Knight of Superius for more years than some in attendance had lived at all.

And while Stannel had never personally been involved in a siege, he knew his military history well—of both Superius and Glenning—and was confident he was making logical choices, given the circumstances.

The only problem, he knew, was that making the right decisions could very well prove inadequate.

Passage V

In contrast to the Celestial Palace in Rydah and the original Fort Valor, this castle was an underwhelming sight.

Drekk't knew there were only eighty or so Knights inside. The defenders had limited munitions, including a few hundred arrows. Their cavalry also was modest in size. Colt had told him as much.

From his tent, the goblin could make out the shapes of men standing along the ramparts, staring out at the massive army that had surrounded them. *His* army.

Despite the Knights' limited resources, Drekk't was faced with no small dilemma when it came to conquering the fort. The humans had the advantage of thick, stone walls, which protected them from the cold and invaders alike.

On an open battlefield, the humans wouldn't last an hour, but inside their fort, the Knights could hold out for weeks, maybe even months. The trick was to get them to come out of their fort, though with each passing minute, that seemed less likely to happen.

Drekk't tried not to think about how much easier it would have been if that damned human hadn't robbed them of their explosives. With winter already taking ahold of Capricon, the goblin army could not afford a lengthy siege.

Truth be told, Drekk't was more concerned with the Emperor's temper than harsh weather.

He was also wary of discord within his army. Some soldiers hadn't seen battle since the attack on the capital weeks ago. Those who had been sent to old Fort Valor had done little more than detonate bombs. There had been few enough human survivors to provide sport, according to reports.

His troops hungered for battle and thirsted for bloodshed.

Scuffles broke out nearly every day, as the soldiers took out their aggression on one another. If he, as their general, didn't find a productive way to channel their aggression, the army would eventually collapse in on itself.

Drekk't continued to gaze out at the silent fortress as he awaited his lieutenants' arrival.

Most enemies of the T'Ruellian Empire mistakenly concluded, after witnessing the goblins' frenzied style of fighting, that the goblins employed no true tactics to speak of. What none of them realized was that, as a people bred for war, the goblins were incredibly organized. The average goblin male saw combat at age fifteen. As a result, every one of T'Ruel's armies was comprised largely of veterans.

The hierarchy for any goblin brigade was intentionally complex. In fact, "officer" was so vague a term that it proved useless in most instances. Everyone in the army took orders from someone, with the smallest company comprised of a mere handful of soldiers. Generally speaking, every goblin—except the youngest—had someone to boss around and, inversely, someone to be bossed around by.

And the goblin military was an incredibly competitive organization. In order to move up the ranks, an individual had to prove himself worthier than whoever currently occupied the post. Promotions tended to occur only after a commanding officer perished, which happened both on and off the battlefield.

It was to prevent assassinations that the Emperor had perfected the system. By placing no fewer than two soldiers at every level of leadership beneath the topmost officer, any goblin hoping to advance through murderous deeds would have to kill not only the officer above him, but also someone at the same level.

Even the slyest, most opportunistic goblin would have a hard time accomplishing that with any discretion. And since the punishment for killing—or attempting to kill—a fellow soldier was death, assassinations were far from common. They were not, however, unheard of.

Drekk't tore his gaze from the fort and glanced at his army, which encircled the castle in a big, dark ring. The war camp was being constructed with methodical precision. Each soldier knew his place in the greater scheme. Drekk't knew that his lieutenants would seek him out only after they were certain their officers knew their orders.

He smirked. Drekk't had little fear that either of his lieutenants would make an attempt on his life. He had served with both of them for many years and was reasonably sure they were content to wait until he died naturally, in battle, to take his place as general. If one of them did end his life prematurely, the murderer would have to face the other in combat to prove himself the better leader.

Since Jer'malz and Ay'goar were equally matched as warriors, Drekk't was safe...at least until one of them became handicapped in some fashion.

By the time the lieutenants arrived at Drekk't's pavilion, the sun was hovering just over the jagged peaks of the neighboring mountains. As was customary, Jer'malz and Ay'goar stood at attention, silently waiting for their general to speak.

While some goblins in superior positions took pleasure in making their underlings suffer—the Emperor, Prince T'slect, and Ay'sek all came to mind—Drekk't treated his soldiers with respect. It wasn't because he feared what they might do to him, but rather what they *wouldn't* do, such as watch his back in the midst of a melee.

And unlike many commanding officers, Drekk't even allowed those directly beneath him to speak their minds.

"It's the midge I'm worried about," Ay'goar said once Drekk't had finished telling them his plans. "Without *n'feranost* Ay'sek here, we have no one to counter his magic."

Drekk't said nothing, silently agreeing with the lieutenant. Between Colt's confessions and what T'slect had told him, Drekk't knew a lot about the fort's residents. T'slect had been obsessed with the Renegades who had come to reside at the fortress, but Drekk't cared nothing about a handful of humans who may or may not have learned about the goblins invasion early on.

The midge, on the other hand, posed a serious problem.

While the diminutive vagrants were notoriously capricious, the midge also happened to be the most powerful wizards in all of Altaerra. That one had allied himself with the Knights of Superius was bizarre to say the least.

"Let's put a bounty on his empty little head," Jer'malz suggested. "The runt can't cast a spell if there are a hundred goblins piled on top of him, trying to grab hold of any part big enough to prove they had a hand in the kill."

Drekk't considered the proposal and found it sensible. The promise of loot was a tried and true goblin method for overcoming reluctance to take on an enemy. In fact, Drekk't was a little surprised he hadn't thought of it first.

Perhaps Jer'malz did warrant watching…

"So be it," Drekk't acquiesced. "Do either of you have suggestions on how to get the Knights to come out of their castle?"

The two lieutenants exchanged blank glances.

Practically all of their technology had been stolen from conquered nations. They knew how to construct catapults and trebuchets, ballistae and battering rams, but the T'Ruellians typically relied on speed and maneuverability. Siege engines slowed an army down, whereas barrels of dwarven blasting powder were far easier to transport. And what the goblins lacked in technology, they made up for in *vuudu*, which was inherently destructive.

Drekk't had neither explosives nor a shaman at his disposal.

"We'll have to flush them out," Drekk't said with a shrug. "We'll throw a quarter of our number at them at sunset to see how they react."

Ay'goar snorted. "If nothing else, it will give the soldiers something to do."

"Those remaining in camp should stay on guard in case the humans ride out," Drekk't added. "Which of you would like to lead the attack?"

The question took both lieutenants by surprise. Drekk't smiled inwardly. Let skeptics call him unorthodox, Drekk't preferred innovation to conformity. Perhaps that was why he had lived forty-seven years, when the average goblin died before thirty.

"Jer'malz, you will head the strike," Drekk't said, answering his own question. "Be sure to take plenty of archers with you in case the midge shows himself."

"Yes, *n'patrek*," Jer'malz said.

Ay'goar said nothing, though he looked disappointed. Drekk't couldn't blame him. He too yearned for combat. Unless the humans were stupid enough to give up their only advantage and come out—which they might do, in the name of honor or some such nonsense—it would be some time before the general's blade tasted red blood.

"You are dismissed," Drekk't said suddenly, and both goblins turned to leave without another word.

He followed them to the egress. Once outside, his gaze came to rest on the tall, dark mass jutting up from the flat land around it. The fort was as quiet and still as a mountain.

The general chuckled to himself. Although few knew it, the goblin race had at one time lived deep within the earth, delving out subterranean kingdoms in the hollows of ancient mountains. Scurrying over rocks, climbing sheer cliff sides—these things came naturally to any goblin.

Soon the defenders of Fort Valor would learn why goblins don't bother bringing ladders into battle.

The Knights called it the Renegade Room because that was where Klye and the others spent most of their time. Klye had no idea what the chamber had been used for prior to their arrival, but the space suited them.

And now that the pirates were there too, Klye no longer felt guilty about the accommodations.

That Pistol and Crooker had been released from the dungeon was no small victory. He had done his best, as Renegade Leader, to improve the pirates' welfare ever since Colt—and Petton—had put them in a cell.

Finally, Stannel had reversed Colt's dictum. With Horcalus, Scout, Arthur, Plake, Pistol, Crooker, and him all together again, Klye might have taken the opportunity to feel pretty good about himself—were it not for the thousands of goblins outside.

Klye had expected the pirates to be relieved and grateful for their freedom, but even Crooker, the more jovial of the two, wore a somber expression on his bearded face. Klye supposed the two of them were still in shock from their unexpected discharge.

Or perhaps they understood the portent of the rapier hanging at Klye's hip.

Thanks to Scout's frequent trips to the dungeon, Pistol and Crooker knew how Lilac and Othello had accompanied Colt and the others to Rydah. However, no one had had the chance to tell them about the army camped outside the fort.

Klye handed the pirates their curved swords and explained the reason—the *only* reason—why the Renegades were being allowed to carry weapons. Frowning, Pistol walked over to the room's only window. Crooker followed.

"Maybe we ought to think about switchin' sides," Pistol quipped, scratching the scar that disappeared beneath his eyepatch.

"I don't think that's an option," Klye replied dryly.

The former pirate king shrugged. "Ah well. It beats dying of old age in a cell. When does the fun begin?"

As though in answer to Pistol's question, a great racket erupted from somewhere outside the fort. His hackles rising, Klye stepped up to the window and felt something drop into the pit of his stomach. A multitude of dark shapes danced against the backdrop of dying sunlight.

The goblins were advancing.

Klye spun around, and his expression must have communicated the truth of the situation. Arthur's face drained of color. Plake swore. Horcalus stared at Klye, expectantly.

He knew no one expected much from the Renegades. They could, perhaps, wait out the attack in Renegade Room and let the Knights repel what would prove to be—according to Horcalus's predictions—the first of many assaults. Who would fault them for sitting this one out?

But Klye's newly discovered conscience would eat him alive if he let the Knights perish in his place. How many speeches had he made—first to Colt and then to Stannel—about how the Knights and Renegades were on the same side? He hadn't pressed Stannel about getting back their weapons so they could sit on their asses...

They were awaiting his instruction. It had been nearly a month since the last time he had issued any orders—aside from "Shut up, Plake"—and while he hadn't felt like much of a leader lately, obviously everyone else did. Well, Klye thought, we survived Port Town, the Knights from Fort Miloásterôn, and T'slect. Let's see how far we can push our luck.

"Horcalus, where will we do the most good?" Klye asked.

The former Knight of Superius thought a moment before saying, "The goblins will likely focus on two points of penetration ...the front gate and the roof. The entry hall will likely be packed with Knights awaiting a breach. Meanwhile, the force on the battlements will be comprised mostly of archers, I would guess, though there will be men ready for hand-to-hand combat up there too."

Klye didn't like the thought of shouldering his way through a pack of Knights, some of whom would just as soon take a swipe at him as at a goblin. He had never been to the battlements, but he imagined they had to be roomier than the front hall.

"The roof it is," he declared.

"I know the fastest way up there," Scout insisted, already moving toward the door.

The keen of goblin voices, shouting and shrieking, filled the room, causing everyone to pause. Klye slammed the shutters closed and started for the door. Over his shoulder, he said, "Arthur, Plake, you wait here. We'll rendezvous back here when it's over...or in the event of a breach—"

"No."

Klye spun around, ready to confront the pugnacious Plake Nelway, but found Arthur instead.

"I'm coming too," Arthur added, his voice quieter but no less firm.

Hands folded before him, a borrowed sword at his hip, Arthur looked not a bit like the frightened runaway who had gotten swept up with rebels and pirates in Port Town. He seemed older to Klye, and he wondered how much Horcalus's mentorship had to do with the change.

Klye had wanted to keep Arthur and Plake out of harm's way, since neither of them had much experience in battle. But if Arthur felt ready to display some of the tricks Horcalus had taught him, so be it. It probably made more sense for them to stay together anyway.

"Lead the way, Scout."

The twilight charge had not taken the Knights by surprise. Neither was the enemy's decision to scale the fort's outer wall unforeseen. However, Stannel had not expected the goblins to be so adept at climbing.

The mob of long-limbed creatures resembled nothing so much as an infestation of overgrown spiders ascending a great web in search of helpless prey.

The first volley of arrows had sent scores of the creatures tumbling back down to the earth. Freefalling bodies collided with those beneath them, causing a living avalanche in some places. But the gaps were quickly filled by eager comrades so that in a matter of seconds, the wall was once more covered with dark, writhing shapes.

After that initial shower of arrows, Stannel ordered the archers to fire at will.

The Commander of Fort Valor waited until the first of the goblins was almost to the top before signaling the Knights with the oversized cauldrons. Using fallen beams as levers—and, in one desperate case, a man's own back—to tip the great vessels, the Knights dumped a deluge of boiling water down upon the goblins.

The enemies' screams were deafening, but the cacophony ended as soon as the bodies struck the ground. The Knights wasted no time in hauling the vats back and out of the way. There wouldn't be time to refill them during this scrimmage, but they would likely need them again in the near future.

Even as the archers fired their bolts down at the grapplers, other Knights were heaving stones that ranged from fist-sized rocks to massive boulders—debris that had been scavenged from the remains of the western wing. The Knights tirelessly tossed the rubble down upon the besiegers, too preoccupied with their work to cheer when they hit the mark or to curse when they missed.

It was then that Stannel first found himself missing Noel. A single fireball from the midge's staff would have dispatched a dozen of the fiends. He pushed the thought away, reminding himself that getting word to King Edward was of greater importance than the defense of one small fortress.

Despite the Knights' valiant efforts, it wasn't long before the first of the attackers reached the crenellated ledge. The rocky missiles were forgotten, as the men began using swords, spears, and shields to shove the goblins from their perches. Stannel winced when he saw one frantic goblin clamp onto a Knight's arm, pulling the unbalanced man to his doom.

Stannel, who had been calling out orders all this time, quickly found himself in the thick of things, swinging his claymore in wide arcs, denting armor and cutting flesh.

He had fractured his shoulder while fighting the rock creature atop Wizard's Mountain, and despite Sister Aric's faithful ministrations, his arm was still stiff. But Stannel ignored the discomfort as he hacked at the murderous throng around him. At one point, he caught sight of Dominic Horcalus and Arthur Bismarc swinging their swords side-by-side. Another glimpse into the fray revealed the pirates, who were fighting with an intensity that rivaled the goblins'.

In the process of executing yet another fatal swing, Stannel noted that the human defenders along one side of the rampart had been forced back by the swelling number of goblins there. Wielding his claymore with both hands, Stannel cut a swath to that area.

He thought he heard someone—Chadwich Vesparis? Klye Tristan?—shout his name, but he ignored the warning. An instant later, he was surrounded by goblins.

A hook-headed spear homed in on his flank. Stannel released his hold on the claymore with his left hand and swung with his right to repel the weapon. At the same time, two more goblins, both carrying curved swords, came at him from the other side. He could only guess how many more blades were aimed at his back.

With his free hand, Stannel yanked his mace from its place at his belt. He felt a tingle pass through his fingers as they clasped the smooth leather grip.

His connection with Pintor, the Great Protector, was instantaneous. The sea of monsters around him seemed to slow dramatically. He even closed his eyes for a second, reveling in the golden warmth that surged throughout his body. He dropped his claymore to the ground.

Taking the blessed mace in both hands, Stannel Bismarc moved his lips in a litany of prayer that his mind could not comprehend but that his heart understood.

Then he was turning so fast that the goblins around him looked like nothing more than a black blur. The living darkness was immediately swallowed up by a blazing bronze light that always reminded Stannel of a sunrise. The heat building inside his body suddenly began to flow toward his arms, through his hands, and into the mace.

When next he was able to see again, Stannel was alone. Those goblins that hadn't fallen over the edge now littered the ground in a ring five feet away. Most of them were dead or dying, judging by their feeble attempts to rise.

The goblins that lay nearest him were barely recognizable as goblins. Their faces—and all other exposed flesh—had fused fast to the bone beneath.

The other goblins paused for no more than a moment before scrambling over their fallen comrades and charging at him. Feeling more than a little fatigued, Stannel backpedaled, careful not to trip over the bodies scattered behind him. It would be some time before he could discharge the mace's power again, but he wasn't worried.

Keeping both hands on the hilt of his god-blessed mace, Stannel waited for the ranks of goblins to reach him.

Amidst the feverish slashing and bashing that followed, he became aware of allies amassing on both sides of him. Most of them were Knights, but here and there he caught sight of a Renegade.

Nearby, more goblins were already pulling themselves up over the wall.

Passage VI

Drekk't watched from a distance as the battle unfolded. The moon, half darkened and half gleaming, illuminated the goblins who were using all manner of axe and hatchet to break down the doors separating them from the fort's delicate innards. There was also a flurry of activity up along the ramparts, near the fort's single tower.

At first, Drekk't had employed the use of a spyglass, a tool he had recently acquired from a human sea captain who had had the misfortune of steering his caravel in the path of Drekk't's warships. But staring through the device had given him a headache, so now he took only sporadic glances through it. In the meantime, he paced from one end of the pavilion to the other and back again.

If Jer'malz's warriors could penetrate the Knights' defenses, the fort would quickly become a slaughterhouse. Yet, as the night drew on, Drekk't knew that would not likely happen. Jer'malz would not sacrifice too many of his warriors. This was, after all, only a preliminary strike to test of the humans' wits and weaknesses.

Even as the Knights threw everything they had into protecting their fortress, Drekk't was using only a fraction of his soldiers. He could send another force the following night and yet another the next. By rotating his forces, he would wear down the humans.

He might even send more troops before sunrise…

Of course, it would have been so much simpler if the Knights simply came out in the open. Drekk't knew his army would inevitably win, but he could ill afford to waste time. He remembered all too well the Emperor's threat of withholding reinforcements until the invasion of Capricon made headway.

Jer'malz's order to fall back came well before midnight. Drekk't watched the warriors scurry back to the camp, their retreat punctuated by a shower of arrows that caused a few goblins to fall.

The survivors would be weary, but not too tired to fight over the meager possessions of the dead. A handful of soldiers would surely perish throughout the night while picking through the bodies within range of the Knights' bowmen.

Jer'malz and Ay'goar returned to Drekk't's tent soon after the retreat. Drekk't listened as the battle-weary Jer'malz outlined the events of battle. When Drekk't asked about the midge, Jer'malz said his archers had seen no sign of the wizard, except for a couple of bright flashes from the battlements. Since none of the troops who had made it to the top of the fort had returned alive, the midge's participation in the battle could not be confirmed.

Drekk't shrugged inwardly. He had seen those golden flares from his tent and had deduced that the midge had caused them. Who else could it have been? Colt had mentioned a second wizard arriving at the fort not long before he left, but the man had had an arrow in his gut. Drekk't figured he was probably dead by now.

Because the Knights had not ventured from their fortress, it was impossible to know how many of them had fallen. Jer'malz estimated the goblins' losses at somewhere near three hundred.

Drekk't's nodded. Losing a few hundred warriors in a battle was not a problem in of itself. Arrows had to go somewhere, and the warriors that were pelted with those bolts paved the road for others who would reach foes bearing empty quivers.

Still, Drekk't had a finite number of soldiers until the Emperor deemed it otherwise.

His aching head full of strategies and numbers, Drekk't sent the lieutenants away. The results of the first attack on Fort Valor had gone predictably, if not perfectly. The midge was likely still alive, and not one goblin had been able to breach the fortress. There were three hundred less warriors in his army, and it seemed as though the Knights had made up their minds to hide inside their fort for as long as possible.

Eager to get some sleep—and to get rid of his headache—the general brushed aside the flimsy curtain that divided his pavilion in two and found himself face-to-face with a human.

Drekk't let out a cry of surprise and alarm and reached for his sword. It was only when he noted the translucent quality of the man.

Angry with himself for letting the shaman get the best of him, Drekk't retaliated with as great an insult as he dared.

"Master Ay'sek, your portrayal of a human is most convincing."

Chuckling depreciatively, Drekk't sheathed his blade. The insubstantial human face tightened into a sour expression, and for a moment, Drekk't feared that he had pushed the shaman too far. Even miles of distance could prove an ineffectual defense against a Chosen of the Chosen.

"Where *are* you, Drekk't?"

It took great effort to keep the smile off of his face, but somehow Drekk't managed. He could have told Ay'sek of his army's march—and how Colt's men were wasting their time in seeking them out in the north—but what fun would that have been?

By Upsinous's black heart, what Drekk't would have paid to see the look on the shaman's face upon arriving at desolate spot that had once accommodated the goblin army!

Taking a deep breath to compose himself, Drekk't said, "The army has moved on to the castle formerly known as Fort Faith."

Ay'sek might have demanded to know why Drekk't hadn't told him about the army's relocation, but dwelling on the subject would only reiterate the fact that the general had pulled one over on him. At least, that was what Drekk't was forced to conclude because Ay'sek said no more about it.

"Then it would appear that Colt has assumed correctly," Ay'sek said.

"What do you mean?" Drekk't asked. When Ay'sek's eyebrows came together, he quickly added, "*N'feranost.*"

"The commander and his men are following your path. At our current pace, we will reach new Fort Valor in a matter of days," Ay'sek said. "If I reclaim *Peerma'rek* tonight, I could reduce this ragtag militia by a third. That might send the rest running back to Hylan."

The human with Ay'sek's voice stopped mid-sentence. "Are you listening to me, General?"

In truth, Drekk't had all but tuned him out. His mind was

already formulating a plan. Struggling to recall what Ay'sek had just said, Drekk't shook his head and said, "You will not reveal yourself...not yet, Master Ay'sek."

The shaman did not bother to mask his anger. "Why not?"

"Because I *want* Colt and his army to come here *without* delay. When the defenders of Fort Valor see us slaughtering their kinsmen, they might leave the safety of their fortress to assist them."

"You risk much. If we miss our chance to reclaim *Peerma'rek*..."

Ay'sek did not need to finish the statement. Recovering the staff had been a direct order from the Emperor. Hence, it was a top priority. And yet Drekk't believed there was a way to accomplish both of his objectives—or, rather, all three.

Not only would he take back *Peerma'rek* and destroy the human armies, but also he would kill Saerylton Crystalus himself.

"Remain with the humans and learn what you can," he told the shaman. "And do whatever you must to convince the commander to attack us."

Ay'sek scoffed, and the sardonic expression on his face strongly resembled the shaman's true countenance. "You needn't worry about that, General."

"When the battle begins, it will be up to you to retrieve *Peerma'rek*." Drekk't walked directly through Ay'sek's illusion and farther into the sleeping section of his tent. "Now, you had best be getting back to your friends. You wouldn't want anyone to grow suspicious, not when we are so close to realizing our goals."

Without a word, Ay'sek vanished.

Despite the throbbing in his skull, Drekk't felt like celebrating. He immediately decided against imbibing anything stronger than water, however. It was all coming together nicely, but there was still plenty of work to be done. He needed rest.

The general crawled into what passed for a bed and fantasized about his reunion with Colt.

Every seat in Fort Valor's dining hall was full, and still the people—almost all of them Knights—continued to filter in. Arthur had to crane his neck to see Commander Stannel

Bismarc, who stood at the far end of the room.

Stannel watched the swarm of activity impassively.

Waves of speculative whispers washed through the crowd. Most of the Knights were blood-splattered, and the stench of sweat was heavy. Arthur heard words like "miracle" and "wizard" repeated over and over.

Beside him, Scout was saying—for the twentieth time—how he had seen Stannel do something similar on Wizard's Mountain. Arthur had dismissed Scout's earlier recounts of that episode as exaggerations, but he now he could not deny what the man had been saying for days.

Arthur had seen the metallic light less than an hour ago, had seen the goblins thrown back like lifeless ragdolls.

He glanced at Horcalus, wondering what the man made of it. Horcalus had said nothing of the spectacle, and it didn't look like he would. When the Renegades—along with everybody else—had been summoned to the dining hall, they had wordlessly followed Klye's lead.

"There are times when I think I was not cut out to be a Knight at all." Stannel had said those words to him two nights ago. Arthur had wondered what the commander meant by them. Now he was afraid to find out.

A woman clad in a white robe and a sky blue cord at the waist entered the room. Behind Sister Aric trailed a man who looked less like a Knight than even Arthur did. A former highwayman, Ruben Zeetan had a lanky frame and wore a gray cloak that had once served as a disguise. Like the Renegades who now called the fortress home, Ruben was allowed to move freely about the castle, though the man spent most of his time in the infirmary with Sister Aric.

Arthur watched Aric say something that caused Ruben to hang back. The healer then wormed her way through the host of Knights to stand beside Stannel.

Whatever the commander's secrets were, Arthur assumed Sister Aric already knew them. The two were old friends by all accounts. According to Scout—who somehow knew something about everything—Stannel and Aric were the only survivors of old Fort Valor.

A minute later, the healer rejoined Ruben, leaving Stannel to stand alone before the crowd once more. When the commander spoke, all mutters and whispers ceased.

"I had planned to give this speech once things settled down, not wanting to introduce further instability in a time of war."

Though Stannel spoke in the same tone he always used, his voice carried to every part of the room.

"I know now that there is never a good time for deceiving one's friends and allies," he said. "You have known me for only a matter of weeks, but today I must reveal to you what the Knights of old Fort Valor had had a dozen years to get accustomed to.

"With the goblins regrouping and likely preparing for a second attack, I shall endeavor to make my explanation brief.

"I became a Knight of Superius for one reason. I wanted to fight in the Wilderness Campaign, that honorable cause which claimed my father's life. But I became a squire late in life, and before I joined the Knights of Superius, I had to resign from a different order altogether."

Arthur glanced at Horcalus and then at Klye Tristan. Both men were frowning. Arthur thought he heard someone say "wizard" again, but he might have imagined it. His heart thudded in his chest with the force of a stampeding steed.

"When my mother made the perilous trek from war-torn Ristidae to Superius, with me growing in her belly, she made a covenant with Pintor, the Great Protector. She promised me to his service if the god saw us safely to Superius, which he did. At the age of ten, I became an initiate in the Church of Pintor.

"For nearly a decade, I trained as a monk. Meanwhile the war in Ristidae raged on, and I was torn between my love for the Church and my desire to participate in the Wilderness Crusade as a Knight of Superius. In the end, I left the monastery for the Knighthood."

A smattering of murmurs broke out in the crowd. Arthur searched the faces of his comrades for an explanation—he didn't even know what a monk was—but none of the Renegades would look away from Stannel. Even loud-mouthed Plake appeared spellbound by the commander's tale.

"I have always done my best to blend both aspects of my training, incorporating what I had learned from the Church with the precepts of the Knighthood. This is one of the few things I retained from my days as a monk."

Stannel drew his mace. The weapon was the length and girth of a man's forearm. Blunt studs covered its round bronze head.

"It's enchanted!" someone from the crowd shouted.

Stannel smiled wanly. "Enchanted. Blessed. Cursed. I suppose it is a matter of perspective. Though the monks preach pacifism, self-defense is a cherished skill. Long ago, before the Knights of Superius existed, it was the priests of Pintor's duty to protect the populace.

"Do you know magic?" one Knight demanded.

After a moment, Stannel replied, "As I understand it, magic refers to the powers granted by the three Goddesses of Magic. All other gods and goddesses may lend their power to us mortals, though the result is called by different names.

"Some might not see any difference between a wizard and a cleric, but they are not the same. For example, a wizard must learn spells from a book. I do not. The energy I can channel through this mace comes directly from the Great Protector. I summon his energy through prayer and meditation."

Stannel returned the mace to its place at his belt. "It took a while for my subordinates at Fort Valor to get used to the idea that I could wield the power of a god—even though that god was the Knighthood's own patron deity.

"There is no law against a priest of Pintor joining the Knighthood, and I will continue leading you until Commander Crystalus returns or, if the gods see fit, I leave this world for the next. I ask only that you think a while about what I have told you."

Arthur held his breath, waiting for the Knights to denounce Stannel and haul him off to the dungeon. But no one said a word. The Knights—and Renegades—exchanged looks, but almost no one spoke. When it was clear that no insurrection was coming, Stannel began issuing orders.

They had staved off the goblins once tonight, but it was hardly a victory worth celebrating. Arthur knew. He had seen soldiers fall and not rise again. He had received a score of scratches and bruises, but nothing that warranted a visit to Sister Aric. Likely, the healer would have her hands full this night.

As the Renegades filed out of the dining hall, Arthur found himself wondering how things would turn out in the end—for the fort as well as for Stannel.

*   *   *

143

Petton had not been privy to either of Stannel's so-called miracles—either the one atop Wizard's Mountain or that which had occurred on the battlements that very night. He had led the Knights tasked with repelling the goblins at the front gates.

He had learned of Stannel's peculiar actions soon after the goblins' retreat, and though he had not himself seen what everyone else was excitedly discussing, Petton was just as eager as anyone to learn the explanation behind Stannel's fantastic feats.

Inside the dining hall, Lieutenant Gaelor Petton listened as Stannel Bismarc told them how he had entered the priesthood of Pintor at a young age, only to join the Knighthood years later. Petton knew that the monks were taught an ancient form of fighting, but he had had no idea that initiates were also instructed in the ways of magic.

Stannel was careful to stress the difference between wizardly magic and priestly magic, but to Petton magic was magic. And spell-casting was dishonorable at best and nefarious at worst.

According to the histories, three kingdoms had once occupied Western Arabond. Canth, Nebronem, and Vast Yehlorm had controlled what was present day Continae, Ristidae, and parts of Thanatan. The three kingdoms had ushered in an era of peace with the signing of a treaty, and all the human lands prospered for generations.

From what Petton could remember of his lessons as a squire, magic also had flourished during this age of peace. It was said that the Three Wise Kings could cast spells. After a territorial clash with the neighboring elves cost Canth much of its land, the three kingdoms turned on one another, ravaging the lands with powerful magic.

What followed was the Wars of Sundering, which ushered Western Arabond into an age of darkness and savagery. Many blamed magic for the revolutions, civil wars, and massacres that stretched from one end of the continent to the other. Petton didn't think magic was solely responsible, but he believed it was a significant factor in the high death count.

A sword could kill but one man at a time; a spell, however, could raze an entire village.

Even though Stannel's powers came from the Warriorlord, Petton thought there was no honor in such magic. And no matter how one looked at it, Stannel had kept a very big secret from them all.

Once finished with his confession, Stannel began giving orders. At last, he dismissed them all. Petton tried to gauge the men's reactions as their comrades filtered out of the room, but most of the Knights remained silent until they were well away from the dining hall.

Petton hardly gave the Renegades a second glance as they passed. It didn't matter what the rebels thought about Stannel. The man could have declared himself Darclon incarnate, and the rebels wouldn't have opposed him—not so long as they retained their pampered status.

He wondered if Stannel's overdeveloped sense of mercy was a result of his time at the monastery.

Not trusting himself to speak with Stannel, Petton exited the room before it was completely empty. He found himself walking behind Ezekiel Silvercrown and hurried to catch up to him.

"Well, that was informative," he said.

Sir Silvercrown smiled uneasily and said, "It certainly caught me by surprise."

"I'll second that," Petton replied, though that wasn't entirely true. He had been suspicious of Stannel for some time now, though he hadn't been able to put his finger on why. "I cannot help but wonder if Commander Crystalus would have handed over his authority to Stannel Bismarc had he known of this little secret."

"Who can say?" After another few seconds, Zeke Silvercrown added, "Of course, Colt wasn't one to condemn others quickly. Take the Renegades for instance…and Noel…"

Petton grunted, not wanting to take the conversation down that avenue. "I have trouble trusting a man who feels the need to keep secrets. He may be our commanding officer, but I, for one, plan to keep an eye on him."

Sir Silvercrown did not reply.

"I can only hope, Subcommander, that I will be able to count on your support if the need to… replace our commander arises, though, gods willing, it will not come to that."

"Gods willing, Commander Crystalus will return soon," Sir Silvercrown said.

The two Knights walked in silence then, and Petton hardly noticed when Zeke Silvercrown veered down a different corridor. Petton's feet took him to the entry hall, where a host of Knights were already making what repairs they could to the front gate. The steel-reinforced doors had taken a beating but had held. He wondered whether they would hold again.

For the nonce, he was almost glad Saerylton Crystalus was away. If the fort were to fall tonight, at least the young commander wouldn't die with the rest of them.

Passage VII

The four-day trek from the deserted goblin camp to new Fort Valor was both arduous and monotonous. Colt pushed his troops, hoping to overtake the enemy somewhere en route, though all signs indicated the goblins were days ahead of them.

The realization that Drekk't was probably waging an offensive against his fort already spurned him on like nothing else could. He was no longer plagued by doubt, but by impatience. Old Fort Valor had been defeated while Stannel was away. He could only pray that the same thing wouldn't happen to him.

Serving among the company's scouts, he followed the Fort Valor-Fort Faith highway until the forest faded. When they reached the open plain, a strange mixture of relief and anxiousness burbled up inside Colt as he took in the massive army that ringed the fortress like a charred wreath.

His fort was still standing—but for how long?

Every impulse screamed for Colt to order a charge. But the goblins would be watching the road. He and his men would be seen long before they got anywhere near the goblin army.

Colt's long sigh swirled visibly before his eyes. The temperature had dropped as they traveled inland. Right then, however, he didn't feel winter's frigid bite. His blood still boiling, he returned to the bulk of his forces.

Though everyone was tired from walking since the dawn, Colt had his army up and moving with a single command. Nearly two hours later, his troupe was positioned southwest of the fort, waiting at a different edge of the woods. By all appearances, the goblins had not seen them.

"They will spot us sooner or later," he said aloud, not taking his eyes off of the black line of tents that stood like a jagged wall between him and the castle beyond. "We should act now."

"The men need rest," insisted Ruford Berwyn, crouched beside him. The captain kept his normally booming voice to a level just above a whisper. "Besides, if we could sneak someone through the ranks and get word to Fort Valor—"

"No." Colt turned to face and Dylan, who was never far from Colt's side these days. "There's no time. If we move now, we can trap the goblins in a pincer attack between us and the fort's troops."

Colt looked to Dylan for support. The Knight rubbed his chin, looking long and hard at the enemy camp. "The element of surprise is still our greatest asset."

Ruford frowned but didn't say anything.

"We'll wait an hour," Colt decided. "If we attack any earlier, the setting sun will hinder us. You and your men will ride out first, Ruford. Hopefully, this will buy those of us on foot a little time. Dylan, make sure the Knights are prepared. They'll form the first line, followed by the Hylaners."

It wasn't an ingenious strategy by any means. Send the cavalry out first, followed by infantry with battle-hardened warriors at the fore to set an example for the skittish novices. This was a battle plan that the Knights of Superius had utilized since the Order's inception, and other armies had employed the same tactics long before Aldrake Superior established the kingdom that bore his name.

If it was good enough for the first King of Superius, it was good enough for Colt—though the charge of Colt's ragtag unit would hardly compare to the legendary exploits of Aldrake's Twelve.

"If we can break through their lines, we'll keep going until we reach the fort," Colt added.

The chances of that happening were slim, but not impossible. They would need help from the Knights at the fort. If Stannel and Petton did not attack from the other side, Colt and his men were doomed.

Dylan saluted sharply and walked away, moving deeper into the forest where the rest of the men waited. Ruford's heavy-browed stare lingered on Colt for a moment longer, and then he too retreated back into the woods. It was only after the men were gone that Colt noticed Opal standing off to his left.

They had spoken very little to each other since leaving

Hylan. With each step taking them closer to Fort Valor—where Opal had wanted to go from the start—he had expected to hear the words "I told you so" from her lips.

But there hadn't been time for good-natured ribbing on the road. Opal had looked too preoccupied and weary to say much of anything. She still did. Colt longed to delve into her mind, and discover what had quenched her spirit—whether it was merely exertion or something more...something he had said or done...

Rather than tread that dead-end road, he approached her and said, "I want you to take this."

She regarded the *vuudu* staff with wide eyes when he held out to her. "Why?"

"I don't want the goblins to get it back," he explained. "I'll be in the midst of the battle. If I fall..."

In the next instant, Colt was face-to-face with the Opal he had come to love. Her cheeks flushed and her eyes narrowed. "And just where do you think *I* am going to be?"

While he was relieved to see the old Opal again, in this instance he hoped she wouldn't prove too stubborn. He cleared his throat. "I would like you to stay here."

"You don't know me very well if you think I'm going to sit this one out. I shouldn't get special treatment just because I'm your friend."

"It's not that. The truth is, you're the only one I can trust with keeping the staff." He paused. "If not for my sake, then please...do it for Cholk."

Opal sucked in her lower lip and stared at the hideous staff. "That was a cheap shot, Colt." Begrudgingly tugging the relic from his grasp, she added, "I'll do it, but you have to promise to take it back after the battle. I don't want to touch this thing for any longer than I have to. It gives me the shivers."

Colt knew what she meant. He had developed an ambivalent relationship with the staff. He loathed its magic, which had forced him to tell Drekk't everything he knew about Capricon. But at the same time, it was a symbol of Cholk's sacrifice and, therefore, precious to him.

Either way, the disembodied skull on the tip was a grim reminder that death was always nearby.

"I want to leave a few men behind with you...not for you," he quickly amended, "but to protect the staff."

"We'll do it."

Colt and Opal turned to locate the speaker. Tryst leaned casually against a crooked elm tree. He had apparently been eavesdropping all along. A sheepish Lucky joined him.

"Sorry for intruding," Lucky said. "We couldn't help but overhear what you were saying, and—"

"We'd like to do our part and help guard the staff," Tryst finished.

Colt didn't quite know what to make of the thieves. He figured that the two of them were looking for any excuse to stay out of harm's way. While neither of them struck him as ideal candidates for the job, he had no better suggestions. Certainly, he would need every available Knight and militiaman for the battle ahead.

Lucky and Tryst were as good a pair as any.

After Colt told the men they could stay behind, Opal said, "I'd like to ask Othello to stay too. He's...he's in worse shape than he lets on."

Colt's face burned in spite of the chilly evening. He wanted to forbid it for no other reason than to keep the two archers apart. But Opal had a point about the forester's injuries. Anyway, Colt had come to realize he was incapable of denying the woman's wishes.

If she had demanded that *he* remain beside her, Colt might have sheathed his sword and let Dylan lead the attack in his stead.

"Very well," Colt said, doing what he could to maintain his composure. To Tryst and Lucky, he added, "You are to keep the staff from the goblins no matter the cost. Once we've cleared a path to the fort, you will make a run for it. Understand?"

Tryst and Lucky nodded. The former looked bored by the conversation.

"If the goblins get the staff, you'll wish you had died," he said to Tryst. "Do you understand?"

Tryst shrugged. "So we keep out of sight and run away if the goblins come after us. Easy as a Kraken whore."

Colt looked away from the infuriating man and turned back to Opal. There was so much he wanted to tell her—there always was—and it occurred to him that despite his promise to return and reclaim the *vuudu* staff, he could very likely die in the battle ahead.

This could well be the last time he saw her beautiful face, his final chance to tell her of the love he had been harboring ever since they met.

But with two thieves encroaching on their privacy, not to mention his suspicion about Othello's place in her heart, Colt simply said, "Be safe, Opal."

Then he was walking past her, Lucky, and Tryst. The sting of tears burned his eyes, but he blinked them away. He had to forget about Opal and concentrate on what lay ahead.

As luck would have it, he crossed paths with Othello on his way back to his army. The forester nodded a greeting, which Colt returned coldly. There was no doubt in Colt's mind that the man was heading for Opal. He might have suspected that Othello had arranged it all—staying behind with Opal and the *vuudu* staff—except for the fact that Colt had planned it himself.

He unsheathed *Chrysaal-rûn* as he neared his men. Though Ruford's troops brought their number up to one hundred and forty, Colt's army made no more noise than a group of ten. Everyone rested in silence, waiting for his order to leave the cover of the trees and confront the enemy.

Colt stared out through the bare branches. The bright orange sun hung like a giant egg yolk in the sky. After waiting so long to find Drekk't and his army, Colt feared he wouldn't be able to endure one more hour.

He remained on the fringe the assembly, alternating his gaze between the sinking sun and *Chrysaal-rûn*. Absently, he ran his fingers over the silver crosspiece, admiring the fine craftsmanship. Taking in the crystalline surface of the blade, he wondered where such a magnificent weapon had come from. According to the stories that had been passed down from one generation of Crystaluses to the next, the crystal sword had been in the family for as long as the family had existed.

Laenghot Crystalus had wielded *Chrysaal-rûn* before retiring from the Knighthood. He wondered why the sword had never worked its wonders for his father, or if it had, why he hadn't told anyone about the sword's magic.

Had Colt done something to unlock the blade's power? Watching the sunlight glisten on the blade's smooth surface, Colt realized the more important question was whether or not he would be able trigger *Chrysaal-rûn*'s magic again.

In less than an hour, he'd need every advantage he could get.

*   *   *

Stannel had fully expected the goblins to make a second strike that first night or, at the very least, return the next morning. When the T'Ruellian force remained in camp all the next day, he assumed the goblins were trying to lull them into complacency. Why else would the massive army give the Knights time to rest and regroup?

After four full days of calm, Stannel did not know what to think.

Surely there was some logic behind the goblins' strategy. It was as though the goblins were waiting for something, and since the Knights had no reason to ride out from their redoubt, he was forced to conclude the enemy expected something else to happen.

Meanwhile, Stannel prayed and meditated, looking to Pintor for guidance, though no revelation came. In the end, Stannel was left to conclude that the goblins were either going to starve them out, or—more likely—they were awaiting the arrival of whatever weapon had destroyed the original Fort Valor.

In the interim, the Knights could only wait impatiently for the inevitable strike.

Sister Aric and Ruben, the highwayman-turned-healer apprentice, treated those who had been wounded during the goblins' initial foray. Thankfully, most had escaped the battle with minor injuries. Eleven Knights had perished during in the fray or shortly thereafter. That wasn't so many when compared to the hundreds of goblins that had died, but to Stannel, the loss of even one Knight was too many.

Every day, Stannel met with Petton, Ezekiel Silvercrown, and Chadwich Vesparis for status reports, though truthfully, little changed from one day to the next. Stannel tried to gauge the attitudes of his officers at the meetings but was unable to ascertain much.

Petton was as curt as ever, and the other two officers acted no different from before Stannel had proclaimed the truth of his relationship with the Great Protector. He wondered whether the men accepted him for what he was, or whether they were simply tolerating him because they had little choice in the matter.

Stannel was trying to lend a hand in the infirmary, enjoying the opportunity to chat with his dear friend Aric, when he heard the first cries coming down from the lookouts. He met Petton and Zeke Silvercrown on the way to his office. The latter had come directly from the sentries on the battlements.

"An army rides from the southwest," Sir Silvercrown said.

"More goblins?" Petton asked, incredulous.

Zeke shook his head. "No, they're human…cavalry and infantry."

Stannel could scarcely believe the subcommander's words. He had prayed almost ceaselessly for a solution to the fort's predicament. It seemed Pintor was providing an answer.

"Who could they be?" Petton asked. "Reinforcements from Rydah? Or Steppt maybe?"

They had no way of knowing, but Stannel thought it safe to say any enemy of the T'Ruellians' was a friend of theirs.

"How many?" Stannel asked Sir Silvercrown.

Zeke's reply caused Stannel's and Petton's faces to fall.

"One hundred…one hundred and fifty at best."

Zeke Silvercrown told what he had learned from the lookouts. Only a small fraction of the mysterious battalion was mounted. Those on foot were decked in all manner of armor—and in many cases, wore no mail at all. Cavalry and infantry alike were charging toward the goblin line.

"They'll be annihilated!" Petton said. "Even if the goblins don't break ranks, there are enough fiends between us and the new arrivals to overwhelm them in a matter of minutes."

"If we can drive a wedge into the goblins and meet this new army halfway, we can at least provide them with a path to the fort," Stannel said.

"But we know the goblins can take on human form," Zeke said. "What if this is a trick?"

Stannel considered the possibility but dismissed it almost immediately. If there were a shaman in the enemy army, why go to such trouble? If what T'slect had done to Fort Faith's western wing was any indication of a shaman's power, the goblins would be better off barraging the fort with *vuudu* than develop such an elaborate hoax.

In any event, Stannel couldn't risk the lives of their unexpected allies.

"I shall lead the cavalry forth," he told his officers. "Lieutenant, ready the bulk of our foot soldiers and await my signal. If this army of humans proves genuine, I will summon you.

Subcommander Silvercrown, you will remain within the fort with the other Knights. The goblins will undoubtedly attempt to break in. Do whatever you can to repel them."

Both men saluted and were off. Stannel went the other way, heading for the stable.

"Commander."

Stannel looked back to find Petton farther down the hall. For a second, Stannel worried Petton would refuse his orders.

But then he asked, "What signal should I watch for?"

Stannel smiled and glanced down at the mace that was always at hand. "You will know it when you see it."

Charging headlong at thousands of monsters who wanted only to kill him, Colt was overcome by an inexplicable calm.

Is it because I have surrendered to his fate? he wondered. Or is this just what it felt like to fight for a righteous cause?

With each enemy he slew, Colt prayed it was one of the goblins who had murdered Cholk. Every swing of *Chrysaal-rûn* sent torrents of black blood spraying through the air. As he pushed through the goblin line, a trail of body parts bespoke his passage.

He quickly outpaced his allies. When he was thrown from his dying horse, he somehow managed to land on his feet. The fiends were all around him, but he hardly cared. He had only one thought: to slay as many goblins as he could before he himself was slain.

Colt almost immediately lost count of how many had fallen to his impossibly honed blade. His movements were automatic, perfect. It felt like he was watching someone else butcher the monsters, one after another. Not a single opponent found an opening in his defenses. *Chrysaal-rûn* cleaved through unguarded flanks and oncoming weaponry alike.

He lost all track of time as he performed his dance of death. Possessed by an all-consuming hatred for the goblins, Colt spared no time pondering how he was accomplishing the complex maneuvers. Every Knight was required to achieve a high level of skill in swordsmanship, but some of the moves he executed would have put a *sai-morí* to shame.

Colt dispatched every goblin within sword's reach, oblivious to where his momentum was taking him. He might have followed the deadly rhythm that had taken ahold of him forever, except he caught sight of something that made him pause.

During his time as prisoner, Colt had scarcely been able to tell one goblin from another. They all looked the same—like evil incarnate. Every crescent-shaped pupil, dark as the Pit, had glared at him with a palpable hatred. Each mouth, lined top and bottom with pointed teeth, had grinned with the promise of horrors to come.

But there was one goblin Colt had gotten to know better than the rest, one who had wanted to keep him alive. Paralyzed by the magic of the *vuudu* staff, Colt had lain lifeless in a tent on the outskirts of the camp with nothing to do but stare upward. The only reprieve from the tedium had been visits from his merciless captor.

Drekk't.

Everything seemed to slow around him as his eyes met those of the general. Drekk't must have seen him too because he suddenly advanced in Colt's direction.

Colt forgot about the surging throng of enemies around him, and the other goblin warriors seemed content to ignore him and his enchanted sword. They gave him a wide berth as they hurried past.

The crystal sword held out before him, its blade slick with dark blood, he regarded Drekk't with a calm that belied the raw emotion gnashing at his soul. This is for Cholk, he thought, as the general drew nearer.

Passage VIII

Stannel could hear nothing above the din of thundering hooves. Gripping the reigns tightly with one hand and holding his claymore in the other, the Commander of Fort Valor urged his mount ever faster.

Up ahead, the unidentified humans and the goblins battled, but in the minute it took Stannel to reach the enemy, he was able to conclude a few things about the fray before him and his men.

To begin with, the goblins forming a ring around the fortress were holding their position. Probably, this was to prevent the Knights in the fort—or the newcomers, for that matter—from escaping. Once the two human forces united within the circle, the goblins would almost certainly close in.

The second thing he noticed was how patiently the goblins ahead waited, even now, as Fort Valor's cavalry galloped toward them. He marveled at the T'Ruellians' discipline, though he suspected their actions—or, more precisely, their *inaction*—portended something sinister he could not yet perceive.

Prayers to the Great Protector drifted in and out of his thoughts as he and his riders struck the goblin line. The collision sent goblins scattering every which direction. Their momentum spent, Stannel and the other horsemen struck their adversaries with swords, lances, and spears.

Then Stannel was holding onto his horse's mane as the beast reared up on its hind legs. On either side, his companions' steeds bucked or fell to the earth. It was only when he saw the arrow protruding from his mare's flank that he realized the T'Ruellians had unleashed a volley of arrows at them.

A company of archers hidden behind a decoy infantry, Stannel deduced.

Clever.

Stannel understood all at once why the archers hadn't loosed their arrows prior to cavalry's collision, as was the traditional method. Those goblins who had hitherto retreated from flailing hooves and sharp blades alike now surged forward to pounce on the unhorsed Knights.

He lashed out at a goblin who came at him with two straight-edged swords. His claymore nearly beheaded the creature. Roughly half of his men had lost their mounts, though Stannel had managed to hang on.

He dared not signal the remaining cavalrymen to fall back and regroup, lest he condemn the others to death. With a roar of defiance, he redoubled his efforts, pushing his way to the archers.

As he swept sword-first through the enemy, he noticed a hole in their ranks farther down the line, where a single human faced off against a lone goblin. From a distance, Stannel couldn't make out much about the man, other than the fact that he wore almost no armor and wielded an unusual sword.

It was the transparent blade that made Stannel pause—a near fatal mistake. A barbed spear homed in on the space between his fauld and tasset. He would have been skewered had his horse not kicked out with its forelegs at that precise moment, caving in the goblin's skull.

Stannel reined the mare back out of harm's way, drawing Pintor's mace as he did so. He held the weapon aloft, and the effect was instantaneous: a golden light burst forth, streaming up into the heavens where it illuminated the darkening sky like a falling star in reverse.

Not even someone as cynical as Petton could ignore that sign, he thought wryly.

Mace in one hand and the claymore in the other, he charged back into the melee. He could only pray Petton and the infantry would reach the battle in time to save Saerylton Crystalus and the ragtag army he was leading.

The sounds of death and dying drifted on the breeze. As dusk gave way to night, it became all but impossible for Opal to make out the details of the battle, though a bronze-hued explosion had lit up the sky a moment ago, providing her with a glimpse at the chaos.

Now she depended solely upon the torches on Fort Valor's rampart, which cast the fortress in a fiery glow Armies of shadow danced before the stone backdrop. And though she could make neither heads nor tail of what she was seeing, Opal couldn't turn away.

Colt was out there somewhere, undoubtedly in the thick of things. She didn't want to think of how slim his chances of surviving were. She hated him for making her feel this way, hated him for asking her stay behind.

I should be out there with you, she thought. *You had no right to—*

A rustling behind her brought Opal's mind back to the present. She spun around and leveled her crossbow at whoever was sneaking up on her.

"Easy there, lady," Tryst said. "It's just us, your faithful bodyguards."

Opal lowered her weapon, and let out a deep breath.

Tryst kept an eye on her crossbow as he stepped nearer. "You know, that thing is very valuable."

It took Opal a moment to comprehend what the thief was saying. She hadn't given the *vuudu* staff a second thought after Colt had led the charge into battle. She glanced down at the talisman and then back at Tryst, who wore an oily smile.

"I can see you're skeptical," Tryst said, taking another step closer. "Well, you'll just have to take my word for it. I've been a thief all my life, you know. Some of my friends might've gotten caught up in Colt's crazy crusade, but there's only one thing I care about in this world. Money."

Though Tryst halted his advance, Opal stiffened. A prickle crawled over her skin. Her crossbow felt heavy and ungainly in her hand. She recalled Tryst's weapon of choice and wondered if she would have time to fire a bolt before he let fly his knives.

Lucky remained standing a few paces behind Tryst, where he had been all along. Of Othello, there was no sign.

"There's quite a market for magical items," Tryst continued, his tone conversational, nonchalant. "If that staff can do *half* of what Colt claims it can…well, let's just say none of us will have to work for a very long time. And it just so happens I know a guy who might be interested in buyin' it."

"It's not ours to sell," Opal told him, putting more bravado in her voice than she felt.

Tryst scoffed. "What, you think Colt's gonna want it back? Well, let me tell you something, darlin'. Your boyfriend's dead. And if he ain't dead already, he will be real soon."

The thief's words were almost enough to provoke Opal to shoot him right then and there. She started to tremble but willed herself to be calm. He's trying to upset you, she thought. He wants you to goad you into making the first move.

"The staff belongs to the Knights," Opal argued.

Tryst's second laugh was louder and dripping with scorn. "And what are the Knights gonna do with it? Lock it in a chest in the far corner of their cellar? Destroy it? What a waste!"

"It's a dangerous weapon," Opal said. "I don't even want to think of what kind of lowlife you'd give it to."

"Not give...*sell*," the thief corrected.

"You're not getting this staff!"

Tryst crossed his arms and frowned. "I feared you might be one of those poor people burdened with a conscience. If you aren't sensible enough to accept a cut in the profit, then we'll take a different route. You can either hand over the staff, or I'll kill you and take it off your carcass. Simple as that."

Opal's heart pounded painfully in her breast. There was no going back now, she realized. She had killed goblins, yes, but never a human...

Tryst uncrossed his arms quickly, and she saw the glint of moonlight on metal. She wrenched her arms up and hastily fired an arrow at Tryst.

Even as she released the bolt, she saw the knife sailing end-over-end in her direction. Tryst jerked awkwardly to the side, but her mind couldn't make sense of what had sent the thief falling; the bolt from her crossbow hadn't reached him yet.

She could do nothing but flinch as Tryst's knife came at her. But the thief's aim proved off, and the blade missed her entirely. Meanwhile, her arrow sped harmlessly through the space Tryst had previously occupied.

Opal stared in confusion at Tryst, who lay on the ground groaning. Her eyes went to Lucky, thinking he had somehow thrown his companion to the ground. That didn't make any sense though. From all appearances, the other thief hadn't moved.

Then Opal saw the green-fletched arrow sticking out of Tryst's leg.

Othello hurried over to her. "Are you all right?"

Opal nodded. A few yards away, Tryst cursed violently.

"He was after the staff," she told Othello.

The forester said nothing. Even in the stingy light of the moon, Opal could make out the deep, verdant green of the forester's eyes as he looked her up and down. She felt their closeness acutely and was thankful for the darkness, certain that her cheeks were ablaze.

"I'm fine," she insisted, looking away from him and over at Tryst. "He just caught me by surprise."

"You bitch," Tryst muttered. "You stupid bitch."

Opal glared at the fallen thief, but Tryst was occupied with the shaft protruding from his thigh. He gave the arrow a slight tug and let out another stream of curses.

"What about the other one?" Othello asked, taking another arrow from his quiver.

Lucky remained rooted in the same spot as before. He took in the suffering of his friend with a detachment that puzzled Opal. She wondered if, perhaps, Tryst had coerced the other thief into helping him steal the staff. From all appearances, Lucky couldn't care less about Tryst's condition.

"Maybe the two of you ought to leave," Opal said. She would have reloaded her crossbow to emphasize her point, but because of the damn *vuudu* staff, she had no free hand.

Lucky mumbled something in reply.

"What?" Opal demanded, thinking Lucky had joined Tryst in insulting her.

Othello gave her a sudden shove, and she hit the ground hard, landing on her crossbow. She rolled over just in time to see the forester pull back on his bowstring.

Lucky shouted something that Opal didn't understand. A flurry of small, dark shapes flew from the thief's palms. Her eyes followed the strange missiles' trail all the way to Othello's chest.

The forester was struck with enough force to knock him off his feet. His arrow disappeared into the night's sky and landed somewhere far away.

Panic rendered Opal's limbs useless. Her mind struggled to make sense of what was happening, but there was only one answer: Lucky knew magic.

And he intended to finish what Tryst had started.

Opal pushed off the ground and dove for the *vuudu* staff,

which she had dropped during her fall. She was no match for a spell-caster, especially with an empty crossbow. Her only option was to run.

She had promised Colt to keep it safe, and by the Benevolent Seven, she was going to keep her word, though it killed her to leave Othello behind…again.

Too scared to swear, Opal fled.

"Lucky…what in the…?"

It was Tryst's voice. She knew she should ignore him and keep on running, but she glanced back in spite of herself.

Lucky walked past Tryst, not paying the other thief any attention. Then Lucky was gone, replaced by a goblin wearing the quiet thief's clothing.

Opal's breath caught in her throat. She took a step backward and tripped over an exposed root. This time, she managed to keep her fingers clamped tightly around the staff as she came crashing to the ground.

Before she could right herself, she heard the goblin shout, "I have a bargain for you, human…the staff for your friend's life."

Since joining up with Klye's Renegades, Lilac had found herself in one sticky situation after another. But never before had she experienced anything like the bedlam around her now.

Everywhere she looked, she saw the hate-filled eyes of her enemy, which seemed to reflect the moonlight with a red-gold glow. There were times when she found herself fighting alongside strangers—the militiamen of Hylan, Knights from Rydah, thieves from the Guild—and there were moments when she saw nothing but foes at every turn.

She clutched the vorpal sword with both hands, swinging the weapon with all of her strength. Pieces of armor, weaponry, and flesh littered the ground wherever she fought. Were it not for the vorpal sword's unnatural keenness, her prowess alone would not have kept her alive.

Even so, Lilac had her share of close calls. There were simply too many goblins.

She had entered the battle beside Hunter, Pillip, and Bly but had lost track of them long ago. Her impetus, fueled by the lethal sting of the vorpal sword, had led her deep into the goblin ranks. She was on the verge of falling back to give her allies time to catch up when she caught sight of Dylan a little farther ahead.

The Knight moved with surprising speed and dexterity considering how many pounds of armor he wore and the hefty broadsword he wielded. Out of the corner of her eye, she watched Dylan Torc dispatch foe after foe with precision, putting into practice the many exercises he surely learned as a squire.

Lilac's own style was similar to Dylan's. She had learned to duel from the same instructor who had mentored her brother Gabriel before he left home to become a squire. But unlike Dylan, who had years of training and experience under his belt, Lilac's training had ended when most Knights' lessons began in earnest.

So while Dylan and the other Knights in Colt's battalion were among Altaerra's finest swordsmen, Lilac could only pray her limited repertoire of techniques would see her through the battle alive.

Suddenly, a goblin came out of nowhere. Having no chance to turn the curved sword, Lilac threw her hips to the side. She winced as the blade grazed her upper leg. Before the goblin could strike again, she hacked the creature's arm off and followed through with a thrust that sent the vorpal sword plunging through the goblin's innards like a warm knife through butter.

The goblin tried to scream but could only gargle as thick black blood spurted from its mouth.

She didn't wait around while the monster wheezed its final breaths. Eager to find a friend, she fought her way over to Dylan, who was contending with five goblins. Between parrying and blocking, the Knight had no opportunity to launch any sort of an offense against his adversaries.

Lilac dropped two of the fiends with a horizontal slash that ripped apart their lower backs. The pair pitched forward, writhing and shouting words she was happy not to understand.

Dylan pitched to the side, evading the downward arc of a pole-axe that was nearly as tall as its wielder. The Knight then pivoted and came back with a thrust that planted his broadsword between the plates of the goblin's armor.

Seconds later, the remaining goblins joined their comrades in dying on the blood-slicked earth. Lilac braced herself for her next encounter, but no one was there. She and Dylan were in the eye of the storm, their nearest combatants several yards away in every direction.

She looked to Dylan for an explanation, but the Knight was already running headlong deeper into the fray. Grateful for the moment of rest—and astonished at Dylan's audacity—Lilac didn't immediately follow. She took the opportunity to look around.

Where she stood now had not always been a place of calm. Dozens of goblin corpses lay strewn across the ground. Lilac squinted into the darkness up ahead, trying to find the source of the slaughter.

Letting out a growl that was two parts frustration and one part determination, she followed Dylan Torc deeper into the goblins' ranks. Once she caught up to him, she found the answer to the mystery.

Before them, Colt faced off with a single opponent. No other goblin ventured into the skirmish, and Lilac and Dylan likewise remained where they stood.

Colt confronted his enemy with a deadly grace that stole Lilac's breath. It seemed to her that the goblin opponent must know of *Chrysaal-rûn*'s powers. The creature put most of its energy into avoiding the crystalline blade, not daring to use its own sword to block the series of precisely placed strokes.

The goblin contorted its body, evading Colt's expert attacks. When the goblin lurched forward, aiming his sword at the Knight's chest, Lilac gasped, certain Colt would not react in time. But then Colt did the impossible.

Releasing his hold on the crystal sword—which was already above his head after completing an upward slash—Colt bent his knees and pushed up and back. Pulling his body into a tight ball, Colt flipped backward.

Lilac had seen acrobats perform similar feats at fairs, but what Colt did next put those professional tumblers to shame. No sooner had his feet touched the ground than Colt leaped forward, performed a perfect handspring, and vaulted over the goblin. Catching *Chrysaal-rûn* in midair, he landed behind his opponent and swung the crystal sword in a whirring arc.

To the goblin's credit, it spun around in time to block the Knight's attack. However, *Chrysaal-rûn* separated all but an inch of the blade from the hilt. The goblin scrambled backward, holding the useless weapon out in front of it.

Colt came in for the kill.

But as he readied to unleash an attack that would tear his opponent in half, a wall of goblins surged forward, engulfing him from behind. The space that had opened for the duelists filled with the monsters, and Lilac had to wrench her attention back to her own precarious situation lest she get impaled.

Even as she and Dylan renewed their assault on the goblin army, she searched for Colt in the crowd. She determinedly pushed her way toward where she had last seen the commander, encountering a goblin at every step. She also did her best to prevent Dylan from falling prey to the numerous weapons homing in on him.

She had no idea how much time passed before they finally reached Colt, but when they finally did, he looked not at all like the champion from earlier.

Colt clutched his side, which was soaked with blood, and with his other hand made desperate swipes at the goblins pressing in on him from all sides. His movements were inelegant and weak, but the goblins watched him warily, careful to avoid *Chrysaal-rûn*.

Judging by the man's pallor and the large red stain on his breastplate, Colt's grip on consciousness—and life itself—was tenuous.

Lilac redoubled her efforts, throwing herself at any goblin that ventured too near the failing commander. Eventually, she and Dylan came to fight back-to-back. Colt ceased his struggles, and she feared he was already dead. There was no opportunity to ascertain the truth, however, and so she and Dylan fought on.

In the back of her mind, she couldn't help but wonder how long before she and Dylan joined Colt on the cold, hard ground.

Passage IX

Pistol felt the difference in his very first swing. Life on a ship kept a person in top physical condition. Even after he and Crooker had thrown in with the Renegades, they had pushed their bodies to the limit, walking for days and battling all manner of foes on the way to Fort Faith.

But sitting in a cell for weeks was not conducive to a healthy physique, and it wasn't long before myriad aches and pains accompanied his every thrust and parry. It was all he could do to keep the goblins at bay. Yet letting up even a little was tantamount to suicide.

Then again, the whole situation seemed suicidal to Pistol. As King of the Pirates of the Fractured Skull, he had orchestrated more than a few battles at sea. Sometimes he had commanded a single ship; at other times, two. In either case, he had always made sure his crew had the upper hand and, more importantly, that the payout was worth the effort.

This battle, however, was a purely defensive one for the residents of new Fort Valor, and he knew how the mariners of those ships he had boarded over the years must have felt. The Pirates of the Fractured Skull hadn't shied away from killing, though it wasn't their primary objective.

The goblins, on the other hand, seemed to have but one thought in their bald, misshapen heads—kill every single human.

Had anyone told him he would one day find himself fighting beside the Knights of Superius to repel an army of monsters, he would have dismissed the speaker as a madman or drunkard. And yet, here he was, flanked by his former enemies and crossing swords with a race of creatures most men dismissed as myth.

As the goblin forces engulfed them completely, the Renegades did their damnedest to stay together. Klye Tristan took to the fore, with Horcalus and Arthur on either side. Scout and to a lesser extent Plake stayed close behind them, dispatching the goblins that survived their confrontation with the Knights' frontline.

Fighting against impossible odds alongside the Renegades, Pistol couldn't help but smile and reflect that this was just like old times.

Which made what he had to do all the more difficult.

"Pistol, your left!"

Crooker's warning came almost too late. Because he had lost the use of his left eye in a mechanical mishap some years back, Pistol had learned to compensate with his other senses over the years. The sudden whir of air alerted him to both the direction and angle of the attack.

He dropped to one knee and twisted his body to the left, stabbing out with his cutlass. The goblin's sword sliced through nothing but air while Pistol's blade plunged into the monster's midsection.

Not sparing the screeching creature a second thought, Pistol quickly righted himself and brought up his sword to deflect an oncoming spearhead. Meanwhile, Crooker swung his own sword in desperate strokes, backpedaling away from a pair of axe-wielding goblins. Pistol kicked his latest opponent in the shin and turned to help Crooker, who was facing four goblins now.

Pistol threw himself at the first fiend, burying his cutlass into the goblin's spine. The creature howled and swung its pole-axe wildly in an attempt to drive Pistol back. He accepted the impact of the hardwood handle against his side and followed through with a left hook to the creature's face.

Crooker let out an agonized cry, and Pistol's heart jumped up into his throat.

Although he would never admit it to anyone, he cared a great deal for Crooker. Pirate vessels were rife with deceit, greed, and violence. He had had to slay a few of his mates to secure his position as pirate king. Crooker had been a friend and ally through it all, helping him dispose of rivals, one after another.

Throughout their years together, Pistol had come to realize Crooker was possessed of qualities not often found in a buccaneer—loyalty being one of them. Crooker had been the only member of his crew to stay behind in Port Town and to save him from the noose.

The thought of losing Crooker nearly blinded him with rage.

Pistol's next stroke severed one goblin's arm at the elbow. He followed immediately with a lunge that sent his cutlass clear through the goblin's leather shirt and into its gut. A second later, he was batting aside the broad head of a battle-axe and ramming his shoulder in the chest of its owner. Both went down, though Pistol landed on top of the goblin.

Since his cutlass was at an awkward angle, Pistol drew his knife and planted it in the creature's throat. Pushing off from the goblin's chest with his hands—a move that caused black spray to geyser up from the hole in the monster's neck—Pistol searched for his companion.

Crooker lay on his back, his blade locked with that of a goblin. Crooker was pushing with all his might against his adversary, but the goblin's considerable strength and gravity made it a losing battle for the pirate. Inch by inch, the blade crept closer to Crooker's face.

Pistol sprang at the goblin, more concerned with getting the monster off of Crooker than scoring any serious damage. The two of them—goblin and human—hit the ground hard. Pistol heard the snap of breaking bones. Since he felt nothing aside from the panic of having his breath blasted out of him, he figured the goblin must have taken the injury.

For a moment, Pistol could only gasp for breath. The goblin recovered quicker. Its blade whirred down at him. Pistol cringed, waiting for the deathblow to land. But it never came.

He opened his eye in time to see the tip of Crooker's blade burst from the monster's chest.

Crooker helped him to his feet. Pistol didn't bother thanking the man, and neither did Crooker express any gratitude for what Pistol had done to help him. They had saved the each other's life countless times before; it came with the territory.

Pistol frowned when he saw a sopping red spot running the length of Crooker's side.

"You all right?" he asked.

Crooker glanced down at the blood as though noticing it for the first time. "I think so."

"We have to get out of here, Crook'."

Crooker glanced at the Knights and Renegades who were slowly pushing back the goblins. "What do you mean?"

"We've got to make a run for it."

"But it looks like we're winning," Crooker said, his face riddled with confusion.

Pistol had seen that expression many times before. While Crooker was as loyal as a watchdog, he lacked a certain pragmatism Pistol had always prided himself for possessing. Crooker wasn't an idiot. He just wasn't good at thinking on his toes.

"Even if the Knights win this battle, we won't," Pistol said. "Once the goblins are gone, they'll throw us back in the dungeon."

"Maybe they won't. Klye and the others get to move around as they like."

"But we're pirates," said Pistol, keeping a wary eye on the battle, which was raging a few yards away. "It's only a matter of time before they get around to executing us."

Crooker's face fell. "But what about Klye? He vouched for us. If we run, he's gonna get in trouble."

"They won't do anything to Klye," he argued. "The new commander seems to like him well enough. Besides, we don't belong with the Renegades, Crook'. Don't you want to get back to the sea?"

Crooker let out a big sigh, and it occurred to Pistol that perhaps Crooker had never considered leaving the fort—and the Renegades—behind.

"Fine." Pistol tucked the black-stained knife between his belt and pants. "You can stay if you want, but I'll not give them another chance to throw me in a cell."

That said, he turned and started to run. He almost felt bad for playing his trump card, as it were, except it was for Crooker's own good—even if the big lout couldn't see it yet.

Two seconds later, he heard Crooker call out, "Hey, wait for me!"

Pistol stopped, allowing the other pirate to catch up. He scanned the distance behind them, making sure that no one—man or goblin—was following them.

"Where...where...are we...going?" Crooker expelled his words between breaths.

Pistol had had plenty of time to think about where he would go if the chance to escape presented itself. "We'll follow the Divine Divider down to Kraken."

He said no more for the time being and was grateful Crooker didn't press him. For one thing, he was already exhausted. For another, he didn't know how much coaxing it would take to get Crooker to go along with his plan.

Pistol had no idea how long it would take to reach the port city of Kraken. His knowledge of Capricon's geography was rudimentary at best. For all he knew, Kraken wasn't even the nearest port to the fortress, but he had other reasons for wanting to go there.

There weren't many places where a buccaneer could spend the spoils of his trade, but from all accounts, Kraken was one of them. Some even claimed that Kraken's mayor had practiced piracy in his younger days.

It was as good a time as any to find out how much of the rumor was true.

What Pistol didn't tell Crooker was that he hoped to find the surviving members of the Pirates of the Fractured Skull there. Their ships hadn't had enough supplies to sail back across the Strait. Likely, the traitors had made for Kraken after leaving him for dead in Port Town.

Pistol would reclaim what was rightfully his—no matter how many throats he had to slit along the way.

Though every muscle in his body ached, Klye willed himself to maintain the intensity that had seen him safely through the battle so far. Petton had been reluctant to let the Renegades accompany the fort's infantry onto the battlefield. Now Klye found himself wondering what had possessed him to argue with the lieutenant.

He had no idea how many goblins he had faced already. He hadn't killed every one of them, but he was no worse off for the encounters. He was still alive, anyway. Each time his eyes met those of Horcalus or caught a glimpse of Scout running past, Klye thanked the gods his friends were still alive too.

After a while, he even forgot to scold himself for praying to gods he didn't believe in.

Eventually, Klye began to notice a gradual dearth in enemies. He looked to either side and saw the goblins falling back.

"We did it," he said breathlessly. "We cut a path through their ranks."

"Now they will close in around us, cutting off our retreat."

Klye turned to find a Knight bedecked in full-plate armor sitting atop a white horse. The rider carried a great sword and a fancy club that looked familiar. The man raised his visor, revealing the countenance of Stannel Bismarc.

Klye wasn't sure if Stannel was answering his comment or if the commander was merely pointing out the obvious.

"Maybe it's time we headed back for the fort," Klye said.

"Indeed…" Whatever Stannel was going to say next was interrupted by the arrival of three people Klye had never seen before.

"Are you from the fort?" asked a woman whose clothes were stained black with goblin blood. She planted the butt of a spear in the earth and looked up at Stannel expectantly.

"I am," replied the commander.

"Can we borrow your horse?"

It was an unusual favor to ask of a stranger, particularly in the middle of a battle. Klye waited for Stannel to shoo the woman away. Instead he asked, "For what purpose?"

"Our leader got hurt bad. If we don't get him to the fort, he's gonna to die."

"Your leader? Do you mean Saerylton Crystalus?"

The woman shook her head. "No, Commander Colt."

Klye might have laughed under other circumstances, knowing full well that the two men were one in the same.

Stannel frowned. "I shall need my horse to rally both your army and mine back to the fort."

"Don't worry about that," said the stout man beside the woman. "Ruford is taking care of that. He said something about crab pinchers."

"A pincer attack," Stannel corrected.

"Yeah…that sounds right."

Stannel sat back a little in his saddle, his face expressionless.

"Who in the hell is Ruford?" Klye asked. "For that matter, who are you guys, and how did you end up with Colt?"

Stannel forestalled any reply with an upraised hand. "This is not the time for tales." To the three strangers, he said, "Please, take me to Colt."

"He's over there." The woman pointed back the way she had come. "Keep going straight. You can't miss him."

Stannel kicked his mount's flank, spurring the beast into action. The three strangers exchanged a look before following Stannel to where they had left Colt. Klye shot a backward glance at the fort, cursed, and ran to catch up with them.

*　　　*　　　*

The goblins were finally falling back, giving her and Dylan a bit of respite. When Lilac was certain it was safe, she planted the vorpal sword deep in the ground and knelt beside Colt, who lay still. Her eyes met Dylan's as she searched for a pulse.

"Is he…?" the Knight asked.

Lilac let out a sigh of relief when she found the steady, though weak, rhythm. "No, but he will be if he doesn't get some help soon."

"We have to get him to the fort," Dylan said. "Should we carry him?"

"I don't think we have a choice."

"He'll leave a trail of blood as wide as a king's red carpet if you drag him there," a familiar voice said.

Hunter, Bly, and Pillip looked grimly down at their commander.

"We gotta get a horse," Hunter added. "He'll still bleed, but at least he'll get to the healer quicker. Am I right?" Before anyone could say anything, Hunter declared, "Come on, guys. Let's find Colt a horse."

After the Hylaners left, Lilac looked to Dylan helplessly.

"We'll give them a few minutes," he said. "If they don't return, we take him to the fort ourselves."

Since she couldn't think of a better plan, she returned her attention to Colt, whose wheezing sent up small puffs of steam into the cold air. She brushed his hair out of his eyes and ran her hand down the side of his stubble-ridden cheek. Hang on, Colt, she begged. Help is on the way.

Despite her silent promise, Lilac was considerably surprised when a Knight on a white steed came trotting up to them. The horseman dismounted and approached them.

"Commander Bismarc!" she blurted, unable to contain her astonishment and joy.

Stannel gave her a look that bespoke a distinct lack of recognition. "Come, help me lift him onto my horse."

Dylan hooked his hands under Colt's armpits and gently lifted his head and torso off the ground. The movement caused Colt's eyes to flutter open.

Now another familiar voice spoke to her. "Lilac?"

She looked up in time to see Klye push his way past Hunter

and Bly.

"Klye!" she shouted, nearly laughing.

When she had left the fort, Klye had been bedridden. She had not expected to find the Renegade Leader back on his feet, let alone on a battlefield.

Beside her, Colt groaned.

"You are hurt badly," Stannel told the young commander. "We are going to place you on my horse and take you to the fort. Brace yourself, lad. This will hurt—"

"No," Colt interrupted, punctuating his refusal with a harsh cough that made Lilac wince. "You must get Opal." Another cough. "I left her with the *vuudu* staff…back in the forest…"

Colt expelled a series of coughs that shook his whole body. When he was finished, Lilac saw that blood speckled his lips.

"*Vuudu* staff?" Klye asked.

"It's a powerful talisman," Lilac explained. "Colt stole it from the goblin general. Opal and Othello and a few others stayed behind to make sure the goblins didn't get it back. They're in those trees way back there."

"Please…" Colt pleaded, his voice failing him.

Lilac, along with everyone else, looked to Stannel for an answer. Stannel took Colt's hand in his.

"I swear I will do all that I can to honor your request," he said, "but you must promise me you will hold on."

Colt's only reply was a drawn-out sigh. His eyes closed and did not open, but Lilac saw his chest rise and fall with each labored breath.

Stannel pulled himself back up on his mount. There were still no goblins nearby—a blessing to be sure!—but Lilac knew it was only a matter of time before they returned. She tore her gaze away from Colt's pallid face and greeted Klye with a sad smile.

The Renegade Leader shook his head, his expression dubious.

Hunter hefted her spear so that it rested against her shoulder. "Looks like we're gonna need another horse."

Passage X

They had entered a forest only moments ago, but already Pistol was disoriented. He hated trees, especially the way they seemed to reach out with their brittle branches, like the fingers of a skeleton. Give me the shaky, slippery deck of a storm-tossed ship over the woods any day, he thought.

The pirate came to a sudden halt, the hairs on the back of his neck bristling. Crooker must not have seen him stop. He came crashing through the brush—making more noise than one might have thought possible—and crashed bodily into Pistol's back.

"Ow!"

"Shhh!" Pistol hissed.

"What?"

"I thought I heard something."

The two men stood motionless for several seconds. At first, Pistol heard only the sounds of the battle they had left behind. The capricious wind caused the bare branches of the trees to creak against one another. Cover or no cover, he was beginning to regret entering the forest.

Pistol strained his ears, trying to find whatever had caught his attention in the first place. Probably just an owl, he thought. He was about to give Crooker the order to start moving again, when he heard a man say, "I have a bargain for you, human…the staff for your friend's life."

"This way," Pistol whispered, moving slowly away from where the voice had come.

He felt a hand on his shoulder.

"Shouldn't we check it out?"

Pistol scowled at Crooker. "We're tryin' to *escape*, in case you forgot."

The next voice that wafted through the trees was a woman's,

and it was louder. "Leave him alone, or I swear I'll destroy it!"

"She sounds like she's in trouble," Crooker insisted, peering into the darkness.

Pistol heard the sound of laughter followed by the first voice. "You couldn't destroy it, fool...not even if you were possessed of the strength of one hundred humans!"

Crooker frowned and shot Pistol a look that reminded him of a mutt that had whined its way into his life many years ago.

"We don't have time for this," he argued. "You're injured for one thing."

Crooker stared out into the night, as though his eyes might somehow pierce the darkness.

"An' you call yerself a pirate," Pistol muttered.

"Huh?" asked Crooker.

"Never mind. If we take a quick look to satisfy your curiosity, could you be persuaded to continue running for your life before the sun comes up?"

Crooker was already tiptoeing toward where the dialogue had originated. Cursing his companion and cursing himself for humoring the soft-hearted fool, Pistol slid his cutlass from its sheath and crept as best he could through the grabbing vines and tripping roots.

The goblin laughed, exposing pointy teeth that glinted in the moonlight. "You couldn't destroy it, fool...not even if you were possessed of the strength of one hundred humans!"

The shaman held Othello against himself like a shield, pressing a short, thick-bladed knife against his ribs. The forester looked like he was already dead. His eyes were closed; his body, limp. Opal sought desperately for signs of life, for any indication the goblin wasn't bluffing.

She wouldn't trade the staff for a corpse, but what if the forester were still alive? Could she betray her oath to Colt to save Othello?

Opal cursed the gods for putting her in such a predicament. How could she live knowing she might have been able to save Othello? Yet if she surrendered the staff, how could she ever look Colt in the eye again?

It dawned on her, then, that if she gave up the *vuudu* staff, there would be nothing to stop the shaman from killing both her and Othello.

If she could not destroy the staff, she would just have to make another attempt at running away with it. If he wanted the staff so badly, the bastard would have to catch her and pry the thing out of her cold, dead hands.

She cast a final glance at Othello—a farewell—and resolved to flee.

Opal cried out as two figures burst from the trees on one side of the shaman. Instead of running, she could only stare in mute wonder as the men confronted the goblin. At first, she didn't recognize her saviors, and when she did, it was all she could do to shake off her many questions and *act*.

She had no weapon except the *vuudu* staff...

The two pirates hacked at the shaman, who was forced to drop Othello to evade their curved blades. The shaman made desperate swings with a knife to keep the men at bay. A trail of black ooze seeped from the places where a cutlass had cut deeply.

The injuries seemed to make the shaman only fight harder.

Opal winced as the goblin landed a solid left hook on the side of the patch-eyed pirate's head. The blow sent the man spinning to the ground and gave the goblin an opportunity to get his bearings. Though wielding only a knife, the goblin turned on the remaining pirate, who, by the look of him, had not entered the battle fresh.

With an unintelligible cry on her lips, Opal charged. The shaman had its back to her, but at the sound of her voice, it began to turn around. The *vuudu* staff connected with the goblin's bulbous head with a loud thwack.

To the monster's credit, it did not fall. The shaman staggered back a few steps, shot her a bewildered stare, and stumbled away like a wounded animal.

Her arm still numb from the impact, Opal watched him go. She looked to the pirate that was still standing, hoping he would finish the grisly task for her, but he was already running over to his fallen friend.

As he helped the one-eyed pirate to his feet, Opal considered scooping up one of the blades lying around and hunting down the retreating shaman herself. T'slect had gotten away because she had hesitated. For all she knew, this shaman *was* the goblin prince.

Opal took one step in the direction the shaman had fled, but that was all. She had no strength left. As all of her aches and pain seemed to catch up with her at once, it was all she could do to keep from toppling over.

She had the *vuudu* staff. That would have to be good enough.

Tryst was gone. The thief had probably hobbled away when the shaman first revealed itself. Opal didn't care. The greedy bastard was the least of her worries.

Holding the *vuudu* staff tightly, she knelt beside Othello, cradling his head in her lap. Whatever magical darts had pierced his chest had vanished, leaving behind gaping holes that continued to bleed.

"Is he…dead?"

Opal glanced up at the pirates. On some level, it surprised her they cared about Othello. They were all members of Klye Tristan's band of Renegades, and yet she found it difficult to picture Othello interacting with the buccaneers.

She put her fingers to Othello's neck, searching for a heartbeat. She begged the gods for a sign of life and was rewarded with the faintest of beats.

"Not yet," she said, "but these wounds…"

Tears blurring her eyes, she looked up at the pirates in desperation. The one with the patch looked away. The other frowned a great frown.

"We gotta get him some help."

The one-eyed man turned on him instantly. "Are you crazy, Crooker? He's done for, and so are we if we stick around."

"But—"

"But *nothing*. It's a damn shame he's gonna die, but there's nothin' we can do about it!"

Crooker looked sheepishly at Opal and then back down at Othello.

"It's time to go, Crook'," the one-eyed pirate said softly. "Either say goodbye to him, or you'll have to say it to me."

The patch-eyed man walked away. Crooker let out a sigh that caused his large frame to slump. Then he turned his back on her, yelling, "Sorry," over his shoulder as he hurried to catch up to his friend.

Opal didn't know whether Crooker's apology was meant for her or Othello. She was too stunned by all that had happened to confront the deserters. What good the two of them might have done, she couldn't say for certain, but they should've at least tried *something*.

When Othello moaned, she gasped in surprise. It might have been her imagination, but his eyes looked greener than ever.

"You're going to be all right," she lied, running her fingers through his hair and giving him the biggest smile she could muster.

"No, I'm not."

A tear trickled down the side of her nose. "You can't go," she whispered. "I have so many questions…"

"Like what?" His voice was gravelly.

She made a noise that sounded a little like crying and a little like laughing. "I don't know…why do you seem so familiar when we've never met before?"

Othello's face contorted in pain. "I couldn't say, but I'm glad we met when we did."

Another tear fell, landing in his blond hair. Othello stared up at her for several long seconds until Opal feared he had passed away. But then he winced again and moved his arms as though trying to get up.

"Don't—" she started to say.

"I want…I want you to have…" He spoke in a whisper now.

She saw him take something from a pouch on his belt. He reached for her hand and dropped something into her palm. She accepted the gift, her eyes never leaving his.

When Othello expelled his last breath, she wouldn't let herself believe he was gone.

Then, for the first time in her limited memory, Opal began to sob uncontrollably.

By the time Ay'sek made it to the battlefield, the two human hosts had already rallied together and were retreating toward Fort Valor.

It was just as well. He was in no condition to confront even the weakest of opponents. In fact, it was all he could do to put one foot in the front of the other. The two men had caught him so completely unaware, stabbing him numerous times. But the sting of those lacerations was nothing compared to the headache that threatened to rob him of his consciousness with every step he took.

He was in too much pain to dwell on his failure. *Vuudu* alone was keeping him alive, and unless he received some proper healing, he wouldn't last much longer.

Ay'sek's keen eyes swept over those who had fallen. Here, at the southern fringe of the battlefield, the bodies of men and goblins alike were cold and stiff. The shaman forced himself to go on, ignoring the thick blood that coated his face like a mask, blinding him in one eye.

Finally, he stumbled upon a survivor, a goblin warrior who clung to life in spite of a missing leg. The soldier let out a hopeful squeal when he saw him. It was possible the goblin recognized him as a Chosen of the Chosen, but Ay'sek thought it more likely the wretch didn't want to die alone.

The soldier peered at him curiously as he drew nearer. Ay'sek did not respond to the goblin's inquiries and pleas until he knelt beside him. Looking the soldier in the eye, Ay'sek said, "Be at ease, brother. Your suffering will soon be at an end."

The warrior's face lit up, and he bowed his head deferentially. Ay'sek took the soldier's hands in his own and began to chant the words of a spell. He continued to speak the powerful mantra even as the other goblin shrieked himself hoarse.

Ay'sek maintained his grip on the crippled warrior's wrists, though it was all he could do to keep his balance. Slowly, however, he felt himself grow stronger—even as his victim struggled less and less. After a minute, the soldier stopped fighting altogether, surrendering to a sleep from which he would never awaken.

When Ay'sek released the soldier, the goblin was decorated with new cuts, and his head was bruised and bloodied. Ay'sek, on the other hand, felt nearly no pain at all.

A sudden dizziness stole upon him when he stood up—letting the corpse of the soldier fall unceremoniously to the ground—but such was the demands of channeling so much of Upsinous's power in one day.

The shaman continued his hike with renewed vigor, heading for the bulk of the goblin army. He was in terrible need of rest, but at least he would live to fight again.

When Stannel found his quarry, he was confronted with a truly perplexing sight.

Opal sat cross-legged before the prone form of the Renegade archer. An item that could only have been the *vuudu* staff lay lengthwise across her thighs.

Othello was most certainly dead. He looked as though he had been pierced by many small knives. Opal, on the other hand, sat erect, her eyes closed and her expression unreadable.

Stannel dismounted and approached the woman warily. Something about the scene demanded caution. If Opal heard his approach, she didn't stir. She appeared to be meditating.

He spoke softly. "Opal?"

Her eyes opened slowly, languidly.

"He's dead." Her voice sounded hollow. It made his skin crawl.

"What has happened here?"

"He's dead," she repeated, "but I can bring him back. I *know* I can."

Stannel was about to ask her how she intended to resurrect the dead when he understood all at once what she intended. The *vuudu* staff. Even from a distance, he could feel the vileness of the thing. It was like a hedge of thistles grazing his skin, a foul stench in his nostrils.

"Evil begets evil." He moved closer, slowly, steadily. "And dark deities always demand a price for their gifts."

If Opal comprehended his words, she didn't show it. She got to her feet and looked into the empty sockets of the skull perched atop the staff. Stannel had the horrible impression she was listening to the thing speak.

Before he could fully comprehend what he was doing, he shot out his hand and tore the staff from her grasp. Opal let out a startled cry. For a moment, she merely gaped wide-eyed at him. He feared she would attack.

But then she seemed to shrink before his eyes. When she began to sway, Stannel caught her with his free hand and helped her to stand.

"We have to go," he said. "Our forces are falling back to the fort. If we don't hurry, we'll be trapped on this side of the goblin army."

Opal's eyes darted over to the Renegade archer. "But Othello …"

"We must leave him. We have but one horse and two riders as it is."

Stannel studied the woman's expression. She looked dazed, and he wondered if she fully understood what he was saying.

The horse whickered, drawing Opal's attention. Her eyes grew even wider than before.

"Nisson!"

To Stannel's surprise, the mare whinnied a greeting back. Opal broke away from him and ran to the mare, draping her arms around the horse's thick neck.

Stannel cleared his throat. "We must hurry."

Opal wiped away tears with her sleeve and mounted. Stannel wasted no time in joining her on the horse, though it was an awkward procedure thanks to the *vuudu* staff. He said a silent prayer for the dead Renegade. Once they cleared the woods, he gave the mare permission to gallop for all she was worth.

After that, all of his prayers were for his and Opal's safe return to Fort Valor.

Passage XI

The atmosphere inside the fortress was nearly as chaotic as the battle outside had been. The retreating armies had flooded into the castle through the main gate. Not knowing where else to go, Colt's men remained in the front hall. While some of the Knights worked at getting the wounded to the infirmary, others kept a wary lookout.

Lilac, among the last people to reach the sanctuary of the fortress, had seen the goblins fall back, thanks in part to the archers on the ramparts. But she supposed the goblins might make another go at storming the castle before dawn.

She considered staying near the gate in case the goblins returned, but apparently Klye had other plans. He hollered something over shoulder—his words were immediately swallowed up by the din—and began fighting his way through the crowd. Not wanting to get separated from her only friend at hand, Lilac followed.

She hadn't seen Hunter, Bly, or Pillip since they went off looking for another horse for Colt. The three Hylaners had succeeded, she supposed, for not long after they left, a mounted Knight trotted up to where Klye, Dylan, and she were waiting. Dylan insisted in personally escorting the wounded commander to the fort.

Not long after that, she, Klye, and the other Knight were running for their lives. The goblins were coming from the left, the right, and behind. She had thought her life forfeit, but somehow they outpaced the goblin host, cutting down any enemy that ventured too near. It was only when they reached the fort she noticed the unknown Knight was no longer with them.

Now, as she forced her way through the throng, keeping an eye on the Renegade Leader's back, Lilac said a prayer for the

Knight who had surely died along the way. She also prayed that Dylan had gotten Colt to Sister Aric in time.

The corridors outside the entry hall were no less crowded the hall itself, but the further they went, the easier time they had of it. Lilac recognized the route they were taking at once. Klye was taking her to the Renegade Room, the obvious rendezvous for their band.

They passed more than a few Knights along the way, but none of them gave Klye and her a second glance. The fort's defenders were too busy to worry about a couple of rebels. Lilac wondered how Klye had talked the Knights into letting him and the others join the battle in the first place, but she kept her questions to herself. For now she would be content with the fact that they were together again.

When they finally reached the Renegade Room, Lilac nearly swooned with joy.

"Lilac!" Scout shouted, pushing himself off of the table he had been sitting on.

Scout wore his silly black hood, which left his beaming face uncovered. As the man bounded over to her, she saw his shirt was soaked with dark ichor. Better black than red, she thought.

He wrapped her in a tight hug. "Thank the gods you're back!"

Scout took a step back, and there was Dominic Horcalus. He smiled warmly and offered her a salute that was usually reserved for those within the Knighthood. Lilac might have given the man a hug—if only to see Horcalus lose his composure—but Plake interceded.

The rancher smelled even worse than Scout had, and his clumsy embrace pinned her arms to her sides. Lilac could only chuckle and hope that Plake wouldn't inadvertently break her ribs.

"You're one hell of a woman," Plake said, still squeezing. "It's a damn good thing you're on our side."

Lilac extricated herself from his grasp and saw Klye grinning. Don't even say it, she silently commanded. Don't even *think* it, Klye.

Then, by chance, she caught sight of Opal passing by the Renegade Room's open door. Without offering an explanation to her friends, she ran into the hallway.

She called Opal's name, but either the woman hadn't heard

her, or she was ignoring her. When Lilac caught up, she grabbed Opal by the arm, forcing her to stop and face her.

"Where's Othello?" Lilac asked. "What happened?"

Had she taken a moment to study Opal's tear-streaked face and haunted eyes, she would have known the truth without asking.

As it was, Opal could only whisper, "I'm sorry…"

The words hit Lilac like a punch in the gut, and Lilac fell back a step. No, her mind argued. It can't be…not after all he had endured…

The two women just stared at each other for a moment. When Opal broke away, hurrying off to wherever she had been going before, Lilac's arm fell limply back to her side. She reached for the wall for support, but the stone was farther away than she had thought. She might have fallen, but someone caught her from behind.

"What's wrong?" Klye asked.

She couldn't reply. Her elation at being reunited with the Renegades had been so suddenly replaced by grief that she was barely cognizant of Klye and Horcalus leading her back into the Renegade Room.

Seated in a hard wooden chair, Lilac tried to find the words to tell them that Othello was dead. She didn't know how it happened, so she started by explaining to the others how Othello had remained with Opal and the *vuudu* staff, guarding the evil relic from the goblins.

From there she worked her way backward, telling them how she had been separated from the forester at the goblin camp and how Othello had miraculously appeared in Hylan. She didn't know how much of what she said was making sense, but now that she had begun talking, she couldn't stop.

At last, she trailed off, her words replaced by sobs.

"He was a loyal companion and died a hero," Horcalus said after a few minutes. "May the Benevolent Seven welcome him into Paradise."

"Amen," Arthur said. It was the first time Lilac had noticed the young man.

"First Ragellan, and now Othello," Plake muttered. "And we weren't a large band to begin with."

Beside her, Klye jerked and took a quick step forward. He looked at the others for a moment and then took two steps toward the door, stopped, and swore.

"What is it?" Lilac asked, rising from her seat.

"When was the last time anyone saw the pirates?" Klye asked, keeping his back to them.

Everyone exchanged glances.

"I don't understand," Lilac said. "Aren't they in the dungeon?"

Klye cursed again. "No, they're not. I persuaded Stannel to let them out so they could help defend the fort."

"They fought in the battle?"

Klye said nothing, but Horcalus nodded.

"Maybe they're dead?" Plake suggested. His comment earned him a glare from everyone, except Klye, who continued to stare at the doorway.

Lilac knew what the man was thinking, what everyone else was thinking. The pirates must have taken advantage of the tumultuous battle and made a run for it. She wondered what the consequence for the pirates' desertion would be, but now didn't seem like the right time to ask Klye for his thoughts on the matter.

"I'll go see if anyone knows anything," Scout volunteered, dashing from the room.

"I should go find Stannel," Klye said.

Lilac thought she saw tears in the man's eyes when he glanced back at them, but then he turned away again.

"I will accompany you," Horcalus said.

Klye hardly acknowledged the other man as he followed him to the door. Lilac continued to stare at the empty doorway after the two men were gone. She had seen how Klye Tristan dealt with disappointment before, and now she found herself wondering what had upset the Renegade Leader more—Othello's death or the pirates' departure.

"You look like you've been to the Crypt and back."

Lilac forced her lips into a polite smile as she faced Plake Nelway. "You don't look much better yourself."

The rancher chuckled, looking down at his filthy attire. "Killing goblins ain't glamorous, but somebody's got to do it."

Lilac continued to smile, not knowing what else to say. Klye had teased her in the past, claiming Plake had a crush on her. She was beginning to fear he was right, though she had done nothing to encourage Plake.

Probably, the most decent thing she could do was simply to tell the rancher he wasn't her type. But Lilac had no ambition to engage the boorish man in so personal a conversation just then.

Her mind grasping for any reason to leave, she said, "If you'll excuse me, I have to—"

She caught movement out of the corner of her eye, and there was Arthur.

"Arthur!" she shouted, "I have to talk to Arthur."

Lilac hurried over to where Arthur had taken a seat by the window. The young man wore an expression of absolute befuddlement as she pulled him back to his feet and hauled him out into the hallway.

Now that it was just the two of them—with his guileless eyes staring back at her—it dawned on her that she had traded one awkward chat for another. She replayed her encounter with Glen Bismarc in her mind and remembered her promise to pass on a message to his son.

She felt guilty for knowing Arthur's secret and felt even worse that she would have to let him know she knew.

"Arthur," she said after taking a deep breath, "when I was in Hylan, I met your father."

Whatever Arthur had expected her to say, that obviously was not it. The youth's eyes went wide, and his face turned a rosy hue.

"What happened between you is none of my business." She spoke softly. Plake was in the adjacent room and, in all likelihood, trying to listen in. "Your father wanted me to tell you that your family misses you, and he hopes you'll come home when you are able."

Arthur, who had been eying the floor, now looked up at her sheepishly. "You didn't...didn't tell him I joined the Renegades ...did you?"

Lilac shook her head, and Arthur let out a sigh of relief. After a few seconds, he asked, "How did he look? My father, I mean."

"He looked well, considering the circumstances." She paused before adding, "He wanted me to tell you something else too. He said it wasn't your fault."

Arthur's gaze returned to the ground, his lips pursed together in a grimace. Deciding it was time to take her leave, Lilac patted his shoulder and walked away.

She didn't know where she was going, but anywhere was

better than back in the Renegade Room with Plake. If she were lucky, she might run into Dylan, who was sure to know more about what was happening than she would learn on her own. She also kept an eye out for Opal. Though it made her stomach hurt to think of it, she needed to learn exactly how Othello had died.

In the meantime, however, she was content to walk alone, sorting through the many thoughts and emotions vying for dominance.

Drekk't dismissed his two lieutenants, cutting Jer'malz off mid-sentence. They hurried from the tent, not bothering to mask their eagerness to leave. Drekk't didn't blame them. They had had a lot of bad news to deliver, not the least of which was the goblins' death toll.

After Ay'goar and Jer'malz were gone, he sat at the edge of his bed. Tired though he was, he would not succumb to the lure of slumber. Neither did he start formulating a new strategy for dealing with Fort Valor, which would have been the prudent thing to do.

Instead, Drekk't relived the battle against Saerylton Crystalus in his mind.

He had underestimated the human commander—that much was certain. And yet, as he watched the battle play, stroke by stroke, Drekk't couldn't find a single error on his part. His swordplay had been near flawless, and he had avoided the enchanted blade up until the very end.

But Colt's performance had been perfect.

Impossibly perfect.

Never had Drekk't faced off against an opponent so nimble and so swift. He prided himself on his skill with a sword. He had never been bested in one-on-one combat, which was a key factor in his advancement to the rank of general. Yet Colt had disarmed him despite his best efforts. Had it not been for the sudden intervention of his subordinates, he would be dead.

The human commander had made a fool of him...again.

Drekk't spotted movement out of the corner of his eye and jumped to his feet. Planting his hands on his hips—ignoring the flare of pain in his injured leg—he glared at the goblin in the shadows.

"I gave the order not to be disturbed," he snarled. When the newcomer stepped forward and narrowed his eyes threateningly, Drekk't recognized the shaman.

"My apologies, Master Ay'sek. Those clothes...I mistook you for a common fighter."

Ay'sek said nothing, which Drekk't took for a good sign. "A silent shaman casts no spells" was an old T'Ruellian proverb.

Drekk't suddenly recalled the trick he had played in not telling Ay'sek the goblin army had relocated to Fort Valor. Alone with the shaman, Drekk't felt more than a little vulnerable. The Chosen of the Chosen had a propensity for getting away with murder. While Ay'sek didn't strike Drekk't as a usurper, every temper had its limits.

Then he noticed the shaman's empty hands.

"Where is *Peerma'rek*?" Flustered though he was, Drekk't was careful not to keep his tone civil.

In an uncharacteristically calm voice, Ay'sek told of his unsuccessful scrimmage with the humans and how he had had to abandon his mission in order to save his life. The shaman made no excuses for his failure. Neither did he sound particularly upset over what had happened.

"Let me see if I understand you," Drekk't said. "Not only have the remnants of the human armies regrouped and retreated to the safety of the fort, but they took the staff *with* them?"

Ay'sek shrugged. "Unless one of your thousands of soldiers managed to stop the woman and her friends, then, yes, *Peerma'rek* is probably within the fort."

"And what would you have me tell our Emperor?"

"Tell him the truth," Ay'sek replied mildly. "Tell him you had me wait rather than take back the staff days ago so that you could manipulate the human armies...a tactic that ultimately backfired."

Drekk't was at a loss for words. Were it anyone other than a shaman standing before him, he would have killed the fool. As it was, there were two reasons why he stayed his hand: he didn't want to give the Emperor another reason to punish him, and he still needed Ay'sek.

"No matter." Drekk't unclenched his fists, revealing deep impressions his fingernails had left on his palms. "We know where the staff is, and now that you're back, we can use *vuudu* to breach the fortress."

An attack at dawn might end the stalemate once and for all.

Then again, an ill-planned operation could end up doing more harm than good. Waiting might give the enemy time to get organized, but in the end, little would change in one day's time.

"It is good to have you back, Master Ay'sek," Drekk't lied. "With Upsinous on our side…and his magic at your fingertips…we cannot lose."

Apparently deciding that their conversation was at an end, Ay'sek removed himself from the tent.

The Chosen of the Chosen would always be headaches for the generals they served, Drekk't decided. Perhaps that was the Emperor's intention. The shamans certainly did their part to keep the high-ranking veterans from aspiring too high.

But who, he wondered, kept the shamans in check?

Opal pushed her way past the solitary Knight barring her way. The man made a half-hearted attempt to grab her, but she squirmed out of his grasp and barged into the infirmary.

Once inside, her senses were assailed by stimuli—people rushing about in a small space, the stench of blood, the hair-raising cries of the wounded. Between the injured and those caring for them, the room was crowded beyond measure.

Her gaze took in the various people only long enough to identify them and dismiss them until she found whom she was seeking. Then she was pressing her way over to Sister Aric and Sir Dylan.

The priestess's eyes were closed, and she spoke so softly Opal couldn't understand what she was saying. Across from them, on the other side of the bed, Dylan looked up briefly and greeted her with a grim smile.

Finally, reluctantly, Opal looked down at Colt. The young Knight writhed beneath the healer's hands. His moans could be heard even above the shrill outbursts of the other patients. Opal took his hand in hers and pressed her lips against it. When Colt's wandering, bloodshot eyes landed on hers, there was no recognition in them.

"You can't die. Fight it, Colt," she pleaded. "Please don't leave me…"

Colt ceased his struggling suddenly, and Opal feared the man was gone. She noted the rising and falling of his chest, however, and almost wept for joy.

"The goddess has granted him respite," Sister Aric said. "He has fallen into a deep slumber."

"Will he live?" Opal asked, grabbing the healer by her sleeve.

Undaunted, Aric tended the gaping wound in Colt's abdomen. "Only the gods can say."

"What can I do?"

Aric paused briefly, glanced at Opal, and said, "You can pray."

The words echoed in Opal's mind for several minutes as she stared down at her dying friend. She couldn't remember the last time she had earnestly addressed the gods. She supposed that she ought to pray to Mystel, the Healing Goddess, but it felt strange to talk to a deity she knew so little about.

Once, when Nisson had taken ill, she had beseeched Cressela, the patron goddess of birds and beasts, to cure the horse's ailment. But that was the extent of her relationship with the gods. She spoke to them only when she needed something.

I know that I have no right to ask anything of you, let alone a miracle, she told Mystel. Never mind that he's the only friend I have in the world these days.

Never mind that I nearly died rescuing him from the goblin war camp.

Never mind that Cholk is dead.

And never mind that I just watched Othello take his last breath.

Don't do it for my sake, Mystel. Do it for Colt.

Hot tears rolled down her cheeks. She squeezed Colt's hand, wishing she could somehow infuse the Knight with her strength. She remained by his side as Aric used needle and thread to stitch his wounds shut. She stayed there even after the healer had moved on, waiting for Colt's eyes to open or any other sign his health was improving.

At some point, Dylan left too, but Opal didn't budge. She had nothing more to say to Mystel—or any other god for that matter—and so remained silent. And the gods, in return, kept their silence as well.

If I had the *vuudu* staff, I could make your own miracles, she thought.

Passage XII

Stannel stared into the hollow eyes of the skull, which, along with the rest of the staff, lay atop his desk.

Sir Dylan Torc had just finished explaining the origin and the capabilities of the *vuudu* staff—or at least what Colt had told him of them. Now the six men inside the cramped office stood in uneasy silence, pondering the hideous rod.

Stannel knew the staff was capable of doing all Dylan had said and probably much more. Just as the mace that hung from his belt filled Stannel with a comforting warmth, the skull-topped staff seemed to emanate a chill that made the hairs on his arms and neck tingle.

Glancing up from the macabre weapon, he took measure of those assembled around him. Klye Tristan and Dominic Horcalus wore grim expressions. Not only had they lost a comrade tonight, but also the pirates had run off.

Petton had said nothing in reply to Klye's news. Stannel appreciated the lieutenant's uncharacteristic discretion, but he assumed Petton hadn't jumped at the chance to say, "I told you so," only because Petton—as well as the rest of them—had far bigger concerns at the moment.

Or perhaps the man was simply too exhausted to engage in verbal combat with Klye. Gaelor Petton had led the fort's infantry into the thick of battle, and as second-in-command, Petton would not soon run out of things to do around the fort.

Next to Petton stood a man of whom Stannel had heard, though the two had never met. Over the years, Ruford Berwyn, Rydah's Captain of the Guard, had earned so much respect from the Knights of Superius that many within the Knighthood considered him an equal, which was no small thing. High Commander Walden had often praised Ruford.

Thinking of Bryant Walden, Stannel sent up a silent prayer for the high commander, Lord Magnes Minus, and everyone else who had perished in the massacre that had wiped Capricon's capital off the map.

That Ruford had survived the Fall of Rydah and the trials that followed was a credit to the hulking guardsman's prowess and wit. And the fact that he and his men had joined Colt's campaign made them all heroes by Stannel's estimation.

Ruford had lost all but eleven of his soldiers on the battlefield outside the fort. Of the Knights who had followed Colt from Hylan, only fifteen remained. By Dylan's estimation, more than half of Colt's army was dead, including most of the civilians and militiamen of Hylan.

Stannel had seen the Hylaners in action—those men and women who wore little or no armor and carried spears, staves, and other odd implements capable of inflicting damage. Whatever the Hylaners lacked in skill, they had made up for in sheer mettle. They had fought as devotedly as any Knight, and their deaths were all the more honorable for the freely given gifts of their lives.

In addition to those losses, nineteen Knights from the fort were unaccounted for, and many of those who had survived long enough to make it to the infirmary weren't likely to live much longer.

That included Colt.

Stannel couldn't suppress a surge of remorse when thinking of all the deaths. Yes, he was saddened by thought that all those men and women would never laugh with their loved ones again, but more than that, he was angered by the senselessness of it all.

They would not know how many goblins had died until sunrise, but even if every human had killed five T'Ruellians—or even ten—they would have hardly put a dent in the goblins' numbers.

"So what are we going to do?"

It was Ruford who broke the silence. Thick arms crossed in front of his broad chest, the Captain of the Guard looked at each of his allies in turn.

No one had had the luxury of cleaning up before the meeting, but Ruford was undeniably the filthiest of them all. His formerly white pantaloons were covered with stains from dirt, sweat, and gore. The rest of his outfit was equally tarnished, as were his exposed hands and face. Were it not for the billowing red-brown mustache that stretched across Ruford's upper lip, Stannel might have mistaken the dried goblin blood on his face for a short black beard.

"What are we going to do?" Petton echoed. "What *can* we do? We will hole up behind our walls and pray to the gods that the goblins aren't in too much of a hurry to finish what they started."

"They have surrounded the fort again," Klye said off-handedly. "Nothing has changed."

"But we have more troops," Horcalus said.

Petton laughed mirthlessly. "For all of the good that will do us."

Ruford gave Petton a fierce look. "I didn't come all the way here to give up."

"Who said anything about giving up?" Petton asked. "Running is not even a possibility, and so we shall continue to defend ourselves. Our deaths will be as honorable and no less tragic than the Knights who were slain here during the Ogre War."

Stannel said nothing for the moment. Petton's comment about the Ogre War had reminded him of something. More than sixty years ago, Toemis Blisnes, a former Knight of Superius had fled Fort Faith and certain death at the ogres' hands.

Toemis had recently returned to the fortress, bringing with him his granddaughter Zusha and the deranged notion that his cowardice those many decades ago had cursed his bloodline. The old man had returned to the fort expecting to find it empty. When that proved not to be the case, he had used a hidden passageway to flee the fortress unnoticed so that he could kill Zusha and himself on Wizard's Mountain.

"There is a way out," Stannel said quietly, "if we wish to flee."

The others listened as he spoke of the route that led from inside the castle to a dried-up riverbed a mile or more to the west. Some—like Petton and Klye—had known of the passageway's existence, but it was news to Dylan and Ruford.

"But where would we go?" Petton asked, posing the question at no one in particular. "The nearest bastion is Fort Miloásterôn, and that's on the other side of the Rocky Crags."

"What about Steppt?" Stannel asked.

"We would never make it," Ruford said. "Even if the goblins didn't find us, the winter snows would."

"Well, if we are going to fight, we must find an advantage." Klye stepped up to the desk and pointed at the *vuudu* staff. "Maybe we can figure out how to use this…fight fire with fire and all that."

No one said anything at first. They all looked upon the foul talisman once more, lost in their own thoughts.

At last Petton said, "Be my guest, Renegade. With the midge gone, you're the only one crazy enough to want to touch it."

Klye glared at the lieutenant.

"This rod may, in fact, hold the power to decimate our foes," Stannel told Klye, "but I warn you, the god who enchanted it will demand a price. Would you, Klye Tristan, be beholden to the deity responsible for creating the goblin race?"

Klye regarded Stannel thoughtfully for a moment before replying. "I don't believe in the gods."

"Be that as it may, please believe *me* when I say you could do more harm than good if you tinker with things beyond your ken. But," he added, addressing the group now, "I am not the one who stands in the way of any who would take the staff. Saerylton Crystalus is the rightful owner. Moreover, I am no longer responsible for decisions concerning the defense of this fortress."

Petton's body jerked. "What do you mean by that?"

"I accepted command of this fortress with the understanding that I would relinquish authority back to Colt when he returned. And he has returned."

At first, there was only stunned silence. Klye was the first to speak up.

"So new Fort Valor is old Fort Faith again?"

"With all due respect, Commander Bismarc," Horcalus said, "it seems as though Commander Crystalus is unable to reclaim his title and duties at present."

"Then, if I am not mistaken, his second-in-command must lead in the meantime," Stannel replied.

Klye and Horcalus exchanged an anxious look. Dylan and Ruford looked very confused.

But no one was more visibly taken aback than Lieutenant Petton himself.

*   *   *

Drekk't found no solace in sleep that night. With the battle so fresh in his mind—a battle that had created new problems instead of solving old ones—the general tossed and turned throughout the early hours of the morning. In his dreams, he encountered Saerylton Crystalus once more, and each time the human commander defeated him with minimal effort.

He awoke with a start, his heart racing. With a curse on his lips, the general started to roll over, dismissing his premature waking as the result of yet another nightmare. But then he felt a shadow fall over him, a silhouette that was all the more sinister for the fact that the interior of his tent was pitch black.

Drekk't sprang out of bed and landed in a defensive crouch, a curved knife clutched in one hand. His first thought was that one or both of his lieutenants had decided to depose him. But when his keen eyes picked out the flowing black robe of the intruder, Drekk't changed his mind.

He was on the verge of lunging blade-first at Ay'sek when something that could only be called a presence washed over him. He knew instantly that the goblin in his tent was not Ay'sek.

Pure, unadulterated terror gripped his insides. The sensation was far more powerful than anything he had experienced, even in his nightmares.

A pair of glowing red eyes that smoldered like living coals levitated in the darkness. Drekk't could *feel* the intelligence in those eyes, a predatory awareness that seemed to reach all the way into Drekk't's soul.

The fiery stare stole Drekk't's momentum, stopping him in his tracks as effectively as any wall. The crescent-bladed knife fell to the ground with a dull thud. In the next instant, Drekk't was down on his knees, bowing low to the Emperor of T'Ruel.

"*N'Kirnost,*" he muttered deferentially.

The Emperor did not deign to reply. In those long seconds of silence, one million frantic thoughts flashed in Drekk't's mind. How much did the Emperor know? Had he come here to dole out instruction or punishment?

"Stand, General."

The Emperor's voice had a hollow quality to it, which was likely an effect of the spell that allowed him to interact with the general as though they were truly in the same room. At least,

Drekk't *hoped* the Emperor was still in T'Ruel. It was impossible to know for sure.

Not that it mattered whether the Emperor was truly there or not. As the most powerful of the Chosen of the Chosen, the Emperor of T'Ruel could likely kill from afar just as easily as up close.

Drekk't scrambled to his feet, keeping his eyes cast downward.

"I have taken the liberty of summoning Master Ay'sek so I will not have to repeat myself." The Emperor's low voice reverberated throughout the tent and inside Drekk't's very bones. "While we wait, tell me how your campaign fares."

Choosing his words carefully, Drekk't reported his army's recent militaristic operations. He did his best to present his recent failures in a positive light and tried to sidestep the issue of *Peerma'rek* altogether. He doubted the Emperor would forget about it, but perhaps he could delay long enough for Ay'sek to arrive and share in the blame.

"Where is *Peerma'rek* now?" the Emperor asked.

Or perhaps not...

"*N'Kirnost*," Drekk't began, struggling to find the best euphemism for "lost."

Drekk't heard the swish of robes as Ay'sek entered the tent. The shaman took no more than three steps into the pavilion before performing the proper show of veneration, imitating the prostrate bow Drekk't had executed earlier. As before, the Emperor told his subject to rise, which Ay'sek did with alacrity.

Under other circumstances, Drekk't might have enjoyed watching the shaman squirm in the presence of someone greater. But the general knew it was only a matter of time before those blazing orbs turned back to him.

"We were just discussing the status of *Peerma'rek*," the disembodied voice of the Emperor declared. "Since neither of you have it, I can only conclude you have not yet recovered it."

Neither goblin replied.

"What happened?"

Despite the lump in his throat, Drekk't forced himself to speak. As campaign general, he was responsible for his subordinates' actions—and he did count Ay'sek as a subordinate, even if the shaman didn't. More than that, he didn't want to give Ay'sek the chance to twist the story in his favor, making Drekk't out to be a bigger fool than was necessary.

When he finished, Drekk't held his breath and waited for the Emperor to react. He knew he deserved death. Not only had he lost *Peerma'rek* in the first place, but he had let it slip through his fingers again.

"I have come to impart important news," the Emperor said. "This war is over."

Drekk't jerked upright, staring at the shrouded form of his ruler with unbridled astonishment. "*N'Kirnost*, you cannot mean—!"

"Silence!"

The single word erupted from the shadow being with such power that Drekk't brought his hands up to his ears, wincing in pain.

"For a campaign general, you know very little of what has been happening while you waste your time at this little fort.

"The Western Army has taken up residence in a place called North Port. Even as you besiege Fort Valor, your compatriots are besieged by humans from the three fortresses west of the mountains."

All of this came as quite a surprise to Drekk't. The last he had heard of his brothers in the Western Army was that they were secretly entrenched in the sewers of Port Town. How—or why—they had traded Port Town for North Port was a mystery to him. And what of the ships the Emperor had promised to end to support the Western Army?

"Give me more time, *n'Kirnost*!" he begged. "I have enough troops to compensate for however many warriors the Western Army has lost. We will destroy Fort Valor at once and press on to North Port, scattering the Knights that surround the conquered city. I swear by—"

"You will swear nothing, General, because unlike me, you cannot see the bigger picture."

"Yes, *n'Kirnost*."

"Even if you could, in fact, conquer Capricon without reinforcements from T'Ruel, where would you go from there, General?

"The conquest of this island was to be a prelude for the invasion of Continae. When the Knights and Renegades had weakened each other sufficiently, we would have marched in and destroyed them both. T'slect's impudence foiled our ruse. Our plans were rushed. Rather than using the Renegade War to drive a wedge between the two human factions, the arrival of a mutual enemy has forced them back together.

"Our first forays into Continae have proven that while the Renegade War has resulted in social upheaval, the humans are still capable of putting up a strong resistance. Instead of sacking towns crippled by civil war, our warships are welcomed by human armies that remain strong and wary."

Drekk't wondered how many warships had landed on the vast coast of Continae. If the goblin navy retreated to Capricon, strengthening the two T'Ruellian armies here...

Couldn't the Emperor see all was not lost? How could the Emperor speak so calmly about calling off the war?

As though answering Drekk't's unspoken thoughts, the Emperor said, "Do not think to question me, General. We T'Ruellians have never waged a war where victory is not assured. And yours is not the only army fighting on foreign soil. Yours is not the only war T'Ruel wages."

"Yes, *n'Kirnost*," Drekk't hissed. "So...we are to retreat?"

The words tasted worse than poison. The thought of letting Colt and his fellow humans win made him dizzy.

"No."

Drekk't wasn't sure he had heard correctly and looked to Ay'sek for an explanation. But the shaman looked as confused as Drekk't was.

"There is still the matter of *Peerma'rek*," the Emperor added. "I would not lose so great a treasure to the humans."

"Yes, *n'Kirnost*. Of course, *n'Kirnost*." A glimmer of hope blossomed in Drekk't's mind.

"You and your army will retrieve the staff, and then you will return to T'Ruel for reassignment."

"Yes, *n'Kirnost*," Drekk't and Ay'sek replied together.

Looking at both goblins in turn, the Emperor added. "Your next failure will cost you both your lives."

Drekk't was about to utter the obligatory "Yes, *n'Kirnost*" when the inside of the tent brightened to a dull gray color. The Emperor was gone, and in his absence, the light of early morning penetrated the flimsy material of the tent.

For the first time since he had awoken, Drekk't was conscious of the gooseflesh on his bare arms and chest. When Ay'sek exited the tent—which he did silently—Drekk't saw it was snowing outside.

The general crawled back into his bed, even though he knew he wouldn't fall back asleep. There was far too much to think about. He wasn't happy about abandoning Capricon, but he was determined to make the most of the time he had left there.

He would reclaim *Peerma'rek* for the Emperor, and he would leave the island, never to return.

But not before killing Colt and as many of his friends as possible.

Part 3

Passage I

Delincas encountered a number of surprised expressions as he descended into the bowels of Castle Borrom.

Very few of the Knights recognized him, he suspected. His attire denoted him as someone of importance—if not a nobleman, then a gentleman at least. And the dungeons were no place for a gentleman.

Those who did know him—or, rather, knew *of* him—were probably even more curious about his presence there. The name Delincas Theta was attached to many a rumor, but it was common knowledge that he was one of King Edward's advisors, the only one who wasn't of noble birth.

Some said he wasn't even a native to Superius, but that wasn't true. Others claimed the king had made him an ambassador because they had been childhood friends. That was pure fallacy.

The juiciest gossip labeled him a wizard. And this was true.

When he reached the gaoler's station at the base of the long, winding staircase, Delincas asked, "Have you a midge in your keeping?"

The gaoler opened his mouth but said nothing at first. His expression suggested he recognized Delincas, and the words he spoke proved it.

"Ambassador Theta!" he greeted, bobbing his head in a quick bow.

Delincas smiled amicably and waited for the dungeon-keeper to answer his question, though the man said no more. His attention seemed fully captivated by the mere sight of his unexpected visitor.

Delincas cleared his throat. "The midge?" he prompted.

The gaoler jerked suddenly. "Oh. Right. Him. Yeah, the Knights brought him in 'bout a week ago."

"May I read the arrest report?" Delincas asked.

The man's face twisted in an odd manner. "Report? There was no report, Ambassador Theta. But word has it the imp was tryin' to get into the palace to murder the king. He was babblin' about an invasion. Wouldn't be surprised if he was workin' for the Renegades."

Delincas swallowed a sour taste in his mouth. As a spell-caster, he had much more respect for the midge as a race than most humans did. The people of Superius—and the rest of Continae, for that mattered—harbored a great deal of mistrust toward wizards, which made them predisposed to dislike the capricious midge, all of whom were spell-casters.

Delincas could empathize with the midge for the prejudice they suffered on a daily basis. While he could discard his telltale robe and walk incognito among the general populace, a midge could never separate himself from his magic.

"Were his captors planning on scheduling a trial for the prisoner?" Delincas asked, endeavoring to keep his voice level.

"Uh," the gaoler stammered. "I don't know. You'd have to ask them, I guess."

"I intend to," Delincas replied, evoking a grimace from the dungeon-keeper. "In the meantime, I should like to examine the accoutrements of our would-be assassin."

The gaoler's brow furrowed in confusion.

"May I see his stuff?" Delincas translated and sighed.

"Oh, sure," said the man behind the counter. "Just a moment."

The gaoler hurried away, exiting through the doorway behind him. Delincas made a mental note to ask King Edward about the prerequisites for gaining employment in the dungeons. True Knights of Superius couldn't be spared for every little chore—especially at a time when rebellion was spreading across the realm—but by Delincas's estimation, there was no reason to scrape the bottom of the barrel just yet.

As he waited for the gaoler's return, he peered through a gate of old, rusty bars. He had never before entered the dungeons proper and was a bit unnerved at the prospect. While King Edward had made use of his expertise in matters arcane in the past, including handling prisoners who could cast spells, the captives had always been brought to him, and not the other way around.

By personally inquiring about the midge, Delincas knew he was lending credence to the rumors that he himself was a wizard, but that could not be helped. The king was too busy to embark on what could very well end up being a fool's errand. The Renegades were growing bolder by the day, and there were reports of mysterious naval attacks along the coast of West Cape.

To top it off, Prince Eliot, Edward's only son, was missing.

Delincas was doing his best to help the king—to help all of Continae—in small ways, but when it came to his magic, small feats were all he could do, unless he wanted to compromise his secret agenda.

Some of the more open-minded citizens might welcome the idea of a wizard serving on the King of Superius's staff, but neither Edward nor Delincas believed the majority would feel that way. For the meantime, Delincas was forced to keep a low profile.

With so much going wrong all at once, he hadn't bothered to tell the king about the midge captive. It might all end up being nothing. And yet, a single word in a Knight's retelling of the little wizard's capture—overheard by sheer chance—had given him pause.

Goblins...

Delincas snapped back to the present at the gaoler's return. The man carried a deep burlap sack in one hand and what appeared to be a straw hat in the other. He held the sack out in front of him, his hold tenuous. He then plopped both hat and pack on the countertop and wiped his grubby hands on his pants.

"There you go, Ambassador."

Ignoring the unusual hat, Delincas reached into the sack. The gaoler took a big step back.

The first thing he discovered was a short staff crafted of a reddish wood and capped with a gleaming blue jewel. He could feel magic emanating from the gem. It was invested with strong spells, though he didn't know which ones.

He withdrew a belt next, followed by a small knife, and a number of pouches and vials. The gaoler took another step back when Delincas started examining the contents of the pouches. Some of the spell components he recognized; others, he did not. From the ingredients he did know—ash, bitzmah root, and shards of obsidian—he deduced the midge in question was a caster of black magic, the most destructive kind of magic.

But he wasn't prepared to write the midge off as an assassin based on that fact. Not every black-robe was a villain, and in the case of midge—who were known to choose their affiliation as impulsively as they did everything else—there was little difference in the temperaments of white-, red-, and black-robes.

He found several scrolls rolled up inside a leather satchel. He was curious about the spells written upon them but didn't look too closely. The gaoler was still watching him warily. He was about to return the scrolls to satchel when his gaze caught some writing that was decidedly not magical in nature.

Delincas unfolded the paper, his eyes quickly scanning its contents.

> *To His Majesty, the King of Superius:*
>
> *Please forgive the unorthodox delivery of this letter, but given the circumstances, adherence to protocol and tradition was impossible. The midge before you, Noel, is a trustworthy ally, having proven himself a loyal and just subject of the Crown of Superius.*
>
> *Let it be known that a foreign nation has invaded the island province of Capricon. As I write this, Fort Valor lies in ruin. I have taken refuge at Fort Faith. We know nothing of the state of the rest of the island, but we fear the worst.*
>
> *The invaders are believed to be goblins, and all evidence leads toward a single conclusion—the goblins intend to conquer Capricon. It is my belief that Superius and the other kingdoms of the Continent United are also in peril. I write this in hopes that you will not be caught unawares.*
>
> *And it is with great sorrow that I report the following news: a goblin shaman came to Capricon masquerading as your son. His mag-*

*ic was ultimately foiled, but we do not know
the location of Prince Eliot Borrom. We pray
that he is safe with you, though the goblins
claim to have taken him captive.*

*Rest assured that we, the defenders of
Capricon, will do all we can to repel the
goblin forces from the island.*

*Yours in loyalty and service,
Commander Stannel Caelan Bismarc*

Gooseflesh rose beneath his coat and doublet. Carefully, he folded the parchment and tucked it in his vest pocket. He glanced up at the gaoler, careful to keep his expression neutral.

"I will see the midge now."

"Uh...yeah...of course...but he's in no condition to talk...if you know what I mean."

Delincas felt his face flush, and he nearly lost control of his temper. He took some solace in the fact that the gaoler was not referring to torture. The Knights of Superius had devised another method for rendering wizards powerless...

"Take me to him," Delincas ordered.

The gaoler shrugged, lifted a section of the counter and positioned himself between Delincas and the barred gate. He removed a ring of keys from his wide belt and fitted the correct one into the hole. With a great shove, the door creaked noisily open.

"Follow me, Ambassador."

Delincas shadowed the man in silence. Strategically placed torches illuminated stone walls covered in mold and cobwebs. As they neared the cells, offensive odors assaulted his nostrils, but the wizard paid neither them nor the unruly prisoners any mind. His thoughts awhirl, Delincas desperately tried to fit the pieces of the puzzle together.

Unbeknownst to the general populace, Delincas Theta was not the only magus in the service of Superius. Even as Delincas Theta served as Superius's ambassador to the Assembly of Magic, another wizard lent his skills to the Knights.

Master Shek Irenistan, a red-robe, currently resided at Fort Miloásterôn in Capricon. The wizard had magically contacted

Delincas more than three weeks ago to report the island was under siege by an unknown menace. Shek had connected with him again a week later, identifying the invaders as goblins.

King Edward had believed the supposed goblins were actually Renegades in disguise, but now Delincas had discovered proof to the contrary...unless the midge was, in fact, a rebel.

When they finally reached the midge's cell, Delincas was greeted by a sad sight. Noel was sitting hunched in one corner. His bright blue eyes stared up at the ceiling. His head swayed slowly from side to side, drool trailing down his chin.

"Noel," Delincas said suddenly, startling the gaoler. "Noel!"

At the second, louder call, the midge's head dropped suddenly, his chin coming to rest against his chest. Slowly, unsteadily, Noel raised his head so that he was staring directly at his visitors. The midge blinked a few times and gurgled, "Avooroo-rooroo."

"See," the gaoler said. "He ain't gonna make any sense. Not that the little imps ever make sense! We make sure he stays good an' drugged at all times. Wouldn't want him to, you know, spout any hocus pocus..."

As though suddenly remembering whom he was speaking to, the gaoler trailed off.

"Let him out."

The gaoler's eyes went wide. A tentative smile tugged at the man's lips, as though he thought Delincas was joking. Then he frowned.

"Sorry, Ambassador, but I can't do that, not unless you got an official order from the Knights' Lord Commander or King Edward hisself."

Delincas opened his mouth to argue but changed his mind. He knew he would get nowhere trying to reason with the dungeon-keeper. The Knights of Superius were known for their strict protocol, and apparently the gaoler's current discomfort was nothing compared to the prospect of displeasing the Lord Commander.

"Very well," Delincas said, turning away from the man and starting back the way they had come. "Keep the midge's possessions on the counter. I shan't be long."

He cast Noel one last pitying look before rushing past the rows of cells and back up the stairs to the surface. He didn't care that he easily outpaced the confused gaoler. He had far greater things to worry about just then.

If King Edward was wrong about Renegades being behind the attacks in Capricon and West Cape, then all of Continae was in terrible danger. As Delincas hurried through the palace, he prayed that the king was right in spite of this new evidence.

He'd rather see young Eliot Borrom in the hands of rebels than monsters.

Arthur was covered in blood, most of it his own. Goblin faces, distorted and howling, surrounded him on all sides. He swung a rusty hatchet in wide arcs to keep the fiends at bay. Although the goblins pressed in on him at every turn, his pitiful weapon never connected.

Now and then, he caught a glimpse of the other Renegades. Klye darted about the battlefield with uncanny agility. Horcalus's movements were measured and polished, sending fountains of black blood into the air. Lilac, Scout, Plake, and the pirates were there too. He even thought he saw Othello.

He shrieked when a pole-axe buried itself in his shoulder. His hatchet fell to the ground, along with most of his arm. He cried for help, hoping one of his friends would hear him over the din of clashing metal and hideous screams.

Rather than finish him off, the goblins taunted him, poking him with their blades, prolonging the kill. At last, one of the monsters hurled a trident at him. The three-pronged javelin homed in on his chest...

Arthur jerked awake. His forehead slick with perspiration, he spent the next few minutes drawing in great gulps of air. He looked around self-consciously, hoping he hadn't disturbed any of his roommates.

The Renegade Room would have served as a spacious dormitory for the five male Renegades, but they were no longer alone. Some of the men from Hylan and Rydah had taken up residence there. Of the newcomers, Arthur knew only Pillip Bezzrik, the owner of Hylan's general store, though the name Bly Copperton sounded familiar.

None of the Hylaners seemed to recognize him, for which he was grateful.

Arthur was also thankful Lilac was lodging elsewhere. He had never had much to say to the woman—to *any* women, for that matter—but now that she knew his secret, he was at a complete loss for words.

At first, he had been ashamed. But she hadn't looked at him like he was some monster. And, according to Lilac, his parents weren't angry either. He supposed he should thank her for bringing word from his family. Gods above, he hoped they were still all right.

Arthur lay on this back, staring up into the darkness. Snores and heavy breathing filled the room. He wondered how any of them could sleep soundly. The battle had exhausted him, but he couldn't close his eyes without seeing the goblins' vile faces.

It wasn't the first time he had been shaken up by a dream. This new one was decidedly preferable to the reoccurring nightmare that made him relive killing the neighbor boy over and over.

Still, he was embarrassed. Brave Dominic Horcalus would never have been bothered by something so childish as a nightmare. How Arthur wished he could be like the Knights of Superius—so fearless, so strong.

Someone stirred, and Arthur squinted into the darkness. He saw a shape sit up and recognized the silhouette as Klye's. The Renegade Leader ran a hand through his hair. Aside from that, the man just sat there. Arthur wondered if Klye had had a bad dream too.

Rather than lie back down, Klye rose and crept toward the door, nimbly stepping over the slumbering bodies in his path. Without looking back, the Renegade Leader disappeared into the hall.

Klye might have gone to answer nature's call, but Arthur had a feeling there was more to it than that. Klye had been tight-lipped ever since the battle. It could be the battle had shaken him up, but Arthur figured it had more to do with the casualties to his band than the goblins lurking beyond the safety of the fortress.

They had been ten when they first arrived at Fort Faith. Now there were but six Renegades left.

Though he had always found the pirates intimidating and unapproachable, he was sorry to see Pistol and Crooker go. And although he had never really talked with Othello, he already missed the forester. The forester had saved his life—all of their lives—on more than one occasion. The band felt incomplete without him.

In truth, they were lucky any of them had left the battlefield alive.

Arthur's insides clenched at the thought of facing the goblins again. The feeling didn't linger, however. He was still afraid of the goblins, afraid of dying, but the fear wasn't as debilitating as before.

He knew that when the time came, he would fight alongside his friends. If he died, he would make Horcalus proud and take as many of the monsters to the grave with him as he could.

Arthur rolled over onto his side and let out a deep breath. He only wished he could see his family one last time. Caitlin had had her eleventh birthday since he'd left. Would his little sister even recognize him?

"If I survive this, I'm going straight home," he promised. "I have to face what happened…and that it *wasn't* my fault."

A strange calm settle over him. Maybe it was the thought of seeing his family again. Maybe he had just needed to acknowledge that killing Llede had been an accident. Or perhaps the peace came from knowing that even if they all died tomorrow, he would be reunited with his friends in Paradise.

Eventually, Arthur's eyes drooped closed. When he opened them again, he was confronted with the light of morning. The dreams of war and goblins were a vague memory now, and somehow he knew he would never again see the bully Llede in his dreams again.

Passage II

Tiny snowflakes wandered down from the sky. At first there were only a few, but as the light of predawn colored the eastern sky a rosy hue, the wind picked up, and the flurries fell faster. To the west, great white clouds draped the mountaintops.

Drekk't could only pray that the snowstorm wouldn't blow down upon his army.

The frozen precipitation that landed among his soldiers melted upon contact with the ground, which was hard as granite and discolored by the blood of men and goblins alike. The soldiers' tents had been erected around the corpses of men and goblins, which lay where they had fallen.

If nothing else, Drekk't thought, the cold will keep the meat from rotting.

The ready supply of food was just about the only good to come out of yesterday's battle. He had lost hundreds of warriors. If a blizzard came down the mountains, he would lose more.

Already, his soldiers were growing sluggish from the chilly air. Drekk't could feel the cold seeping into his body like some intoxicant, slowing his blood and his thoughts. But not even a blizzard could have cooled the burning in his breast.

The Emperor's decree to abandon Capricon echoed mercilessly in his mind, molding his lips into a permanent frown. He was angry with the Emperor for having so little faith in him, and he was still livid over the fact Saerylton Crystalus had bested him in battle. Mostly, though, he was confused as to why he was questioning the Emperor's decision.

Why should I want to stay a moment longer than necessary? he wondered. The climate was not in the least hospitable, and he had no clear advantage over the enemy. Even the least of his underlings would see the wisdom in retreating, abandoning the entrenched Knights for easier prey.

Drekk't had always prided himself on being a brilliant strategist. He could shape a battlefield to his advantage in a matter of minutes, using his army's assets to rout his foes. A goblin's enemy was supposed to be a faceless thing—an obstacle, a victim, a meal. And yet, as he walked through the camp, he found himself studying the features of the dead humans, half hoping and half dreading that he would discover Colt among them.

Goblin warriors hurriedly saluted their general as he passed by, but Drekk't hardly heard their flattery. When one warrior prostrated himself before Drekk't and swore to personally deliver the midge's head to him, Drekk't was momentarily confused. Then he remembered the bounty his lieutenants had placed on the fort's resident spell-caster.

For a moment, Drekk't merely stared down at the warrior, whose promise seemed as empty as Drekk't soul that morning. Perhaps the goblin truly was determined to kill the midge. More likely, he was just trying to win the general's favor.

Drekk't brought his foot up in a quick jerk, catching the unprepared goblin under the chin and sending him sprawling on his back. Shock, followed quickly by rage, contorted the warrior's features. For a moment, Drekk't expected the goblin to attack him. He would have welcomed it.

Instead, the humbled warrior spat out a tooth and skulked away. Drekk't paid no heed to the stares and muttering he left in his wake. The more he thought about the peon who had dared block his path, the more he wished he would have slit his throat.

At last, he came upon a tent that rivaled its neighbors in size and quality. The surrounding tents gave this one a wide berth, and the barren ground—empty except for a couple of corpses—resembled a moat around a palace.

Drekk't paused but a moment before approaching the opening of the tent. There was no telling what fell incantations secured Ay'sek's dwelling. He very much wanted to barge in like Ay'sek and the Emperor had been intruding on him lately. But this small dose of revenge was not worth putting his life at risk.

Thanks to *vuudu*, Ay'sek would always have the upper hand, so long as he lived.

"Master Ay'sek," he called, carefully controlling the tenor

and the volume of his voice.

As he waited for a response, his breath streamed out of his mouth like smoke. He ignored the urge to shiver. Ay'sek would not find him trembling like a terrified virgin upon his doorstep!

He was on the verge of calling out again when the flaps of the tent curled back on their own. The interior of the tent was as dark as Upsinous's black heart. Gods-damned showoff, Drekk't thought.

As he crossed the threshold, Drekk't expelled a deep breath. As much as he loathed the shaman, he knew he needed him too. If he lost his temper even once, his entire plan would be forfeit.

A solitary candle atop a yellowed skull shed a little light inside of the tent. Drekk't stared into the vacant eyes of the candleholder and was reminded of *Peerma'rek*. There were other oddities strewn about the place, including metal tools of esoteric design and a small, empty cage that hung from the ceiling.

Ay'sek sat behind a crate that functioned as a table. Atop the crate lay a serrated knife and the entrails of an animal Drekk't couldn't identify. The air in the tent was rich with blood.

"Master Ay'sek," he said. "I pray the morning finds you well."

The shaman didn't bother to look up. His eyes were fixed on the bloody organs at his fingertips. Ay'sek extracted what might have been the creature's heart. He carved the thing in half, examining first one part and then the other, paying no mind to the red liquid dripping down his hands.

The impudence of the shaman—ignoring him like the invalids who serve because they cannot fight—had Drekk't reaching for his sword. But he checked himself before his hand reached the hilt.

He needed Ay'sek alive…for now.

The shaman discarded the heart halves, setting them aside with the rest of the gore. He fixed his attention on the red puddles that stained the top of the crate. Ay'sek then closed his eyes and dipped the index finger of his left hand into the viscera. He muttered unintelligible words that conveyed dark promises.

A shiver passed down Drekk't's spine.

As he chanted, Ay'sek ran his finger over the surface of the crate. The bloody smears became sharp angles. The angles became symbols. Drekk't recognized only the final rune, the goblin cipher for Upsinous and the emblem of T'Ruel.

When the shaman opened his eyes again, he glanced down at the mess he had made and nodded absently. There were myths about the earliest shamans having had the ability to divine the future. Could Ay'sek see the future? If so, what did the bloody shapes foretell?

Drekk't wanted to ask the shaman, but Ay'sek spoke first. "You have a plan for regaining the staff."

He nodded. "I have need of your help."

Drekk't silently dared the shaman to insult him, but his expression remained neutral. As the general shared his strategy, Ay'sek neither interrupted nor reacted negatively. At last, when Drekk't had finished, the shaman let out a sigh.

"It would be easier to bring the fort down on top of the humans. But," he quickly added, not giving Drekk't the chance to cut him off, "we would risk losing *Peerma'rek* in the process."

Drekk't waited.

"Very well," Ay'sek said at length. "I will aid you in any way I can."

Drekk't checked a sigh of relief. Having said all he needed to say, he turned to leave.

"This course will bring both good and bad to our cause," Ay'sek said when he reached the exit.

Drekk't did not turn around. He recalled the blood runes on the top of the crate and considered asking the shaman to elaborate. Yet somehow he knew Ay'sek would tell him no more.

Walked away from the shaman's tent, Drekk't's thoughts even more muddled than before. He fought to keep doubt at bay. In the end, he would have to trust Ay'sek's insight. After all, Ay'sek wouldn't engage in a course he knew to be futile.

Not when he had as much reason to fear the Emperor's wrath as Drekk't did.

The fortress was eerily quiet. With the arrival of Colt's army, the fort's population had nearly doubled, and yet the heavy silence made Klye feel like he was the only one there.

It was closer to dawn than sunset. He had slept only a few hours before waking up for no apparent reason. There were many things he needed to sort out, however, so instead of tossing and turning for the remainder of the night, he had decided to take a stroll through the corridors of Fort Valor.

Or was it called Fort Faith again?

Stannel's decision to hand his authority over to Petton had taken everyone by surprise. Klye had fully expected the lieu-tenant-turned-commander to banish him and the rest of the Renegades to the dungeons as his first order of business.

But Petton had made no changes as of yet. The Renegades were still allowed to bear arms and walk about freely. Petton had a lot on his mind right now, but at any moment, the order to relocate the Renegades to the dungeon might come. And there would be nothing Klye could do about it when it did.

Unless they used Toemis's secret passage to escape. Arthur knew where it was…

Klye dismissed the thought with a sigh. Running away would only prove what Petton had insisted all along. Besides, he didn't want to run from the law anymore. And Horcalus would never desert the Knights, not even if the fort were overrun with goblins.

He chuckled. Things had certainly gone from bad to worse. The original Fort Valor and Rydah were both destroyed. No one had any idea what was happening on the other side of the moun-tains, but Klye knew for a fact there had been goblins in Port Town's sewers.

He worried for his friends in Port Town—Father Elezar, Veldross the half-elf, and Leslie Beryl.

Why am I worrying about her? he scoffed. She's probably a hell of a lot better off than I am right now!

Ever since becoming a Renegade Leader, he had had to shoulder a lot of responsibility. His band had encountered many obstacles en route to Fort Faith. When Chester Ragellan had died, Klye had been assaulted by equal parts anger and sorrow, but his resolve hadn't wavered for long.

It was hard for him to accept Othello was gone now too. He half expected the stealthy forester to step out of the shadows and offer a silent greeting. Losing Othello made him feel helpless and confused. Of course, there was nothing he could have done for the archer.

Whenever Klye thought of Pistol and Crooker—imaging them someplace safe and comfortable, laughing at his expense—fire scoured his insides. He had trusted them, and they stabbed him in the back. He wanted to call them cowards, but Klye feared it was something else.

Maybe *he* had failed *them*.

Klye banished the idea at once. It wasn't his fault the sons of bitches had fled. He had done all he could to argue the pirates' case with the Knights. Probably, the two men had stuck with the Renegades as long as they had out of convenience. They were both wanted men, after all, and there was safety in numbers.

And yet, with Ragellan and Othello dead and the pirates gone, Klye couldn't help but feel that his ever-shrinking band was a direct reflection on his ability to lead.

Klye scolded himself for dwelling on things he couldn't change. The pirates were gone, and so was Othello. He should be focusing on the present. What could he do to resolve the current dilemma?

What difference does it make what I come with? Klye groused. Petton isn't going to listen to me. The Renegades will do exactly what they're told, or they'll end up in the dungeon. Hell, we'll probably end up there anyhow.

Klye's feet seemed to stop of their own volition outside the bedchamber of Saerylton Crystalus.

On the battlefield, he had seen Colt's wounds. It was a miracle that the young commander was still alive. The last he had heard, Colt was in the infirmary, being treated by Sister Aric.

Klye grabbed the doorknob and turned it slowly. He opened the door an inch and peeked in, expecting to find the room empty. It wasn't. The modest-sized apartment had two occupants. Someone was sleeping in the bed; another slept in the chair beside it.

Surprised to find Colt out of the infirmary already, Klye took it as a very good sign or a very bad one.

He entered the room as silently as a cat and stole up to the bed. Although the room was dark, Klye could discern the man's features. Colt's face was expressionless. He might have been dead, except for the slight rise and fall of the blankets over his chest. Maybe it was the light beard that covered his cheeks, but Colt looked much older than before he had left for Rydah.

Klye glanced over at the figure in the chair, already certain he knew who it was. His suspicions were confirmed as he took in the woman's long red hair and generous curves.

In sleep, Opal could have easily been mistaken for a proper lady—and not the loud-mouthed adventurer whom he and his band had taken hostage more than a month ago. Opal had yet to forgive the Renegades for how they had treated her—Klye personally had punched her in the face during a later encounter—and according to Lilac, Opal had never warmed up to her during their mission with Colt.

Despite their differences, Klye felt sorry for Opal. As far as he knew, Colt was her only friend at the fort these days.

A moan from Colt sent Klye back on his heels. The Knight's head rolled from side to side. His next groan crescendoed into a cry.

Opal jolted awake at the sound. She acknowledged Klye's presence with a scowl but didn't say anything. Leaning over Colt, she brought her hand up to the man's face. She spoke soothingly to the wounded Knight, stroking his cheek with the palm of her hand.

Klye considered leaving—probably, he should go fetch Sister Aric—but he couldn't bring himself to move.

Colt's eyes popped open, which made Opal flinch. She stopped speaking for a moment, staring hopefully into the man's eyes. A tear glistened its way down the side of her face.

Colt was silent as he looked around. When his eyes landed on Opal, he groaned again.

"Colt," Opal whispered. "You're all right now. You're safe."

"Opal," Colt said, or at least he tried to. The word had sounded like a croak, but Klye had seen the word on the Knight's lips.

"Shhh," Opal pleaded. "You need your rest, Colt. You need to—"

"No," Colt told her. "I can't...can't..."

Opal shushed him again, but Colt shook his head, either defying the woman or attempting to clear his head.

"I won't recover from this," Colt said.

Opal uttered the most pitiable sound Klye had ever heard.

Saerylton Crystalus had spent the night fighting the demons that preyed on his delirious mind. The demons often took the shape of goblins. He must have faced off against Drekk't a hundred times. Arrows pierced him. Spears impaled him.

But then, in an instant, the battle ended. A sensation that was both warm and cool enveloped him, evaporating his pain like dew in the morning sun. He found peace for a time, but after a while the demons began poking and prodding at the border of his sanctuary.

The hoard returned with a vengeance. Colt wondered how he would ever find the strength to face them again. He considered giving up and probably would have done so if he had not spotted a familiar face in the midst of his enemies.

Opal.

The creature dragging her by one foot was twice her height. In place of its head was the skull of the *vuudu* staff.

Colt could do nothing but watch as the abomination unsheathed a machete as long as a lance and swiftly, callously cut Opal in twain from shoulder to shank.

He heard himself scream. The sound came from far, far away. Then the scene began to drop away. He tried to focus on the skull-headed behemoth, but the image vanished suddenly, replaced by darkness.

He heard Opal's voice before he saw her face. He was no longer on the battlefield, but lying in a bed. He wondered how it could be real but didn't want to question it, lest she disappear.

"Colt," Opal whispered. "You're all right now. You're safe."

At the moment, his own safety was the furthest thing from his mind. Damn the goblins and their accursed staff—all that mattered was Opal was alive and well.

He tried to say her name but couldn't find his voice.

She shushed him. "You need your rest, Colt. You need to—"

"No, I can't...can't..."

With a clarity that caught him unawares, Colt realized the truth of things: he was dying. He had precious minutes left. There could be no more delay. If he didn't tell her he loved her now, he would never have another chance.

When she tried to quiet him a second time, he said, "I won't recover from this."

Opal let out a cry, and Colt saw tears glistening in her eyes.

It was then that Colt knew she loved him too.

It no longer mattered whether she loved him as a friend or as something more. It didn't matter whether she had a romantic interest in someone else. He and she would never live happily ever after as man and wife.

A deep sadness washed over him. However, it left as quickly as it came. His life was forfeit, freely given to a great cause. But Opal would live.

"Opal," he said, his lips stretched in a smile. "I'm so glad…"

Opal's tears were falling freely now. She dropped her head onto Colt's chest and cried, "You can't leave me, Colt. Please don't leave me!"

Embarrassed for intruding upon the intimate scene, Klye wanted to walk away, but he couldn't. Colt's eyes had fixed upon some distant spot. The man no longer spoke, no longer made any sound.

Beneath Opal's sobbing form, Colt's chest ceased its rise and fall.

"Nooooo…" Opal moaned. "Oh gods, no…"

Klye's own eyes welled up with tears. He had never watched a man die before, and for several long minutes, he could only stare at the body that had one housed the soul of Saerylton Crystalus.

Was there even such thing as a soul? he wondered. Was Colt already enjoying the bliss of some afterlife? Or was his essence just…gone?

Opal jumped to her feet, and her gaze met his. Klye was mortified. What could he say to comfort the woman? The awkward silence didn't last long.

"Why were you skulking around in here? Huh?" she demanded, grabbing hold of his collar and shaking him. "What did you *do* to him?"

Klye was too stunned to react. When Opal started pounding her fists against his chest, he snapped out of his stupor and seizing her wrists. All at once, Opal stopped struggling and collapsed against him, weeping.

He wrapped his arms around her shuddering body and whispered words of comfort to her, including sentiments he couldn't bring himself to believe. And when he told her everything was going to be all right, he knew he was trying to reassure himself as well.

Passage III

Word of Saerylton Crystalus's death circulated quickly throughout the fortress. By noon, everyone had heard the sad news.

Lieutenant Gaelor Petton had been notified immediately.
Roused from an uneasy sleep, his brain still foggy, he had
followed Sir Silvercrown to Saerylton's room.

Sister Aric and Opal were already in the room. The healer
greeted them with a cheerless smile. Opal barely acknowledged
them; she sat in a chair beside the bed, her puffy red eyes betraying her sorrow.

Petton approached the bedside and gazed down at Saerylton.
Like everyone at the fort, he had known the commander for only
a short time. The two of them had had their differences, but
Petton respected the man's determination.

And he had secretly envied his unabashed optimism.

Lying in the bed, cold and still, Saerylton looked far too
young to have left this life behind. While there were many
youthful Knights in the Order, Saerylton Crystalus had been the
youngest commander in recent history.

The decision to promote Saerylton directly to commander
while Petton, a more experienced Knight, stayed a lieutenant had
struck Petton as unjust. Being stationed to far-flung Fort Faith
had felt like a punishment at the time.

He thought back to the times he had begrudged Saerylton his
rank and felt guilty. He was the Commander of Fort Faith now,
and it was a hollow promotion indeed.

With the goblin army camped outside the castle—and logis-
tical chaos inside—he almost envied Saerylton Crystalus, who
had died as every Knight hoped to die.

Petton remained in Saerylton's quarters only long enough to
say a prayer and offer his condolences to Opal, who didn't seem

to hear his words anyway.

Rather than attempt to gain another hour or two of sleep, he transitioned to his duties. Even something as routine as breakfast had become a complicated affair. The men and women of Colt's Army—as it was being called—had to be integrated into the equation. Portion sizes and dining schedules needed to be adjusted.

Petton threw himself at the problem. He could have assigned the task to one of his officers, but he welcomed the opportunity to escape his thoughts and sorrow for a short time.

He must have dozed off eventually because the next thing he knew he was being awakened by a gentle prodding. He straightened in his chair, his neck and back stiff from lying slumped over his desk. His face flushed as he eyed the man who had entered his office—formerly Saerylton's office—and found him asleep.

At a loss for what to say, Petton bade the man sit, which he did without comment.

"I trust you have heard the ill tidings?" Petton asked.

Stannel Bismarc nodded. "It was not unforeseen, but that makes it no less tragic. Moreover, Colt's passing is a detriment to morale. He was well-liked by all, and those who followed him from Hylan are hit all the harder by his death. Despair has settled over the fortress like a fog."

What do you want me to do about it? Petton snapped inwardly, but he said nothing. Why are you here? That's what he wanted to ask—nay, demand—of the strange Knight. Even before Stannel had confessed his unusual relationship with the Warriorlord, Petton had found the man peculiar.

"Even if Saerylton were still alive, I fear a cloud of misery would haunt this place," Petton said at last. "There is little hope as long as the goblins remain outside."

"What will you do?"

Petton chuckled humorlessly. "I will pray to any god who listens for our survival."

Stannel's lips pursed into a frown. "Perhaps you need pray to only god."

Petton realized his error at once. As a cleric of Pintor, Stannel surely took offense at any irreverence to the gods.

"Perhaps you are right," Petton replied. "But I have always believed the gods help those who help themselves."

"I too have come to that conclusion," Stannel said with a slight smile. "So...how are we to help ourselves?"

Petton paused, once again uncertain what to say. It seemed as though Stannel had a solution on the tip of his tongue and was simply toying with him.

"We have but two options...the same two options we had before the arrival of Colt's Army," Petton said. "We can either hole up in the fort, repelling the goblins' attacks as they come, even as we fight off starvation. Or we can follow the example of Fortunatus Miloásterôn at the Fall of Merekeep."

"Sir Miloásterôn and his Knights died to a man," Stannel pointed out.

Petton shrugged. Even the freshest squire had heard of Miloásterôn's Charge. Although the ogres had slaughtered General Miloásterôn's army, the man was considered a hero for facing certain death with uncompromised valor—so much a hero, in fact, that the grand fortress built to replace Merekeep was named in honor of him.

Petton didn't expect King Edward would erect a Fort Petton anytime soon, but he could think of worse things fates than following Miloásterôn's example. Toemis Blisnes's cowardice came to mind.

"I, for one, would rather die in battle—"

Petton was interrupted by the arrival of Sir Vesparis, who burst into the room without knocking.

"It's the goblins," the breathless Knight said. "It looks like they want to parley."

The general consensus was that it was a trap.

After all, neither side seemed to have anything to say to the other. And even if the language barrier weren't an issue, what was to stop the goblins from killing the messenger if he said something the goblins didn't want to hear?

Stannel had been the only one to volunteer to serve as the fort's emissary. Everyone else was against the idea, and yet everyone wanted to know what the goblins were up to. If it were truly a snare—and Stannel had to admit that was a real possibility—then they ought not waste one more life than was necessary. For that reason, Stannel chose to go alone.

Of course, he was not truly alone.

Covered in armor and wrapped in a thick coat, Stannel made his way to the pair of goblins who had positioned themselves halfway between their army and the fort. Even without the use of a spyglass, Stannel saw one goblin's dark robes flapping in the wind. Surely this was the shaman who had infiltrated Colt's Army.

Stannel had never seen a shaman in action, but he had heard accounts of the battle against T'slect, the *vuudu* priest who had impersonated Prince Eliot Borrom. For all Stannel knew, this *was* T'slect.

As he drew nearer, he was able to make out the thick plate armor that covered the adjacent goblin's torso and the open-faced helmet resting atop his head. A hefty, two-handed sword hung from the warrior's belt, along with several other blades of varying lengths.

Both goblin crossed their arms as they waited for him.

When Stannel finally reached the T'Ruellian envoys, he saluted, showing them he had no weapon in hand. The goblins did not return the gesture, did not respond in one way or another. Stannel was completely ignorant of the goblins' customs, military or otherwise. He had never heard of anyone parleying with goblins, for that matter.

"I am Sir Stannel Caelan Bismarc, Knight of Superius, Continae, and the Alliance. I have come as a representative of this fortress and, as such, am authorized to speak on behalf of its defenders."

He spoke loudly and clearly so that his words were not carried away on the wind. The goblins did not reply. Stannel wondered if they could understand him, though he suspected they could. Why would they have orchestrated a meeting if they had no way of communicating with humans?

The goblin on right—the one with the sword—began to speak, employing a language that sounded like gibberish. To his amazement, Stannel found he could understand the meaning behind the words, if not the words themselves. He supposed *vuudu* was responsible.

"I am General Drekk't," the warrior said. "I command the army that has surrounded your fortress. I have come to state our demands."

"We have not surrendered," Stannel replied. "On what grounds do you make your demands?"

The general's lips tugged upward into an ugly smile. "On the grounds that we"—he indicated the shaman with a nod—"could cause your fort to come crashing down on you. You are at our mercy, human. If you want to live, you will do as we say.

"And if you doubt that we are capable of following through with our threats, I suggest you speak with Saerylton Crystalus. Ask him about the city of Rydah."

Stannel's thoughts had not been on Rydah, but rather on Fort Valor. He had seen the wreckage of that castle with his own eyes. His pulse quicken when he realized the creature before him was the one responsible for the massacre of his men. General Drekk't had ordered the destruction of Rydah, Fort Valor, and possibly other cities.

The urge to attack Drekk't overcame Stannel. The suddenness and intensity of the desire caught him completely off guard, and he had to force himself to calm down. A single misstep would not only render his own life forfeit, but it would also kill the humans' chances of negotiating with the goblins.

This was not a personal matter. He had a duty to perform, and he would do it to the best of his ability—which was not to say he was ready to grovel for the goblins' mercy.

"If you had full advantage of the situation, you would have destroyed us already," Stannel stated. "Obviously, there is something you desire that you cannot gain by violence alone. Otherwise, we would not be here now. So what is it you want?"

The general glowered at him for a moment. Stannel feared that he had pushed Drekk't too far. If it came down to a battle, Stannel was confident he could hold his own against the general, but the shaman's presence worried him.

"You are correct in your assumption," Drekk't said finally. "You *do* have something we desire, something that was stolen from us. I can see by your expression you know what I speak of."

The *vuudu* staff, Stannel thought. How ironic that the only thing keeping the goblins from storming the fort was that evil, skull-topped rod—that the Knights' saving grace was an instrument of evil Upsinous.

Whoever had first quipped that the gods worked in mysterious ways was truly a master of understatement.

"What do you propose?" Stannel asked.

The general stepped closer. Stannel held his ground, his hand remaining near the grip of his mace.

"I would give you your lives in exchange for the staff. My army will leave your fortress unmolested once I have *Peerma'rek* in my hands," the general said.

Stannel studied Drekk't, searching the goblin's countenance for clues. If Drekk't was speaking truthfully, then Stannel had underestimated the *vuudu* staff's worth.

Oh, he doubted the goblins would simply turn and walk away once they got the staff. In all likelihood, the Knights would only be giving the T'Ruellians another weapon with which to attack them.

But while the arrangement sounded too good to be true, it also seemed too obvious to be a deception.

"If we gave you back the staff, there would be nothing to stop you from using it against us," Stannel said. "And even if you kept your promise, your army would only move to another battlefield in Capricon, and we would be forced to ride out against you."

Drekk't did not hesitate. "If you give us the staff, we will leave the island altogether, attacking no one along the way."

"Pardon my suspicion, General, but I find that difficult to believe."

The goblin's smile widened, revealing a row of pointy teeth. "What can I say or do to convince you?"

"Probably nothing," Stannel answered. "You have not proven yourself to be an honorable foe. By all accounts...and judging by the god you serve...you are far more likely to tell lies than the truth."

The general was visibly taken aback by the blunt statement. Again, Stannel worried that he had gone too far. The two warriors stared at each other for a long moment. Then Drekk't smiled again.

"You are right. We goblins do not put much stock in honor. You have no reason to believe anything I say. And yet you have little choice but to do as I have ordered. Anything less than absolute compliance will result in the annihilation of you, your comrades, and your castle."

Stannel did not flinch. "That outcome could cost you the staff."

"Perhaps," Drekk't said with a shrug. "And perhaps not. I came here to present a scenario that profited both sides...one that saved lives instead of squandered them. If you would rather die needlessly, so be it."

The fact that the general remained rooted in place—a mere three feet from Stannel—told him the conversation was not over.

"You have not offered a very compelling proposal," Stannel told Drekk't. "Perhaps if you sent half of your army away in a sign of good faith—"

Drekk't was already shaking his head. "So that you can divide my army and defeat us one piece at a time? I think not. However, there is another solution in which you might find merit. The Knights of Superius formerly used one-on-one combat to decide matters of justice..."

"A *duel*?"

"Yes, that's the word for it," Drekk't said. "I propose a duel. I, the commanding officer of this army, would do battle against Saerylton Crystalus, the leader of yours."

Although he heard the meaning of the goblin's words in his mind, the only thing his ears could understand was "Saerylton Crystalus." The name sounded queer coming from the lips of a goblin—sibilant and coarse. Drekk't's eyes seemed to light up as he spoke the name, reminding Stannel that the two would-be duelists were not strangers.

This is what he really wants, Stannel deduced. The *vuudu* staff wasn't the only treasure to escape Drekk't's clutches...

"Let the gods decide which side is the worthier," Drekk't announced. "If Commander Crystalus strikes me down, my armies will leave you in peace. If I slay your commander, you will relinquish the staff willingly, and my army will leave just the same.

"You say you cannot trust me, Knight, and you are right. Perhaps we will destroy your fort in either case...that is what you are thinking, yes? But I am willing to trust you...to trust that you will return the staff to me if I kill Saerylton Crystalus in combat.

"I am willing to put the outcome of this dispute in the hands of the gods. I have faith that Upsinous will give me victory. Do you put so little stock in your Warriorlord?"

Stannel felt the weight of his battle mace at his side. He wondered if the general had any idea just how much Stannel had come to depend on his god. At that moment, he wanted nothing more than to demonstrate how intimately he was connected with the Great Protector, but Stannel knew when he was being manipulated.

"What say you?" Drekk't pressed. "Are you prepared to put all of your precious principles to the test?"

Letting out a sigh that left a trail of steam behind, Stannel replied, "I will relay your challenge to the commander."

Drekk't's eyes narrowed. "I thought you said you were authorized to speak on behalf of the fort's defenders."

"And so I have," Stannel said, "but I cannot make a decision as heavy as this on my own."

The goblin general scoffed. "Very well, Knight. Deliver my challenge to Saerylton Crystalus, who hides behind the walls of his castle. Ask him if he has the courage to come out and face me again."

Stannel nodded, though he knew that order was impossible to obey. It was not his place to tell the goblins that Commander Crystalus was dead, however. In fact, volunteering such information would likely have proven to be a fatal mistake.

"I will have your answer at noon tomorrow," Drekk't called as Stannel turned to leave. "And make sure Colt brings the staff with him."

Stannel maintained a vigorous pace en route back to the fort. All the while, his conversation with the goblin general replayed in his mind. He had learned a lot about the enemy, but he wondered what good would come of it. The Knights had two things that the goblins wanted, and they couldn't deliver one of them.

And Stannel prayed to the Great Protector that Petton wouldn't surrender the other.

Passage IV

Ay'sek watched the Knight return to the fort. His gaze had not left Stannel the entire time. There was something uncanny about the humans' emissary, though Ay'sek couldn't say what. All he knew was the tingling sensation—like hundreds of tiny spiders crawling under his skin—had come and gone with Stannel.

And that feeling had intensified when Drekk't mentioned the gods.

Ay'sek was left to conclude that Stannel Caelan Bismarc was god-blessed. Throughout the centuries, T'Ruel's armies had encountered warrior priests from other cultures, though—followers of Celon-Tor, Javell, and even dreaded Darclon. He had never heard of a Knight of Superius wielding magic. Then again, he knew very little about the men of Continae.

They had no way of knowing how dangerous Stannel was, but Ay'sek was determined to find out.

"He sends out an underling," Drekk't muttered. "I should have expected as much."

Ay'sek glared at the general. "You revealed too much."

Drekk't responded with a glare of his own. "What do you mean?"

"Your desire to battle Saerylton Crystalus is what drives you. If that Knight is half as intelligent as I fear he is, now he knows this too."

Drekk't's countenance darkened. "Commander Crystalus leads our adversaries. By killing him, I will strike a major blow against the Knights and, at the same time, retrieve *Peerma'rek*."

Ay'sek glanced at Fort Faith. How easy it would be to topple the unimpressive redoubt. The goblin army was bereft of explosives, but Ay'sek's arsenal of spells would make short work of the small castle.

He had agreed to support Drekk't plan to regain *Peerma'rek*, though Ay'sek couldn't forget what the omens shown told him. Both good and bad would come of Drekk't's scheme. A victory and a failure. By Ay'sek's reasoning, they could not achieve both objectives.

He would ensure the staff's return—Drekk't's vengeance be damned!

Drekk't studied him, perhaps searching for signs of wavering. Ay'sek turned back to the general.

"I can think of another general who lost sight of the greater purpose because he was fixated on a handful of individuals," Ay'sek said. "He ended up going out of his way to track down some Renegades who probably knew far less than the obsessed general imagined."

Drekk't's jaw tightened, and he spat his next words. "I am *not* like T'slect. That fool had no business coming to this fort. I am a military strategist, not some spoiled prince. My judgment is sound!"

"If you had let me take the staff when I first infiltrated Crystalus's troops, we wouldn't be in this predicament," Ay'sek reminded him. "You wanted nothing to stop the commander from returning to this fort. You wanted him to deliver *Peerma'rek* to you—"

"Enough!"

If looks could kill, there would have been nothing left of Ay'sek to tempt even the hungriest of scavengers. After a series of heaving breaths, Drekk't calmed enough to say, "I erred in the past. That much is true. But you can find no fault in my plan. If I defeat Saerylton Crystalus in battle, we will take the staff... whether the Knights are prepared to give it up or not. And if I lose, you can use your *vuudu* to snatch it away from them."

"If the Knights agree to bring the prize out with them."

"They will," Drekk't said. "It's a condition of the match."

"What if they don't agree to your terms?"

"Then we will bring the fort down on top of them and sift through the rubble until we find *Peerma'rek*!"

Ay'sek was starting to think that that was the wiser course in any case, but he kept silent. Let Drekk't have his duel. If the general perished, Ay'sek would step in as commander of the army. Jer'malz and Ay'goar wouldn't dare stop him, a Chosen of the Chosen. Unlike Drekk't, the two lieutenants respected their betters.

It occurred to Ay'sek he could easily rid himself of Drekk't while the general was dueling. Something as simple as making him dizzy at a crucial moment would be a simple enough feat, thanks to his magic.

On second thought, the shaman wasn't so eager to be promoted. As long as Drekk't was alive, Ay'sek would be spared the brunt of the Emperor's ire.

"Do I still have your support?" Drekk't asked, his tone under tight rein.

Basking in the other's discomfort, Ay'sek paused, as though considering the matter carefully. Finally, he said, "Of course, General."

Drekk't gave a swift nod and departed for the camp. Ay'sek's smile widened as he watched him leave. *Finally, you are beginning to learn your place,* he thought.

The shaman lingered a moment longer before following Drekk't back toward the encampment. Drekk't wouldn't need his services again until tomorrow when the Knights either accepted or refused his challenge.

Or perhaps they wouldn't come out at all. Ay'sek doubted that the Knights were stupid enough to send out a messenger with a negative response. The rider wouldn't live to see sunset.

Drawing his cloak about him tighter, Ay'sek didn't care whether the duel took place or not. He didn't care about the Knights, and he didn't care about this war, which was as good as over. He wanted only to reclaim the staff and return to T'Ruel— to be away from the freezing climate of Capricon and warm himself in the breeding tents.

Yet Ay'sek didn't intend to squander the time between now and noon tomorrow.

He had agreed to go along with Drekk't's self-serving plot, but that didn't mean he was without a plan of his own. If there were an easier way to take back *Peerma'rek*, he would find it. Then he alone would get credit for retrieving the relic.

Commander Petton, Dylan Torc, Ezekiel Silvercrown, and Ruford Berwyn listened, engrossed, as Stannel reported his meeting with General Drekk't. There wasn't room for everyone to sit, but the office wasn't as crowded as earlier. Stannel noted that Petton had not invited Klye or Horcalus to attend.

Perhaps the Renegades had a right to know what was going on. Perhaps not. Either way, it was no longer Stannel's decision to make. Petton finally had the authority to toss the rebels into holding cells beneath the fort. Yet for some reason, he did not.

That fact gave Stannel hope that Commander Petton would make the right decision regarding Drekk't's offer.

"A duel?" Ruford asked, his voice brimming with incredulity. "What, are we living in the days of Aldrake Superior?"

No one replied. Everyone, including Stannel, looked to Petton, waiting for the commander to state his views on the matter.

"We are not honor-bound to accept this challenge," Petton said after a moment. "For that matter, we couldn't agree to their terms even if we wanted to. Saerylton Crystalus is dead."

"Gods rest his soul," Ruford muttered.

"I will take his place," Dylan volunteered. "It would be an honor to fight in Colt's stead. There is no doubt in my mind that the goblin Colt fought out on the battlefield was General Drekk't. Colt would have slain him, if not for the swarm of goblins that suddenly rose up to protect their leader."

Petton raised a hand to forestall further comments from the younger Knight. "If Drekk't was there when Commander Crystalus fell, he knows we cannot comply with his demands."

"Then why the farce?" Zeke Silvercrown wondered. "To confuse us?"

Dylan shook his head. "After Colt wounded Drekk't, the general retreated. I don't think he saw what happened next."

"That doesn't change the fact we can't give him what he wants," Ruford said.

"Can't we?"

Everyone turned back to Gaelor Petton. The commander reached for something that lay behind his desk. The Knight held the *vuudu* staff out before him, examining the macabre object with a grimace. Petton set it on his desk, and he looked relieved to put it down.

"The goblins claim they will leave if we give it back to them," Petton said. "Obviously, they value the staff, but we would be fools to take them at their word."

"We'd be giving them another weapon to use against us," Ruford said.

"It has to be a trap," Dylan added. "Why would the goblins want to arrange a duel...to fight one on one? It's not consistent with the tactics we've seen thus far."

"Unless Drekk't just wants a rematch."

Now Stannel was the center of attention.

"The general made no mention of Saerylton in the early part of our conversation," Stannel explained. "But when he finally did bring up the duel, it seemed to me that he had had it in mind all along. When he spoke of facing Colt in battle, there was a hunger in his eyes."

"Well, sorry to disappoint the general, but it's a bit too late for that," was Ruford's bitter reply. "What a waste of time!"

Stannel did not agree with the captain's assessment. If nothing else, they had learned a lot about the enemy that afternoon. Ruford probably realized that too. He was just frustrated. They all were. Colt had made an impression on everyone, and they were all feeling the loss and coping in different ways.

Dylan stepped forward. "I don't care if it is a trap. Commander, I ask for your permission to fight in Colt's place."

Petton stared into the younger Knight's eyes as though measuring the man's mettle. At last, he said, "No."

Dylan frowned. He looked ready to argue, but either he remembered his place in the chain of command, or he realized Petton's mind would not be changed. Deflated, Dylan fell back in line with Ruford and Zeke Silvercrown.

"It's a testament to your valor that you would fight a battle for the sake of honor," Stannel told Dylan. "It is also a testament to your devotion to the memory of Saerylton Crystalus. But there has been enough death here, and we have nothing to gain by agreeing to Drekk't's terms."

"That is not quite true," Petton said. His face had softened, and when he spoke, it sounded to Stannel as though he were thinking aloud. "The goblins killed our leader. Now we have a chance to kill theirs. I doubt slaying Drekk't will send their army into a state of chaos, but it would be no small victory for us."

"So you will let me duel the general?" Dylan asked eagerly.

Stannel held his breath.

"No," Petton said. "It is not your place to serve as Colt's substitute. It is mine."

*　　　*　　　*

Ay'sek heard himself speaking the words, though he no longer had no control over his mouth. A rush of energy burst into his mind, a sensation he always likened to getting struck by lightning. It wasn't all pain—but it wasn't all pleasure either.

In these moments when he made contact with the Goblinfather, Ay'sek felt like he could do anything. There was always the temptation to take more than was being offered, just as there was always stark despair when the connection was inevitably broken.

His lips ceased moving, and the tent was quiet once more. Ay'sek let out a sorrowful sigh, but the breath did not come. He couldn't breathe at all. The leather walls of the tent blurred as he turned his head and looked directly into his own eyes.

The shaman's body sat behind his makeshift altar, seeing nothing, hearing nothing. His chest rose and fell in a steady rhythm. His eyes stared straight ahead, blinking occasionally, but there was nothing behind them.

It was a most disconcerting sight.

The intangible essence of Ay'sek backed away from his body and floated through the secured entryway of his tent. Although the flaps appeared to be held together merely by straps of boiled hide, the sharpest of knives would not have been able to cut them. Likewise, the canopy itself was protected from intruders by a powerful *vuudu* enchantment.

Such precautions were necessary when one's left one's body helplessly behind.

Ay'sek felt only the smallest insecurity at leaving his corporeal form behind. He trusted his magic. Had there been another Chosen of the Chosen in the camp, he might not have been so bold, but none of the warriors in Drekk't's army had the ability to get to him, including Drekk't himself. So he drifted away from his tent, leaving the camp behind.

In one of his early campaigns, Ay'sek had had to plunge into a frigid river to escape his foes. Goblins weren't graceful swimmers, but he had managed to hold his breath long enough to propel himself away from danger.

Now, navigating without a body, he was reminded of swimming in that nearly frozen water. He wasn't cold now, exactly, because he had no sense of hot and cold. But as he drifted nearer and nearer to the fort, Ay'sek had to will his thoughts to stay focused, just as he had struggled to stay awake while swimming in that ice-cold stream.

When roaming about ethereally, there was always the danger of losing control, and Ay'sek had no intention of being drawn away from the world or dissipating into nothingness or whatever it was that happened to hapless souls.

No longer limited by gravity or fatigue, the shaman quickly found his way to Fort Faith. He passed through walls, furniture, and even people. It took a lot of concentration to see anything because in reality he was sensing, not seeing. He had no eyes.

To stay rooted in the here and now, Ay'sek used a sense beyond those the body employed. It was like squinting into a fog, trying to make sense of the shapes and colors therein. That he could hear nothing was also disorienting.

Depending fully on his mind's eye, Ay'sek flitted through the halls of the fortress. He didn't pay any attention to the people whom he passed. Most humans looked alike to him, and thankfully, he wasn't looking for one in particular.

His search was neither orderly nor thorough. The longer he remained outside of his body, the more difficult it would be to return. Already, he felt the strains of maintaining constant concentration. He might have described the sensation as light-headedness, except he didn't have a head.

Then there was a familiar hum in the air, buzzing around him like static electricity.

Ay'sek followed the invisible thread through wall after wall, ignoring the hazy figures of the living, which flitted around him. The tug grew stronger, and he did not hesitate. Like the smell of meat to an empty stomach, *Peerma'rek*'s presence was palpable.

He passed through yet another wall and ceased his flight all at once. Five blurry figures stood inside the room, but Ay'sek paid them no heed. There, in plain view, was *Peerma'rek*.

Ay'sek could barely make out the vague outline of the skull and the long shaft protruding from it because the relic was shrouded in violet smoke that roiled around it like a storm cloud. Upsinous had invested much of his power into the staff; that dark haze surrounding it was like the fingerprint of a god.

He wanted desperately to go to the staff, to bask in the terrible glory of the Goblinfather. But a silent warning prevented him from drawing too near. If his essence touched that of the staff, he knew he would be destroyed.

Ay'sek couldn't touch the blessed item in his current form,

and since he had no tongue, he could not call upon the power of Upsinous to aid him otherwise. This stalemate was not unforeseen, however. He was already considering which human would make the best temporary host when he noticed that something was amiss.

One of the five humans was looking in his direction, and unlike the others, whose translucent bodies encased a swirling white light, the mortal shell of this particular human contained a yellow globe that shone like an earthbound star. The brilliance of that light caused Ay'sek to draw back.

The shaman would have held his breath if he had any. As it was, he held himself as still as he could, focusing his mind's eye on the strange being that stood before him. The physical features of the man solidified slightly as he concentrated.

Stannel Bismarc took another step toward him, his hand reaching for something at his side. Ay'sek tried to make out what the object was, but the thing was surrounded by such radiance he had to look away.

The disembodied shaman considered charging into the body of one of the other Knights. Catching the man off-guard, Ay'sek would certainly be able to wrest away control of the body, if only temporarily.

He needed only enough time to grab *Peerma'rek*…

But such an endeavor was risky. Taking possession of a foreign body required an incredible amount of power, and Ay'sek had already been away from his body a long time. If he proved the weaker and failed to usurp the Knight's body, he might not have enough energy to return to his own.

Stannel drew nearer, positioning himself between *Peerma'rek* and Ay'sek. The man's brightness blinded him, and Ay'sek felt his strength ebb still more. Spewing a stream of silent curses, Ay'sek dropped through the floor, abandoned the fort, and raced back toward the goblin camp. He sailed through the air with the speed of an arrow in flight.

He was reunited with his body with a force that sent him falling backwards, hitting the ground hard. He gasped for breath, his heartbeat thundering in his ears. He lay there for several minutes, watching the canopy spin around him. Even when the dizziness subsided, Ay'sek couldn't bring himself to get up.

With a trembling hand, he wiped the cold sweat from his brow. It occurred to him that he was on the verge of swooning, but there was nothing he could do about it. As the darkness closed in on him, Ay'sek's dark lips drew into a knowing smile.

Passage V

"Your point is moot because the goblins will regain the staff in any event," Petton argued. "Anyway, I am taken with the idea of letting the gods decide our fate."

Petton waited for Stannel's rebuttal, but the other Knight was no longer even looking at him. Stannel took a step toward the middle of the room. Petton followed Stannel's stare but saw nothing but empty space.

"Sir Bismarc?" Petton prompted.

Stannel's hand dropped to the mace hanging from his hip and took a few steps closer to where the *vuudu* staff lay. For a second, Petton worried Stannel would make an attempt for the much-disputed staff, but he just stood there, staring.

Petton glanced at the others, who had said nothing since he announced he would personally accept Drekk't's challenge. Ruford, Dylan, and Ezekiel Silvercrown didn't seem to know what to make of Stannel's odd behavior either.

"What it is?" Petton demanded, his patience dwindling.

Stannel turned and met his eyes. The older Knight had gone very pale, which gave Petton gooseflesh. "I…I am not sure. I felt…a presence."

Petton saw Stannel release his hold on the mace. The former Commander of Fort Valor—both Fort Valors—then let out an audible breath.

"Are you saying someone was here?" Ruford asked cautiously, eyeing one of the empty walls.

"A presence?" Dylan asked. "Like a spirit?"

"Or a shaman," Stannel ventured.

Petton pressed his lips together in a line. Stannel had spoken of a black-clad goblin whose magic enabled Drekk't and Stannel to communicate. It was conceivable Drekk't had sent his wizard to spy on them. It was also possible Stannel was creating a ruse of some sort. Stannel was awfully anxious about the *vuudu* staff.

What Stannel said next only deepened Petton's suspicions.

"The shaman was drawn to the staff. We need to hide it or, better yet, be rid of it. We could send someone through the secret passage…"

"You are no longer the commander of this fortress," Petton said. "This staff"—he gestured toward the leering skull—"is the only thing keeping us alive at the moment. And you know as well as I that the general will not go through with the duel unless the staff is present."

"We do not know whether Drekk't will accept you in Colt's stead," Stannel replied, calm and collect as ever.

Petton's face flushed. "He will fight me."

"What makes you so certain?" Stannel asked.

Petton looked over at the others, who also waited for his answer. Looking each in the eye, one after another, he said, "The goblins are devious. We all know they would lure us into a trap if they could. This is why we cannot abide by their terms.

"Tomorrow morning, at first light, I will ride out to the place where Drekk't and his shaman had come to parley today. Stannel, Dylan…I would like you to accompany me. We will bring the *vuudu* staff with us. If the army comes out against us, a hard ride will see us safely back inside the fort. If the shaman comes alone to steal the staff, we will do battle.

"But since the goblins are so desperate to get the staff back, I predict they will not react so hastily. Though we arrive well before the appointed time, I am confident that General Drekk't and his shaman will meet us. Then I shall dictate my terms.

"If they do not comply, if a battle for the staff ensues among us, we will fight them, and we will win. If Drekk't agrees to duel, then he and I will let our sword arms decide who is worthier."

"And if the general loses?" Ruford asked. "The shaman will make a play for the staff, or I'm a drunken midge."

"Of course he will," Petton said. "At which point Sir Bismarc, Sir Torc, and I will kill the shaman."

"And what if you lose, Commander?"

Petton's gaze darted back to Stannel. "If I lose, then you will be free to make whatever decisions you like."

The four men took a moment to digest the intricacies of his

plan. Petton crossed his arms, waiting for someone—anyone—to speak out against him. Ultimately, they would have to do as he said. He was the Commander of Fort Faith, after all.

And yet Petton didn't want to bully them into this course of action. He hoped they would realize his plan had merit. Couldn't they see this was the only way to strike out against the invaders?

Dylan cleared his throat. "It is a desperate plan, but I, for one, am for it."

Ruford grunted what might have been grudging approval.

Petton turned to Stannel, whose sober expression did not waver. It occurred to him the unusual Knight could refuse him. Petton had no true authority over the Commander of Fort Valor, even if Fort Valor was just a mountain of rubble.

Stannel and his enchanted mace were integral to Petton's plan. He needed them as a foil against the shaman's magic. Petton's pulse quickened as he waited for Stannel's reply.

"This is a great gamble," Stannel said at last. "We risk much by bringing the staff to the goblins."

"The staff is in peril as long as the goblins remain camped on our doorstep," Petton stated, doing his best to keep his exasperation in check. "The Warriorlord has given us this one chance. We cannot squander it!"

Stannel sighed, and Petton thought the Knight looked older all of the sudden. "I can see that you are resolved to this course, and so I shall do my part to help."

Petton could not keep a smile from his face. "Then it is agreed. We ride tomorrow at dawn!"

Stannel left Petton's office with a heavy heart. He was confused, uncertain whether he had made the right choice in complying with Petton's plot. As he walked, Stannel weighed the pros and cons until it was clear the latter would always outnumber the former.

How he wished Petton had taken his advice to send the *vuudu* staff away from the fort. And how he wished he had been able to impress upon everyone just how dangerous the talisman was. None of them, Stannel included, could comprehend the many mysteries of the staff, but Colt had been right to deprive the enemy of its power.

That Drekk't was so eager to regain the staff was enough to

convince him the Knights should do whatever it took to keep the general from obtaining it. And he had not forgotten the queer look in Opal's eye when he had found her in the woods with it.

"He's dead, but I can bring him back," she had said.

The problem with Petton was he could not see beyond the immediate situation. Fort Faith's new commander had already given up hope, and so he was content to take any small victory he could.

And because Petton saw himself and his men as doomed, he would unknowingly do great harm to countless others.

Stannel continued walking, not knowing where he was heading. Lurking beneath his thoughts was the knowledge that if he had not given up his authority, he would have been able to do whatever he wished with the staff. He had had his reasons for stepping down, but in light of recent developments, they all seemed petty and selfish.

When Stannel realized where his feet had taken him, he was not at all surprised. Although he needed to meditate and seek wisdom from the Great Protector, it seemed he needed the advice of a friend more.

He entered the infirmary and was greeted by a scene far less distressing than the one he had seen the night of Colt's return.

All of the sickroom's beds were filled, but there were no screams, no smell of blood. The infirmary's chief healer had brought swift order to the bedlam that followed the wounded into her workplace. Those who still lived owed their survival to Sister Aric and her goddess.

When their eyes met, Aric's face brightened. She left the bedside of an unconscious woman and hurried over to him, wrapping him in a hug. They hadn't had a chance to talk for some time, and Stannel realized now how much he had missed their soul-searching discussions.

"Are you well?" she asked, stepping back and taking measure of him.

Stannel examined her in return. Bags under her eyes and unkempt hair served as evidence of late nights and constant work, but aside from that, Aric looked none the worse for her labor. In Stannel's estimation, the woman looked far more beautiful because of her evident sacrifices.

"My shoulder is still a bit stiff," he told her, "but Pintor saw me safely through the battle."

Aric's eyes veritably twinkled as she said, "The Great Protector may have had some help. At least one person was asking Mystel to watch over you Knights."

"Then my thanks to the Healing Goddess…and to those who do her work," Stannel said with a bow.

Stannel spotted Ruben Zeetan on the far side of the room. He acknowledged Stannel with a shy smile and quickly looked away again, busying himself with smoothing out one patient's blankets.

"Ruben has been a true blessing," Aric said, following Stannel's gaze. "He is a tireless helper, and I daresay he has a gift for helping the wounded."

Stannel suspected Ruben's diligence had more to do with admiration for Aric than an interest in serving Mystel, but he didn't voice his suspicions. In the end, it made little difference. Whereas Ruben Zeetan had previously made a living out of robbing people, he was now helping strangers. To Stannel, it mattered not at all that Ruben had found his salvation through loving Sister Aric in lieu of her goddess.

Aric spoke of what she and her assistant had overcome in the past twenty-four hours. Stannel knew each loss of life affected her more than she let on. Though her faith was strong, Aric could not completely distance herself from death's toll.

"The key is to remind yourself you are not succeeding or failing," she had told him once. "The gods alone know when and how any of us will die. No man or woman can thwart that destiny."

The catch was that no mere mortal could comprehend the deities' designs. Sister Aric might dedicate an entire day to nursing a man back to health, only to watch him die.

Likewise, Stannel thought, we Knights could debate for hours about defenses and counterattacks, but if Pintor—in his unlimited wisdom—does not deign to interfere on our behalf, nothing we do will save us in the end.

"Stannel," Aric said, her voice quieting some, "there has been talk that you went out to speak with the goblins earlier today. I know you probably can't talk about the specifics, but can I ask you one thing?"

Stannel nodded.

"Is there any hope for us? Any hope at all?"

If he told her they would all die to a man, the priestess would continue to see to her duties. She would serve Mystel until her last breath was spent. While Stannel's dark prediction would certainly make the healer sad—self-preservation is a reflex of the living, after all—her faith in Mystel and the gods of good would remain strong until the very end.

Even so, Stannel was not about to destroy what little optimism Aric harbored.

"There is always hope, my dear," Stannel said with a forced smile.

"It's that bad, eh?" she replied with a wink.

Stannel chuckled softly, not knowing what else to say.

"Is there anything I can do to be of service?" Aric asked.

"You have done more than your share already."

"I wish I could do more. Mystel gives me the power to mend flesh, but some wounds fester far beneath the surface."

Stannel raised an eyebrow, not understanding what she was getting at.

Aric let out a sigh. "I don't want to trouble you further… because I know you are troubled, Stannel, even though you do your best to conceal it…but I worry about Opal. I don't know if she has any friends at the fort now that Colt and the dwarf have passed on. I think she is very lonely. Please keep her in your prayers…and say a kind word if you happen upon her."

Stannel promised he would, but as he walked away, he began to wonder what good it would do when all was said and done. Unlike Aric, who would labor over a dying man until his soul departed, Stannel was starting to wonder if perhaps it wasn't worth the effort. They would all be dead soon anyway.

He shook his head ruefully. Clearly, Petton wasn't the only one who had given up hope.

Noel squirmed in the long-legged, tall-backed chair, trying to find a comfortable position. Leaning back meant he'd have to stretch his legs out straight or sit cross-legged, both of which would make his feet fall asleep again.

But sitting at the edge of his seat was beginning to take its toll on his spine. He didn't want to slouch, but he didn't have much of a choice after a while. His feet, which seemed miles above the floor, kicked rhythmically at the air.

He glanced longingly at the fine chalice that rested on the

wide armrest beside him. It was empty and had been that way for some time. At first, Noel had enjoyed the throne-like chair, but it was hard to pretend you were a king when you couldn't even ask for some more water.

As it was, Noel dared not make a peep. He had promised Delincas Theta he would be on his best behavior. His solemn oath had evoked a skeptical expression from the human wizard.

Ingrates! Noel silently grumbled.

He had spent the better part of an hour explaining to the King of Superius—and all of his aides, counselors, advisors, ministers, and chief staff members—why he had come to Castle Borrom. King Edward had had plenty of questions, which Noel had happily answered. But as time went on, he had grown more and more frustrated with the whole situation.

The impatient humans had interrupted him constantly. When it became clear the monarch and his snooty cronies had no interest in his tale's many fascinating facets, Noel was tempted to deprive them all of its ending. Didn't they realize that details were what made the story interesting?

Across the room, King Edward Borrom III, Ambassador Theta, and the other men spoke in hushed tones. Noel knew that they were talking about him as much as his story. Every once in a while, one of the long-bearded men glanced in his direction. Meanwhile, Noel had nothing to do—and nothing to drink.

Explaining all about Klye and his friends and Colt and *his* friends and then about Stannel and how Fort Faith had become Fort Valor left Noel's throat as dry as the Desert Ahuli-Okx. On top of that, his head felt like someone had dropped an anvil on it. He had woken up that morning with a pleasant, fuzzy sensation between his ears—with no memory about the past week—but as the day progressed, the pleasant feeling fizzled out, replaced by a throbbing ache.

Well, Noel thought, I'll have a thing or two to say about Superian hospitality if anyone ever asks me!

He must have dozed off because the next thing he knew, someone was prodding him awake. Noel reached for his knife, which wasn't where it was supposed to be, and then for his spell components, which weren't there either. After a few blinks, the face of Delincas Theta came into focus, and Noel remembered where he was.

"It's time to go," the wizard told him.

Looking past the man, Noel saw the room was now empty. The king and his friends had left. None of them had bothered to say goodbye or even a proper thank you.

Delincas must have discerned his displeasure for he said, "The king is a very busy man, but please accept my gratitude as his own."

"From everything I'd heard about King Edward, the founder of the Alliance of Nations, I thought he'd be a friendly guy," Noel grumbled as he vaulted out of the chair.

Delincas's smile tightened. "The king has not been himself lately. First it was the Renegades…and now the goblins. And I'd remind you he was just informed that his only son is likely the goblins' captive. I daresay the king is holding up very well given the circumstances."

Noel smoothed out the wrinkles in his robe and adjusted his hat. "Yeah, I guess you're right. I probably should have said, 'I am sorry for your loss,' huh?"

"You have already done a great service for Superius and Continae," Delincas replied.

Noel smiled and decided he liked Delincas Theta.

Even though the man wore no robes of red to denote his affiliation, Noel knew Delincas got his spells from the goddess Quess. Not only could he *feel* it, but also he had confirmed it earlier with a question.

Delincas Theta had been visibly uncomfortable during their conversation about magic, which led Noel to believe he didn't want everyone to know he *was* a wizard. He supposed that made sense. After all, Delincas lived in a country swarming with Knights—Knights who were afraid of magic, even if they'd never admit it.

Noel felt sorry for the human wizard and wondered why Delincas didn't just leave Superius and head to neighboring Ristidae, which was, generally speaking, a more tolerant country. Though it seemed to Noel he had only just arrived in Superius, *he* was certainly ready to leave.

"You'll have to say goodbye to King Edward for me," Noel told Delincas. "Or, if you want, you can come back to Fort Valor with me. My friends will need all the help they can get if more shamans show up."

Delincas's smile faded as he looked down to the floor. "I'm sorry, Noel, but I must ask you to remain with us a little while longer…until we are certain we've learned all we can about the goblins from you."

Noel placed his hands on his hips. "What if I don't wanna stay?"

Now Delincas met his gaze. "You are a spell-caster of no small talent, Noel. I know we could not keep you here without taking drastic, deplorable measures.

"I convinced the king to let you stay inside the palace by promising I would look after you. I will not force you to stay. Instead, I beg you to remain for as long as the king has need of you."

And what about my friends at the fort? Noel wanted to argue. But it was hard to stay mad at the wizard with him looking all sad and everything.

Noel sighed loudly. Klye, Colt, and the others would just have to watch their own backs for the time being. How could he say no to the King of Superius?

"All right," Noel said. "But can I have my stuff back? I don't want to lose that staff. I made it myself, you know."

Delincas smiled again. "Of course. Is there anything else you require for your stay?"

Noel thought hard for a moment before replying, "Can I get a drink of water?"

Passage VI

Lilac folded her hands on her lap and pretended to examine something out the window. She could feel Plake's eyes on her. The rancher sat directly beside her. She was running out of excuses for the man's behavior. Sooner or later, she was going to have to admit to herself that Plake Nelway fancied her.

And sooner or later, she would have to do something about it.

The rebels had spent most of the day in the Renegade Room. Every now and then, people would pop their heads in, as though looking for someone. Lilac recognized some of the men and women from Colt's Army.

Klye, who was seated on floor, brooding, was certain Petton was checking in on them. The Renegade Leader was not at all pleased at being left out of the Knights' meetings. Hunter, Bly, and Pillip, who were also holing up in the Renegade Room—and who were no happier about being left in the dark—sat in contemplative silence.

"Well, it could be worse," Scout ventured. "We could be in the dungeon."

Lilac flashed the hooded man a smile. Scout's mood was unsinkable. Even in the grimmest circumstances, she had never seen him despair. Scout had as much cause to be depressed as the rest of them and perhaps more. She had heard him talk about his friends in Port Town and how badly the man wanted to go and make sure they were all right.

"If you want, Klye, I can go snoop around the fort and see what I can learn," Scout said.

Klye waved his hand dismissively. "The Knights aren't going to let anything slip around you. You're a Renegade, and they still think we're the enemy. Besides, if they see you sneaking around, they might just throw us in the dungeon after all."

"What about us?" Hunter asked.

The question clearly took Klye by surprise. When he did not answer her, Hunter went on.

"We ain't Renegades. Maybe we could pry some information outta them tight-lipped Knights."

Klye shrugged. "Do what you want. I'm not your boss."

Hunter planted her hands on her hips and frowned. She looked as though she was going to say something else but instead glanced over at Bly and Pillip. Neither man acknowledged her. They appeared to be as content with wallowing in self-pity as Klye was.

Lilac reminded herself that both men had reason to wallow. They had both lost loved ones to the goblins. Colt had given them hope that they might strike the enemy a lethal blow. Now he was dead too.

Her stomach clenched at that thought. She had shed her share of tears upon learning of the commander's fate. Her brain could not yet fathom that she would never see the young man again. She, Opal, and Othello had risked everything to rescue Colt from the goblins. It all seemed so pointless now. Colt and Othello were gone…just like her brother…

Across the room, Hunter chewed at her lower lip. Suddenly, she perked up.

"I got it," she said to Lilac. "What about that blond Knight…Dylan? You spent some time with him, didn't you? I'm sure he knows what's goin' on. And with a little persuasion, he might fill ya in."

Plake sat up straight. "What the hell do you mean by 'persuasion'?"

Lilac was speechless. On one hand, Hunter was volunteering her for a reconnaissance mission. On the other, Plake was making an ass out of himself and her.

She was unspeakably grateful when Klye said, "Shut up, Plake."

Her thankfulness evaporated, however, at the Renegade Leader's next words.

"Is that true, Lilac? Would Dylan tell you what that meeting with the goblins was all about?"

"He might."

Before Klye could ask the question—and before Plake could make her feel even more uncomfortable—she stood and walked briskly to the door. Of course she would go. Even if her conscience objected to the idea of using Dylan for information, she was all too happy to remove herself from the Renegade Room.

Her pace slowed considerably once she had left Klye, Hunter, and Plake behind. Making her way through the chilly hallways, she rehearsed what she would say to Dylan. Nothing sounded right.

Dylan probably had been instructed not to tell anyone—least of all a Renegade—about what was transpiring. No one could fault her if Dylan refused to share what he knew. After several minutes of fruitless searching, she doubted she would even be able find the man.

Lilac was already thinking of how to break the news of her failure to Hunter and the Renegades when she rounded a corner and walked headlong into Dylan Torc.

She reflexively brought an arm up to prevent from colliding with the Knight, who had only enough time to pull a surprised face.

"Pardon me, madam," he said while trying to navigate his way around her.

"Dylan!" Lilac called before the man could get away.

He stopped and looked at her more closely. She supposed he hadn't recognized her because of the poor light in the corridor. Not to mention he likely had a lot on his mind.

"Lilac," Dylan greeted with a bow. "Please pardon my rudeness. I didn't see it was you."

"Ah," Lilac stammered, frantically searching for the words she had been practicing. "I don't want to keep you if there is somewhere you must go…"

Dylan glanced off in the direction he had been heading, and it looked like the man was trying to recall where he had been going. "I am free at the moment. I have only just come from a meeting with Commander Petton. I don't expect I'll be needed again until tomorrow morning."

Lilac put on a smile, though she almost wished he hadn't been so forthcoming about where he had been. But there was a part of Lilac that *was* terribly curious about what the new leader of Fort Faith was planning. When she had been with Colt, she had been privy to a lot of information—more than was proper, really—and she had gotten used to being in the know.

"I trust you are well?" Dylan asked. It was a polite inquiry. It also served to nurture the floundering conversation.

"A little sore, but I can't complain," she replied. "What about you? I suppose Petton...*Commander* Petton is keeping you busy."

"With so many civilians in the fort, it falls to us Knights to keep order."

"The 'civilians' that followed Colt from Hylan are no strangers to harsh conditions, Dylan. They came here because they wanted a chance to fight the goblins, not to be corralled like livestock."

Dylan scratched his head and said, "None can question the valor of the men and women of Colt's Army, but it is a Knight's duty to defend the realm. We will not endanger more lives than necessary."

"Then you are not using all of the resources allotted to you," Lilac argued.

Dylan laughed, probably trying to dispel the tension. She hadn't meant to make Dylan the target of her frustration, but he was the only Knight available at the moment to listen to her complaints.

"We're all ready to do our part," she continued. "But many are beginning to think they have come here only to be coddled. They watched their family get butchered in Rydah and their friends fall outside this fort. They yearn for another chance to face the enemy."

He nodded resignedly, as though none of it came as any surprise to him. Recalling how impatient Dylan always was during times of inaction, Lilac wondered if Dylan felt the same way. Had he had been pacing when she came upon him?

"Defenders' Plague," Dylan mumbled.

"What?"

"No one likes having his life placed in the hands of an enemy. It's human nature for the besieged to want to fight the besieger, even when the odds are against him. Better to die on your own terms than someone else's. The Knights call this Defenders' Plague, and more than one Superian commander has succumbed to its symptoms over the years."

Lilac considered Dylan's words and found that she agreed. It was the waiting more than the inevitability of their deaths that rubbed everyone's nerves raw. Still...

"Dylan, you've had Defenders' Plague ever since I met you. Why are you suddenly in favor sitting tight?"

She might as well have said, "What are the Knights planning?" She no longer cared. If Petton wasn't going to let Colt's Army fight, he owed them an explanation.

Dylan stared into her eyes for a moment. Probably, he was taking into account everything he knew about her. She was from a noble family, but she was also a Renegade, which usually trumped everything else.

The Knight must have come to a favorable conclusion, however, because he let a long breath and then told her about the goblin general's challenge and Petton's pending counter-challenge. Nothing she had witnessed of the goblins suggested they would honor the rules of a duel, but Dylan seemed confident that he, Stannel, and Petton would be able to handle anything the general and his shaman threw at them.

"It's a desperate plan," Lilac said at last.

Dylan grunted. "My words exactly."

"But you're going through with it?"

Dylan's eyebrows shot up. "Of course. It is my duty to help Commander Petton in any way I can. My only regret is that I cannot fight Drekk't in Petton's place. I'm sure that was the goblin we saw Colt fighting."

He didn't have to say more. The events were already playing in her mind—Colt fighting with superhuman skill, accomplishing feats that Lilac would not have thought possible. She had seen Colt spar before. Hell, she had dueled him herself. But never before had the young commander displayed that level of expertise.

If he had, Lilac wouldn't be alive today.

"Will Petton carry the crystal sword into battle?" she asked.

Dylan looked puzzled by the question. "I don't think so. For one thing, it's not his to take, and for another, he desires a fair fight against Drekk't. Neither *vuudu* nor the magic of Colt's sword will be allowed to sully the sanctity of the duel."

"What about you? Stannel has his mace, which is possessed of the power of his god. Please…take this."

Dylan's eyes were drawn to the blade she unsheathed and held out to him. Aside from its antiquated stylings, the vorpal sword looked common enough, but Dylan had fought beside her outside the fort. He had seen her cleave through solid steel.

"I...I couldn't accept," Dylan replied, his eyes lingering on the vorpal sword.

"I insist." Lilac returned the blade to its sheath, removed the scabbard from her belt, and handed the weapon to Dylan. "Since I cannot lend my sword arm to this enterprise, then at least allow me to lend my sword."

Dylan hesitated.

"Unless, of course, you're afraid of its magic," Lilac teased.

The matter resolved, Dylan wasted no time in removing his own sword. When he handed it to her, accepting hers at the same time, he said, "Please take care of my blade in the meantime. Though it has no magic, it has seen me through many battles."

Lilac took Dylan's sword and affixed it to her hip. It was much heavier than the vorpal sword, and she wondered if she'd even be able to wield the weapon if it came down to it. She also wondered what had possessed her give up the treasured vorpal sword.

He's not my brother, she reminded herself. Protecting him won't bring Gabriel or Ragellan back. Or Colt.

They stared at each another for a few seconds, not quite sure what to say next.

"You must rise with the dawn," Lilac said suddenly. "I shouldn't keep you."

Dylan smiled. "I shouldn't wonder if I stay up half the night. My heart quickens at the thought of seeing Drekk't tomorrow."

"Be safe, Dylan."

"I will, and I'll keep your sword safe as well," Dylan promised.

Without another word, the Knight bowed stiffly and walked away. Lilac watched him go, silently praying Dylan would not prove to be the next friend of hers to die.

Passage VII

Drekk't awoke to cries of alarm. By the time an officer reached his tent, he was more than half-dressed in his battle gear. As the goblin relayed what the sentries had seen, Drekk't fastened the buckles of his plate armor and pulled his sword partway out of its sheath to make sure the thing hadn't frozen in place.

"You are certain that there are only three of them?" Drekk't asked after the officer finished his report.

"Yes, *n'patrek*."

"And all three are Knights?"

"As far as the lookouts could discern."

Drekk't tugged at the straps of his breastplate, testing for signs of wear. Mentally, he ran through scenario after scenario in an attempt to understand the humans' treachery. The duel was not to take place until noon, but here it was, shortly after dawn.

Perhaps the midge had cloaked a cavalcade of Knights in a spell of invisibility, and even now they waited behind the three emissaries. But if that is the trick, why bother to send any visible troops? he wondered.

In the end, Drekk't deduced the Knights' early arrival was planned, in part, to catch him off guard. All he could do was take the morning one step at a time.

Drekk't told the officer to keep the troops back. He was on his way over to the opening in the tent when a familiar silhouette darkened the threshold. Ay'sek didn't wait to be invited in. The obsequious officer scrambled out of the shaman's way, bowing repeatedly and mumbling a litany of greetings and praises.

Drekk't wanted nothing more than to backhand the sycophant, but he settled for a sharp glare that silenced the goblin as effectively as a blow to face.

If Ay'sek had even noticed the officer, he made no sign. To

Drekk't he said, "They bring with them *Peerma'rek*."

"Is the midge among them?" Drekk't asked.

"No."

"What about his magic? Are they ensorcelled?"

"No," Ay'sek said again, but after a moment's hesitation, he added, "Which is not to say the Knights don't possess magic of their own."

Drekk't crossed his metal-covered arms, waiting for the shaman to explain himself.

"Some god of good watches over Stannel Bismarc," Ay'sek said. "I can sense it even from afar. And there is something else…"

"What?"

"I do not know yet," Ay'sek snapped. "*Peerma'rek* has an aura of its own, one that overshadows whatever other magic the Knights have with them."

Drekk't could barely keep the grin from his face. Surely it was Colt's crystal sword.

"But we needn't to walk into the trap in order to spring it," the shaman added. "Allow me to gather a small force—"

"No."

Ay'sek's gnashed his teeth.

"If we give them cause to doubt us," Drekk't said, "they'll run back to their fortress, and we might never get another chance to retrieve the staff."

"They'll not flee," Ay'sek argued. "If you give me a chance, I will prove that the Chosen of the Chosen are superior to all other spell-casters."

Drekk't was already shaking his head. "I have made up my mind, Master Ay'sek."

To Drekk't private relief, Ay'sek did not argue further. The shaman's lips curled into a slight smile. He wondered what the other goblin found so amusing but had no time to ponder it.

Regardless, nothing was going to dampen his spirits today, not when Saerylton Crystalus had accepted his challenge and at that very moment was waiting his arrival.

Petton absently patted the neck of his piebald charger. He knew not the name of the beast nor where it had come from. Had it sailed to Capricon with Petton and the other Knights, or had it arrived with Colt's Army?

He thought the unknown horse a fitting representative of the fortress, a bastion of inconsistency that was currently being called by no less than three names.

Out of the corner of his eye, he saw Dylan looking at him. He ignored the younger Knight and continued to stare straight ahead at the camp that had sprung up around them like weeds around a lake. With each passing minute, Petton's nerves tightened.

He let out a breath and watched the vapor undulate before him. Until the goblins made a direct move against them, he would hold fast, though he hoped to Pintor they wouldn't still be sitting there at noontime.

He would sooner die than show weakness before monsters threatening Fort Colt.

Petton scoffed at the notion. As much as he respected Saerylton Crystalus, the young commander's death did not warrant having a fortress named after him. Not that the Knighthood would ever officially sanction something as ridiculous-sounding as "Fort Colt."

Fort Crystalus on the other hand…

Petton knew the real reason the idea irked him was because he was jealous of the dead man. Saerylton's style of leadership had been unconventional at best. And he had abandoned his post at a crucial junction before dying as a result of an ill-planned battle he himself had initiated.

While Petton was the better commander, he knew he would never enjoy the same degree of love and respect the men bestowed upon their Commander Colt.

Petton snapped out of his daydream when three dark shapes emerged from the goblin camp. Although they were on foot, the envoys approached with haste, covering the distance between them in a remarkably short span.

As the goblins drew closer, Petton studied his adversary. The one in the middle, clad in suit of armor that would have made any Knight proud, was surely General Drekk't. Like Petton, the goblin wore an open-faced helm, though he did not carry a shield. Petton could not help but notice Superius's sun-and-sword standard emblazoned on the broadsword's scabbard hanging—along with an assortment of smaller blades—from the general's belt.

It was only when Drekk't drew near enough for Petton to

look into the goblin's eyes—eyes both bestial and intelligent—that the new Commander of Fort Faith tasted his first sip of doubt.

Before Petton could make any introductions or utter a greeting, Drekk't exchanged glances with the black-robed goblin on his right and shouted something Petton would have understood even without the shaman's enchantment.

Drekk't's predatory eyes shot daggers at Petton. "Where in the hells is Saerylton Crystalus?"

Drekk't's glare told Ay'sek the general suspected he had known of Colt's absence from the start. This, of course, was true. And now that Drekk't realized he was being robbed of his revenge, Ay'sek enjoyed another dose of spiteful delight.

"Where in the hells is Saerylton Crystalus?"

All three humans kept their composure, a testament to their mettle. Ay'sek, for one, fully expected Drekk't to draw his sword and lunge at the nearest Knight.

"He is inside the fort, of course," the Knight in the middle said. "I am Sir Gaelor Petton. I have come to accept your challenge in the commander's place."

Drekk't fumed. Ay'sek tensed, waiting for the general to charge headlong at Gaelor Petton. Silently, he urged Drekk't to do it. While Drekk't—and the random soldier whom Drekk't had dragged along with them—kept the Knights busy, Ay'sek would make a play for *Peerma'rek*.

He glanced at the staff, which was tied to the saddle of Stannel Bismarc's horse. He looked up at the man. The warrior priest stared back.

Drekk't let out a stream of curses. At least some of them must have been translatable, for the three Knights' faces hardened at the foul declarations and filthy promises.

"My terms were to fight Saerylton Crystalus, not his lackey!" Drekk't roared.

"Yet here I am," the human shouted back. "If you will not face me as a substitute for Commander Crystalus, then you will have no duel, and we will take the staff back into our fort."

Ay'sek privately commended the Knight for his audacity. He had put Drekk't in a delicate position. Obviously, the general had betrayed too much of his hatred for Saerylton Crystalus to

Stannel. By denying Drekk't what he desired most, the humans fueled his rage without giving him any outlet aside from themselves.

One way or another, there was going to be a battle, though at that moment. The only question was whether Drekk't would bother with a formal duel or simply dive right in.

For several long minutes, the general did not speak. Ay'sek was astonished by Drekk't's self-control in the face of the human's trickery. The Knights had used their leverage as cunningly as any goblin. Drekk't could not deny Petton's offer unless he wanted to admit to himself, Ay'sek, and the Goblin-father that he had arranged the duel for vengeance's sake.

"Very well," Drekk't growled, "You and I will fight."

As the two combatants negotiated the rules—a battle unto the death, no magic of any kind, victor gets the staff—Ay'sek stole another glance at *Peerma'rek*. The yellowed skull smiled back at him.

There were rumors about that skull. Some said it was the skull of the greatest shaman Altaerra had ever known. Others insisted it had belonged to a demigod, the half-mortal son of Upsinous. Ay'sek could not take his eyes off of the staff. He longed to hold it, to learn its secrets, and to supplement his own *vuudu* with its power.

Meanwhile, Gaelor Petton dismounted, and the duelists prepared for combat.

Petton expected Drekk't to immediately take the offensive. Yet the general held back and crouched low, his knees bent and back hunched. Despite the knives and dirks at his disposal, Drekk't unsheathed only his sword, which, upon closer inspection, was a hand-and-a-half sword.

Hand-and-a-half swords—or bastard swords, as they were sometimes called—could be wielded with either one or both hands. For the moment, Drekk't's left hand remained empty, his fingers splayed, ready to grab.

The insignia engraved on the sword's crosspiece reminded Petton that Drekk't had stolen the weapon from a dead Knight. Petton planned to avenge that unknown warrior, along with Saerylton Crystalus and the other Knights who had lost their lives to Drekk't's army.

Petton held his broadsword out before him. The weapon had been a gift from his father, a present bestowed upon him the day he was knighted. Unlike many within the Order, Gaelor Petton was a first-generation Knight of Superius.

He had known none of the benefits that came with a famous surname. Some of the squires in his class had been taught the ways of the Knighthood since birth, thanks to fathers or uncles whose only wish was for their kin was to follow in their footsteps.

Petton had known next to nothing about the laws and customs of the Knights of Superius, but he quickly absorbed the Knights' culture like a sponge. His favorite lessons had always been about swordplay. After many hours of physical testing, shedding sweat and blood on a daily basis, Gaelor Petton had excelled beyond most in his class.

Twenty-three years later, he would put those lessons to the test.

He came at the goblin with a roar, swinging his broadsword at the fiend's flank even as he plowed his ovular shield into his opponent's face. At the last moment, Drekk't's knees straightened, propelling the goblin sideways. Petton planted his left foot in the ground to slow his charge and altered the angle of his shield, holding it in front of him to block any surprise attacks.

But Drekk't was more interested in deflecting Petton's sword, which he did expertly, the hand-and-a-half sword connecting with Petton's broadsword midway between hilt and tip. Petton was about to pull back for a second swing, but he felt a sudden pressure behind Drekk't's sword as the goblin tried to push Petton's sword aside.

Instinctively, Petton pushed back. Using every ounce of strength he possessed, he managed to stop the goblin's progress. The two combatants remained locked together for several seconds. Drekk't's orange eyes burned with an intensity that cut through Petton's mind like a razor. He knew, suddenly, that the goblin wasn't using his full strength—just enough to keep Petton at bay.

Drekk't wanted Petton to tire himself out.

Petton seethed. He was no weakling, but goblins were innately stronger than men. On top of that, Drekk't was proving to be far more cunning than Petton had expected. The goblins Petton had fought prior had thrown themselves at him with abandon, hoping to overwhelm him with brawn alone. Drekk't, however, had been gifted with an attribute few of his kind displayed—patience.

Knowing *he* could not afford to be patient lest he wear himself out, Petton pulled back. As he took a few steps away from his opponent, he swung his shield in front of him to defend against Drekk't's counterattack. Petton braced himself against the stroke that battered his shield like a hammer upon an anvil.

He gritted his teeth and shifted his weight forward. As his shield deflected Drekk't's sword, he made swung his broadsword again. To Petton's surprise, Drekk't accepted the blow. In fact, he stepped into it, thrusting forth his breastplate as though it were a shield.

The impact hardly slowed the goblin. Before Petton could react, Drekk't's left hand struck out, going for Petton's exposed right flank.

He had not seen Drekk't draw the knife. He spotting the glint of sunlight on metal at the last second and swept his sword arm out, trusting his gauntlet to deflect the blade. At the same time, he pushed his shield outward in hopes of forcing Drekk't back.

The two adversaries connected on both fronts simultaneously. The knife grazed Petton's arm, his armor protecting him from the jagged blade. Petton had put all of his weight behind his shield. Had he been facing a human foe, the maneuver would have landed the man on his ass. As it was, Drekk't merely grunted and recoiled back a step.

The maneuver had bought Petton a little time but naught else.

He took a swing at Drekk't's head. This time, the goblin did not rely on his armor. Drekk't ducked, returning to his low crouch. Petton's blade sailed over the goblin's head. He had not expected to connect. With Drekk't on the defensive, Petton took the opportunity to put more space between them.

The first exchange was over, and while no damage had been scored, Petton felt beads of sweat trickling his skin under his armor. The hair beneath his helmet was matted to his scalp. He was breathing hard, and the muscles in his sword arm had already begun to burn.

It was in that brief moment of respite that Petton realized he had underestimated Drekk't.

The knowledge that the goblin general would almost certainly kill him filled Petton with shame. And yet he had never questioned at least one aspect of his life: Sir Gaelor Petton, Knight of Superius, would one day die in battle.

Along with the certainty of his imminent death came a feeling of acceptance. If he were destined to fall to Drekk't's sword, then so be it. He would fight honorably and die honorably. What more could be asked of a Knight?

No one would ever sing songs of his courageous sacrifice, and there would never be a Fort Petton, but by all the gods of good, he would fight as hard in this, his final battle, as he had in every battle leading up to it.

Petton charged forward, initiating the second encounter. He came at the goblin with a series of heavy strokes, giving Drekk't no time to do anything but dodge and parry. Abandoning strategy, he surrendered to his most basic instincts.

As they traded blows, Petton found that his mind was far removed from the fight. His body acted and reacted, but his thoughts roamed free. He wondered if, when he saw his father in Paradise, the old man would be proud of him. He thought about his mother back in Superius and about the children he would never have.

He barely noticed when his shield flew from his grasp. Without questioning the course of events that had led up to it, Petton unconsciously brought his hands together. With both hands gripping the hilt, he swung his broadsword like a woodsman's axe. Drekk't cried out as the blade produced a sizable dent in his pauldron and the top of his breastplate, but even the goblin's vile curses weren't enough to bring Petton's mind back to the present.

His thoughts turned next to the two Knights who had accompanied him onto the field. A pang of guilt struck him when he realized he had likely doomed Stannel and Dylan to share his fate. Yet they were Knights too, and as such, dying was part of their duty.

Ezekiel Silvercrown would be the new Commander of Fort Faith—the fourth commander of the castle in so short a time. Zeke would likely be the last Commander of Fort Faith; when the goblins got their staff back, nothing would stop them from laying waste to the fort and its defenders.

That bitter realization was a poison to Petton. Giving his life to a cause was one thing, but he had pitted more than his personal welfare in this contest. He knew then that Stannel had been right. Leaving his men to die at the hands of the goblins was tragic, but allowing the enemy to walk away with the *vuudu* staff...

That was unforgivable.

Now that he had gotten it into his head that he was to die honorably in battle, Petton was reluctant to shrug off that strange comfort. However, when he looked at Drekk't's face, he no longer saw the goblin's sneering visage, but rather than hollow-eyed skull from the *vuudu* staff.

If the goblins reclaimed the staff, his death would be the first of many. What would he tell Colt when he saw him in the after-life? How could he admit he had given up what the young commander had fought so desperately to keep?

He had to end this.

Although it went against every instinct, Petton broke away from Drekk't, brought his sword down to his side, and yelled, "Hold!"

Drekk't didn't hesitate in the slightest.

The general leaped forward, and it was all Petton could do to bring his sword up in time. It was an ugly block, but somehow he managed to stop with Drekk't's blade. The two weapons met with a crash. Then, inexplicably, Petton was overbalanced.

Petton's confusion lasted only as long as it took for Drekk't to plunge the bastard sword into his breast. The Knight looked down at the goblin's sword, which was planted hilt-deep in his chest. He then looked at his own sword. The blade had been severed just above the crosspiece.

Thick, warm liquid welled up in Petton's throat. He coughed, sending a spray of blood into Drekk't's face. The goblin pulled back abruptly, ripping his sword from Petton's body. The move hurt Petton far more than the initial stab had. The pain was so overwhelming he didn't feel himself fall.

The goblin loomed over him. Petton braced himself for another blow. He must have closed his eyes, though, because complete darkness replaced the monster. The anticipated agony from a final stab never came.

Then pain itself became a fast-fading memory.

Passage VIII

Stannel felt a sharp pain in his chest as he watched the goblin general impale Gaelor Petton. Stunned by how quickly and brutally the duel had ended, he could only hold his breath as the Knight slumped to the ground and died.

Beside him, Dylan leaped from his horse and drew his sword in one swift motion.

Before Stannel could react, Dylan rushed Drekk't. Stannel cried out to his companion, but Dylan paid him no mind.

Stannel expected to find the shaman already casting a spell. But the dark-robed goblin merely watched him, possibly waiting for him to make a move. The third goblin, however, reached for his axe and ran to his general's side.

Drekk't met Dylan's onslaught with measured strokes, deflecting the Knight's sword again and again. If Drekk't had tired at all during his match with Petton, he showed no signs of it. Dylan's assault was relentless, and even when the axe-wielding goblin came at him from the side, Dylan turned his attention away from Drekk't only long enough to force the other goblin back with a wild swing.

The situation was rapidly deteriorating, but Stannel dared not interfere. The shaman was still staring at him, as though daring to break the unspoken stalemate. Provoking the shaman into launching his spells could easily doom both Knights.

Dylan shouted at Drekk't, emphasizing his words with every swing of his sword. "You *bastard*! He said, '*Hold*'! He wanted to *talk*!"

Stannel silently petitioned the Great Protector for a way out. Was there any scenario where he and Dylan left the battlefield unharmed and with the *vuudu* staff?

Dylan pressed forward, keeping Drekk't occupied with a

series of swift strokes. It was all Drekk't could do to block them. The other goblin came at Dylan again, this time from behind. The goblin swung his axe in a horizontal arc aimed at the Knight's lower back.

Stannel's breath caught in his throat, certain Dylan would soon join Petton in death.

But Dylan must have heard the goblin coming. Pivoting with his right leg, the Knight spun around. His sword connected with the head of the axe.

Stannel winced, expecting the goblin's mighty swing to knock the sword aside and keep on going.

The axe struck Dylan's sword, and a part of it did keep going —the broken portion. Somehow, Dylan's sword had cleaved through the flat, broad blade of the axe, sending the majority of it flying off to the side.

At the sudden shift in weight, the goblin's momentum sent him pitching forward. Dylan followed through with a second stroke that bit deep into the goblin's back. The creature fell face-first to the ground, where he lay screaming in pain.

Stannel's gaze shot back to the shaman, certain the axe-wielder's death would spur him into action. But the shaman simply watched the two remaining combatants. Stannel thought the goblin looked perplexed.

In that moment of distraction, Stannel saw his chance to run. His first priority was to keep the staff away from the goblins. The shaman would certainly notice if he turned his horse around and retreated at a full gallop. Yet he had to try, even though it might cost Dylan his life.

Stannel hesitated.

Something was amiss. Why wasn't the shaman helping his general? And how had Dylan managed to decapitate that battle-axe? As Stannel tried to unravel those mysteries, his hand sought the comfort of his mace.

Nearby, Dylan threw himself at Drekk't with abandon. When presented with an obvious opening in Drekk't's defenses, the Knight took it. Stannel saw the ruse for what it was, and he mentally urged Dylan to pull back.

Dylan's sword connected with Drekk't's left pauldron. Stannel expected the goblin to accept the blow—as he had done during his duel with Petton—and to then counter with the same deadly lunge that had killed the commander.

As the sword smacked into Drekk't's protected shoulder, the general made no attempt to block it. At the same time, Drekk't thrust his sword at Dylan's midsection. If the manner in which Petton had been dispatched was any indication of Drekk't's strength, Dylan was about to find himself skewered like a boar on a spit.

Stannel prayed.

Drekk't's sword homed in on Dylan's belly. But Stannel could see the attack had been compromised. Both warriors let out a cry and fell back. Dylan's free hand went to where Drekk't sword had grazed his side, penetrating his mail and the flesh beneath. Drekk't inspected his shoulder, which was covered in black blood.

It was unlikely the younger Knight would have time to get back to his horse before Drekk't came at him again. It was even less likely the two of them would be able to escape the shaman's magic. Yet they had to try.

"Dylan!" Stannel shouted.

The younger Knight made no reply. For the moment, everything was unnaturally quiet. Neither Drekk't nor Dylan showed any signs of renewing their attacks. After measuring the severity of their wounds, both warriors looked down at their swords.

Wounds that should have been prevented by armor, and swords with the power to cut through metal, Stannel thought.

For the first time, Stannel noticed that Dylan's weapon was smaller and lighter than the one he usually carried. It wasn't *Chrysaal-rûn*, but the crystal sword wasn't the only enchanted blade at Fort Faith. The female Renegade who had accompanied Colt to Rydah also owned a sword of remarkable properties...

All at once, Stannel realized what had happened.

"Foul play!"

Stannel dismounted and hurried over to where Petton lay. He passed by the commander's broken sword, noting the impossibly straight edge of the break. Then he crouched beside Petton. The only damage that had been done to Petton's breastplate was the single puncture in its center, the fatal blow.

Drekk't sword had not found the space between plates, as Stannel had initially thought. The general had penetrated a quarter-inch of solid steel.

Stannel had seen holes in armor like this before. However, those had been dealt by nine-foot lances with the force of a charging steed behind them. The goblins were a strong people, but they were not *that* strong.

By this time, Dylan had joined him, alternating his gaze between the dead Knight, Drekk't, and the shaman. Stannel rose and took appraisal of Dylan's wound, which bled freely though the man's fingers and down his side. By all appearances, the goblin's sword had missed any vital organs, but Stannel worried the younger Knight would bleed out if the wound were not treated soon.

The hole in his cuirass was similar in size and shape to that in Petton's armor.

Fully aware that he had his back to the shaman—and keeping his hand near his mace—Stannel took a step closer to Drekk't.

Pointing an accusing finger at the general, he said, "There was to be no magic in the duel, but clearly your sword has magical properties. Therefore, the match is forfeit!"

Stannel tensed as the words left his mouth. When Drekk't made no move against him, he glanced back at the shaman. The robed goblin said nothing, for which Stannel was thankful. The third goblin lay unmoving where he had fallen, the yellow grass stained by his dark blood.

He looked back at Drekk't in time to see the general plant his blade deep into the frozen ground with ease.

"It is true!" Drekk't snarled.

The startled confession took Stannel by surprise. When Drekk't withdrew his sword from its earthen scabbard and stormed over to him, Stannel loosed his mace and prepared for the attack.

But rather than confront him, Drekk't strode past him and demanded of the shaman, "What have you done, Ay'sek?"

Thanks to the *vuudu* enchantment, Stannel understood the goblins' words. During the course of the argument that followed, it quickly became clear that the shaman, Ay'sek, had acted without Drekk't's consent—the general was not at all happy about it.

Ay'sek must have cast his spell during the duel, when no one was paying him any attention. Probably, he had had the incantation prepared from the start; the spell would have been invaluable if Drekk't had been pitted against Colt and his crystal sword.

"Why are you shouting at me?" Ay'sek snapped. "We have but to dispatch these two humans, and the prize is ours!"

Stannel tightened his grip on his mace, as Drekk't's bestial eyes fixed on Dylan and him. He resisted the urge to glance back at where the *vuudu* staff was secured to his horse's saddle.

Drekk't's gaze lingered on him for a moment longer. What the general said next surprised everyone, especially the shaman.

"We have violated the terms of the duel. We will not compound our treachery by killing those who accepted our oath in good faith."

Stannel was speechless, as was Dylan. The two Knights exchanged a puzzled look, though neither put his weapon away.

"What foolish babble is this?" the shaman demanded. "We have a mission to—"

The shaman's words were cut off when Drekk't turned on him and positioned his blade mere inches from the other goblin's neck.

"I am your leader," he said calmly. "You will obey me, or this sword you enchanted will be the instrument of your death."

Ay'sek's eyes widened. Stannel saw in his expression first surprise, then indignation, followed almost immediately by visceral malice.

"To make amends for my *unintentional* breech in combat, I will ensure your safe return to the fortress," Drekk't told the Knights.

"With the staff?" Stannel asked.

Drekk't nodded. "You may keep it for now. If my initial demands are not met, then my army will bring your castle to the ground, and I will pry the staff from your stiff, dead grip."

"Initial terms?" Dylan asked.

"I *will* have my duel with Saerylton Crystalus...his magical sword against mine. If your commander does not appear on this spot at dawn two days hence, the blood of everyone in that castle will be on his hands."

"I will relay your order to our commander," Stannel said.

As much as he despised being deceptive—even to a goblin— he had no intension of informing Drekk't that Colt was dead. He wondered why Drekk't had given them two full days to prepare, but the dark blood covering the general's shoulder seemed to explain Drekk't's supposed charity.

There were no more words exchanged between the two parties. Dylan and Stannel dragged Petton's body over to his horse and draped the dead Knight over the horse that had brought him out onto the field. It would be slow riding back to the fort for Stannel, who held the reins of Petton's horse.

Dylan would not be convinced to ride off ahead, despite his injury.

"I trust the goblins as far as I can smell them," he said to Stannel. "If they make a play for the staff, I'll not leave you to fight them alone."

Stannel nodded. Wary though he was of further betrayal from the goblins, he fell into introspective silence. There were many matters weighing heavily on his mind, not the least of which was the senseless death of Gaelor Petton.

So distracted was Stannel by the predictably dire future for the defenders of the fort, he didn't even notice when large, heavy snowflakes began falling from the sky.

General and shaman departed the battlefield, a heavy silence between them. Neither gave their dead comrade a second glance. The wretched goblin would rot where he lay, as was dictated by the Code of the Crusade.

Unlike the sentimental humans, a goblin would never take a carcass he didn't intend to eat. The dead never inconvenienced the living, and often a goblin served a purpose even in death. A pile of slain warriors at the base of a wall provided a ramp for the rest of the army—even as fallen officers served as figurative stepping-stones for those of lower ranking.

Ay'sek resisted the urge to launch a spell at Drekk't as they walked back to camp. Even with the *vuudu*-enhanced sword, the general was no match for him. A single spell would spill Drekk't's guts upon the ground.

If the humans had not been there when Drekk't had threatened him, Ay'sek might have killed him then and there. But Ay'sek would not risk inciting a battle that pitted him against Drekk't and the two remaining Knights.

By the time the humans left, Ay'sek had regained his composure. Drekk't would survive the day, but Ay'sek swore by the Goblinfather that in two days, the general would die. Ay'sek could remove the enchantment as easily as he had created it. Nullifying the spell during the upcoming fight with Colt would rob Drekk't of his revenge as well as his life.

Ay'sek wondered if Saerylton Crystalus would show up for

the duel. Maybe the Knights would send another substitute. Or maybe they wouldn't come out at all. In that case, Drekk't would attack the fortress again.

That possibility was problematic for Ay'sek. While he could kill Drekk't in the confusion of battle, there was always the chance his treason would be discovered. Therefore, it was in Ay'sek's best interest for the duel to occur. The number of witnesses would be minimal…

Even as he plotted Drekk't's murder, Ay'sek suspected Drekk't was doing the same for him.

Once they reached camp, they parted ways without comment. Despite his serious injury, Drekk't's did not ask for any magical treatment. It was just as well. Ay'sek needed all of his strength for what lay ahead.

Let Drekk't die from an infection, Ay'sek thought. It's better than he deserves!

The shaman made haste for his private tent, ignoring the curious expressions he met along the way. None of the warriors would learn what had happened on the battlefield that day, but each and every soldier already must realize their general's behavior was atypical.

How long before the warriors see Drekk't for the imbecile he is? Ay'sek wondered. How long before one of them assassinates him for the good of all?

Not soon enough.

Once inside his tent, Ay'sek wasted no time in channeling the power of Upsinous into various wards of protection imbued upon his tent and his body. He didn't think it likely Drekk't would try to kill him—Drekk't couldn't talk to the humans without him—but neither would he take chances.

Even the meekest prey became a predator when backed into a corner.

Ay'sek took a seat behind the crate containing the various ingredients he would need for the spell. He recalled then what the far-sight ritual had revealed. Both good and bad would result from Drekk't's plan. Perhaps the Goblinfather had meant that things would end well for Ay'sek but bad for Drekk't.

He shrugged. Prophecy was simply a guide. He would devise his own destiny.

Pushing augury from his mind, Ay'sek opened his soul to Upsinous, eager to enter the trance that would give him with the words to the spell he needed.

The small room that had served as Petton's office seemed far too empty to Stannel as he informed Ezekiel Silvercrown and Ruford Berwyn of that morning's tragedy.

Both men had surely suspected bad news was to come; Petton and Dylan had been taken to the infirmary straightaway. But it was up to Stannel to tell Zeke and Ruford that the commander was dead.

When Stannel finished his account of the duel, Zeke Silvercrown said, "He died bravely, fighting for what he thought was right. A Knight could wish for no better fate."

Stannel did not necessarily agree, but he held his tongue. He wondered how close Petton and Zeke had been. Moreover, Stannel wondered whether Zeke Silvercrown shared Petton's low estimation of the *vuudu* staff's worth. Perhaps the new commander would trade the staff for the goblins' empty promise to leave the island in peace.

Stannel reminded himself that the matter was beyond his immediate control. He had willingly stepped down as the Commander of new Fort Valor. Guilt, doubt, and fear had prompted the self-demotion. He could see that now. He hadn't wanted to hold so many lives in his hands, not after the Knights of *old* Fort Valor had slipped through his fingers, one and all.

If he hadn't relinquished his command, Gaelor Petton might still be alive. But then again, maybe not. Since Stannel would never have agreed to a duel with Drekk't, the general would have probably ordered a full assault on the castle already.

If nothing else, Petton had bought them some time. It was up to Ezekiel Silvercrown, the next in line for command, to decide what to do with it.

"General Drekk't still believes Saerylton Crystalus leads us," Stannel said to Zeke. "I can only pray that Commander Silvercrown will not ride out to face the goblin general, as Commander Petton did before him."

Zeke Silvercrown opened his mouth to respond, but no words came out. Stannel pitied the man. While being promoted to such a high rank should have been the honor of a lifetime, Ezekiel Silvercrown could take little joy in his advancement, which had resulted from not one, but two untimely deaths.

Would Zeke's uncertainty cause him to overcompensate, making bold decisions like Petton had? Would he too ride out to find death rather than live with the seemingly hopeless situation he was presented with?

It had never sat well with Stannel that a single man should determine the fate of so many. From commanders to kings, they were all just men—susceptible to fear and capable of error.

Zeke Silvercrown took a deep breath. "I concede to your wisdom and experience, Sir Bismarc. Please lead us as the Commander of Fort Valor once more."

Whatever he expected Zeke to say, that was not it.

In his mind, Stannel saw the ruins of the first Fort Valor, imagined the horrible manner in which his men had died. He had failed that fortress. Now he was being asked to carry the burden of command again. How easy it would be to say no, to let the responsibility fall on someone else's shoulders.

For a split second, he hated Zeke Silvercrown for putting him in that position, but he hated himself more for his cowardice. Someone had to take control of the fort, and he was the most qualified.

Was Pintor giving him a chance to redeem himself or simply testing his faith?

"Very well," Stannel said in a near-whisper. "I accept."

Zeke did not mask his relief.

Ruford grunted. "A fort with an identity crisis, an army of thousands demanding what can't be delivered, and our lives hinged on a staff that I, for one, can't wait to be rid of...so what's our next move, Commander?"

Stannel noted the helplessness and frustration in Ruford's words. Though a leader in his own right, Ruford would abide by whatever the Knights of Superius decided.

"I do not know," Stannel admitted, "but neither do I intend to determine that on my own. I will host a council this evening, inviting key members of our united army to speak their minds.

"If we are to find hope in our darkest hour, we must find it together."

Passage IX

Jer'malz's eyes widened at the sight of the general's injury. As Drekk't snarled at the whelp of a soldier trying to bandage his arm, Jer'malz glanced at Ay'goar. The other lieutenant's expression was as guarded as his own.

Neither of them had had any say in Drekk't's decision to engage the fort's commander in one-on-one combat. When they had first been told of the duel, Jer'malz had thought Drekk't was joking—not that the general was known for his sense of humor.

Jer'malz lowered his gaze when Drekk't turned his full attention back to Ay'goar and him. Judging by the general's temperament, the duel had not gone well. Jer'malz did not expect to get a full account of the battle, though they deserved an explanation.

Yet none was forthcoming. Instead, Drekk't started giving orders.

Jer'malz analyzed the commands, trying to piece together what might have happened between Drekk't and the human commander. Drekk't didn't have the staff, and since the general was not rallying the army for an attack, he was still planning to recover the talisman on his own.

The fact that Ay'sek wasn't tending to Drekk't's wound meant the two of them still weren't working in concert. Drekk't and Ay'sek's mutual hatred did not concern Jer'malz, but the consequences of it did.

Whatever the general and the shaman were planning—separately or together—it meant the rest of the army was going to have to wait two more days before the chance to fight presented itself. And even then there was no guarantee.

Two days were not so long when compared to how much time they had already invested in the campaign. But two days felt an eternity when you were living in hell.

Winter's chill had wrapped itself around Jer'malz bones like a constrictor snake. According to the legends, goblinkind had once dwelled in deep caverns far beneath ancient mountains in the West. Goblins could survive in even the coldest weather, though it slowed their blood and made them sluggish.

Some of the warriors had fallen ill. Thankfully, the ailment was not contagious. The fever of dissent, however, had spread through the ranks like wildfire. In circumstances such as these, mutiny was not unheard of.

At least we have food, Jer'malz thought. The most recent battle had provided fresh meat, but already they were operating on reduced rations. When the food ran out, the soldiers would almost certainly turn on each other; the army would literally cannibalize itself.

As a veteran officer, Drekk't had to know all of this. So why did it seem as though he no longer cared about the war?

When Drekk't finished listing what needed to be done to prepare for the second duel, Ay'goar bowed and said, "Yes, *n'patrek*."

Jer'malz echoed the automatic response, but when Drekk't turned his back to him—a clear indication the meeting was over—Jer'malz could no longer hold his tongue.

"*N'patrek*, while we wait for the moment to strike, the army is exposed to an enemy more formidable than the humans. The brunt of winter assails us—"

"What is your point?" Drekk't snapped.

"Some of the soldiers are ill. If we relocated a fraction of our forces to the nearby woodlands, we could rotate the troops and lessen the casualties."

Drekk't took a step closer to Jer'malz. "You would have fall back? Now?"

"No...no, *n'patrek*," he stammered. "I'm saying we should designate a place to keep the sick. The sickness does not seem to be catching, but why take chances?"

The general only glared at him, prompting Jer'malz to add, "If nothing else, it would give the soldiers something to do."

Drekk't let out a terrible laugh that made Jer'malz flinch. "You are bored, are you, Jer'malz?"

"*N'patrek*, no—!"

"I know of just the errand for you. There is an abandoned

village to the southwest. It used to be a mining town. You will take fifty goblins to appraise the location for possible habitation."

"Me, *n'patrek*?"

Drekk't grinned evilly. "It was your idea, Jer'malz. Maybe you will come to appreciate periods of calm after you have walked there and back *without rest*."

Jer'malz opened his mouth to say something in his defense, but the dark glare Drekk't fixed on him stole the air from his lungs. He could only bow, whispering a deferential "Yes, *n'patrek*" before hurrying out of the tent.

He stormed away from the tent, pointedly avoiding Ay'goar. The other lieutenant had said nothing to support Jer'malz's perfectly reasonable suggestion. Of course, Jer'malz probably would have handled the situation the same way if Ay'goar had overstepped his bounds.

Jer'malz decided he would have to be wary upon his return to the camp. If something happened to Drekk't while he was gone—the general was injured, after all—Ay'goar would probably welcome Jer'malz home with a dagger in the dark.

As he gathered his squadron, Jer'malz cursed himself for a fool. Even though Drekk't was making one poor decision after another, it was not his place to question his superior—at least not publicly. In fact, he might have gotten worse for his meddling than the command of a pointless mission.

All fifty of the soldiers Jer'malz handpicked readied themselves for the journey without complaint. Not a one of them questioned the reason for the errand. They had been taught from birth to do as they were told. Jer'malz thought he could learn a lot from the least of them.

The farther they walked from the camp, the heavier the snowfall became. Jer'malz's anger toward Drekk't only increased when they met their first real obstacle. A wide river, covered in translucent ice, separated them from the foothills—and the mining town—beyond.

The goblins followed the eastern bank of the frozen river for a time, heading due south. After an hour, Jer'malz felt the jaws of indecision gnawing at his mind. If they kept going south, they might miss the village entirely. Yet backtracking would only add more time to the pointless mission.

As it was, they might not make it back to the army before the next battle—a thought that soured the lieutenant's mood a little more each time it occurred to him.

Jer'malz stared at the dark, still waters for a moment longer before announcing that they would walk across it.

The first goblin, a low-ranking soldier on his first campaign, inched his way across the delicate covering. One false move would plunge him into the deadly cold waters. No one would save him in that event, and even if he managed to drag himself out of the water, he would inevitably die from hypothermia.

The remaining goblins were assailed by mixed emotions when the young soldier made it to the other side. If that first goblin had fallen in, none of them would have been expected to risk a similar fate. The ice had proven strong enough to support one of them…but would it hold out for the others?

Jer'malz sent two more soldiers across, making sure they remained a safe distance apart. Both warriors—who were considerably larger than the first—made it across without incident. Thinking every footfall weakened the fragile walkway, Jer'malz went next. He heaved a visible sigh when his feet landed once more on solid ground.

Crossing the river proved to be a time-consuming endeavor. By the time there were but five goblins remaining on the opposite shore, Jer'malz had run out of patience. He ordered the lot of them to come over at once. The soldiers hesitated only a second before complying.

They were midway across when a crunching sound made them pause. After a moment's hesitation, three of the soldiers tried to make a run for it. Two of those warriors lost their footing and came crashing down to the ice. The third managed to stay on his feet, but he didn't get far before the long, snaking fissures caught up with him.

Within a minute, all five of the goblins were bobbing in the water, flailing and screaming.

Jer'malz cursed his ill luck. Drekk't would not be pleased when he returned to camp with five fewer soldiers. Without a glance back at the doomed goblins, Jer'malz resumed the march.

By the time they found the abandoned town, the sun had vanished behind the wall of rock that formed the western horizon. Jer'malz supposed he should have been thankful for finding the place at all, but he was tired from so much walking as well as the chill that had invaded his body like an unseen enemy.

Jer'malz was dividing his contingent into groups of five when one of the soldiers shouted. He searched the crowd for whoever dared to interrupt him. He never discovered the guilty party. Realizing that all of the warriors were looking, as one, at something behind him, Jer'malz spun around and drew his machete.

He had expected to find a pack of wolves or maybe a cavalcade of Knights. What he had not expected to see was a young human female.

"What have we here?" Jer'malz mumbled to himself.

The girl was alone, and since the village appeared to be otherwise unoccupied, Jer'malz was left to conclude the whelp had wandered away from home—wherever that was—and gotten lost.

There wasn't enough meat on her bones to make a decent snack, but Jer'malz could think of other uses for her. Despite the inherent repulsiveness of human females, their anatomy was comparable to their goblin counterparts.

In spite of the freezing wind, Jer'malz's blood began to burn.

Certain that the little girl would run the instant he came nearer, Jer'malz signaled for his men to fan out. Jer'malz took no more than three steps toward her before stopping again. The girl made no move to flee, and Jer'malz was fairly certain the sound coming from her mouth was laughter, not crying.

It wasn't the girl's strange behavior that had caused the lieutenant to stop, however. It was the way her eyes seemed to flash white in the darkness. The eyes of animals did that sometimes, but Jer'malz had never seen a human's do it.

The girl's laughter ceased suddenly and was replaced by a disembodied voice that spoke in a language Jer'malz couldn't understand. It might have been the human tongue, but somehow he knew he was hearing the words to a magical rite.

Jer'malz watched, transfixed, as the girl walked up to him. Her hair was as black as the night. Her eyes no longer shone white, but even in the waning light, Jer'malz saw that one eye was blue and other brown.

He decided to deal with the uncanny human in the way goblins traditionally handled potentially dangerous surprises. Tightening his grip on the machete, he took a swing at her.

Or, rather, that's what he had intended to do. A searing pain erupted from somewhere inside his skull. He heard himself scream, heard the cries of his men. It felt as though someone was snuffing out a torch with his brain.

The pain consumed his mind, and his last conscious thought was a prayer to Upsinous, begging for death to come quickly. But his prayer went unanswered.

The girl giggled.

Ay'sek knew there were risks in casting the incantation again so soon.

A fish might survive out of the water for a time, but if it spent too much time outside of its natural habitat…well, there was a point of no return with such things.

With every separation of Ay'sek's corporeal and ethereal halves, the invisible cord that bound them together grew weaker. Yet he couldn't afford to wait. He had to act before the Knights did something drastic.

The fort's defenders probably couldn't destroy *Peerma'rek*—even with a midge's help—but hiding it away somewhere would prove just as disastrous for Ay'sek, who couldn't forget the Emperor's threats.

His resolve bolstered, the shaman fell into a trance. The Goblinfather's words washed over him. The sensation reminded him of being scalded by water so hot it felt cold—or vice versa. With an excruciating, exquisite cry, Ay'sek expelled his soul.

Leaving his body far behind, the shaman steered his spiritual essence across the snowy field and into the fortress, passing through hallways and solid walls alike. He could already feel the pull of *Peerma'rek*, as though the staff were calling out to him.

Any elation he may have felt upon fixing his mind's eye on the staff's thick, shadowy aura was instantly quenched by the presence of an all-too-familiar form. Stannel Bismarc, the self-appointed guardian of *Peerma'rek*, had the staff strapped to his back.

It took all of Ay'sek's will to hold himself back. His spirit yearned for a shell—any physical shell. Invading Stannel's body would bring Ay'sek that much closer to obtaining *Peerma'rek*.

But the golden glow that surrounded Stannel like a cocoon reminded Ay'sek how dangerous a direct attack would be. Whatever god protected the Knight would certainly lend him strength if Ay'sek engaged him in spiritual warfare.

Ay'sek needed to find someone who was not favored by any one deity or, better yet, a human who had no use for the gods at all. As Stannel walked down one of the fort's hallways, Ay'sek followed at a distance, invisible and intangible. The shaman's patience was rewarded when he spotted the hazy figure of another human up ahead.

Unlike Stannel, this newcomer possessed no wreath of holy radiance. An unremarkable white light swirled within the man's chest. Ay'sek wasted no time in advancing on the unsuspecting man. Whizzing past Stannel, the shaman drew himself around the stranger.

Eager as he was to usurp a body, Ay'sek did not force himself upon the random human. Even if Stannel weren't a cleric, he surely would have noted something amiss when the other man's body began to twitch and shudder. Instead, Ay'sek attempted something that, as far as he knew, had never been attempted before.

Slowly, gently, he eased his spirit inside, careful not to interrupt the delicate symbiosis of soul and body. The arrangement was uncomfortable for both parties, but Ay'sek's spirit was allowed to remain. He was aware of Stannel coming nearer, could feel the irritating warmth of Stannel's golden aura.

All he could do was pray that the Knight would not interfere.

Shutting out everything else, Ay'sek focused all of his will into a single objective. As he concentrated, a tiny part of his essence formed itself into a needle-like tendril. Holding his breath—figuratively speaking—Ay'sek then thrust the dark thistle into the ball of white light that was the unknown man's soul.

The man's body jerked, as though stung by an insect, but Ay'sek detached himself before the human could repel him. So sudden was his retreat that the injected fragment of himself—the metaphysical stinger—remained where it had been injected.

Stannel gave the oblivious victim an odd look, but to Ay'sek's relief, the Knight did not stop. Turning his attention back to the other man, Ay'sek was pleased to find a tiny, dark filament squirming worm-like within the glow of whiteness. Like Ay'sek's own soul, that wisp of black smoke bore a distinct resemblance to the storm cloud that swirled about *Peerma'rek*.

Ay'sek did not know if the desired effect would come about, but one thing was for certain: he had left a lasting impression on the unwary human.

Suddenly, Ay'sek's spirit was wracked by a series of convulsions. Struggling to keep the fibers of his being from unraveling, Ay'sek burst from the fortress and soared back to the goblin camp. He knew with certainty he would never be able to cast this particular spell again, could never roam free outside the confines of his physical being.

But that no longer mattered. All he cared about now was getting back to his body before his soul dissipated into nothingness.

As his spirit homed in on its body—both halves desperately seeking the union they needed to survive—Ay'sek could only pray that his subconscious command to the miscellaneous man would be obeyed.

Passage X

When word of Petton's death reached the Renegade Room, Plake studied the reactions of his companions. Everyone wore solemn expressions, even Horcalus, whom Petton had regularly referred to as a traitor. Klye and Petton had had their share of arguments, but rather than gloat, the Renegade Leader looked as glum as everybody else.

Plake didn't feel much of anything. He had come to hate the haughty Knight, and Petton's death didn't change that. Still, he hated the goblins more.

It was Lilac who broke the reverent silence that had settled over the room.

"Where is Dylan now, Pillip? Was he injured badly?"

The man who had delivered the news about Petton's duel was a lanky fellow. Although he—along with some other refugees from Hylan—had been lodging in the Renegade Room for the past couple of days, Plake had never heard anyone address the man by name.

He might have been suspicious of Lilac and Pillip's familiarity, but he knew Pillip and Hunter were a couple. Sir Dylan on the other hand…

Plake had noticed at once the strange sword hanging from Lilac's hip when she returned from her chat with Dylan last night, and it wasn't hard to put two and two together. Dylan and Lilac had traded weapons.

The woman obviously cared a great deal for Dylan if she had handed over her precious vorpal sword just like that.

Plake barely listened to what Pillip said in reply to Lilac's question. He was too busy staring at Lilac, gauging her expression for clues. He did, however, catch the word "infirmary," so when Lilac walked past him and out of the room, he knew exactly where she was headed.

His face burned. If she was so in love with Dylan, she should at least have the guts to tell him!

Klye, Horcalus, and Scout fired question after question at Pillip, though the Hylaner knew few details. Pillip repeated much of what he had already said, probably repeating the very words that had been given to him.

With the information passing through so many people, Plake thought that the story could be all wrong by now. He hoped it was Dylan who had died, not Petton.

Klye, Scout, and Horcalus began talking among themselves, speculating about what the commander's death meant for the residents of the fort. Arthur was content to sit there and listen. Plake, however, was bored with idle chatter.

"Where are you going, Plake?"

He stopped midway between where he had been sitting and the door. He glared back at Scout, who regarded him innocently. He would have just ignored the question, but he was all too aware of Klye's and Horcalus's eyes on him also.

"Thought I'd stretch my legs," he muttered.

"A walk? Mind if I join you?" Scout asked. "If I stay in this room too long, I start feeling a little crazy, if you know what I mean."

Plake thought Scout had been "a little crazy"—or more than a little—since the day they met, but he kept his opinion to himself. He had more important things to do than argue with Scout, who never got tired of talking and who would likely change the subject halfway through the debate anyway.

And if he had to listen to one more of Scout's history lessons, he would be the one losing his mind.

"I kind of just want to be alone," he told Scout.

The answer didn't seem to faze the other Renegade at all. "Oh, all right."

Plake glanced at Klye, hoping he had bought the story. Klye's expression betrayed no emotion at all. Not giving him a chance to stop him, Plake left the room.

Probably, the Renegade Leader hadn't believed him. Klye Tristan was pretty good at figuring things out—even if he hadn't figured out how to get them away from the damned fort yet!

He had hoped to follow Lilac to the infirmary because he wasn't sure he could find the place on his own. But the woman had gotten a head start, and Plake soon found himself wandering aimlessly. Mumbling curse after curse, he tried to get his bearings. Maybe I should have let Scout come with me, after all, he thought.

Finally, he found himself in a familiar stretch of corridor. He crept up to the door to the infirmary, which was open. Inside, he saw a Knight standing at the bedside of a man he didn't know—probably a wounded comrade. There was no sign of Ruben, the highwayman who had gone from being one of Sister Aric's patients to her assistant. The healer was there though, praying over the occupant of another bed.

Plake's gaze took them all in and dismissed them in less than a second. He fixed his attention on Lilac Zephyr, who was standing with her back to him and talking to someone in a bed. It had to be Dylan.

He craned his neck, trying to get a good look at his rival for Lilac's affection, but the woman was standing in his way. He supposed it was for the best. If he couldn't see the Knight, then the Knight couldn't see him either.

With his back pressed up against the wall and his head turned at a sharp angle, Plake forgot about any physical discomfort as Lilac's words drifted over to him.

"You're far too reckless. If I hadn't lent you my sword, Drekk't would have shattered yours and scored a hit far worse than this."

"If I hadn't had an enchanted sword, I might not have attacked the general at all," Dylan countered.

"Oh, I think you would have," Lilac said. "You're drawn to battle like loadstone to iron. It's like I said before, you've had Defenders' Plague since the day I met you."

Plake tried to remember how Lilac and this Knight had met. She had told the Renegades about her trip to Rydah and back, but now he couldn't recall this one detail. Had Dylan been one of the men to save her, Colt, and Opal from getting captured at the goblin camp?

Gods damn it, he was, wasn't he? No wonder why she was so taken with him!

"Maybe you're right," Dylan said after a moment. "But I couldn't sit this one out, not when Petton had clearly signaled a halt to the duel. Striking the killing blow was probably a fair move, according to the ancient rules of the contest, but it was a wretched way to win nevertheless. Anyway, Drekk't's sword was fortified with *vuudu*, so he did cheat after all."

"But you didn't know that at the time," Lilac pointed out.

Plake imagined that the Knight shrugged his shoulders—his broad, muscular shoulders…

Gods damn it all!

Dylan laughed. "And here I thought you had come to wish me well. Instead, you're scolding me like a brat who strayed too far from his mother."

Although he could not see Lilac's face, Plake was certain she was smiling.

What was so special about Dylan anyway? he wondered. Yes, the Knight was a brave warrior and all that, but Plake was no stranger to battle. Had Lilac already forgotten the fight against T'slect in the war room? That had been no minor tussle, and afterward he had ended up in sickbed himself.

Not that Lilac had ever come to visit him. Oh, she had come to see Klye, but he never would have gotten so much as a glimpse of her if his bed hadn't been next to Klye's.

"So," Lilac said after another long pause, "how long are you going to have to stay here?"

The Knight lowered his voice, so Plake had to strain even more to hear what he said next. "Sister Aric says I must spend the night here. But I'll not lie here for much long after that. I've come too far to wait the war out in a sickbed."

"There's that Defenders' Plague again."

A sound from behind him made Plake jump. He spun around, certain his face was radiating guilt. He was so alarmed by the presence of the newcomer that he didn't recognize him at first. In fact, he was having a hard time seeing anything due to a sudden dizziness. When his body ceased its trembling, Plake dismissed the sensation as severe embarrassment.

Or maybe, he thought, this is what it feels like to be in love.

Plake planted his hands in his pocket and tried to look natural. As the man drew nearer, he was able to identify him as Stannel Bismarc. The Knight nodded politely at him as he passed by and entered the infirmary. Plake was going to nod back, but he found that he could do nothing but gape.

As Stannel made his way to Dylan's bedside, the skull on the staff stared back at Plake. He'd seen a human skull only once before in his life, and it had given him nightmares for years. But although the *vuudu* staff was a ghastly sight, Plake couldn't turn away.

It was ugly to be sure, but it was also somehow…fascinating.

Somewhere in the back of his mind, Plake understood that Stannel's entrance would likely result in Lilac's exit. Unless he wanted her to find him there, spying, he had better hightail it back to the Renegade Room. It was the smart thing to do, yet he couldn't quite look away from the disembodied head that grinned perversely in his direction.

The sound of Lilac's voice—saying goodbye to Dylan—sobered Plake right up. Tearing his eyes away from the staff, he turned and ran down the hallway. As he sprinted back to the Renegade Room, his mind was aflutter with possibility.

Before, there had been no hope for winning Lilac's love. Not with Sir Daring and Dashing Dylan in the picture. But now he saw a solution. All he had to do was find a way to show Lilac he was every bit as brave as the Knight.

Dylan had thrown himself at Drekk't, mindless of his own fate. It shouldn't have surprised Plake that Lilac was attracted to the selfless warrior. She herself had sailed all the way to Capricon to save Ragellan and Horcalus.

Plake knew he would find a way to impress her—and he was equally certain the *vuudu* staff would be part of the solution.

She couldn't help but notice how, even in a large crowd, people formed distinct groups. There were many pockets of Knights, and the Renegades, of course, stood together. Hunter, Pillip, and Bly had positioned themselves off to one side, talking among themselves. Even Aric and Ruben had each other.

But Opal was alone.

She had kept close to the door, uncertain of whether she would stay long. At the opposite end of the room, Stannel was signaling for silence. She listened halfheartedly as the Knight—who, apparently, was the fort's commander again—explained their current situation.

After he finished his speech, Stannel asked those gathered for their thoughts. Voices familiar and foreign to Opal chimed in at various intervals, taking the discussion in different directions, but her mind was no longer on the topic at hand.

Another important meeting had taken place in the fort's

dining hall. The gathering had been called after Stannel returned from the ruins of the first Fort Valor. And it had been at that meeting that Colt stepped down as Commander of Fort Faith in order to join the party bound for Rydah.

Opal had demanded to go with him. So had Cholk.

Now, with Colt and Cholk both dead, she felt as though she had wandered into the wrong fort by mistake. Never had she felt so alone—not even when she had first realized the extent of her amnesia. She even missed Noel.

The thought made her laugh in spite of herself, which earned her a confused look from a man standing next to her.

She realized that she must have been daydreaming for some time because Stannel Bismarc was once again addressing the group as a whole. As the commander spoke, Opal was able to put the bits and pieces of information together and figure out what course of action had been decided.

And though she could see the logic behind it, Opal hated the plan.

As she understood it, the Knights, along with Ruford and remaining guardsmen, would take up defensive positions inside the fort at dawn two days from now. As the defenders prepared to repel the assault that would come once the goblins realized the duel was not to be, everyone else—the Renegades, militiamen, thieves, the wounded—would hide in the subterranean passageway that Toemis Blisnes had revealed weeks ago.

With its great numbers, the T'Ruellian army was guaranteed to win. The Knights and guardsmen would probably all die—dutifully, of course—while the rest of the fort's residents cowered under the ground, praying that the enemy wouldn't realize they were missing. And there they would remain until the goblins moved on.

"Everyone who is able to fight should be allowed to," Klye Tristan insisted. She had the feeling that this was not the first time the Renegade Leader had made the argument.

But Stannel was shaking his head before Klye even finished.

"Those who cannot fight will need the protection of those who can," was the commander's firm reply. "Those who wait out the battle in the tunnel will not find an easy route to safety. Between the elements and the invaders…"

Opal shuddered at the thought of emerging from the passage and finding bodies strewn all about the fort. The Knights apparently had no problem with trading their lives for the civilians'. How damned chivalrous of them, she thought bitterly.

Having heard enough, she pushed her way past a group of Knights who had been listening to the dialogue from out in the hallway. She stormed away, refusing to look them in the eyes.

How could Stannel expect her to sit this battle out? She owed those monsters for what they did to her friends. And if she had stayed by Colt's side instead of remaining with the *vuudu* staff, she might have been able to save him.

Hurrying away from the dining hall—her rage increasing with every step—Opal soon found herself in the one place that still felt familiar. The air was warmer here, but not stiflingly so.

At that moment, she wouldn't have traded the smell of manure for even the most precious bottle of Huiyan perfume. Nisson whinnied a greeting as Opal approached her stall. As she combed her fingers through the horse's mane, Opal spoke softly to her. She was only vaguely aware of the tears trickling down her cheeks.

"You're a brave one, aren't you, girl?" she whispered. "I don't know what I would've done if...if..."

Opal had wanted to stay angry with Stannel for riding Nisson into battle, but she was convinced it had been Nisson who found her in the woods. Alone in the woods...with Othello's corpse...

Thankfully, Nisson's wound hadn't been deep, and the horse was already on the mend. She knew Nisson would run for her if she commanded it. Even if every hoof-fall sent a jolt of agony through the animal, Nisson would run for her.

"If they think I'm going to hide in some stinking hole and leave you to die here, they're in for a surprise," she told the mare.

Absently stroking Nisson's snowy white flank, Opal remembered the confidence she had felt when facing the whole of the goblin army in order to rescue Colt. She didn't remember being afraid. Had her concern for Colt overpowered instinctual fear?

No, it had been more than just bravery...

Her boldness had been bolstered by an exquisite display of swordsmanship. In her impromptu battle with Drekk't, she had wielded the crystal sword with a talent seemingly beyond her.

According to Lilac and Dylan, Colt's final fight, too, had been a remarkable display...

Like sunlight piercing the darkest of storm clouds, understanding hit her. It was the sword—it had to be. *Chrysaal-rûn* had displayed an assortment of magical properties during the short time Colt had carried it.

She had seen Colt cut through solid steel with it. On one occasion, the crystal sword had emitted a blue beacon of light. Another time, it had scalded Klye's hand so that the rebel couldn't wield it against Colt.

And apparently, *Chrysaal-rûn* also had the ability to enhance its wielder's fighting abilities.

Still petting her beloved horse, her only friend, Opal muttered, "If I'm going to face those ugly bastards again, I'm going to need that sword."

Plake spent the first part of the meeting staring at Lilac, trying to come up with a way to win her affection. During the silence dedicated to the late Lieutenant Petton, Plake saw the woman close her eyes and bow her head. She looked so sad.

How he wanted to take her in his arms and comfort her!

Stannel then said something about the goblins proposing a second duel, but Plake immediately tuned the commander out. Strategy bored him, and because Klye, Horcalus, and Scout had been discussing what they would do if they were in charge almost nonstop before the meeting, Plake thought he'd prefer a goblin spear to the gut than to have to listen to more talk.

If Lilac hadn't come, he probably would have sat this meeting out in the Renegade Room.

"What if someone were to don the late commander's armor and brandish his sword?" someone near the front of the room asked. "The goblins might unwittingly accept a substitute."

Stannel looked over at the man who had spoken, as did Plake. The rancher's worst fears were confirmed when the man proposing the daring plan turned out to be none other than Sir Dylan Torc.

"Perhaps," Stannel told Dylan, "but General Drekk't is cunning, and as you know, he employs the services of a *vuudu* priest. Any charade on our part would quickly unravel, I fear. Aside from gaining the opportunity to slay one goblin out of thousands, I cannot see what we would gain by the ruse."

Stannel spoke with calm assurance and obvious intelligence. Plake hoped Dylan would argue with him just so the new Commander of Fort Faith—or was it Fort Valor again?—could put him in his place. But the younger Knight did not say anything else.

"A decoy is not without merit." The paunchy man who spoke had a thick mustache that curled up at both ends. He reminded Plake a little of his uncle. But instead of worn leather duds, this man wore a uniform of some sort. Faded red and white stripes could be seen in the few places that weren't discolored by dark stains.

"A false Colt would make a nice diversion," the same man added. "If the goblins are all looking in one direction, we could strike from another."

"We couldn't beat 'em when we had two armies," argued a man that Plake couldn't see. "What chance do we have now that there's even fewer of us?"

Several people, including Pillip and the burly fellow beside him, condemned the defeatist sentiment. Above the sudden clamor, Lilac's friend Hunter could be heard shouting, "Well, dyin' out there sure beats suffocating in some tunnel!"

That comment evoked even more shouts—some in agreement, some against—and provoked Stannel to raise his voice to be heard above the din.

"Order!" Surprisingly, everyone quieted down. "You will all have a chance to speak, but you must do so one at a time."

The argument raged on for a while, with Stannel playing mediator and devil's advocate. But Plake was no longer following the discussion. He couldn't stop thinking about Dylan and how the Knight had one-upped him again by volunteering to fight in Colt's place.

Though it didn't seem likely Dylan would be allowed to impersonate Colt, Dylan had certainly scored points by suggesting it. The only thing Plake could do to trump Dylan's bravado was to go through with the heroic deed.

Hmm…

He was about the same height and build as the late Saerylton Crystalus. Wrapped in a suit of armor, his face hidden behind the visor of a helm, Plake would easily dupe the goblins. If he could get his hands on Colt's stuff—including that magical sword—the goblin general would never be the wiser!

Plake imagined his triumphant return to the fort, carrying the general's head. If the goblins kept their word, they would leave, and he would be a hero. If they didn't go, he'd use the crystal sword to hack apart any goblin foolish enough to get too close to him and Lilac.

When Stannel turned his back to the Renegades, addressing someone on the other side of the room, Plake caught sight of the *vuudu* staff.

He had known earlier that day that the staff would be part of his plan to win Lilac's heart. At the time, he had supposed he might use its magic to force Lilac to love him back. But now he realized the staff would play an indirect role.

He needed the staff to entice Drekk't to come out and fight him.

Throughout the rest of the meeting, Plake pondered how he would accomplish what he was now determined to do. Later, he found himself following the crowd as everyone slowly filed out of the dining hall.

His heart was beating so quickly he thought it might burst. Gods below, how he wished he had a drink! Liquid courage would certainly hit the spot. Back in Param, he had never brawled without having emptied a few mugs first. Was he really brave enough to go through with it?

A glance behind him revealed Lilac talking with Dylan.

Plake vowed to any god listening that he would do whatever it took to accomplish his mission. And in two days' time, no one—not Lilac, not anyone—would be able to deny his bravery.

Heedless of how people were pushing to get around him, Plake took the opportunity to sneak another look at the *vuudu* staff. His skin no longer crawled when he looked into the empty sockets of the skull. He felt only excitement.

As he made his way back to the Renegade Room, Plake began thinking up ways to get the staff from Stannel Bismarc.

Passage XI

The first corpse Plake had ever seen was his mother's. That had been so long ago he couldn't remember what the woman had looked like alive, let alone dead.

More recently, he had seen the beheaded body of Chester Ragellan—a grisly sight to be sure. And of course, he had seen more dead bodies than he could count during the recent clashes with the goblins. The horrified expressions of the dying, not to mention their piteous screams, would live on in Plake's nightmares.

But unlike those others, Colt looked peaceful. The dead Knight lay with his arms crossed over his chest and his eyes closed. The longer Plake stared at the man's pale face, the more he was able to convince himself that Saerylton Crystalus was only sleeping. He half feared the commander would open his eyes and discover him sneaking about his room.

"We should go," Scout whispered.

Plake had all but forgotten the other man, and when he turned to face him, he found Scout looking at him, wearing an uncharacteristically serious look on his face. He was about to agree with Scout—eager, as he was, to send the other Renegade on his way—but he feared that that might come off as suspicious.

When had he ever agreed with Scout?

"I dare you to touch him," Plake said, speaking as loudly as he dared.

He watched in satisfaction as Scout flinched. The hooded man's eyes darted over to the door, as though he expected someone to barge in and discover them.

"Shhh!" Scout hissed. "We could get in trouble. We really shouldn't be here…"

"So you *are* afraid," Plake said with a smug smile.

Scout might have rolled his eyes, but it was so dark in the room that Plake couldn't tell for sure.

"You're about the most unsneaky person I've ever met," Scout shot back. "I've already stayed in the dungeon here, and I don't care to go back. Feel free to stick around if you want, but I'm leaving!"

Having said that, Scout walked over to the door, glanced left and right, and slipped into the hallway. Plake shut the door behind him.

He let out a deep breath and walked back over to the bed where Colt's body lay. As Plake approached the bedside, he kept one eye on the body. In the gloominess of the room, it was easy for his eyes to play tricks, and he stopped in mid-stride when Colt's arm seemed to move.

It was then that Plake remembered he believed in ghosts. He suddenly regretted sending Scout away. For all of Scout's faults, the man was absolutely fearless. Plake on the other hand...

He looked longingly back at the door.

Oh no you don't, Plake scolded. You have to do this your-self, and you have to do it quickly. The longer you're away, the more suspicious Scout and the others will get.

He had not wanted to involve anyone in his quest, but he had encountered an obstacle early on. Because stealing from a dead man was easier than robbing Stannel, Plake had decided to go to Colt's room first—only, he had no idea where that was.

Manipulating Scout into taking him there had been all too easy. Between his trusting nature and his willingness to please, Scout had demanded that Plake follow him so that he could prove he *did* know where Colt's room was and that he *most certainly was not* afraid of dead bodies.

Knowing that Scout could, for any number of reasons, return, Plake forced down the lump in his throat and hurried over to the far wall of the room. To his relief, he saw Colt's armor stacked neatly on the ground; the visored helm sat atop a small table. Plake was about to try it on when he realized something was missing.

The sword.

Setting the helmet down, he frantically searched the room. As he explored the dark corners of Colt's quarters, he kept his gaze away from the corpse, adhering to the childhood rule that prevented supernatural things from occurring as long as one didn't go looking for them.

Instead of hiding beneath a blanket, Plake now found himself kneeling on the floor, peering into the abyss beneath the bed.

But there were nothing but dust bunnies dwelling in the realm of imaginary monsters—just as Auntie had always assured him. With a sigh, Plake twisted around and ended up in a sitting position with his back leaning against the bed.

The crystal sword wasn't there. Some Knight—maybe Stannel himself—had taken the precious weapon and hidden it from would-be thieves. The crystal sword could be anywhere in the fort. How would he ever find it in time for the duel with Drekk't?

Cursing his ill luck—and whoever had gotten to the sword first—Plake stood up once more and started walking toward the door. Lingering in the dead Knight's bedchamber made no sense. *I might as well go back to the Renegade Room and get some sleep,* he thought miserably.

He stopped short halfway between the bed and the door, however.

There was *one* place he hadn't searched.

Swallowing the brassy taste in his mouth, Plake turned to confront the body of Saerylton Crystalus. Small, hesitant steps brought him to the Knight's bedside. Careful not to look at the man's face, Plake examined the blanket that stretched up to Colt's shoulders. Plake's trembling hand reached out and tugged at the covers.

He did his best to pull the blanket down without touching the man's cold, dead skin. The round pommel of a sword rested at the base of Colt's neck. A little more pulling revealed the cross-piece and the lip of a scabbard.

Unfortunately for Plake, the Knight's stiff arms, folded as they were, held the sword and the rest of the blanket tight against his breast. For a second, Plake considered moving Colt's arms, but when he imagined the sickly crunching sound of bones breaking, he almost lost his nerve and his dinner.

Steeling himself against the fact that he was going to have to get closer—much closer—to the dead man, Plake wrapped his hands around the top of the scabbard and pulled. When his arm pressed up against the side of Colt's face, he muttered an apology. He yanked at the weapon, but it budged only an inch.

He was about to make another effort at slipping the sword out of death's embrace, when he heard the distinct sound of a door creaking open behind him.

Opal's body reacted far quicker than her mind. Up went her crossbow, training in on the center of the intruder's chest. After what seemed like several minutes—but what was actually no more than two full seconds—she regained mastery of her voice.

"Who in the hells are you, and what are you're doing here?"

Whatever the man had been doing to Colt, he now withdrew his hands and held them up to show he was unarmed.

"I can explain," the man blurted, his voice full of fear.

Opal's finger itched to squeeze the trigger, to send a bolt into the monster who dared to desecrate Colt's resting place. What could he have been up to, anyway? she wondered. Although he was the son of a nobleman, Colt possessed no jewelry that Opal knew of. In fact, the most valuable thing Colt owned was…

"*Chrysaal-rûn*! You're trying to steal the crystal sword!"

"Now wait just a minute!" the man yelled back. "I wasn't going to steal it…I just…just needed to *borrow* it…that's all."

Opal couldn't suppress a wry chuckle. The man called Lucky was dead, and maybe Tryst was too, but they weren't the only members of Rydah's Thief Guild to join Colt's Army. No one would fault her for shooting the burglar.

"We can talk this out, Red," the man pleaded. "If you'd just put down that bow of yours and let me explain—"

"What did you call me?"

"W-what? Oh, sorry…you're name's Opal, right? I didn't mean any dis—"

"You're a Renegade!" When the man didn't deny the charge, she squinted, trying to make out his features. She recognized him then, though she didn't know his name. "Did Klye Tristan send you here?"

The rebel started to stammer again, assuring her that Klye had nothing to do with his being there. Opal listened impatiently as he explained why he was after the crystal sword.

At first, Opal was determined to dismiss it all as a lie. The guy expected her to believe he was stealing the crystal sword to impress a woman? It seemed too ludicrous to be true. And yet it was too ridiculous to be invented.

Her arm was starting to cramp up, so she lowered the cross-bow. The Renegade must have taken that for a good sign because he relaxed visibly, and his voice lost its panicked, desperate edge. As he finished his story, Opal looked him up and down. She supposed his body type was similar to that of Colt's. But his voice and accent were off.

Even if he were hidden beneath in a ton of armor, the rebel would never fool Drekk't.

Or could he?

"What's your name, Renegade?"

"Plake Nelway."

"And what, Plake Nelway, makes you think you can best Drekk't in a swordfight?"

"The crystal sword can cut through anything," he replied confidently. "I lost a perfectly good blade the one time I crossed swords with Colt...back when we kidnapped you...and..."

He went silent, probably noticing the scowl on her face.

Why am I still here talking with him? Opal wondered. She knew she should report Plake to the Knights. Even if the rebel weren't lying to her, she'd be a fool to get caught up in his scheme.

"You are committed to this course?" she asked, surprising both Plake and herself with the question.

Plake thought for a moment before crossing his arms. "It's not that big of a risk, as I see it. With the crystal sword in hand, how I could lose?"

"According to Stannel and Dylan, Drekk't also wields an enchanted sword. The keen blade of the crystal sword alone won't win the duel."

A few seconds later, Plake said, "Well, I have to try. It's the only way she'll ever notice me."

Opal resisted the urge to scoff. Even if Plake did somehow defeat Drekk't, the goblins would still sack the fort. Thanks to the shaman, Plake would never even make it back to the castle. The love-struck Renegade was willing to throw his life away to get Lilac's attention.

But she could stop him. She could save his life.

"The way I look at it," Plake said, "it's better to die out there, trying to do some good than to wait for the goblins to come and find us trapped in a tunnel."

Or she could help him.

Opal avoided Plake's eyes as she spoke. "I carried *Chrysaal-rûn* for a time. I believe there is more to the weapon than its incredibly sharp edge. When I confronted Drekk't near Rydah, the sword took control of the situation...of me. I think the crystal sword has the ability to protect its owner."

After a long pause, Plake asked, "Does this mean you're going to let me take it?"

"Even if you kill Drekk't, you'll be no match for the shaman," she told him. "He'll kill you, and the crystal sword will be lost."

"So you're *not* going to let me take it."

"What I'm saying is you can't go out there alone."

Plake laughed derisively. "Yeah, like Klye's gonna go along with my plan. He thinks I'm an idiot."

"I wasn't referring to Klye."

"Scout?"

"No, you idiot. *Me!*"

Plake's face scrunched up in confusion. "You? Why would you want to come along?"

Opal was asking herself that very question. She knew it was an incredibly foolish idea—and probably suicidal as well—but then again, Stannel's plan wasn't much better.

Maybe their actions could benefit the Knights. There was a lot that needed to be done to prepare the secret tunnel for occupation. The illusion of Colt's acceptance of the duel would buy the fort's defenders a little more time.

And there was something to be said for taking out the goblins' general and shaman.

Opal sighed. "For one thing, I'm going to make sure *Chrysaal-rûn* doesn't fall into the goblins' hands."

"And for another?" Plake prompted.

Opal smiled. "Revenge."

Plake nodded grimly. "Yeah, I guess you owe those bastards for what they did to Colt. Me, I'll be avenging Othello."

Opal looked away when the man mentioned Othello. As she saw it, her grudge with the goblins was threefold: Cholk, Colt, and Othello. But there was no reason to tell Plake that.

"All right," he said. "We have Colt's stuff. Now how are we gonna get the staff?"

"The what?"

"The *vuudu* staff," Plake explained. "We need it to lure the general to the battlefield."

Opal hated to admit it, but she had forgotten all about that part of the arrangement. Her first thought was to make a decoy, a false rod, but she knew that that would be pushing their luck too far. Even if they managed to convince Drekk't that Plake was Colt, there was no way the shaman would mistake a fake for the real staff.

"We *have to* bring the staff," he said urgently. "We have to get it away from Stannel."

"And how are we going to do that, Plake?" she snapped.

"I don't know yet!" Glancing nervously at the door, Plake added more quietly, "I hadn't gotten that far."

Now Opal was beginning to have some serious second thoughts. Borrowing Colt's armor and sword was one thing, but stealing from Stannel Bismarc, a priest? The thought nauseated her.

Perhaps sensing she was wavering, Plake added, "It's not like the staff belongs to Stannel. *He* didn't steal it from the goblins. You did."

That much was true. If it hadn't been for her, Drekk't would still have in his possession both Colt and the voodoo staff. She had as much right to the staff as Stannel did—arguably more.

As she attempted to sort through the emotions pulling her in two very different directions, she glanced over at the body of Saerylton Crystalus. What would you have me do, Colt? she wondered.

Recalling her final days with the man, she supposed that Colt would have been in full support of Stannel's plan. Colt would have wanted her as far from danger as was possible while he and the Knights futilely threw themselves at the enemy.

Well, she told her friend's ghost, that was unacceptable when you were alive, and it's unacceptable now.

To Plake she said, "All right, but I'm not going to steal the staff like a damned crook."

"What do you have in mind?" Plake asked eagerly.

"I'll talk to him. I don't know what I'll say, but I'll think of something."

In the end, she knew she'd have to lie to him. That didn't make her feel any better, but what else could she do?

"What about Colt's things?" Plake asked. "Where are we going to stash them?"

"Why stash them anywhere? We'll leave them here until we need them."

"What should I do in the meantime?"

A slew of sarcastic replies came to mind, but Opal resisted voicing them. "You can go back to the Renegade Room and keep your mouth shut. We'll meet here three hours before dawn in two days."

"And you'll bring the staff?" Plake pressed.

"Don't worry about me. Just don't do anything suspicious in the meantime."

Plake scoffed, as though such a thing were inconceivable. "We shouldn't be seen leaving together. I'll go first, since the Renegades are probably already wondering where I am."

The man slinked over to the door, opened it the tiniest bit, and stuck his eyeball up against the crack. After a full minute, the Renegade turned back to her and said, "Don't let anyone see you leaving."

"*I* have a reason to be here!" she hissed.

"Oh yeah...I guess so..."

Plake then shouldered through the doorway and disappeared into the corridor. To her dismay, she heard each of his heavy footfalls as he sprinted down the hallway.

She brought her hands up to her face, rubbed her eyes, and wondered what she had gotten herself into.

Passage XII

While a flurry of activity had seized the fort early that morning, the Renegade Room remained much the same as before. Some of the refugees from Rydah and Hylan had already cleared out, perhaps leaving early to find a good place in the tunnel that would serve as the castle keep.

As the day wore on, it seemed obvious to Klye that Hunter, Bly, and Pillip—like the Renegades—were procrastinating. He didn't know the Hylaners very well, but even if he were inclined to chat with them, he wouldn't have tried today. A somber air had settled upon the room, and the trio spent the day talking quietly among themselves.

As for Klye, he had little to say to anyone. Both he and Horcalus had said their piece at last night's meeting, for all the good it had done. None of the Renegades were happy about being forced to miss the impending battle. They had come so far—all the way from Superius—only to be told to stand aside and let the Knights handle things.

Why, Klye thought, if it hadn't been for us, the Knights would still be following T'slect's orders!

Naturally, Horcalus had taken Stannel's decree with the poise of a man accustomed to following orders. Like Stannel, Horcalus had pointed out the importance of their role. Someone had to protect those who planned to escape.

Having thought of Stannel Bismarc as an ally, Klye felt more than a little betrayed by the commander's decision. He might as well throw us in the dungeon, as Petton had wanted, Klye thought with a frown.

Some small part of Klye realized that he was less angry with Stannel than he was with the fact he may never see the man again. For some reason, Klye had wanted to get to know Stannel better, if only to learn glean some of the wisdom that veritably radiated off of the commander.

Stannel's confidence in a crisis, his grace under pressure, reminded Klye of Father Elezar back in Port Town. Even if Klye didn't believe in the gods, he knew faith was a real thing, and it seemed to him that men like Stannel and Elezar were made strong by their beliefs.

At some point in the afternoon, a Knight glanced into the room and upon noticing the lot of them sitting there, entered.

"Shouldn't you be heading for the tunnel?" There was no remonstration in the man's voice, which reinforced Klye's opinion that Zeke Silvercrown was a friend to the Renegades.

"We will," Klye assured the Knight, "but not yet. We'll be the last ones to be sealed in that tomb…just in case the goblins find a way through. If the passage is as narrow as Stannel says, the six of us should be able to hold the monsters off for some time, giving the others a chance to run.

Zeke Silvercrown flashed him a warm smile. "An honorable course of action. We Knights are grateful for your cooperation."

"It's the least we can do," Klye replied with a forced smile. He reminded himself that none of the Knights deserved to be the target of his anger. They were already being lenient by overlooking their past crimes.

As though noticing the Hylaners for the first time, Zeke turned to the three and asked, "What about you?"

"We're in no hurry either," Hunter said.

"Pray don't tarry too long. We Knights are depending on you all to keep order in our absence. Good luck."

As the Knight departed, Klye heard someone say, "I don't believe in luck."

The cocky words had been spoken quietly so that only Klye could hear. To Klye's astonishment, they had been spoken by none other than Dominic Horcalus.

His expression caused the former Knight to chuckle. "Well, that is what you always say, is it not?"

Klye smiled—something he hadn't done all day. "I suppose I do…because it's the truth. Either we'll live, or we'll die. It's as simple as that."

"A fifty-fifty shot?" Lilac asked. "Those aren't bad odds, considering."

"There's a difference between luck and probability," Klye

pointed out. "Our chances of surviving are far lower than fifty-fifty."

"But if we survive in spite of those terrible odds, then we'll be lucky," Lilac argued.

"We'll have beaten the odds, yes, but I don't see that as luck. It's like playing dice." He pointed over to where Plake, Scout, and Arthur were throwing two wooden dice over and over again. "Scout seems to have an uncanny habit of winning, but it's not because he's lucky. He has a strategy. He knows when to bet big and when to back off."

"Well," Lilac said, "I've played dice with Scout, and I'm inclined to disagree with you. Never in all my life have I seen a man roll doubles as often as he does. He's just lucky."

"Or a cheater," Horcalus said with a laugh.

"Rolling the same number eight times in a row is not only beating the odds, it's throwing them out the window," Lilac continued. "To me, that's luck."

"Some might say we're lucky to have lived as long as we have," Horcalus said, "though I'm inclined to believe the gods have had a hand in it."

"Ha!" Klye exclaimed. "I'd sooner put my faith in a midge than the gods. At least I can *see* a midge…but speaking of dice, does something strike you as odd about our three friends over there?"

Neither Lilac nor Horcalus said anything as they once more regarded the game of dice.

"It looks to me like Scout is winning," said Lilac at last. "Nothing unusual about that."

"Yes, but Arthur usually only watches," Horcalus interjected. "He is not wont to play with Plake because the rancher taunts and ridicules him."

Klye, Horcalus, and Lilac watched for another few seconds.

"I don't think I've heard Plake curse once!" Lilac whispered to her fellow conspirators.

"Maybe he's trying to impress you," Horcalus teased, and he received an elbow in the ribs from Lilac for the comment.

Klye didn't say anything. Now that he thought about it, Plake hadn't said much of anything all day. He hadn't complained once, and in Klye's estimation, that was a sure sign that something was amiss. When the rancher apologized to Arthur for grabbing the dice when it was Arthur's turn, Klye was convinced Plake was up to something.

Eventually, Horcalus and Lilac started talking about something else, but Klye's attention remained fixed on the dice game and—more precisely—on Plake.

Opal lay in bed long after the sun had risen. She was only partly aware of the outline of the shutters moving across the wall. Every so often she would awaken, only to roll over again, ignoring the fact that day had broken. This sequence might have continued well into the evening, but for a knock on her door.

The sound wrenched Opal from her restless sleep, causing her to jolt upright in bed. For a moment, she didn't know what had roused her. A heavy cloud had settled in her head, and it showed no signs of dissipating. After a few seconds, however, last night's chat with Plake Nelway burbled up through the fog. The memory was nearly enough to send her reaching for the pillow.

The knock came again.

Opal shivered, suddenly chilled. She had inadvertently sundered the seal of insulation that was her quilt when she sat upright. Now, wearing only a thin shift, she was loath to throw back the heavy blanket and confront the wintry day—not to mention whoever was at the door.

"Just a moment," Opal called out groggily, stalling for time.

With a sigh of surrender, she extricated herself from the warm cocoon. The cold stone floor sent another shiver through her body. Her feet were instantly numb. She considered pulling on some pants and her coat but reached for the blanket instead.

She hurried over to the door, stumbling over the quilt, which had bunched up at her feet. As she turned the key in the lock—a luxury Colt had provided for her even before the fortress became overridden with Renegades and thieves—she supposed it was Plake standing on the other side.

Opal was forced to bite back her scathing words when she found herself face-to-face not with Plake, but with the one man she had been avoiding all day.

"Pardon my intrusion, Miss Opal," Stannel Bismarc said. "I did not mean to wake you."

The Knight glanced down at her attire, taking in the sheer nightgown that had been revealed when she had reached for the doorknob. Self-consciously, Opal pulled the quilt tighter to her chest. To the man's credit, his eyes did not again wander from hers.

"I…didn't realize it was so late," she replied.

"I would like to speak with you," Stannel said. "I shall come back a little later."

"That's not necessary. Please, come in," Opal told him, taking a step back from the doorway to give him room to enter.

She nodded toward a vacant bed even as she took a seat at the edge of her own. Opal's once-private quarters had been converted into a women's dormitory, thanks to the unexpected influx of female residents. Having had the bedroom to herself since first arriving at the fort, it had been quite an adjustment having to share her room with strangers—not to mention her bed!

Lilac, Hunter, and the other newcomers spent their nights in the cramped chamber. But since the room was now empty, Opal was left to assume the other women had already headed for the hidden passageway—which, she thought wryly, was bound to be even more crowded.

With a wry smile, she wondered if the Knights planned on constructing dividers to separate the males and females within the tunnel when it came time to sleep.

Stannel must have mistaken her smirk for a sincere smile because he bestowed upon her a warm smile that made her feel guilty for her sarcastic musings. To top if off, she was already scrambling to think up a way to swindle him out of the *vuudu* staff.

"I hope I find you well this morning?" Stannel asked. Whereas most people uttered those words as an empty greeting, the Knight's inquiry had been said in earnest.

She brushed back a few strands of hair that had fallen against her face. "I'm doing all right," she said.

She wasn't sure if it was a lie or not. Now that her life had purpose again, the string of tragic losses pained her a little less. And yet knowing she would have to stoop to unscrupulous tactics to obtain the staff made her feel ill.

So as not to appear too eager, Opal avoided looking at the staff, which was strapped to Stannel's back.

"I am glad to hear it." Stannel's smile faded when he added, "I realize that you are already carrying a heavy burden, but I must ask a favor of you."

"What is it?" she asked, grateful for any avenue of conversation that would delay her unsavory agenda.

"As you well know, we Knights will face the full might of the goblin army tomorrow morning. Since I will be in the thick of it, I can no longer be the bearer of this."

Stannel reached around and told hold of the *vuudu* staff, removing the leather harness he had fashioned for it. He set the accursed thing lengthwise across his lap. For a moment, Opal could not understand his meaning.

"I must confess you were not my first choice," Stannel continued. "I asked Sister Aric to keep the staff safe, but she will have no part of it. On the one hand, she will be busy enough looking after the wounded in the tunnel, and on the other, she cannot bear to look at the thing."

Opal could only stare stupidly at the object of her desire—and her deepest loathing.

"You…you want *me* to take it?"

"In all fairness, I ought to have asked you first," Stannel told her. "You and Colt were the ones who stole it from the goblins. Colt saw fit for you to safeguard the staff while he and his army went into battle. Now I must ask you to do the same."

Opal could not bring her mouth to speak.

"I can see you are reluctant to take on this grim responsibility, and I do not blame you," the commander said. "Alas, I have yet to tell you the worst of it. I believe that the goblin shaman has already tried to reclaim the staff once within the fort. You will find yourself in great danger if he makes another attempt."

"Unless the shaman dies," Opal muttered, her eyes never leaving the hideous yellow skull.

"Yes, that is true," Stannel agreed. "My men know the shaman is the most dangerous member of Drekk't's army. Should any of them have the chance to slay Ay'sek in battle tomorrow, they will not hesitate to take it."

"Are you so certain that the goblins will attack?"

The question had come unbidden to her lips. To Opal, her voice sounded like that of a frightened child.

Stannel nodded, his expression severe. She understood, then, how much she had wanted him to assure her the Knights' plan was just a precaution and that tomorrow morning would be as blessedly uneventful as the past few had been. More than that, she had wanted him to tell her there was no reason for her to go through with the crazy plan she and Plake had concocted.

Of course, the Knight could not do that.

"Will you take the staff?" Stannel asked, holding it out to her.

Opal leaned forward and wrapped her hands around the cold, gnarled wood, trembling as she brought the evil relic to her lap. She had held the staff like this once before, sitting cross-legged, the rod balanced across her knees...

She remembered the pirates running away. She remembered sitting beside Othello's dead body. And she remembered a distinct presence—no, not presence, an *awareness*. She had known then that with the staff, she could give life back to the forester.

How long she had sat there, contemplating whether or not to resurrect Othello, Opal could not say. Finally, Stannel and Nisson had come for her. In retrospect, the entire episode seemed more like a dream than reality.

She looked up at Stannel, who appeared relieved to be rid of the staff.

"You may feel compelled to use its magic," Stannel told her. "Don't look so surprised, my dear. I am convinced that the staff will lend its power to anyone, whether she would use the magic for good or for evil. I too have endured temptation while carrying the thing. Yet I know that despite my noble intensions, the staff would twist my purpose into something dark."

He rose suddenly to his feet. "I must bid you goodbye. There is much to do before dawn."

Opal made to follow, but he motioned for her to remain seated. When he reached the door, Stannel turned to look at her again.

"Pray remember this, my friend...that weapon serves a wicked god, and the Nefarious Seven always demand a price for their gifts."

Stannel looked as though he wanted to say more, but with a resigned sigh, he left, closing the door behind him. Opal stared at the spot where he had been for several minutes, trying to make sense of what had just happened.

Then she glanced down at the *vuudu* staff to find the empty eyes of the skull staring up at her. She half expected the damned thing to start talking, but the room remained dreadfully silent.

She supposed she should be grateful Stannel had given her the staff freely and that she hadn't had to lie to him to get it. But now that she had the foul thing, she wanted only to give it back.

Opal set the staff on the ground, wiping her hands on the blanket afterward. The temptation to go back to sleep was great, but she resisted. Instead, she brought her knees up to her chest and wrapped the quilt around her in an attempt to banish the cold that had seeped into her bones.

She sat there for two hours more. When she finally got dressed, the sun was nearly set, and her stomach groaned for want of nourishment. After so many hours of soul searching, Opal had set her mind to the course ahead.

But even as she made her way to the dining hall, the *vuudu* staff secured to her back, she couldn't decide whether her decision was one of great bravery or immense cowardice.

Passage XIII

Klye groaned and swatted away the hand that was jostling him back to the world of the wakeful. He rubbed his bleary eyes. It was still dark in the Renegade Room, which told him it was too early to be awake.

"It's time we headed for the tunnel," Scout said, hovering above him. "The Knights are waiting to conceal the passage-way...though it'll take all of one minute to close the wall and hang that old tapestry back up again."

Klye muttered an incoherent reply. As he pulled on his boots and weapons—the rapier he had acquired in Port Town and a knife Stannel had given to him—he glanced around at the others. Horcalus was standing impatiently near the doorway. The man looked as though he had been up for hours.

No matter how much Klye wanted to stay and fight, Horcalus wanted it that much more. He couldn't imagine how difficult it was for Horcalus to remain separated from the other Knights—the "rightful defenders" of the fort.

Klye's glance landed next on Arthur, who was busy search-ing his sword for imperfections. How different the young man looked compared to the skittish runaway who joined his band three months ago. Klye suspected Arthur's adventure atop Wizard's Mountain was partially responsible for the transfor-mation, but he also knew that Horcalus had worked wonders in building the boy's confidence.

Arthur had certainly changed as a result of his journey across Capricon—but couldn't that be said of them all?

"I already went and woke up Lilac." Scout sounded much too chipper for Klye's liking. "The funny thing was, she wasn't the only one in the room. Opal still hasn't gone to the tunnel. She was awake, though, and she had all of her gear on."

Klye absorbed the news with an absent nod. Out of the corner of his eye, he saw that Bly, Pillip, and Hunter were seated together, eating hardtack and drinking from water skins. He wondered what the three of them were waiting for but figured like the Renegades—and like Opal, apparently—the Hylaners were just putting off the inevitable for as long as possible.

His attention was drawn away from the trio when Lilac entered the room. The first thing he noticed was that Lilac carried the vorpal sword once more. She mumbled a sleepy hello to the others and then asked, "Where's Plake?"

A damn good question, Klye thought. He cursed himself for not noticing Plake's absence right away.

"Relax, Klye. Plake said he had to answer nature's call," Scout said. "But now that you mention it, he's been gone a long time. Maybe the hardtack's not agreeing with him."

And maybe I'm Almighty Aladon, Klye groused. He had supposed that the rancher was up to something yesterday when Plake had gotten along so well with the others. But Plake never gave any hint as to why he was acting so peculiar.

"He actually said 'nature's call'?" Arthur asked skeptically.

"Yeah," Scout said, his eyes looking somewhere far off. "Now that you mention it, that's a bit weird. The man has no shortage of colorful phrases to describe his bodily functions, and most of them are too crude to repeat in the presence of a lady."

Lilac rolled her eyes.

If Plake had spent the previous day cursing the goblins and making outrageous promises to personally kill them all, Klye could not have been more alarmed than he was now.

"He's going to do something stupid," Klye said.

"How do you know?" Horcalus asked.

Klye threw his hands into the air. "Because he's Plake!"

He was about to give the order to split up and search for the missing rancher when a distant cry wafted into the room from the corridor. Although he could not make the words, Klye detected a distinct note of alarm in the shout.

What had Plake done this time? he wondered.

When Drekk't finally found Ay'sek, he nearly drew his sword and beheaded the shaman on the spot.

"What is the meaning of this?" he roared, gesturing at the

warriors dressed for battle and lined up in rigid rows all around them. "I gave no order to form ranks!"

Ay'sek didn't flinch. "But I did, General."

"Wha—"

"Someone had to take the proper precautions," Ay'sek continued, "and since you have apparently lost your mind, I took the liberty of assuming control of the army."

"How dare...how *dare* you!" Drekk't growled. "You've gone too far this time, shaman!"

Ay'sek took an aggressive step forward, looking Drekk't squarely in the eyes. "Jer'malz has not returned from the fool's errand you sent him on, and for all of my spells, I cannot locate him. Likely as not, the lieutenant and his squadron are dead."

Drekk't opened his mouth to say that Jer'malz's situation had nothing to do with the present circumstances, but Ay'sek did not let him interrupt.

"As for the other lieutenant, Ay'goar, he was killed during the night. Naturally, no one seems to know what happened."

An assassination, Drekk't deduced. Some ambitious officer—or several of them—had taken advantage of Jer'malz's absence. With both lieutenants gone, there were now two positions that needed filling...and even a third promotion if someone were bold enough to strike at him.

Someone like Ay'sek.

The shaman pressed on. "The warriors are numb and frostbitten, and this snow threatens to bury us alive. We have tarried too long here, General."

"In one measly hour, we will know whether Saerylton Crystalus has accepted the terms of the duel!" Drekk't argued. "To attack now would be madness!"

Ay'sek let out a laugh so full of ridicule that Drekk't's hand dropped to the hilt of his sword. Upsinous damn him for eternity, but he *must* kill the shaman!

"Saerylton Crystalus will not come," Ay'sek sneered. "I am now convinced the commander is d—"

The shaman's words were cut off as the sound of many voices speaking at once rippled through the army around them. General and shaman broke off their baleful stare and turned to regard the preoccupied soldiers.

"What is it?" Drekk't snapped, grabbing one of the warriors by the arm. "What's going on?"

The goblin blanched. "I dunno, *n'patrek*. Can't see much of anything back here, but it sounds like the humans are coming out."

Drekk't was on the verge of charging through the lines, forcing his way to the front to see what was transpiring, but Ay'sek's words stopped him.

"Well, I'll be a son of a dwarf," the shaman chuckled.

Drekk't turned to find Ay'sek levitating five feet off the ground. His eyes glowed with a strange light as he gazed out at the fort.

"It looks like you'll have your duel after all, General. Two riders approach, and one appears to be your rival, the indomitable Saerylton Crystalus."

Wicked delight welled up from inside Drekk't. The realization that he was finally going to face the hated Knight in battle hit him like a heady brew. He almost let out a celebratory whoop, but feeling the shaman's eyes upon him, Drekk't was careful to keep his expression dispassionate and dignified.

"What about the staff?" he asked Ay'sek. "Do they bring *Peerma'rek*?"

A dark smile stretched across Ay'sek's face. "They do."

The Emperor had declared an end to the war, but Drekk't was determined not leave the island without one last victory. He would kill Colt, or he would die trying.

"Hold still," Opal snapped, doing her best to secure the shiny piece of metal to Plake's leg.

"Don't sass me, squire," Plake told her in an exaggeratedly regal voice. This earned him glare from Opal—not the first one she had given him that morning.

But she bit back the sharp words that came readily to her tongue and concentrated instead on the task at hand. The problem was neither she nor Plake knew much about armor. By sheer luck, they had managed to drag Colt's gear from his bedchamber to the stable without being seen. But now she felt like she was putting together an oversized puzzle.

"How in the hells did you expect to do this by yourself?" Opal wiped the sweat from her brow and retrieved the helmet. None too gently, she put the thing on Plake's head.

"Do I look dashing?" he asked.

Opal slammed the visor closed over his face. "Much better," she muttered.

"Very funny," he replied, his voice echoing against the face-plate.

Seconds later, they encountered their next obstacle—getting Plake up on a horse.

"If you insist on touching me there, milady, we will have to be wed at once!"

Opal—who was bracing herself against the unfortunate horse with one hand and using the other to push against the man's backside—was in no mood for jokes. The fact that Plake was enjoying himself immensely only made her angrier.

"Shut up, Plake!" she said between clenched teeth.

Finally, the Renegade managed to right himself. He opened the visor again. "Oh, I almost forgot. Could you hand me my canteen?"

"Yes, *milord*," Opal said under her breath.

She handed him the item and watched as he took a long drink. She then led Nisson over to the stable's entrance, which she had opened earlier. The white mare greeted her with a whicker as she mounted. When Opal glanced back at Plake, he was taking another drink.

"That's not water in there, is it?"

Plake flashed her a mischievous grin. "Nope."

"Where did you get...? Never mind. I don't want to know. Just put a stopper in that and come on. We haven't much time."

The Renegade defiantly took one last swig before dropping the canteen onto the ground, the deep-red liquid dribbling out onto the ground.

"A terrible waste," Plake said with an exaggerated sigh.

Opal had just about had it with the man. She was on the verge of calling everything off when she heard voices coming from inside the fort. Probably, it was the Knights who were to guard the stable from any goblins attempting to breech the fortress.

"Too late to look back now," she thought aloud.

She gave Nisson a firm kick to the side and told her to run. At this stage in their partnership, Opal suspected that the horse probably would have responded to vocal commands alone, but now was not the time to test her theory.

Horse and rider burst from the stable and into the frigid outdoors. A backward glance confirmed that Plake, atop a chestnut charger belonging to the Knights, was following close behind. Opal looked back a few seconds later and saw men standing in the doorway, watching her and Plake as they raced away.

In her haste, she hadn't tied back her hair. Now, the red strands blew wildly, whipping at her face. Tears welled up in her eyes as she squinted against the cold wind. The first rays of morning crested the eastern horizon, casting the snowy plain in a dull gray light.

But the bulk of the landscape was blotted out by dark shapes. It appeared as though the goblins were all lined up, ready to surge forward and throw themselves at the fort.

This could well be the biggest mistake of my life, Opal thought—not to mention the last. She slipped one hand behind her to make sure that the *vuudu* staff was in place. She was both comforted and troubled when her fingers closed upon the stiff, gnarled wood.

"It's too late to go back," she repeated, though her words were blown away the moment they left her mouth.

If this ends badly…if I die, she thought, at least I'll get to see Colt and Cholk again.

And yet, she couldn't help but wonder if her friends would welcome her into Paradise with open arms or curse her for handing the abomination back to their hated enemy.

Klye followed the sound of excited voices to the fort's front hall. The rest of the Renegades and the trio from Hylan followed closely at his heels. Klye entered the vast chamber to find an assembly of Knights gathered there. The lot of them were talking at once.

He thought he heard the word "riders" being repeated, and as he forced his way into the throng, he could have sworn one Knight said, "It was Commander Colt, upon my honor!"

Klye looked around, searching for a familiar face, but even though he had been a guest of Knights for more than a month, he knew precious few of them. When he noticed Stannel standing on the lower section of the large stairway, he altered his course, shoving fully armed Knights out of his way without a second thought.

When he—and the trail of Renegades and Hylaners behind

him—finally made it to Stannel, he saw that Dylan and Zeke Silvercrown were conversing with the commander.

"What's going on?" Klye demanded.

Both Zeke and Dylan looked surprised to see him, but not Stannel.

"By all appearances, Opal has left the fort on horseback, taking with her the *vuudu* staff," the older Knight explained.

"What?" was all Klye could think to say. He had all but forgotten about the redheaded archer until Scout had mentioned her earlier that morning. In fact, he had done his best to avoid the woman ever since he had seen her looking so vulnerable at Colt's deathbed.

"That's not the best part," Dylan added. "The Knights who were sent to the stable claim they saw Colt riding beside her."

Klye had no response to that, and so he looked to Stannel for an explanation. The Commander of Fort Valor regarded Klye with a perfectly unreadable expression, betraying none of his thoughts.

"Maybe Colt didn't die after all?" Scout ventured from somewhere behind Klye.

"The body of Saerylton Crystalus is accounted for," Stannel assured them. "The late commander's belongings, however, are missing."

"But who would dare to take Colt's place?" Klye wondered aloud.

He might have suspected Sir Dylan if the Knight had not been standing right in front of him. Stannel started to say something, but Klye didn't hear him because it suddenly occurred to him who the culprit was.

"Plake!"

"Pardon?" Stannel said.

"Plake...he's one of my Renegades. Damn it all, it *has* to be him."

Within minutes, they had pieced it together. Plake, who shared a few characteristics with Saerylton Crystalus, had taken it upon himself to challenge Drekk't in Colt's place. The rancher had convinced Opal to help him because he needed the *vuudu* staff to make the scenario as credible as possible.

But how Plake had managed to talk the stubborn, Renegade-hating woman into going along with his scheme, Klye couldn't guess. When Stannel asked him whether he knew why Plake would do something like this, Klye shook his head.

Behind him, Lilac said, "Defenders' Plague?"

Casting Lilac a knowing glance, Klye chuckled and said to Stannel, "I can think of only one reason why Plake would want to play hero."

"It doesn't matter *why* they are doing it," Dylan said. "Their actions are paramount to treason. They might as well just *give* the staff back to the goblins. Unless that Renegade is a better swordsman than Petton and I combined, he hasn't a chance at defeating the general."

Klye heard several groans behind him. Klye silently shared in the sentiment. Out of everyone in his band, Plake was probably the worst fighter.

"We have to stop this," Klye said to Stannel. "If we hurry, we might be able to drag Plake, Opal, and the *vuudu* staff back to the fort before the goblins make their move."

"The goblin host is already lined up and prepared for battle," Stannel said. "If we show any signs of aggression, they will charge, and we will be caught out in the open."

"So you're just going to let them die?" A pang of guilt stabbed at Klye's stomach when he saw Stannel's expression soften.

"You cannot ask me to lead my men out there to be slaughtered," Stannel said evenly. "And the *vuudu* staff is not worth the lives of all of those in the tunnels who are depending on us."

Klye could appreciate Stannel's point of view. He too was a leader of men. But it was precisely because he was a Renegade Leader that Klye could not agree with Stannel on this.

"Fine," Klye said, "but let me and the Renegades go out alone. If we're lucky, the goblins will mistake us for Colt's entourage."

Stannel's brow creased ever so slightly as he considered Klye's offer.

"Please," Klye begged. "Plake is a huge pain in the ass, but he's a Renegade, gods damn it. I can't stand by and watch him die!"

Everyone was silent then as they awaited Stannel's answer.

"Very well," he said at last. "I will not stop you from going to your friend, though I urge you to reconsider."

Klye was too elated to speak. He wanted to thank the commander but was interrupted by Hunter.

"We're goin', too!" she declared.

"No," was Stannel's quick reply.

Klye glanced back at Hunter. The woman was practically trembling with rage. "Whaddaya mean—"

"Too many attendants will rouse the goblins' suspicion," Stannel told her. Hunter looked ready to argue with him, but Stannel was quick to add, "However, because you are so intent on finding battle today, I will allow you to supplement the ranks of Knights and guardsmen within the fort."

Hunter looked first to Pillip and then to Bly. Seemingly satisfied, she said, "All right, it's a deal."

Klye didn't bother waiting around to see what happened next. Trusting that Horcalus, Lilac, Arthur, and Scout would follow, he pushed his way through the mass of Knights and made for the stable. His mind was so jumbled with thoughts he couldn't concentrate long enough on any of them to come up with a decent plan. There were simply too many variables to do anything but play it by ear.

If Plake survived the day, Klye swore he'd kill the insubordinate rancher himself.

Passage XIV

Plake heard Opal let off a stream of curses. He was stunned and entertained by the woman's vocabulary—which rivaled any tavern talk he had heard in Param—but his amusement evaporated when he turned in the saddle to find what had made the woman swear.

A handful of riders were crossing the plain, quickly approaching the spot where he and Opal had stopped to wait for the goblins. A glance back at the goblin lines revealed a small procession making its way toward the two of them from the opposite direction.

He looked to Opal for an answer, but the woman just shook her head and repeated the same dirty word over and over. The humans—whoever they were—would reach them first, but the goblins' arrival would come soon after, despite the fact that they had no horses.

"What are we going to do?" Plake asked.

"Why ask me? They're *your* friends."

It took Plake a few seconds to understand what she meant, but another look at the oncoming riders showed him the truth of things. Naturally, Klye was in the lead. As the group neared, Plake was able to distinguish the armor-clad Dominic Horcalus as well as Scout, whose silly black hood flailed in the wind. The other two would have to be Arthur and Lilac.

Plake felt his heart beat faster. While he was happy to have Lilac there to witness his valorous deed firsthand, Klye would probably try to stop him.

He was unable to give the matter more thought for the Renegades were upon them then. Klye shot an incredulous look at Opal but walked his horse over to Plake.

"What in the fiery hells do you think you're doing?" he

shouted.

Maybe it was the wine coursing through his veins, but Plake was not at all intimidated by the self-made Renegade Leader. Or maybe it was the crystal sword hanging at his side that emboldened his tongue.

"Isn't it obvious?" Plake shot back with a smirk.

Klye's expression darkened, and Plake thought that the Renegade Leader might hit him. The man's jet-black hair danced in the wind like black flames. After a moment, Klye broke eye contact and looked back at Lilac, who accepted the signal for what it was.

Lilac urged her mount forward and said, "Plake, this is the stupidest thing you've ever done!"

The words stung—there was no denying that—but at the same time, Plake saw true concern in the woman's face. And that was a good thing. Not knowing what else to say, Plake replied, "Well, no one ever accused me of being smart."

"We have to go," Lilac said. "The goblins—"

"Are all but here," Opal interrupted. "If we turn and run now, they'll attack, and I'm willing to bet that not even Nisson can outpace a *vuudu* spell."

Klye looked like he was ready to argue with the archer, but Horcalus spoke first.

"She is right, Klye. It is too late to go back."

"Then let's make a stand," Scout suggested, an eager gleam in his eyes.

"We haven't a chance against the shaman," Lilac argued.

"Our only hope is to fool them," Opal declared. "Go along with our ruse, and maybe some good can come out of this."

Plake looked to Klye, who would make the decision for all. Plake could only hope that his face didn't appear too desperate. The goblins were so close he could make out the harsh syllables of their speech.

"Fine," Klye said angrily. "Now shut your visor, Plake."

And he would say no more. The goblins came to a stop a few feet away from them. Plake counted ten in all. Two of the more distinguishable goblins stepped forward. One wore a long, black robe. The other was bedecked in an assortment of mismatched armor. That he had obviously collected his equipment from the corpses of his enemies made General Drekk't all the more intimidating.

"You keep strange company, Commander."

Although the general spoke in his native tongue, Plake heard the meaning of the words in his head. Compounded with the effect of the wine, it was most disorienting. For a moment, Plake could only stare in awe of the general. But the sound of Opal clearing her throat brought his mind back to the here and now.

"Ah…well, you already know my good friend Opal," he improvised. Pointing at the others, he said, "These are the Renegades. We've become pals too…ever since T'slect tried to kill us all."

"What of Stannel Bismarc?" Drekk't asked.

The words that penetrated Plake's brain were wrapped in a sly tone. The general was suspicious.

"The Knights did not want him to partake in the duel," Opal said quickly. "After what happened to Sir Petton…"

"Yes, I see," Drekk't said, a toothy smile splaying his face.

"Well, should we get started then?" Plake asked.

Drekk't's eyes narrowed, and Plake wondered if the general could distinguish between human accents.

"Lift your visor, Commander, so that I may look you in the eye."

Plake considered refusing the order, but refusing might prove even more dangerous than complying. To Plake, all goblins looked alike. He could only pray the same was true the other way around.

He lifted the visor of Colt's helm and stared defiantly at the goblin, daring him *not* to see Saerylton Crystalus looking back.

Drekk't scrutinized his face for a moment. He must have seen what he wanted to see because he then said, "Dismount, Commander, and draw your sword. It is time to end our rivalry."

Plake almost fell while trying to extricate himself from the saddle. Having been a rancher for most of his life, it was an acutely embarrassing moment. But Plake had never worn anything like the suit of armor before, and he supposed he was lucky to have dismounted without breaking his neck.

Plake unsheathed his sword. He could not help but marvel at the glassy blade, which looked as delicate as the wayward snowflakes drifting down from the heavens. Of course, Plake knew that the crystal sword was not at all fragile.

Silently, he implored the blade's magic to work for him.

Drekk't turned to confront him, positioning his feet in a

battle-ready stance. Plake had no stance. He had never met an opponent in prearranged combat. Plake's preferred method of attack was from behind with a bar mug in hand.

Looking into the demonic eyes of his enemy, Plake felt all of the courage drain from him like a drunkard pissing in public. For that matter, he had to make a conscious effort not to wet himself. The seriousness of the situation struck him all at once, and he considered throwing off his helmet, declaring the match forfeit.

He never had the chance.

"If I should fall, do whatever you must to regain *Peerma'rek*...for the redemption of both our souls!"

Drekk't's words echoed in Ay'sek's mind as the duelists faced off. Ay'sek had barely contained his mirth at the time, but now that Drekk't was preoccupied with the much-anticipated battle, the shaman chuckled to himself.

If you should fall? he silently taunted. Oh, you will fall, General. If the human does not slay you, then I will!

Ay'sek could have arranged Drekk't's death from the start. How simple it would be to remove the enchantment from his sword. He longed to see Colt's crystalline blade pierce the general's chest...

But Ay'sek wanted to relish the insolent warrior's demise. He would enjoy the bloody sport that was unfolding for as long as it lasted. If Drekk't fell to Colt's superior swordsmanship, then the general's death would be of his own making. If Drekk't won, Ay'sek would make sure Drekk't knew who it was that robbed him of his moment of victory—and his life.

Ay'sek took a moment to observe the unusual escorts the human challenger had brought with him. There was no sign of the warrior cleric, which made Ay'sek's grin grow. Stannel's absence would make regaining *Peerma'rek* all the easier.

He recognized only two of Colt's company. The female with the yellow hair had been with Colt in Hylan, back when the shaman had stolen the identity of the thief Lucky. At least, Ay'sek was fairly certain it was the same swordswoman.

As for the other female—oh, Ay'sek certainly knew her.

Once before, this woman with hair was the color of human blood had stood between him and *Peerma'rek*. Although she possessed no magic, the archer—and her unexpected allies—had prevented him from reclaiming the staff. If it hadn't been for her, he and the rest of the army could have departed days ago.

If I can't kill Stannel, he thought, I'll just have to settle for the bitch.

Plake watched in horror as the goblin leaped forward. The monster's broadsword came down in a diagonal slash, aiming for the place where his neck met his shoulder. Plake saw it coming. In fact, time seemed to slow down, affording him the opportunity to imagine the goblin's sword cutting him from shoulder to shank.

Plake closed his eyes, bracing for what would surely be the first and last blow of the duel.

A loud clang resounded, accompanied by a jolt that ran up the length of his sword arm. Plake opened his eyes. To his absolute astonishment, he found the crystal sword situated between himself and Drekk't's blade. It took him a moment to realize he had blocked the attack.

Remembering what Opal had told him of the crystal sword, Plake could only assume that the magic of the sword had been activated.

The revelation—and the relief that came with it—was nearly enough to knock him over. He might have shut his eyes again, surrendering his fate to the miraculous sword, but he wasn't certain whether the crystal sword could see on its own or if it needed to use his eyes. When Drekk't took a second swing, directing his weapon at his midsection, Plake resisted the urge to move.

Once again, the crystal sword snapped up, knocking Drekk't's blade aside. Plake then took a step forward and jabbed his weapon at the general's breast. Drekk't sidestepped the lunge and countered with another stroke.

In a maneuver that belied the fogginess in his brain, Plake altered his stance, shifting his balance to his back leg, and yanked the crystal sword in an upward motion. The blade clipped Drekk't's sword, knocking the goblin's blade up above his head and providing Plake with a more-than-generous opening.

Plake plunged the crystal sword into the center of Drekk't's chest—or rather, where it would have been if Drekk't hadn't leaped back out of range.

With no control over his actions, Plake pressed his attack, flinging himself at the goblin general with a series of cross-body slashes. Drekk't could do nothing but parry the attacks, back-pedaling with every collision of the two blades.

Content to be the crystal sword's instrument, Plake heeded the unheard commands of the crystal sword. He knew with all certainty that the weapon would find a way to defeat Drekk't on its own.

If not, he was a dead man.

With an unintelligible cry on his lips, Drekk't threw himself at Colt, putting all of his strength behind his swing. He ignored the doubt that lurked in the back of his mind, threatening to steal his resolve.

Colt had bested him twice, but by Upsinous's black heart, it would not happen again!

He saw Colt hesitate, but at the last possible moment, the Knight reacted. The glassy blade whirred through the air, striking Drekk't's sword. The collision of the two weapons caused Drekk't to recoil slightly. Despite the goblin's superior strength, Colt had not budged in the least.

He took another swing, which Colt effortlessly blocked. Drekk't marveled at Colt's technique. It was as though the man was calculating the probable result of every possible move and executing the action that would have the greatest effect with the least amount of motion—all within a fraction of a second!

In no time at all, Drekk't found himself on the retreat, dodging and parrying the deadly blur of the crystalline blade.

Every time he managed to block the sword, pain shot through his left arm. His wounded shoulder was bound tightly in a tour-niquet, but that did not protect him from the waves of agony that assailed him with every parry.

Drekk't would have preferred to face Colt with a sword in one hand and a knife in the other—as he had during his duel with Gaelor Petton—but he dared not use his left arm for any-thing other than keeping his balance. And since there was noth-ing he could do to stop the pain, he gritted his teeth and fought through it.

Drekk't quickly grew frustrated with his opponent's ability to flawlessly defend against his every attack. It didn't seem fair—didn't seem *possible*. He recalled then how Colt had jumped clear over him during their last fight...

He could not hope to match Colt sword for sword, but he was not ready to give up. A plan was already unfolding in his mind, and he seized it with the desperation and zeal of a hyena biting into a lion's neck.

Drekk't waited for his chance, and when it came, he let out a roar.

Plake's muscles were sore and cramped. Beneath his armor, his sweaty skin was beginning to chafe. He breathed heavily, and his heart pumped so fast he feared it would explode in his chest. But Plake dared not deny the will of the crystal sword.

Better to *feel* like you're on death's doorstep than actually cross the threshold, he thought.

Despite the fact he was gaining ground, Plake worried the goblin would end up winning from stamina alone. With every stroke of the crystal sword, Plake prayed to the gods that the weapon would reach its target. Yet Drekk't expertly evaded the string of attacks, blocking those swings that he could and avoiding those he could not.

How long could it go on?

Plake thought he found his answer when Drekk't presented him with a wide opening. He thrust the tip of the crystal sword at Drekk't's chest. The goblin had no time to sidestep the attack. Plake was sure he had won.

But then Drekk't roared and thrust out his own sword. Even to Plake, who knew next to nothing of sword fighting, the move seemed incredibly foolish. It was as though Drekk't was willing to accept Plake's blow, even as he dealt one of his own.

Plake cringed, waiting for the cold steel to pierce his body.

The tip of Drekk't's sword met with that of the crystal sword. Plake expected both weapons' momentum to carry them past each other, sliding onward toward their new fleshy sheaths. The result would see them both skewered. Plake could only watch Drekk't's blade draw nearer.

Rather than aim for Plake's body, however, the goblin kept the tip of his blade tight against the crystal sword, encircling the blade again and again. Plake mindlessly mimicked the movement, his wrist straining to maintain hold of the sword. Meanwhile, Drekk't's blade swirled ever closer. The look of it reminded Plake of an uncoiling snake.

It occurred to Plake that, if unchecked, the goblin's sword would soon reach his forearm. Reason had it that the crystal sword would find Drekk't's sword arm too. Was this a game of chicken then?

Or would the winner be the one with the longer blade?

All of these things flashed through Plake's mind as the entwining blade wound its way toward him. Plake winced, imaging the excruciating pain that would come with losing his hand. But then, suddenly, his wrist jerked outward.

Drekk't's sword went flying harmlessly to the side.

The crystal sword went with it.

Plake stared stupidly at where the two weapons landed. He saw Drekk't lunge at him, but did not immediately react. He had grown accustomed to his body moving without his command. Plake uttered a quiet whimper an instant before the goblin plowed into him, knocking him onto his back and blasting the air from his lungs.

Plake struggled to draw in air, but none would come. Shadows closed in around the visage of the grinning goblin general, who had landed on his chest.

Drekk't released his hold on his weapon. As the goblin had predicted, Colt did the same, surrendering his own sword instead of losing a hand. For some unknown reason, Colt just stood there.

It was as though the man had been caught by surprise by the outcome, as though, for once, Colt had lost control of the situation.

Drekk't charged into his unprepared foe. The layers of armor worked against the human. Off-balanced, Colt toppled like an ancient wall under the assault of a battering ram. Drekk't let gravity carry him down on top of the Knight, sending the full brunt of his weight into Colt.

He heard the man expel his breath and then gasp for air.

Drekk't rained a few blows against the side of the man's head. He knew that, thanks to the helm, he was scoring no real damage, but he was adding to Colt's disorientation.

Frantically, Drekk't searched for a weakness in the armor, for a way to quickly end the contest. He brought his hands down to the man's neck, hoping to throttle him, but his fingers found only the solid steel of the Knight's gorget. Colt was covered almost head to toe in armor. Drekk't would break his hand before he even bruised Colt.

Drekk't found the end to their stalemate in Colt's visor. It was as though the Goblinfather had put the idea in his head. He would yank open the visor, gouge out Colt's eyes. Then, while the human screamed and screamed, he would regain his sword and beheaded the helpless human.

A triumphant cry burst from his mouth as he wrenched open Colt's visor. Drekk't would have taken nothing but purest of delight from the fear emanating from the man's eyes.

Except they were not Colt's eyes.

His brain could not fathom how it had been accomplished, but Drekk't realized two things at once. In his lust for vengeance, he had allowed himself to be duped. And he would never face the real Saerylton Crystalus again.

Plake squinted against the light that pierced his eyes. Now that the visor was up, he had an unobstructed view of the goblin. He saw the hand hovering above him, fingers drawn together like the blade of a knife. Wide-eyed, Plake looked into the face of his murderer—

—and saw an expression so full of confusion that, under other circumstances, he might have laughed.

Not questioning his good fortune, Plake pushed himself into a half-sitting position and did what came naturally.

His gauntleted fist struck the goblin's nose with a sickening crack. The force of the blow knocked Drekk't off of him. Struggling beneath the weight of his armor, Plake managed to get to his feet. He ran over to the crystal sword and, holding the weapon in two hands, came to stand over Drekk't, who cradled his bloody face his hands and moaned.

Plake felt a moment of revulsion for what he had to do, but before he could think twice, the crystal sword acted on its own.

Chrysaal-rûn ripped clean through Drekk't's torso, cutting the goblin in half.

Passage XV

Hardly breathing as she watched the battle unfold, Opal could almost believe the man inside the armor was Saerylton Crystalus. She had orchestrated this, the illusion of Colt's retribution, and for the time being, it was enough to bring solace to her soul.

When Plake lost his hold on the crystal sword, she feared she would have to watch her beloved friend die in effigy, but then, miraculously, the man regained the upper hand. She held her breath as he dealt the deathblow. Drekk't's body hit the ground in two beats, darkening the already muddy snow to coal black.

Just like that, it was over.

Colt was avenged, but he was still dead.

She felt no better than before.

There was no time to ponder the emptiness that lingered inside her. The unnatural stillness of the scene was instantly banished by a single word from the shaman.

"Attack!"

The Renegades reacted immediately. Leaping from off their mounts, Klye and his band drew their weapons and engaged the nearby goblins warriors, who were already scrambling forward. Still standing over Drekk't, the glassy blade of *Chrysaal-rûn* dripping black slop, Plake lowered his visor and waited for the monsters to come.

Beneath her, Nisson pounded her hooves nervously against the ground. They were in great danger, and Opal was half tempted to turn the horse around and race back to the fortress, but at that moment she made eye contact with the shaman. She couldn't be certain, but it looked as though he was talking to himself.

"Oh shit!" She quickly brought the butt of her crossbow up to her shoulder.

There was no doubt in her mind the shaman would aim his spell at her. She carried the *vuudu* staff, after all. Her only hope was to take him out before he completed his spell. She hurriedly pulled the trigger, wincing against the recoil. The bolt flew true, homing in on the middle of the shaman's chest.

Mere inches from its target, however, the arrow bounced off of an unseen barrier and went ricocheting impotently off to the side.

Opal swore again.

Stannel watched the duel through a spyglass from the ramparts of Fort Valor.

In the days of yore, the legendary Knights Exemplar had developed trial by combat as a means to determine justice between two warriors. The Knights of Eaglehand and the Knights of Superius had carried the tradition into the modern age, though duels were now a rarity in both orders.

The premise behind the duel was simple: the Gods of Good would intercede on behalf of the innocent party, giving him the strength to defeat his opponent.

Stannel had read enough histories and journals, however, to know that many innocent men had lost their lives dueling not because they were in the wrong, but because they were inferior swordsmen. Following the Wars of Sundering, unscrupulous Knights had challenged weaker rivals to duels in order to dispose of contenders for land.

On some level, Stannel respected the idealism that the duel represented. The combatant was forced to depend fully upon his god, trusting that truth and justice would win out in the end. There were stories of mere stable boys trouncing dishonest Knights in armed trials.

Watching the duel between the false Knight of Superius and the goblin general, Stannel wondered what had gone wrong in those other cases. How had the gods allowed deceitful men to vanquish the honest and upright?

He supposed it had something to do with faith—or the lack thereof. It was one thing to appeal to the gods' mercy, directing an aimless plea at the heavens, but it was quite another to believe that you would win because your god was truly on your side.

"Faith without works is not faith at all."

That maxim that had been one of his first lessons as a monk-in-training. In spite of their innocence, those blameless contestants of yesteryear probably had gotten their affairs in order prior to the duel. They had made preparations in the event that they failed, which—according to the proverb—meant that they had lost before they even began.

Faith was believing you would win no matter what the odds were and acting accordingly.

While he trusted the Great Protector with his immortal soul, Stannel realized he had not demonstrated much faith lately. He had all but given up on his own life, not to mention the lives of his men. Doubt was a greater foe to him than the goblins ever were.

"Faith without works is not faith at all," he muttered aloud.

"Pardon?"

Stannel lowered the spyglass and looked at Sir Dylan Torc, who had remained by his side all morning.

"Has something happened?" the anxious Knight asked, squinting futilely out at the small gathering on the plain.

"Perhaps Fortunatus Miloásterôn's only fault was that he did not believe he would win."

"Commander?" Dylan prompted, his brow furrowed with confusion.

Stannel felt something warm growing inside of him. The uncertainty and fear that had plagued him for the past few days vanished at once. His hope restored, Stannel couldn't help but smile.

Before Dylan could again question his cryptic words again, Stannel signaled for the other Knights on the battlement to follow him down into the fort. Dylan kept close to the commander, looking more perplexed than ever.

Klye fell back a few steps, sparing a quick glance at the wound that dribbled hot red blood down his arm. Unlike the Knights of Superius—and unlike Plake, for that matter—Klye wore minimal armor. The Renegade Leader depended on his speed and dexterity to defeat his foes.

He also depended on his wits.

Pretending not to notice as a goblin reared back with two curved swords, Klye cradled his injured arm. Out of the corner of his eye, he saw the blur of the blades. Both swings were high. Klye crouched low.

He nearly lost his footing. The ground was slick with melting snow. He heard the hum of the swords as they tore through the air mere inches above his head. In the same motion that nearly had him doing the splits, Klye lashed out with his rapier, cutting the goblin across the thigh of one leg and the knee of the other. When the goblin pitched forward, Klye followed through with a thrust that pierced the creature's throat.

Klye paused for a moment to regain his balance and his breath. Nearby, Scout lured another goblin between him and Lilac, and the swordswoman promptly chopped off the monster's arm. Horcalus and Arthur fought side by side, the former Knight's technique more than making up for the younger man's inexperience.

As Klye dived out of the way of a falling battle-axe, he caught a glimpse of Plake running headlong at the shaman.

Ay'sek watched as the sphere of violet light hit the female full in the chest, launching her clear off of her horse. While it could not compete with the sight of Drekk't being skewered as the highlight of his morning, seeing the woman fly from the saddle and hearing her cry of pain was still satisfying.

He heard more than saw her hit the ground, though, for the stupid horse was standing between them. The shaman walked over to where the female human had landed, his pace unhurried. Either the horse was paralyzed in fear or it was suicidal for it did not run away.

Ay'sek came to stand over the woman, who writhed in pain, her shirt singed by the spell. Before he could finish her off, however, Ay'sek saw a solitary Knight rushing straight at him, crystal sword held high above his head.

Ay'sek spoke the words that would launch a second missile at the imposter. He released the spell at the same time the crystal blade collided with his magical shield.

A blinding light burst from the crystal sword, and Ay'sek shut his eyes. When he opened them again, he saw the Knight had fallen on his back. The man's armor was blackened as though touched by fire. Ay'sek did not bother to check if the man was alive. It no longer mattered because he was no longer a threat.

The crystal sword was gone, apparently destroyed by Ay'sek's *vuudu* enchantment.

The explosion of light caused all of the combatants to pause momentarily, but Klye stared at Plake and shaman for a bit longer than his opponent—a delay that nearly cost him his life. As he made a desperate swing at the axe-wielding goblin, Klye tried to make sense of what he had just seen.

He was certain that if he were to close his eyes, he would see, emblazoned across the backdrop of his eyelids, the thousand sparkling shards of the crystal sword. Could *Chrysaal-rûn* really be destroyed so easily? he wondered.

Leave it to Plake to find out…

As though Klye didn't have enough to contend with just then—with Plake possibly dead and with him barely avoiding the heavy fall of his enemy's battle-axe—Klye heard a sound like the rumbling of a timpani beneath the discordant melody of the melee.

He didn't have to glance up at the bleak, gray sky to know that the thunder had come from below. The ground shook beneath his feet, and all around him, the wall of dark shapes was growing larger little by little.

The entire goblin army was advancing.

Stannel reined in his mount, taking in the scene with one quick glance. The Renegades were busy fighting Drekk't's entourage, which was already being augmented by more troops. The bulk of the goblin host would be on them in seconds, but Stannel did not let that distract him.

First things first, he thought, as he urged his horse over to where the shaman stood.

One of the Knights in the vanguard must have had the same thought for the man steered his horse in the direction of the dark-robed goblin, his sword held high and ready to strike. When that Knight was almost upon the *vuudu* priest, the goblin faced him at last.

Dark flames billowed up from the frozen ground, engulfing horse and rider alike. The suffering animal reared and raced off, carrying the screaming warrior away.

Stannel pushed the lamentable image of the living torch from his mind and dismounted. Before the shaman could turn his attention back to Opal and the *vuudu* staff, Stannel charged in, the blessed mace of Pintor glowing wildly in his hands.

Ay'sek was astounded that the Knights had actually come out of their fortress—astounded and annoyed.

He was wondering how many flies he would have to swat in order to reclaim *Peerma'rek* when he spied Stannel Bismarc. Though Ay'sek would enjoy killing the troublesome cleric, he would have gladly postponed the encounter until after he retrieved the staff.

Vuudu flowed through his body like a million wriggling worms. The release of the spell was a mixture of relief and distress. He watched eagerly as the purple glob of light soared unerringly toward its target. So large was this magical missile that Stannel could not hope to avoid it.

The Knight did not attempt to dodge the spell. Gripping a small mace with both hands, Stannel brought the weapon down in an arc that left a visible trail of golden light. When the mace connected with the magical blast, the sphere hissed and fizzled away as though it had never been.

Stannel paused only long enough to deflect the supernatural attack. Then he was once more running full speed at Ay'sek, who quickly cast another spell.

Stannel swung his mace at the shaman, but the weapon collided with an unseen barrier. Not knowing whether or not his efforts would weaken the invisible shield—but hoping and praying he was doing some good—Stannel kept on swinging. Meanwhile, the shaman spoke a stream of words that, apparently, had no translation.

He nearly lost his balance when the mace finally did penetrate the *vuudu* barrier. He brought the mace up defensively as the shaman pounced on him. During the struggle, the goblin managed to get both his hands around Stannel's wrists. The commander assumed that the maneuver was meant to prevent him from swinging his mace.

Stannel did not understand his true peril until it was too late.

On separate occasions, Colt and Klye had told Stannel of their battle with the goblin prince. T'slect also had been a shaman, and he had nearly killed the Renegade Leader with a spell that drained Klye of his strength.

Now Stannel gritted his teeth as a hungry fire flooded into him, pouring in through his wrists and spreading slowly—ever so slowly!—throughout his body. The pain was too much for him to think of anything else.

Soon the sneering countenance of the shaman was replaced by a pulsating white light that reflected the agony threatening to destroy Stannel's sanity. But beneath the pain, an inkling of a thought was being nourished into certainty: if he surrendered, the pain would end.

Nisson lowered her neck, providing Opal with the support she needed to pull herself up from the ground. The woman winced and sucked in a loud breath through her teeth as pain shot through her hip. She had broken something, but now was not the time to worry about it.

She nearly fell over when Nisson jerked away. The mare's hind legs launched a goblin ten feet away. Opal thanked Nisson, who had chosen to fight beside her rather than flee. Now there was nowhere to run. The goblins were all around them.

Well, she thought, if I'm going to die today, I'm taking that son-of-a-bitch shaman with me.

It took all of Opal's concentration to reload the crossbow. She pulled back on the drawstring, demanding her mind to stay focused despite the pain that was scorching her upper leg like lava. Thankfully, the area where the goblin's spell had struck her had already gone numb.

She spread her legs far apart in a stance that, while not beneficial to balance, kept the weight off of her wounded hip. She brought the crossbow up to aim at the shaman, whose long, bony fingers grasped Stannel's wrists like manacles.

Gods above, she prayed, guide my arrow.

The kick from the discharge sent Opal staggering backward, and she fell to her knees with a cry. Paying no heed to Nisson, the Renegades, or the hundreds of goblins around her, she stared at the shaman, who remained exactly where he had been standing.

At first, Opal assumed she missed. Then she spotted the bolt protruding from the shaman's neck.

The shaman glared at her, but somehow he stayed on his feet. Dropping Stannel to the ground, not bothering to remove the arrow, the goblin staggered over to her. She saw his lips were moving and knew she had but seconds left to live.

Colt, Othello, I hoped you saved a spot for me in Paradise.

A spasm rippled through the shaman, and he crumpled to the ground. Stannel stood with his mace positioned at the precise place where it had connected with the shaman's back. Even from a distance, she could see how shaky Stannel's legs were.

The shaman did not rise.

Opal let out a laugh. Or maybe it was a cry. The next thing she knew she was lying on her back. Not understanding how she had gotten there—and not caring either—she could no longer fight back against the darkness that enveloped the pale sky above her.

Klye was completely cut off from his allies. A ring of monsters were toying with him, jabbing at him with spears, pole-axes, and weapons he had never seen before. They cursed at him, though whatever spell had translated their words earlier had expired.

"Come on, you heartless bastards!" Klye shouted, holding his rapier and dagger out in front of him.

The circle of fiends tightened, but before the lot of them could strike, one side was overtaken from behind. Klye did not question his fortune. He instantly turned and began fighting off the goblins behind him.

"Looks like we got here just in time," Hunter said as she buried her spear into the breast of a goblin she had tripped a moment before.

Klye might have gawked at the three Hylaners—along with the company of Knights they had brought with them—but there wasn't time for anything but combat. For next few minutes, the Renegade Leader fought beside the newcomers, concentrating solely on keeping the ever-increasing goblins at bay.

When the immediate threat had been repelled, Klye tried to

catch his breath. That's when he noticed that the sky was being swallowed up by black, roiling clouds. Crimson streaks of lightning danced from thunderhead to thunderhead, and the thunder nearly deafened him.

"—the hells is going on?" Hunter gasped.

The sight reminded Klye of how a priest had once described the end of the world. Of course, Klye didn't believe in the gods, so he was ready to dismiss the phenomenon as an effect of the shaman's *vuudu*.

But what he saw next was nearly enough to convince him that gods truly existed—that they existed and that they were vengeful beings, to be sure!

Passage XVI

Ay'sek lay in the filthy snow, his heavy robes soaking up the cold moisture around him. He felt none of winter's chill, however. Nor did he feel any pain. The commander's glowing mace had shattered his spine, paralyzing him from the neck down.

If he hadn't leeched so much of Stannel's strength beforehand, the shaman was certain he would already be dead.

He coughed and gasped for air, expelling flecks of bloody froth with every labored breath. Storm clouds swirled above him, and what he saw next confirmed his suspicions that Death was coming for him.

A mammoth raven hovered overhead, its silhouette made murky and nebulous by the darkening sky above it. The creature's wingspan stretched from one horizon to another. Its oily feathers seemed to suck up the vivid flashes of lightning. Talons the size of ballistae reached out from beneath the nightmarish bird. A pair of ruby-colored eyes glared down at the shaman.

At first, Ay'sek feared the Goblinfather had come to carry him off to the Pit to be tortured endlessly for his failures. He watched, spellbound and terrified, as the awful bird tucked back its wings. But rather than plummet to the earth, the bird defied gravity while its gigantic legs stretched down toward the ground.

Feathers rained down, covering the creature's legs in a veil of darkness. The oily plumage also formed a cowl around its neck. Eventually, the hood concealed the bird's head and beak—though no shadow could extinguish the fiery eyes smoldering within.

Now the Emperor of T'Ruel no longer resembled a bird at all.

Ay'sek tried to call out to his sovereign, who floating a few yards above the ground. He would have begged for mercy, begged for life, but he could manage no more than a soft whimper. He could feel his strength draining like water through a sieve.

Any moment now, his spirit would fly free from his body— only this time, there would be no coming back.

A moment before, Stannel could barely keep his eyes open. Now he could not tear his gaze away from the great black bird suspended above the battlefield.

The vileness of the thing made the hairs on the back of his neck stand on end. He could feel the malevolence, the *hatred*, pelting him like balls of hail. His rational mind told him that what he saw could not be real, and yet he knew it was more than an illusion.

Stannel shielded his eyes from the blinding darkness and glanced around the plain. Each and every goblin had broken off his attack and was regarding the bird with an expression of awe and terror. Thousands of them had fallen to their knees—some to their faces—paying homage to the enormous raven.

He looked up in time to see the bird take on a more upright form. A coat of coalescing shadow now clothed the being as completely as the feathers had before. The hateful red eyes alone remained unchanged.

The dark giant, whose height rivaled that of nearby Fort Valor, seemed content to stare down at the warriors for the moment. Stannel tensed, waiting for the storm of spells that would wipe him and his allies from the face of Altaerra.

Several long minutes passed, and nothing happened. Then, as one, the goblin army began to stir. Despite the dizziness that threatened to steal his consciousness every time he moved, Stannel forced his body into a defensive stance. His strength was spent, but Pintor's might was endless. As though in response to that very thought, a refreshing sensation surged from the mace into his arm.

But the goblins did not attack. In fact, against all reason, the invaders were walking away. Some turned around, heading back the way they had come. Others—those who had been heading north—resumed their march, falling to either side of Fort Valor like a stream parting before a great stone.

Goblins who had been fighting for their lives only moments before turned their backs on the humans. The injured did their best to keep up. One unfortunate goblin was forced to drag himself along, having lost one entire leg and a part of the other.

Like the other humans, Stannel could only stare, dumbstruck, as the foreign army made an orderly retreat. He expected that the goblins would take action against the fortress, but as far as he could tell, none of them were giving the fort a second glance as they passed by. He looked to the shaman for an explanation, but the dark-robed goblin was dead.

Above him, the cloaked figure watched the goblin army march away. When the last of the soldiers had passed beyond Fort Valor, the towering creature lowered its huge, hooded head to stare down at the humans.

It occurred to Stannel that the godlike figure had sent his minions away so that he could rain down fire and brimstone without fear of taking out his own followers. But it was too late to do anything about that now. He could only wait to see what happened next—wait and pray.

You should consider yourself very lucky.

The words exploded into Stannel's mind, and he reflexively covered his ears in an effort to shut out the loud and painful rumbling.

This war is over. My armies will leave your lands without further incident.

Although he understood the giant's words, Stannel could not fathom the reasoning behind them.

You could not begin to comprehend the complexities of the situation. I have ruled over T'Ruel for countless centuries, expanding the empire with each passing year. This was not our first attempt to take land in the East, and it will not be the last.

But for now, you need not fear invasion...at least not from us.

"Why suffer us to live?" Stannel demanded, not knowing whether or not the goblin monarch could hear him. "If you think we would willingly relinquish that accursed staff—"

Stannel clutched ay his head again, as the Emperor of T'Ruel's sudden laughter threatened to split his skull.

You may keep the staff, Commander. Consider it a consolation. I know how much you Knights value honor and valor, and your victory in this war is bereft of both. This ends only because I say it does.

As for the staff, I have seen the future...distant and near. Peerma'rek will be of more use to our cause if it remains with you.

The human nations are powerful...so long as they remain united. But that which is gathered can be scattered once more, and it is always easier to destroy than to build.

One day, the goblin empire will span the entire world. We will rule over all other races, even as Upsinous enslaves the lesser deities. In the meantime, I suggest you celebrate your hollow victory while you can.

"We will be ready for you when you return," Stannel promised.

The terrible, mocking laughter filled his head again, but Stannel refused to take his eyes off of the twin orbs of red.

You will be long dead by the time T'Ruel again lays claim to this land, Commander. The consequences of this war are beyond your understanding. Before long, your nation will again feel the caress of war.

The massive shape of the Emperor began to fade. In a matter of seconds, it was as though the Emperor had not been there at all. Some of the Knights let out a cheer, but Stannel did not join in. He was not prepared to trust the Emperor's word that he and his army would withdraw in peace.

And yet the Great Protector *had* shepherded them through their darkest hour...

With the goblin army gone, Stannel could make out the snowy landscape in the distance, and he thought that he had never seen so lovely a sight. The grisly scene of the battlefield, however, reminded him that if the humans had really won, their victory had come at a high price.

Then again, by Stannel's estimation, there were no such thing as a happy ending when it came to war.

By the time Klye got back to the fort, his legs were so tired they could barely support him. From noon to dark, they—the Renegades, Knights, and the men and women who had hidden in the passageway that morning—had spent the majority of the day carrying the wounded back into Fort Valor and gathering the dead.

Klye had wondered why Stannel would bother with corpses

of the enemy. The goblins themselves didn't care about their fallen comrades. But the commander had insisted, and so every dead goblin was added to what became a massive funeral pyre.

"We will treat our foes with the honor they could not achieve in life," Stannel had told him. "But there is also the matter of sanitation. Who could say what diseases would fester here during the spring thaw?"

Klye wouldn't have been surprised if Stannel had lumped the dead humans and goblins together. The commander seemed to respect the goblins a hell of a lot more than Klye did. But as it was, the fallen men and women would be buried, not burned.

Saerylton Crystalus was to join that number. Othello might have been placed in the mass grave too, except that no one—not Stannel, not Opal—could say precisely where the forester had died. By all reason, some forest predator had already dragged the body away.

Though that prospect was better than being eaten by the goblins, in Klye's opinion, he thought Othello deserved the honor of being buried with the other defenders of Fort Valor. And seeing the forester one last time would have made it easier for them all to accept that they would never see their friend again.

Klye briefly considered visiting Plake in the infirmary, but after hauling corpses around all day, he headed to the Renegade Room to retire instead. According to Ruben, who had carried word from Sister Aric, Plake's injuries were superficial anyway. Mostly, the rancher's muscles were just cramped.

Klye could believe that, having witnessed Plake's unbelievably coordinated movements during the duel with Drekk't. Klye knew now that the crystal sword had guided Plake's actions.

Pity the thing had exploded...

Horcalus, Arthur, Scout, and Lilac followed him into the Renegade Room, none of them saying anything. They were all ready to call it a day. Tomorrow would be even worse, Klye figured. It would take a long time to dig the mass grave.

The Renegade Leader had not forgotten that he and his band were still the Knights' prisoners, and who better than prisoners to help with hard labor? Klye's lips curled into a wry smile. At least after being cooped up in the fort for so long, we'll be getting some fresh air, he thought.

One by one, the Renegades slumped to the floor with a

chorus of groans and sighs. By all rights, they should be celebrating. The goblins were gone, and the war was over. The arrival of the Emperor had been a surreal event, however, and he could not yet wrap his mind around the idea that they were no longer in peril.

"Pardon my intrusion..."

Klye looked over at the door and found Stannel Bismarc standing there. Although Klye had not witnessed Stannel's clash with the shaman, he had heard tell of it again and again throughout the day. The goblin had been in the process of draining Stannel's life when Opal had fired an arrow into the shaman's neck. Stannel had finished the job with his enchanted mace.

That Stannel could still stand was a miracle, as far as Klye was concerned. He had been the victim of that same *vuudu* spell and had been bedridden for weeks after the incident. Stannel had undeniably come through in better condition.

Either Stannel had not been as close to death as Klye, or the commander's god had protected him from the brunt of the magical assault. Since Klye wasn't ready to allow for the existence of a pantheon, he decided the former must be true.

"It's no intrusion," Klye said. "Won't you please have a seat?"

He motioned at the floor—the furniture had been chopped up for the Knights on the battlements to throw at the goblins scaling the walls—but although Stannel exuded weariness, he declined the invitation with a wave of his hand.

"I will not stay long. We all need our rest." Stannel glanced to the right of the Renegades, at the empty half of the room. "Where are the Hylaners?"

"Hunter was dealt a nasty blow," Lilac said, "though she didn't realize it until after the battle. I saw Ruben escort her to the infirmary. Bly and Pillip are probably with her."

"And what about your friend?" Stannel asked.

Klye scoffed. "Plake? He'll live...which is more than he deserves."

"Perhaps it's more than any of us deserves," Stannel said.

Shrugging, Klye replied, "You're probably right. But then again, who's to say the goblins are really gone for good?"

"I was thinking the same thing," Stannel sighed, "which is what brings me here, actually."

"What do you mean?"

"I am granting you Renegades a full pardon for the role you played in defending this fort."

Klye opened his mouth, but he couldn't find the words to express his...what...surprise? Gratitude? Apprehension?

His eyes met those of Lilac's. The woman's smile stretched clear across her face. Arthur and Scout grinned too. Klye wondered if Scout would want to leave for Port Town right away. The prospect of seeing Leslie Beryl again filled Klye with an unexpected feeling of anxiousness. He wondered how he could get out of going back there without splitting up the band.

"Do you have the power to pardon us?" Klye asked, almost accusingly. "I mean, I wouldn't want you to get in trouble. You've already done so much..."

"As Commander of Fort Valor...and this place will be called Fort Valor unless someone goes to the trouble of changing it to something else...I have the authority to make a great many decisions."

Stannel turned to face Horcalus. "Unfortunately, I cannot reinstate you as a Knight of Superius. However, you have my promise that I will do all in my power to convince those who can that you and the late Chester Ragellan are worthy of your previous titles."

Dominic Horcalus could not hope to hide his joy at Stannel's promise—though the man tried his damnedest. "You have my gratitude, Commander."

Even when he had been at the mercy of Gaelor Petton's command, Klye had maintained control over his and the Renegades' situation. But now, Klye felt powerless. The events of the Renegade War, followed immediately by the Goblin War, had dictated his actions.

Now that the fighting was over, what would he and his men do?

"So...we are free to go?" Klye asked.

"Of course," Stannel began, "but I had rather hoped you might do me one final favor."

"Name it."

"I need a small party to follow the goblins and make certain they truly leave Capricon without wreaking further havoc."

Klye nearly declared an oath to do so but caught himself at the last minute. He looked to his Renegades, few as they were, praying they felt the same way he did.

"Well, I really did want to go and see Leslie," Scout said with a sigh, "but if the goblins are leaving, she's probably not in danger anymore. All right. I'm up for it. It seems like we've been sitting around this fort for ages."

Lilac and Horcalus answered with nods, which was enough for Klye.

"We'll do it," Klye told Stannel. "We'll leave at first light."

"I would have liked for Opal to join you," Stannel said. "She has few enough friends these days. But I fear it will take some time for her leg to heal."

Klye thought it was just as well—Opal was no friend of the Renegades, after all—but he said nothing to the concerned Knight.

"You might find that much has changed by the time you get back," Stannel continued. "I have spoken with Ruford Berwyn, and there seems to be an interest among the refugees to repopulate Port Stone."

"Really?" Scout jumped to his feet. "No one's lived there for a long time. Why the sudden interest in it now?"

"Many from the East have lost their homes. Those who survived the ruination of Rydah must start over, and those who have lost their loved ones in Hylan want to start afresh."

An image of the ghost town flashed in Klye's mind. Port Stone would need a lot of work, but he couldn't blame the refugees for wanting a place of their own. After all, the members of Colt's Army weren't the only ones who lacked a home.

After Stannel left, Klye decided he ought to go see how Plake was faring. If nothing else, he needed to confirm whether or the rancher would be well enough to join them in shadowing the goblin army. A part of him hoped that Sister Aric wouldn't allow it. Then again, gods only knew what kind of trouble Plake would get into while the other Renegades were gone.

When Klye announced his intentions to go to the infirmary, Lilac quickly rose. "Maybe we'd be better off not telling Plake about the mission. It would be cruel to tell him we're going without him."

"Who said we're going without him?"

The color drained from Lilac's face, and Klye had to bite his lip to keep from grinning.

"You can't avoid him forever," he said at last. "Besides, if this band gets any smaller, I'll be a Renegade Leader of one."

"Technically, none of us are Renegades," Horcalus pointed out.

Klye supposed that was true, but if he wasn't a Renegade Leader, then what was he? He decided he wasn't ready to give up his title, not just yet. Klye offered Horcalus a shrug before leaving the room.

As he made his way through the fort, he quickly forgot about the insubordinate Plake Nelway. Not knowing—and not caring—where his feet were taking him, Klye couldn't believe how good it felt to know they would be setting out on a new mission tomorrow morning.

Who could say where the journey would take them?

Epilogue

Delincas Theta brought his fingers to his temples, massaging away the tension building there. Across from the ambassador sat Noel. Though the midge loved chitchat, Delincas feared he would never be able to separate the truth from exaggerations and creative amendments Noel added to his stories.

He didn't believe the midge was outright lying to him. Probably, the midge really did think he had saved an alternate reality from four archfiends…

In retrospect, Delincas saw Noel as a mixed blessing. The midge had brought word of Prince Eliot's abduction to Superius, and even now the Assembly of Magic was sending out agents to hunt for the young nobleman. Delincas supposed that, if nothing else, the war with the goblins had strengthened the ties between King Edward and the Mastermage, who had been all too willing to aid Superius in its time of need.

Rumor had it the Assembly of Magic had had its share of altercations with the goblin empire. But Delincas knew that the Assembly's agenda had more to do with politics than vengeance. If Superius came to openly accept spell-casters, perhaps the rest of the world would follow.

Or so the Mastermage hoped.

The Assembly of Magic owed Noel a debt of gratitude for bringing both sides closer. Delincas wondered if, perhaps, Noel would be the first midge allowed to visit the Seminary of Wizardry, the first of his kind to join the august enclave.

Regarding the midge's infuriatingly innocent countenance— Noel had absolutely no idea how many headaches he had caused him—Delincas was forced to admit that there were undeniable benefits in keeping the Assembly of Magic midge-free.

"Why do you keep asking me about Albert?" Noel asked,

wearing a perplexed expression. "Is he a friend of yours?"

Delincas leaned back in his chair and almost chuckled in spite of himself.

"Not likely," he replied.

The ambassador's thoughts trailed off before he could say more. Noel too fell silent, as he searched for the answer to the question Delincas had asked earlier.

After several days with Noel—trying days, to be sure—the ambassador was convinced he had learned all he could from Noel about the goblins and the missing Prince of Superius. In fact, he would have already sent Noel on his way, except that the midge had mentioned something that had stuck in Delincas's mind.

Delincas had communicated his concerns to the Mastermage himself. A missive—magically delivered from halfway around the world—told Delincas that the Mastermage had discussed the news with the High Masters of the Three Orders. To Delincas's dismay, the highest-ranking wizards in the Assembly seemed to share his suspicions.

After chewing at his lower lip for a few more seconds, Noel finally said, "I don't know *how* I knew Albert was a wizard in disguise. It's like how your nose can tell you if there is a freshly baked pie in the next room. Only, I didn't *smell* Albert. It was more like a pull. And then I found his spell books and stuff—"

"And you are certain that they contained spells of black magic?" Delincas interrupted.

"Yup," Noel chirped. "And I should know because *I'm* a black wizard."

"And then 'Albert' confronted you?"

"Uh-huh." Noel nodded. "He didn't cast any spells or any-thing, though, because he didn't want the Knights to know that he was a wizard. Kind of like your situation. Are you sure he's not a friend of yours?"

Ignoring the question, Delincas asked, "Can you tell me again what he looked like."

Noel let out a longsuffering sigh. "He looked like an old, old man. His face was all wrinkly, and he had a long, white beard. And he was real skinny. But like I said before, none of that matters because he was wrapped in a spell of illusion.

"Opal said that some of the Renegades...you know, Klye's friends...I told you all about Klye already...well, some of them saw Albert's true form. That was when he told them not to ever, *ever* climb Wizard's Mountain. I guess he was planning on living there…"

Delincas held up a hand to silence the midge. Since Noel never told a story from beginning to end—but rather from middle to end to beginning—Delincas took a moment to sort out some of the midge's earlier reports.

"Later, some of the Knights did trespass on Wizard's Mountain, correct?"

"Actually, it was only one Knight…Stannel…and some other people, but, no, Albert didn't show up. Maybe he was napping. Are you ever going to tell me why Albert Simplington is so darn important?"

Delincas seriously considered honoring Noel's request. But what would he tell the midge? That supposed surgeon Albert Simplington might very well be the most dangerous wizard to have ever walked the earth? And that Wizard's Mountain was the *last* place anyone wanted him to be?

If only you hadn't mentioned him at all, Delincas thought. You could already be back with your friends in Capricon, helping them fight the goblins.

But it was too late for that now. If Albert was who the Assembly feared he was, the situation was far too volatile to allow a midge get mixed up in it.

To both Delincas's and Noel's chagrin, it looked as though the midge would be staying in Superius for some time to come.

"I'll have the Knights send someone back with the horse," Arthur told Stannel, as he pulled himself up onto its gray-white back.

The commander did not reply. The return of one horse was probably the least of his concerns. Everyone, Arthur included, had heard what the goblin emperor said about another war on the horizon…

Arthur felt his cheeks burn and did his best to avoid Stannel's eyes. Despite all that needed to be done in the wake of what some were already calling the Goblin War, Stannel was taking the time to see him off.

He had said his goodbyes to the Renegades two days ago when Klye, Horcalus, Lilac, Plake, and Scout had left to follow the goblins. Now Arthur found himself wondering if Horcalus had asked Stannel to make sure he didn't chicken out.

"It's funny," Arthur said, eager to banish the awkward silence. "I really haven't been here all that long, but it feels more like I'm *leaving* home than returning to it."

The older Knight smiled warmly. "A man may find many homes in his lifetime."

Was Stannel referring to his new command, to the second Fort Valor? Arthur couldn't be sure. The man always seemed to talk in proverbs.

Arthur looked into the distance and let out a long sigh. "I think I was less afraid when the goblin army was closing in on us."

"Fear is a natural reaction to uncertainty," Stannel quipped. "So long as you do not let it rule your decisions, you will be all right."

The words washed over Arthur; his mind was on other things. "I guess it's not just fear. I'm eager to see my family again, but it's...it was very difficult saying goodbye to my friends."

Stannel waited for him to go on.

"I know we weren't together for very long...a matter of months, really...but I really felt like I *belonged* with them."

"But you do not belong with them anymore?"

Arthur smiled and looked out the open stable door once more. "I have to go home...to Hylan. There are some things I need to settle. Anyway, I was the most useless member of the band. Except for Plake maybe."

"Why do you say that?"

Arthur thought that maybe the Knight was teasing him, but a glance at Stannel revealed a sincere expression. "Well," Arthur said, "I've only just learned the basics of wielding a sword. Before that, I just watched as the others fought. Horcalus would spend more time protecting me than anything else."

"You are a neophyte in the ways of combat," Stannel summarized. "But that does not make you useless. You were...you *are* their friend. Even as you needed to be defended, Dominic Horcalus needed someone to protect. A friend, you see, is valuable in his own right."

"I guess you're right." Arthur suspected there was a deeper meaning to Stannel's words. Oh well, he thought. I'll have plenty of time to ponder Stannel's riddles on my way to Hylan.

"I probably won't stay there long...Hylan, I mean," Arthur said. "I don't want to be a farmer. I don't think I *could* be a farmer. I've seen too much, experienced too much since I ran away."

"What will you be?" Stannel asked.

Arthur averted his eyes again. "I want to leave Capricon ...and become a Knight of Superius."

He shot a glance down at Stannel. To his relief, the commander did not appear to be fighting off fits of laughter. Arthur hadn't told any of the Renegades of his plans, not even Horcalus. Plake would have surely laughed at him, but he could only speculate about the others' reactions.

"Do...do you think I will make a good Knight?" Arthur asked. "I know Horcalus was already a squire by my age, but maybe if I work hard, I can catch up?"

"You already have the heart of a Knight, Arthur. Or perhaps it is more accurate to say that you have a heart that reflects the ideals of the Knighthood."

Since Arthur could not grasp the difference between, he merely accepted the compliment for what it was.

"I don't suppose I'll be seeing you or anyone else at Fort Valor for quite some time," Arthur added, staring out at the snow-covered landscape. "Maybe I'll never see you any of you again."

"The gods only know," Stannel replied, and Arthur heard the smile in his voice. "Who can say where any of us will be tomorrow? I would not give up all hope, however. It might be that the Knighthood will see fit to station you in Capricon one day. And who is to say that your friends will not visit you in Superius?"

Arthur laughed in spite of himself. "I'm sure *that* would go over well with the Knights...a band of former rebels showing up on my doorstep!"

The feeling of heaviness came upon Arthur in the silence that followed. He had delayed long enough. It was time to face his family again, to leave the Renegades behind, and to look to the future.

"I will deliver your letter at once," Arthur promised. "Sir Dale Mullahstyn, right?"

Stannel nodded. "Sir Dylan said that if the Knights he left in Hylan have moved on, they will probably be in Kraken. If that is true, then give the letter to Quillan Dag. The mayor will know what to do with the information.

"If the Knights have evacuated *everyone* from Hylan, can I depend on you to track them down and deliver the news of the goblins' unexpected withdrawal?"

Arthur brought his fist up to his heart, a gesture he had seen some of the Knights perform when giving an oath. "I may not be a Knight yet, Commander, but I swear on my honor that I will give the letter to the proper person."

As there seemed nothing left to say—and since he was wasting precious daylight—Arthur bade Stannel farewell and urged his horse out of the stable. His heart beating loudly in his chest, he spurred his mount into a gallop.

The air that whizzed by his face was cold, but he welcomed the sensation. It seemed to wake him up, preparing him for a strange, new day.

He made for the road that would bypass the ruins of old Fort Valor and take him on a strictly easterly route. When he reached the place where the road met the forest, he looked back and said one final farewell to new Fort Valor.

Later—in the days, months, and even years that followed—Arthur would dismiss the thought as wishing thinking, but at that moment, he knew he would return. One day, he would see the Renegades again.

ACKNOWLEDGMENTS

To properly recognize every person who supported The Renegade Chronicles since I first put fingertips to keyboard in 1997 would fill another entire book. To spare the lives of a few trees, I'll attempt to keep my kudos concise and thank everyone who encouraged my creativity throughout the years, including:

Family members who nurtured my imagination by making sure I always had paper and pencils to map out new worlds and by exploring those places with me.

Dear friends who called me "weird but in a good way," indulged me when I spoke of made-up people and strange plots, and provided feedback along the way.

Educators who taught me the craft as well as bolstered my confidence—even though I was only interested in writing stories with swords and magic.

Comrades-in-arms whose critiques made me the writer I am today, especially the Allied Authors of Wisconsin.

To recognize a few of those individuals by name:

Robyn Williams, who motivated her little brother to try his hand at the written word and who inadvertently helped invent two main characters in this series.

Stephanie Williams, my incredible wife, whose interest in Altaerra and its populace in 1994 prompted me to record those stories in copious notebooks and who has supported me in so many ways over the past two decades.

Judith Barisonzi, who taught me the fundamentals of storytelling, how to write on deadline, and the truth that great writing transcends genre.

Alan Hathaway, who inspired me to pursue my dream and also made accommodations so I could make it a reality.

Jake Weiss, a good friend and brilliant designer who exceeded all expectations for the cover art.

Fern Ramirez, who always sees the best in a story even while seeking out its flaws.

And last but not least, Tom Ramirez, who has played a variety of parts since we met at that auspicious rummage sale in 2005—from surrogate grandfather and role model to tireless cheerleader and invaluable friend.

It's been a long, strange journey, and I consider myself very blessed indeed.

Photo: Jaime Lynn Hunt

DAVID MICHAEL WILLIAMS was exposed to sword-and-sorcery fantasy at the tender age of 12. He dove headlong into fiction writing when he competed in a short story contest in sixth grade. While the tale—a glorified battle scene, really—garnered no accolades, two of its characters survived for many years thereafter and appear in The Renegade Chronicles.

David lives in Wisconsin with an amazing wife (who somehow puts up with his storytelling addiction) and two larger-than-life children.

Visit his website at david-michael-williams.com.

Made in the USA
Middletown, DE
02 September 2017